I0823971

leave it on the track

MARGOT FISHER

DUTTON BOOKS

DUTTON BOOKS
An imprint of Penguin Random House LLC
1745 Broadway, New York, New York 10019

First published in the United States of America by Dutton Books,
an imprint of Penguin Random House LLC, 2025

Visit us online at PenguinRandomHouse.com.

Library of Congress Cataloging-in-Publication Data is available.

ISBN 9780593858394
1st Printing

Printed in the United States of America
BVG

Design by Anna Booth
Text set in Sabon LT Pro

The authorized representative in the EU for product safety and compliance is Penguin Random House Ireland, Morrison Chambers, 32 Nassau Street, Dublin D02 YH68, Ireland, https://eu-contact.penguin.ie.

For all my teammates, past and present,
on Wreckers and High Rollers.
And for Hannah, who waited for me
to reach the same chapter.

leave it on the track

chapter one

WE WAIT IN LINE at the roller rink for fifteen minutes, even though Papa made a point to get here early. The chaotic line for the Finney's Mesa Rollerdome always stretches around the corner on Friday nights. There's a family of four behind us—a dad on his phone, a mom trying to stop her little kid from putting on their plastic Fisher-Price skates outside, a preteen in a hoodie avoiding looking at the rest of his family. The preteen has reached that phase of waiting outside the rink that comes with stoic patience. He's too old to be running around like the little kids and too young to be huddled in a group of his friends being obnoxious on their phones. So he's standing, slightly apart from his embarrassing family, clutching his skates and probably looking forward to getting inside and being able to roll away from them. That was me a couple years ago, awkward and unsure of myself even though I'd been skating at the Rollerdome all my life.

Dad is completely unbothered by the queue and falls into conversation with the guy in front of us, a dance skater who's new to Finney's Mesa. Dad's always been able to do that—zero in on someone new, say just the right thing to get them smiling, opening up, dip so suddenly into conversation that they don't notice when the line's moving. I've never managed to figure it out.

"Dad made another friend," Papa says to me with a bemused look. His skates are slung over his shoulder, laces tied together, the black suede striking against his bright red jacket. Papa always dresses nice when we go skating—*nicer than church*, he'd say, even though we've never been to church. *This is our church,* he said once when I was little, skating between him and Dad and clutching both their hands. *The church of eight wheels*. He'd ripped it off the name of a famous roller rink in San Francisco, polished wood laid down in the shell of an old church with makeshift lights and a DJ booth set up every weekend. Papa's always showing me old skate videos from the famous roller rinks, pointing out the way the floor is curved or the types of wheels people used in the '90s as though I can see them in the grainy footage.

We get inside to the ticket stand, where Dad hands our skate passes to Gemma. She's slouched in her scuffed wooden booth, grumpy expression contrasting with the sequined top hat and glow-stick necklace someone made her wear. "Happy Friday, Gemma," Dad says smoothly, and Gemma cracks a rare grimace.

"It'll be happier when I can go home," she says as she stamps our passes. "Hey, Moose," she says to me, "nothing better to do on Friday night?"

It's our usual routine—Gemma acts like seeing a sixteen-year-old at the Finney's Mesa Rollerdome with her parents on Friday night a month before school lets out is an affront to human nature. I ask her if she knows of any other exciting social activities happening in dead-end Finney's Mesa; she rolls her eyes, stamps my well-creased pass, and slides it back to me, along with a Tootsie Roll from her stash under the counter.

On Fridays, the rink comes alive. The neon carpet underfoot vibrates from the speakers, the space crowded with people lacing up their skates and half rolling, half stepping awkwardly around the benches. The ugly stained carpet around the edges of the rink is there to slow you down and keep you from plowing at full speed into a little kid with a plastic tray of nachos. It's like a gentler introduction to moving with wheels on your feet. *See?* Papa said to me once when I was little and just learning, clutching his hands with white knuckles as I wobbled to my feet. *It's not so different from walking on the carpet, right?* He'd gently pried my hands off his and made me roll along the lace-up area, letting me stumble over a crease in the carpet and slapping his thighs in approval when I steadied myself without help.

Tonight, the overhead lights are shut off in favor of flashing lasers and a disco ball, and the floor is packed with a slow-moving ring of skaters decked out with glow sticks. We squeeze through the crowd to our usual spot by the lockers, a carpeted bench between the DJ booth and the arcade. Papa uses a key from his belt to open our locker, tossing in his wallet and jacket. "Where'd your friend go?" he shouts to Dad over the music, and Dad gives him a playful shove.

"Can you move?" I press, waving my coat in Dad's face. "Some of us are here to skate."

"Okay, Your Majesty," he says, taking my coat and stuffing it into the locker with his. "You gonna keep up with these old men tonight?"

"Are *you*?" I ask, reaching out to spin one of the wheels on his skates. "Sounds a little crusty. Cleaned your bearings lately?"

"Not since *someone* lost the bearing press."

"My turn," Papa proclaims, dramatically fake shoving both of us apart so he can squish his bag into the locker.

Dad and I sit on the carpeted bench to pull our skates on. There's an eyelet near the toe of my left skate that's started lifting out of the leather—probably just from these skates being three years old—and I use my pinkie to pop it back in before I slide it on my foot. "I need new skates," I tell Dad, threading the laces in the special pattern he showed me years ago, the one that helps lift my arches so my feet don't cramp. "These are gonna fall apart soon." The lights, in the shapes of pink flowers and stars, rove over my hands.

"Oh, come on," he chides, reaching down to pinch the toe of my skate and check the fit. "We can just slap some duct tape on there and buy you another year at least."

"*I* will buy you new skates when I'm in SLC next month, favorite child," Papa says, sitting down on my other side to put his skates on.

"That's why you're my favorite dad."

"Pushover," Dad says across me, and Papa gives him one of those annoyed-yet-lovesick looks. They always flank me like this when we lace up—when I was little and first learning to skate, it was so they could each grab a hand and pull me to my feet. Now it's ritual. I finish lacing my own skates and give Dad's a tug to make sure they're tight, but not too tight. Dad and I like the high-top rhythm skates with dance plugs instead of toe stops, but Papa still wears sleek black artistic skates from his figure roller skating days and refuses to let either of us touch them.

I'm always ready first, and I stand and pat Dads on the head. "Too slow!" I tell them over the music, and they wave in lazy acknowledgment as I head to the skate floor.

The minute my wheels hit polished wood, I'm sailing. I weave in and out of the throngs of other skaters, deftly maneuvering my way around the floor and scanning for familiar faces. While Friday-night skate always draws a handful of newbies from Moab proper shuffling across the floor, the regular crowd is the heartbeat of the rink. I wave to Sam and Mike, the two old dudes who show up every night to skate slowly around the outside and talk about sports, no matter how crowded it is.

"Hey, Moose," Sam says, barely audible over the music, and I turn to skate backward in front of them.

"Who's losing this weekend?" I ask.

"Cougars are a fucking mess this season," Mike sighs. "Your dads follow the Cougars?"

"They definitely don't." Dads—the only gay couple in Finney's Mesa (*that we know of,* Papa always reminds me)—probably don't even know what sports season we're in.

"Good. Fuckin' painful this year."

I leave Sam and Mike to their griping as Lorraine, the artistic skater with impossibly long silver hair, skates past and catches my hand to spin me in a circle. She nearly takes out a teenager struggling to stay upright on peanut butters, the battered tan-and-orange rental skates that separate the regulars from the newbies. The teenager flails, and Lorraine steadies him easily before twirling away into the crowd. Skatemare, the only other rhythm skater in town besides Dad and me, rolls up next to me, stepping smoothly in time to the music. His real name is Shawn, but since I was a kid he's always introduced himself as *Skatemare*, the alter ego embroidered across the shoulders of his jacket.

"Fall in, kid!" he calls, and I roll into step with him, following the familiar pattern. The trick with rhythm skating is making it look easy and carefree, like you're dancing at the club, when really you're sweating your ass off and trying to find your edges in your skates and match the pattern of the person you're skating with, all while avoiding uncoordinated little kids flailing around on peanut butters. Skatemare is one of those rhythm skaters who makes everyone skating with him look good—he grooves his shoulders in just the right way, laughs the whole time like he's never had more fun. Dad always talks about taking me to the rinks in California, where folks clear the floor to watch people skate off against each other, backflipping and spinning and dancing in perfect time. Someone skates past me too close, and I lose the beat for a second—Skatemare easily takes my hand and points down, showing me how to spin my foot to find the pattern again. Dad made me watch a documentary about the Black roller rink scene once, pausing it every three minutes to add commentary on the history of adult skate nights. "There you go," Skatemare says, dropping my hand now that I've found the pattern again. I cross over in time with Skatemare, then lift my crossing knee, raising my hands to pivot on one foot so we're skating backward. Dad wanted to show me the specific type of wheel jam skaters use and the racist roller rinks in LA that banned jam skating as a roundabout way of banning Black skaters. Dad is there suddenly, falling easily into step with Skatemare and me, but his moves are even smoother, his smile wider, a slinkier version of the rhythms Skatemare and I are already doing.

"You know your daddy's a show-off, yeah?" Skatemare yells to me, and I roll my eyes, but everyone in the vicinity slows to watch Dad skate. Where Skatemare makes it look easy, Dad makes it look like breathing—so fluid and simple even though he's throwing out patterns that would send most skaters to the ground.

Rinks aren't the same in Utah, Dad always insists, though the Rollerdome is where he met Papa. Papa was a freshly excommunicated Mormon (*and a baby gay*, he liked to say) who did artistic skating all his life—Dad tried to get him into rhythm skating, but he prefers to swirl around the rink with Lorraine in his artistic skates, both of them twirling and jumping around the peanut butters like figure skaters on wheels.

When the music pumps like this, the sweat and foot cramps feel insignificant. I'm twisting and dancing and moving in time with the music, in time with Skatemare and my dads. Lights and heavy bass reverberate through the rink, and we all fold into the music and the consistent clap and whisper of our wheels on smooth, polished wood. At a certain point on Friday night, the other skaters all blur into each other—a frenetic mix of rink staff in neon shirts yelling at parents not to pick up kids in skates, the rhythm skaters, the artistics, the peanut butters, the single annoyed speed skater with big-wheeled inlines, who inexplicably chose this night to skate—it all just turns into wheels on polished wood and heat under the disco ball.

The current song ends, and an old-fashioned alarm bell plays over the speakers. "*Happy Friday night, Finney's Mesa,*" the DJ announces. "*It's time for the couples skate! You must be holding hands with a partner to skate, so singles who aren't ready to mingle, please clear the floor.*"

I join the mass of people rolling off the floor while some cheesy '80s ballad starts to play, practically blowing out the rink's ancient speakers. It's good timing—I'm slick with sweat from trying to keep up with Dad and Skatemare.

"You want something to drink, Moose?" Skatemare asks, gesturing to the snack bar as we glide onto the carpet together.

"I'm good." I'm parched, and the snack bar has fizzy lemonade on Friday nights, but Jenna from freshman English—beautiful, shiny-haired, incredibly hetero Jenna from freshman English—is working the counter. I've had this debilitating crush on her since middle school without ever having really talked to her, until we were in the same group for the Huck Finn project. I spoke probably three words to her the entire time, mostly staring at my notebook and praying nobody noticed me. I don't know what I was hoping for—that Jenna would casually mention being attracted to girls, notice me, and tell off the kids who call me a dyke behind my back, while simultaneously sweeping me off my feet in some grand romantic gesture? Somehow, being the only child of the only gay couple in Finney's Mesa (*that we know of*) has made me the latest target for hurling unimaginative slurs. Even if they're right. *They* don't have to know that.

Skatemare rolls toward Jenna and the snack bar, and I skate to our locker instead, pulling a five out of Papa's wallet for the vending machine in the arcade. I hover for a moment by the carpeted half wall that separates the locker areas from the skate floor to watch the couples skate. Dad and Papa skate hand in hand, so close their shoulders touch, even though Papa has half a foot of height on Dad. The couples skate is the only time they're not actively trying to out-skate each other—they both roll easily along the outside, talking in hushed tones, grinning at each other and giggling, squeezing hands the whole time. Dad takes Papa's other hand and turns so he's skating backward in front of him, singing along to the power ballad with embarrassing bravado. People are looking, but Dads have been gay in Finney's Mesa for years now. The stares don't seem to faze them anymore. I used to imagine skating with Jenna during the couples skate, holding her hands and singing to her and not caring who watched.

The arcade is just off the main skate floor, occupied by a trio of middle schoolers daring each other to play *Dance Dance Revolution* in their rental skates. I slide the bill into the vending machine, and a can clanks into the chute. My chest is still heaving when I crack the Coke, perching sideways on the peeling chair of a racing game to drink it. I usually retreat to the arcade anytime I need a break from the pumping music and flashing lights of the skate floor. There are two small windows in here that they prop open regardless of the weather. The cool air trickling in is always a reprieve.

It takes me a while to smell the smoke.

It's so insignificant at first, a weird undertone that I barely notice. Until it grows, and then the acrid smell fills my nose. I look up suddenly—the middle schoolers are gone, and people on the skate floor are starting to falter, looking around for the source of the weird smell. In the flashing lights above the skate floor, I see a gathering haze of black smoke.

Then there's a blaze of white, a growing streak of fire in the snack bar. People on the floor start to notice and swerve away from it, pointing.

The windows shatter, glass spraying out onto the floor.

Screams fill the rink out of nowhere, and I feel cold soda splash my legs as I drop the can. *Dads!* I skate to the edge of the floor, scanning the panicked faces. There must be hundreds of people on skates, and they all start surging toward the front of the rink.

Fear wells up inside me, and the smoke pouring out of the snack bar stings my eyes. It's too hazy to see the floor now—I have to look for them myself.

"Dads!" I shout, propelling myself onto the wood. Glass crunches under my wheels, but I keep my footing, shoving upstream through the panicked crowd. *"Dads!"*

"Moose!" someone yells—I whirl around, but it's Skatemare. "Moose, let's go!"

"Have you seen my dads?" I shout, grabbing his arms. I can taste the smoke, and I feel it filling every part of me, choking me. I cough.

"Come on!" Skatemare drags me with the crowd.

"I have to find my dads!" I yank my arm out of his grip.

"Everybody's outside, kid," he tries.

"They wouldn't leave me!" I shove my way through the throng before Skatemare can protest, bile rising in my throat as smoke stings my eyes, my lungs, every part of me. The blaze is spreading now, catching on the carpet around the skate floor, and the heat surges toward me.

Then I'm through the end of the crowd, spinning on the emptying skate floor, squinting around through the smoke and rippling heat. There's a crush of people at the door, and panicked shrieking overpowers the music.

They have to be in the crowd somewhere—Dads wouldn't leave knowing I might still be in here. I start to skate back to the crowd, barely visible now through the smoke.

The laser lights overhead flicker and go out, and fresh cries well up from the crush of people at the exit. The fire is the only light source now, all around us, reflecting off the disco ball.

I'm slowing down, my wheels sticking on something. I keep pushing toward the exit, but my skates roll to a complete halt, stuck. My eyes sting from the smoke as I squat to check my feet with shaking hands.

The wheels have melted. No, not the wheels—I've *skated* through something that's melted, smeared across the skate floor and turned to tar from the heat. I pull against the floor as hard as I can, but my skates are cemented to the wood.

More yelling. More fire, ringing the edges of the floor, creeping toward the wood. The wood that they always polish right before Friday-night skate, with varnish that smells like jet fuel.

I fumble with the laces of my skates, heart pounding. Sweat drips off my forehead and onto my hands, shaking as they yank the laces out. The second they're loose enough, I wiggle my foot out of the boot, my sock landing on the tar.

The floor's searing hot, and I scream, jerking it upward and nearly tipping over. I squint through the smoke—I can't see, but I know the fire's getting closer to the floor.

I pull my other foot out of my skate and jump, landing on my knees and elbows on the other side of the tar puddle. The wood is just as hot, but it barely registers as I scramble to my feet, running blindly. Fire swirls in out of nowhere, feeding on the floor polish and setting the rink floor ablaze.

"*Dad!*" I scream hoarsely, dissolving into coughs. I swing my arm around, trying in vain to clear the smoke enough so I can see. "*Papa!*" Abruptly, I realize that the screaming of the crowd has stopped. Music still blares over the speakers—the fire hasn't reached the DJ booth yet. It's an old Beastie Boys song, the rap verses distorted in the smoke and crackle of fire.

They're not here.

I have to get out.

The arcade. The windows. They're always open. I stumble through the smoke, pressing the inside of my elbow to my mouth and nose. My face is slick, and I can't tell if it's sweat or tears. Everywhere I turn is a haze of smoke, and I smell acrid, burning plastic.

I drop to the floor, scrambling for carpet. There are decals on the space print, arrows pointing toward the snack bar or the wavy floor or the ticket booth. My hands find a peeling red arrow marked *Arcade*, and I crawl toward it, ignoring the searing pain on my palms. Beside me, something explodes.

I curl into a ball, shielding my face as heat hurdles over me. Sparks catch my shirt and poke my skin like needles. I roll toward the arcade, trying to disperse the fire, and fall into a fit of coughs again, feeling blindly for the wall.

Window, I think weakly, repeating it like a prayer. *Window, window, window, window.*

There's fire here too—it's everywhere, closing in on me, choking me. I find the edge of an arcade game, the plastic twisting and melting in the heat, and I use it to drag myself upright. The arcade's on fire now. It's pressing into me, and I smell my own burning hair, so hot it feels like my skin is searing off my bones. The music still pulses overhead, taunting me.

My hand finds something white-hot, and I yelp, careening backward. Coughing, choking, I stumble back toward it. Cool air leaks through. *Window.*

But the flame has closed in now, pressing me into the wall. There's a carpeted pillar between me and the window, with six inches of space on one side. I feel like I'm on fire—like I can smell it, my own flesh twisting and burning and melting, but I can't tell if it's real or not. I make a run for it, fixing my gaze on the window, that little black rectangle of safety. I reach for the pillar to steady myself as I pass it, hooking one arm around the stapled carpet.

Pain explodes through the inside of my arm where I grabbed the pillar—the carpet is half melted away already, nearly burned down to the metal. My vision blurs and pitches sideways as I struggle to stay upright. Someone is screaming—is it me? I think it might be me. My throat feels raw, filled with smoke.

The music distorts, then drips into silence like it's melting too. There are no screams now, not even from me—just my own haggard breath and the dull roar of fire.

I drag myself back upright, a frustrated gurgle escaping my throat at the effort. The spot where I hooked my arm around the pillar is raw, pulsating. I don't look at it, afraid I'll see my own skin melting off. All I can see is fire now, fire and black, black smoke. I rely on my hands to find the window, to pull myself up despite my burning body screaming in protest. Mercifully cold air hits my face. My arms give out, and I'm slumped there, half out, half on fire, smoke closing my throat. I can't think—can't breathe—can't move.

When my eyes close, I can't fight anymore.

chapter two

THEY SAID THE RINK FIRE only killed six people.

Only. Like the six that died were an acceptable tragedy. The social worker in the hospital told me that Dads died in the women's restroom, trapped by a beam that fell in front of the door. Looking for me.

I wish I was still unconscious in the hospital.

It's all I can think, over and over, gripping the edge of the passenger seat as the car grinds slowly up a hill. Rock ledges rise on either side, and thick snow glints in the headlights' beams. Eden sits uncomfortably close to the wheel, one white-knuckled hand on the steering wheel and the other on the parking brake.

"Sorry," she says without looking at me, gritting her teeth. "I haven't driven this road since I moved out here."

"It's fine," I say, and even after nearly five months, my own voice still sounds foreign. There's a rasp that was never there before, a faint feeling like I swallowed a mouthful of glass. I can talk now, can breathe without a tube in my throat, but it still feels wrong.

"Once we get through the Cascades, it's a straight shot," Eden says for the fourth time in the past hour. "No more hills."

"I don't mind hills." Utah's full of hills—I'm used to scrambling up steep rock, clothes stained with orange dust. It's the fear that's making me want to throw up. I can feel Eden's anxiety radiating off her.

I look down at the backpack at my feet, searching for something to distract myself. A crumpled brochure pokes out of the side pocket, the last thing they gave me at the hospital in Moab. *Understanding and Improving Body Image After Burn Injury.* I hadn't known what to do with it when the doctor handed one to me and one to Eden—it's not like I have grafts all over my body like some of the people in the pamphlet. One mottled patch of skin on the inside of my elbow, barely visible, and the long red scar in the hollow of my throat. I had shoved the pamphlet into my backpack without opening it.

Eden's talking, chattering nervously about a show she watched at the hospital, or a podcast, or something. I can see her flushed cheeks in the reflection from the headlights. I consider telling her that she doesn't have to talk to me while she drives if it's making her more anxious. But maybe telling her that would make her more anxious. And I don't *really* want to say anything. So I let her keep talking.

"Going down," Eden says suddenly, interrupting her own monologue. I look back up through the windshield, and my stomach drops. The car crests the hill, tipping down a steep slope with a sharp turn into a tunnel at the bottom.

"Eden," I warn, clutching the dashboard. "Can your car do this?"

She doesn't answer, but I see her jaw shaking as the car starts down the hill slowly, then gathers speed.

Panic grips me, and I'm not in the car anymore—I'm reaching for the latches of a window, hair sticking to my face. Smoke presses in around me, filling my lungs, stinging my eyes. I can feel it deep inside my chest, the rattle as I gasp for air. I touch the window latch, and it's white-hot. I hear a scream—*Was that me?*—and I reel backward, into the flames.

Eden brakes a little too hard, and I gasp as I'm thrown back into the present. My shoulder hits the passenger door, a faint sting running down my arm from the impact. Eden's turning the wheel, and we're in the tunnel, and then the car bursts out on the other side.

We both breathe a sigh of relief as she straightens the wheel, letting the car slide to a gentle stop on the stretch of flat road beyond. "Are you okay?" Eden asks.

"Yeah," I breathe, massaging the feeling back into my arm. I twist around in my seat to look at the hill and picture our car flying off the cliff, disappearing into the snowy pine trees. *Would it really be so bad?* It would probably hurt less than the smoke, be easier than spending all summer propped up in a hospital bed unable to speak.

"We shouldn't have taken Deadman Pass," Eden murmurs, grabbing her phone to check directions. The blue light illuminates my sister's long face, the anxious frown lines around her mouth. "I'm an idiot. I just didn't want to make the trip in two days."

"It's fine, Eden," I insist, and she glances up at me. "Really."

I can tell what she's feeling. Guilt, at making me fear for my life months after I almost died. It's what anyone would think.

"Can we just keep going?"

We sit in brief silence, watching snow swirl around the car. Somehow, this feels like the first hurdle I've cleared. A minivan turns the corner we barely survived and goes around us, a little slow in the snow but nowhere near spinning off the cliff. Over Eden's arms, I see the driver texting, calm. We watch its taillights disappear—me and this half sister I barely know, who is now, somehow, my guardian.

Eden puts the car in drive, and we slowly slide back onto the road. "Well," she says, tucking her phone away, "welcome to Oregon."

It's past midnight when we reach Eden's house, a tall Craftsman with a bare porch and weeds poking up along the walls.

"It's a duplex." She says this quickly, like I might judge her for living in a big house by herself. "No way I'd be able to afford a whole house in this neighborhood. I live in the upstairs half."

"Cool." The snow turned to rain as we drove out of the mountains, and Portland just seems to be dark and wet. As soon as I get out of the car, the damp presses in, clinging to me. The rain is more like a mist here, fog settling along the dark street. I didn't know air could feel like this. I take a breath, imagining the mist filling my lungs, steeling me. At least it isn't smoke.

I follow Eden through the front door and up a narrow set of stairs, where she unlocks another door and ushers me through. "I'll grab your other bag," she says, setting my backpack inside the door. "Make yourself at home."

I click on a lamp. Eden's apartment is cute—old bay windows with gauzy curtains, a couple potted plants, a knit blanket on the couch and a few half-melted candles on the coffee table. There's a bricked-up fireplace on one wall that she's filled with messy stacks of old horror paperbacks. I pick a book up off the stack, flipping open the cover. *Property of Eden S.,* she's written in glittery silver Sharpie—kid handwriting. At the bottom of the page, a note in lighter pen strokes, familiar spiky handwriting that makes my throat feel dry. *Eden, This one's a classic. Don't tell your mother I'm letting you read Stephen King. Happy Birthday.*

Love, Dad

I hear Eden's footsteps on the stairs and quickly replace the book. It feels like I'm snooping, in this cozy apartment that belongs to a sister I barely know.

"You hungry?" she asks, kicking the door shut and pulling off her wool hat. Her hair is shaved close on one side and was once dyed blue—it surprised me when I first woke up in the burn unit, but lying in a hospital bed for weeks on end, unable to speak or move or do anything, really, Eden's hair fading from electric blue to washed-out green quickly became one of the ways I gauged time passing.

"Uh—no, I'm good." The burger I'd gotten from a drive-thru after Deadman Pass is still sitting in my stomach, a solid lump.

"Cool," Eden says, unzipping her coat and gesturing for me to do the same. She hangs our coats by the door, slipping off her boots. "Well, it's not much of a tour. There's just one bathroom in the hall there. My room's on the end, yours is on the other side. Oh, shit." She pads past me, heading for the hall. "You're not allergic to cats, are you?"

I follow Eden to the bedroom, where she flicks on a lamp. There's a huge drafting table by the window and a bulletin board full of landscape sketches. A deflated air mattress sits on the carpet with a gray cat curled on top, blinking sleepily in the light.

"That's Typo. She'll sleep on your chest if you leave the door open." Typo meows tiredly, stretching and curling around my ankles.

"I'm not allergic." I offer her my hand, and she rubs her head against it. "She's cute."

"Yeah. Annoying, too. You can't sit down without her inviting herself onto your lap."

"Who's been taking care of her?"

"A friend who—uh, owes me a favor," Eden says awkwardly. "Catsitters cost a freaking arm and a leg these days." She steps past me into the room, digging in the closet and pulling out a pump for the air mattress. "I'm sorry, Moose, I wanted to have all this ready when you got here. I've only been home a couple times since I got the call—I didn't want to leave you alone there any longer, and I just kind of dropped everything and—"

"It's fine," I say quickly, my cheeks hot. Eden feels sorry for me, and I hate how weak it makes me feel. "I can pump that up myself."

Eden turns around from the closet with a stack of sheets. "No, no, I'll—"

"Really, Eden," I say, a little firmer. "I just—I kind of want to be alone. I'm exhausted."

I see the pity in her eyes again. "Of course. Totally." She looks around the room. "We can go to Ikea or something this weekend. Get you a real bed. I'll move my drafting table out of here tomorrow."

I feel bad. This was clearly Eden's office before I got dumped on her out of nowhere. I don't even really know what she does for work, I realize. She could be single-handedly making all her income at this desk in this room that I'm taking over. But I really do just want to sleep, so I say, "Okay."

She leaves the sheets on the desk chair, then hesitates a moment before resting a hand on my shoulder. "I'm glad you're here, Moose."

I muster a smile that I know looks fake—big facial expressions sometimes pull at the skin of my throat, remind me of the thick red scar currently hidden under an old gray scarf Eden gave me. She'd pulled it out of the backseat and handed it to me wordlessly before we left the gas station, and even though it wasn't cold, I'd wrapped it around my neck. "Yeah. Me too."

Eden looks like she wants to hug me but seems to think better of it. "You can leave the door open if you want Typo to sleep with you. She loves new people."

I nod, and Eden disappears into the bedroom. The door clicks shut, and I hear the mattress squeak. I wonder if she collapsed onto her bed, overwhelmed and exhausted from spending the past five months by the hospital bed of a sister she hasn't seen in years.

I sit down on the chair by the drafting table as the air mattress inflates, spinning to look at the drawing pinned there. It's a half-finished mountain sketch, every stroke precise and neat. I have distant memories of her constantly drawing anime characters when I was little. It was dorky, but she was good. It's weird to see her careful, clean drawings of hills and lakes instead of bug-eyed magical girls. I should ask her if this is what she does for work. Or if it's a hobby. Or what she's been doing with her life for the past ten years since I've really seen her. Besides sitting in a hospital room with me.

Typo leaps onto my lap and settles there, purring. I scritch her head as my eyes fall on the mirror on the back of the door, currently angled away from me so all I can see is my foot and the slowly inflating air mattress. I know I shouldn't do it. I've been avoiding mirrors for months, staring hard at my hands at the sink in the hospital bathroom instead of the unfamiliar girl looking back at me. *You may not look different,* the therapist had said carefully, weighing every word, *but your body probably* feels *much different. Take it slow with mirrors.*

I brace my foot against the wall and push off it, rolling the desk chair into the mirror's view.

The girl looks like me. She has my eyes and my nose, my frizzy curls, my freckled cheeks and resting bitch face. But I don't recognize her. She's softer around the edges from the long immobile months with a feeding tube. There are dark circles under her eyes that were never there before. The tan from the Moab sun is gone—she looks pale and tired.

I pull the scarf off from around my neck and unzip my jacket to see the dark red scar on my throat, nearly two inches long, still raised and shiny. It's better than the gaping hole after they removed the plastic tube that let air into my smoke-swollen throat. I haven't been able to bring myself to touch it, even though the doctor told me to massage it with scar oil every day. It's too angry, too red and fiery, too much of a reminder of the past five months.

That's me, I tell myself, staring hard at the mirror—but really just staring at the scar. I should make myself touch it, run a finger along the ridge—maybe then it would be more real. As I stand there, fixated on it, I suddenly feel a tightness in my chest, an overwhelming urge to gulp in a huge breath of air. When I try, it feels like my lungs can't fully expand, like my throat is still swollen shut from breathing too much smoke. A panicky feeling starts to bubble up, and I try three more times before I finally take a big enough breath to feel satisfied. The panic ebbs away, my finger hovering near the scar.

I throw a blanket over the mirror.

When I leave my room the next morning, I hear Eden's voice in the kitchen, pinched.

"I just can't today, Prince," she's saying. I pause in the hallway, peering around the wall. She has her back to me, phone to her ear. "No, no, I just— Look, I just got back into town in the middle of the night, and I'm just fucking exhausted, okay?"

I feel my cheeks flush. Eden didn't ask to be suddenly saddled with raising a teenager. I try to remember what day it is—time seems so weird and immaterial since the fire. Is it a weekday? Is she supposed to be at work?

"I think it's too soon," Eden's murmuring into the phone as she wanders aimlessly around the kitchen. Typo winds between my ankles, meowing loudly, and Eden turns. She smiles quickly when she sees me, but she still looks drawn.

"Lemme call you back," she says into the phone. "Hey! Did you sleep okay? I know that air mattress isn't exactly comfortable." She's trying too hard to sound perky.

"It's fine," I assure her, stepping shyly into the living room. The blinds are open, sunlight pouring through gauzy white curtains. Eden has hung colorful glass bulbs from the curtain rod, and they toss patterns of purple and blue across the floor. There's a cup of coffee on the counter, a half-eaten bagel smeared with cream cheese. The calmness of her apartment should ease my nerves, but I feel more on edge than ever. "Eden, you don't have to . . . I mean, you shouldn't cancel all your plans because of me."

Eden's smile fades. "Oh, Moose—it's really okay. I don't want to leave you here by yourself after . . ." She trails off, not wanting to say *the fire*, as though it would send me into a debilitating panic attack. It might—I can't seem to figure out what's going to trigger me these days.

"I don't— Wait, were you baking?" I realize that she's wearing an apron, a wooden spoon in one hand.

"Oh! Yeah." She turns, picking up a baking dish on the counter. "I made flan for us."

My throat hitches. Spanish flan, the weird, custardy dessert that Dad loved. There was a bakery in Moab that he was obsessed with, and when they closed down, he learned how to make it himself. Every other week, there was flan after dinner, a trail of sticky eggshells left behind on the counter.

"For Dad," I say.

Eden starts to speak, then closes her mouth, looking like she's about to cry. "I hadn't talked to him in a couple weeks," she says quietly, staring down at the flan. In the last few months she spent with me in Moab, Eden barely talked about Dad. I assumed she thought I wouldn't want to talk about him, but seeing her now, staring down at her lumpy homemade custard, I realize she probably didn't want to talk about him either. Or maybe she *needed* to talk about him, but couldn't with me. I feel another pang of guilt and look away.

"Go see your friend," I insist, leaning down to pet Typo. Mostly because I don't know what else to say. "I can hang out here."

"You should come with me," she says cheerily, though her voice sounds strained. "It would be good for you to get out of the house."

"I just got here," I point out, pulling a bagel from the plastic bag on the counter. I twist the halves apart and drop them in the toaster.

"And you spent all summer not going anywhere or doing anything."

"I was busy being in the *hospital*," I say incredulously, but Eden's already pulling off her apron and tossing it over the back of a kitchen chair.

"It won't be super long, just an hour or two to get some fresh air."

"I don't want to go, Eden."

When Eden doesn't answer, I look up. She's biting her lip, fiddling awkwardly with the edge of the baking pan. "Moose, I . . . I can't leave you here by yourself."

"I'm really okay," I say, a little annoyed now. I'm sixteen, and I haven't been babysat in years. "Dads let me stay home alone all the time in Utah. I'm not going to trash your apartment."

"No, Moose, that's not—" She sighs and rubs her temples. "Fuck. Moose, the therapist at the hospital told me you're a suicide risk right now. They didn't even want to discharge you yet."

The air seems to leave my lungs. Silence stretches between Eden and me.

"I'm not" is all I can seem to say, though I'm not sure I believe myself. After all, I *was* thinking about Eden's Subaru flying off the cliff in Deadman Pass less than twelve hours ago.

Eden comes around the counter, stepping over Typo to gently touch my shoulder. I flinch away, and she drops her hand. "Hey. We just need to—you know—take these first couple months slow. You've been in the hospital a long time, and . . . and Dr. Greene said it's going to take a while to process everything."

I don't answer. *Process*. The word seems to be following me around. Dr. Greene said it a million times in my sessions with her. It's plastered all over the insides of the hospital pamphlets. *Process* doesn't feel like a real word anymore.

"Fine," I say, squaring my shoulders. "Where are we going?" As soon as the words leave my mouth, it occurs to me that Eden might have had a date, or a work meeting, or something equally important where it would be weird to bring your little sister who you barely know.

"It's a surprise."

"Eden."

"Moose."

"Seriously? I'm sixteen."

"So? I'm twenty-six, and I still like surprises."

"I just wanna be prepared for . . . I dunno, how many people I'm going to have to talk to." For the first three months after the fire, I sounded like I'd swallowed gravel when I spoke, and every sound made my throat burn. It's mostly back to normal now, but I still don't sound like *me*. There's a lingering rasp, and talking too loudly makes my trach scar vibrate in a weird way, like it doesn't want me to forget it's there.

"Don't worry about that."

It's easy for her to say, but I can tell Eden's not budging on this, so I sigh in resignation.

"Let me just change real quick," she says, tossing her wooden spoon in the sink. She gives my shoulder a squeeze as she passes me, slipping into her bedroom.

"What about the flan?"

"Put it in the fridge!" she calls through the door. "It probably sucks anyway!"

chapter three

"IS THIS A WAREHOUSE?"

Eden turns off the car. She's driven us down a winding road past a closed amusement park, through a gate, and up to a parking lot in front of a huge metal building. There are a surprising number of cars around for what looks like a creepy abandoned factory. She seems almost giddy, like she's letting me in on a secret.

"A hangar," Eden answers.

"Like for a plane?"

"Yeah. But we don't use it for that."

A woman around Eden's age passes the car, waving at her. The woman's eyes slide to me, and I can see her processing. Do Eden's friends know about me, where she spent all summer? Do they know how our dad died? But the woman just grins at me too before heading toward the building. As she passes, I see the huge bag on her shoulders. Strapped to the outside of the bag, a pair of roller skates.

Memories rush at me. Dad kneeling at my feet when I was six, lacing up a pair of pink quads. Clutching his hand as I shuffled awkwardly around the rink, other skaters sailing past us with ease.

Seeing smoke through the colored disco lights. Hearing screams as people fought to get to the doors. Scrambling for that window in the arcade.

"Moose?"

I realize I'm breathing hard, clutching the leg of my pants. That tightness in my chest is back, like I can't get enough air. And Eden's staring at me.

"What the hell, Eden?"

"This isn't a roller rink," Eden says quickly.

"It sure fucking looks like one."

"No. Totally different. Roller derby."

At her words, the panic releases my ribs slightly, letting me breathe. "Like—the Elliot Page movie? You skate around and hit people?"

"No, this is the real thing. But I guess we do skate around and hit people."

I study the big metal hangar, the people bundled in hoodies and raincoats headed to its doors with skates dangling over their shoulders. "I have no idea how to play roller derby."

"Oh, you're not playing. You're not even gonna be on skates. Just watching."

"You still skate?" I have a few hazy memories of a gangly teen Eden at the rink with us—our dad and her mom separated before I was born, but she used to spend summers with us when I was a kid, when we practically lived at the Rollerdome. Dad and I drove from Moab to Boise to pick her up one year, and I spent the whole nine-hour drive grilling Dad on my distant older sister, making a list of her favorite food and TV shows and whether she liked Taylor Swift or not. *You don't have to impress her, Moose,* Dad had said eventually, arm draped over the steering wheel as we drove through the blank brown desert north of Salt Lake City. *She's family.*

"Yeah," Eden says now. "I never stopped skating." I guess it's one more thing I didn't know about her.

I look back out at the airplane hangar. A sign on the side of the building reads ROSE CITY ROLLERS, with two fists punching toward the viewer. The whole building seems defiant—a run-down-looking warehouse tucked in the corner of a dreary, closed amusement park. The people gathering at its entrance look strong.

"Okay, I can see now that I shouldn't have sprung this on you," Eden's saying, running a hand through her frizzy curls. "But can you just hear me out?"

I give her a look, which she takes as a yes.

"Roller derby is not like rink skating at all. You use totally different skills, you wear all this special protective gear—hell, you even use a different type of skate. There's no lasers or disco balls or anything like that. It's a serious, competitive full-contact sport that just happens to be played on roller skates."

"And what makes you think I want to watch that?" I ask. My voice has an edge, but I'm still trying to wrap my head around the fact that Eden thought it would be okay to bring me *skating*, of all things.

"Because it's powerful," she says firmly. "And the people who play roller derby are resilient, and badass, and wonderful. I just . . . I thought maybe you should see that you don't have to give up skating forever." She catches my eye, and I can see that she's excited to show me this. "Moose? Is this okay?"

"It's fine," I manage, even though it's not.

"Watch us skate for five minutes. If you hate it, give me a signal, and we'll go." She's staring at me nervously, like she's praying I'll say yes. I close my eyes and take a deep breath, trying to dispel some of the anxiety roiling in my stomach.

"Let's go in." I open my door and scramble out of the car before I can see Eden's reaction.

The inside of the Hangar is dominated by a huge oval track, marked by neon orange tape on blue plastic tiles. Bleachers are crowded around the sides, where people talk loudly as they strap on helmets and protective gear.

"You can sit wherever," Eden tells me, so I climb to the top of the bleachers where it's empty, making sure my scarf is covering my trach scar. I watch Eden sit between two other women, greeting them loudly. One hugs her, and the other tousles her hair.

In the few years that Eden spent summers in Utah with us, she looked a lot like me—awkward and kind of scrawny, with frizzy brown curls and glasses, like she didn't quite fit anywhere. Now she seems at home, laughing as she pulls kneepads out of her bag. Everyone here looks like they could snap me in half—tall, short, heavy, or tiny, they all have muscles. I see dyed hair like Eden's, piercings, tattoos.

Someone turns on music, and an upbeat Lizzo song fills the Hangar. I watch one woman stand, wearing full protective gear and a helmet with a whistle around her neck. She jumps easily over the low foam barrier around the track, skating smoothly to the middle.

"Get your asses on the track!" she calls, and more skaters stand and hop the barrier. "Let's scrimmage!" I watch Eden skate in a group of four on the track, laughing with them as they warm up.

Even though the Hangar's freezing and my butt quickly goes numb on the bleachers, all I can do is stare in awe. I've spent practically my whole life at the roller rink in Utah, but I've never seen skating like this. Some of them move like Olympic weight lifters on wheels, slamming a shoulder or a hip into someone else so hard that they go sliding across the track. Some are like water, threading themselves easily between the other skaters and ducking out of hits impossibly fast.

I try to work out the rules from watching—it looks like a sort of race, with five skaters from each side on the track at once. Two of them wear stretchy fabric helmet covers emblazoned with a big star on each side, and when the whistle blows, they fight their way through all the other skaters to lap the track. I can't figure out everything that's happening, though—there are whistles and penalties and skaters screaming at each other, but there are also brutal hits that the referees don't seem to mind.

Eden never wears the helmet with the star, but she commands the rest of her team every time she's out, barking orders and darting around to catch other skaters. She's small like me, but she's outgrown her scrawniness to look wiry, tough. On the track, moving her teammates where she needs them, she's like a different person. I don't recognize her as my awkward older sister.

I can't get over how *strong* she looks, how I can hear her voice from the back of the bleachers.

One of the referees blows a long whistle.

"Cooldown laps!" someone shouts, and the skaters high-five one another, retrieving their water bottles and skating slow circles around the track. They're all flushed and sweaty, but they look exhilarated as they roll out their arms and stretch their legs.

It's over? I glance at the clock on the wall and realize an hour has passed. I watch the skaters return to the bleachers, stripping off their sweaty gear and pulling sweatshirts over their jerseys.

I haven't been on wheels for five months now. It's the longest I've gone without skating since I was a kid, and I haven't missed it. My skates had burned with the rest of the rink, and I was glad. I tried to block any thoughts of it from my mind, scared to remember the flames and the searing pain and the feeling of my wheels melting to the floor as I tried to find my dads.

"Hey," Eden says when I join her at the bottom of the bleachers. She's standing in a knot of other chatting skaters, a half-eaten protein bar in hand. She's shiny with sweat, and her hair is a mess from the helmet, but she's grinning, looking more at ease than I've seen her all summer. She loops an arm around my shoulders and turns to her teammates. "Y'all, this is my little sister, Moose."

"Is that your derby name?" asks one, a stocky skater with her hair in two braids. " 'Moose'?"

"It's short for Morgan," I answer, feeling weirdly shy. "But it's only one letter shorter."

The skater laughs. "Nice. I'm Prince Harming. You transferring in?"

"This is literally the first time she's seen derby, Prince," Eden says, and I get the impression that Prince has pressured people into derby before.

"Ohhhh, okay. So if we give you a cool derby name, will you skate for us?"

"She's also sixteen," Eden adds.

Prince shrugs. "We have a junior league. Oh, what about *Moose-a-rita*? Or *Moose Knuckles*? Oh!" she exclaims, nearly smacking a nearby skater in the face. *"Moose on the Loose!"*

"Chill, Prince," another skater says. "Let the kid breathe."

These women all look so strong, carrying themselves like they own the world. I want to say something witty or impressive.

"Um. That was really cool."

They smile indulgently at me, and I wish I could sink through the concrete floor and disappear.

"My girlfriend's here," one skater says, and I feel a little jolt at the word *girlfriend*. She said it so casually. "See y'all next week. Prince, Fist, you two want a ride?"

As Prince follows the other skaters to the door, she gives me a playful nudge. "I'll see you at practice, Moose on the Loose."

Eden stares after Prince for a second, then hefts her skate bag on her shoulder. "You ready?"

"Yeah." I glance back at the track—another group is skating on it now, warming up. I want to stay and watch, but Eden's already headed for the door. I follow her out to the car as the rain starts back up.

"We can grab lunch on the way home," Eden's saying as she opens the trunk to dump her skate bag in. "I have to catch up on some work emails, but maybe tomorrow we can hit Ikea."

"Eden."

She pauses, one hand on the door of the open trunk. "Yeah?"

My chest feels tight, like it's clawing down the words I want to say. It's the same feeling I get before the panic sets in, dragging me back into the fire and the window and the rink. I finally manage a deep breath, calming me enough so I can talk.

"Why did you bring me here?"

"I told you. I thought seeing a different kind of skating might help. See that you don't have to give it up entirely."

"Maybe I *want* to give it up entirely." I say it without thinking, and I'm surprised by the way my stomach clenches at the words.

"*Do* you want to give it up?" Eden's saying now. She has one hand on the trunk, and she looks nervous. I don't answer. "Look, there's a juniors' intake next weekend. I think you should do it, Moose. It could be really good for you."

"Junior roller derby," I repeat dully. "Have you seen me? I couldn't knock someone down if I wanted to." Maybe before the fire, when I still had muscles from rock climbing and full lung capacity.

"Sure you could. You just have to learn how." Eden's face is brightening, excited.

"Do I have to pick a derby name?" I ask as we climb into the car.

"Not yet. You have to earn it."

"What's yours?"

She chuckles as she turns the key. "Ripley Riot."

I'm not surprised. Eden only lived with us for a few summers when I was a kid, and I remember a good chunk of that time was spent watching *Alien* over and over.

I buckle my seat belt and glance out the window as she backs out. When I catch sight of my own face in the side mirror, I'm almost startled. For a second—just *one* second—the girl in the mirror looked like me. Fuller, brighter, stronger. My gray scarf is still in place, trach scar still hidden, voice quiet enough to hide the rasp. Eden's teammates must know what happened—you don't just randomly show up with a long-lost half sister after being gone for almost half a year. But it didn't feel like they pitied me the way everyone else has.

Maybe Eden has a point.

Eden drives us to Ikea the next day, where we load the cart with sheet sets and hangers and a fake vintage botanical print. "That's cool," I mentioned, pointing to it, and Eden immediately grabbed it for the cart. "Can you afford all this?" I ask when she wedges a rolled-up carpet into the cart, angling it so it's sticking out in front of us like a battering ram.

"Sure," Eden says breezily, but I stop mentioning things when I like them anyway. I don't need to be the reason Eden drains her bank account.

I keep stealing glances at her as we wind through the fake kitchens and bins full of shrink-wrapped pillows. I was always completely enamored by Eden when she spent summers with us in Utah—I idolized her skull necklaces and emo band T-shirts and skinny jeans, convinced she was the coolest person to walk the planet and overwhelmed with panic and pride when she deigned to hang out with me. We look a lot alike, even though we're only half related. Under her faded blue curls, her cheeks are dusted with freckles, spilling onto her upper lip. I reach up to touch my nose absentmindedly, wondering what I would look like if I had a septum piercing like her. I think about the trach scar, thick and red and hidden under my scarf, and I pull my hand away, shoving it in my pocket.

We order meatballs and desserts in the cafeteria, dropping our trays at a table near the window. "The finest view in Portland," Eden says grandly, gesturing to the parking lot.

"Do you even know what this is?" I pick up a little green cookie half-dipped in chocolate, skeptical.

"Yeah," she says, fishing the receipt out of her purse. "It's a . . . *damm-su-ga-ree.*"

"Flawless Swedish."

When I agreed to try derby, it felt like something finally broke between Eden and me, like a dam giving way. Suddenly, she was my sister again, and some of the awkwardness faded as we both remembered what it was like to have a sister. We shared a dad, who married Eden's mom right out of high school and taught architecture at the community college. I'd only met Eden's mom a few times, but Eden had always treated Papa like a fun uncle she got to stay with for the summer. Hers was the first familiar face I saw at the hospital, the first person not in scrubs, who sat by my bed and slept on the uncomfortable rolling cot at night. I couldn't talk yet when I first woke up, but I remember my eyes stinging as soon as I saw Eden so close to me, her eyelids swollen. Eden being there meant my dads weren't.

I shake off the memory as Eden spears a meatball on her fork. "So, the juniors' intake is on Saturday, after my scrimmage," she says. "I coach one of the junior teams, and I help out with the introduction class, so I'll be around."

"An *introduction* class?" I haven't skated since the fire, but I practically grew up in the rink before that. Learning to skate into someone else hard enough to knock them over couldn't be *that* difficult, considering I already know how to skate. I'm still not sold on playing derby in the first place, but I promised Eden one practice before I decide.

"Everybody starts in the class, even if you've been playing derby for years. They need to evaluate your safety before tryouts. That's when you join a team." Her brow furrows. "Hang on—do you know the rules? Like, how the game works?"

"Kind of. It's like a race, right?"

"Yeah." Eden slides her plate to the middle of the table, scooting her meatballs around so they're in a cluster on one edge. "A derby game is called a *bout*, and it's split into segments called *jams*, which last up to two minutes." She stabs toothpicks into five meatballs. "Okay, pretend the ones with toothpicks are wearing a different color. Each jam has ten skaters on the track, five from each team. Four of them are called blockers, and the fifth is a jammer. The jammers wear a helmet cover with a star on it, and they start behind this line." She slides her fork in a straight line through the pooled gravy.

Eden goes on like this for fifteen minutes, shuffling the meatballs around on her plate and explaining complicated scoring scenarios and rules and positions. I quickly lose track of the meatball gameplay, but Eden's so animated that I let her keep going—her eyes are bright, and she almost knocks her drink off the table because she's gesturing too enthusiastically. I realize I'm watching Eden more than the meatballs, trying to remember the last time I saw her this excited about anything. The past few months with Eden have been so heavy, and now, explaining this weird contact sport on roller skates, she seems weightless.

I realize Eden's looking at me, waiting for me to say something.

"So . . . you're a blocker, right?" I ask. I remember that there are two positions—jammers, who wear the star, and blockers, who don't—but that's about it.

"Usually, yeah. I like blocking. I get to yell a lot."

I scrutinize Eden's plate, trying to wrap my head around the meatball game she's created. "Is that it?"

"Well, no. There's a ton of rules. It's a game where you can get a concussion or a broken ankle, like, anytime, so the referees are pretty strict to try to keep everyone safe."

"Have you ever gotten hurt?" I can't picture the shy Eden in my head taking a hit big enough to put her in an ambulance.

"Sure, but I've been lucky. Just a sprained ankle a couple years ago and your average bruises. Everybody gets hurt," she adds nonchalantly. "It's a rough game. But that's why we train skaters on the basics so much—to keep everybody safe."

To my own surprise, I want to keep talking about roller derby—a million questions immediately come to mind—but I can tell Eden's about to change the subject.

"So . . . school."

The word puts a lump in my throat. "Let's talk about derby some more."

"You still have to go," Eden says slowly.

"Can't you drop out at sixteen?"

"Not in Oregon. Eighteen."

I slide my hands around the back of my neck.

"Can I be homeschooled?"

Eden sighs. "I get it, Moose." Though I'm not sure she does. "But I don't have time to homeschool you. I have to go back to work, and I've already missed so much—" She stops herself. "I'm sorry."

I briefly consider all the cruel ways I could hurl this back at her—she could have just put me in foster care in Utah, still has time to turn around and drop me off—but I can tell she feels bad by the way her shoulders sag and she avoids my gaze, picking at her meatballs. *She's trying.*

"Do I get to choose which school?"

"There are some private high schools in Portland—"

"I don't want to go to a private school." It might be fine—there's only one private school in Moab, so I wouldn't know—but I get the feeling Eden isn't swimming in cash, and I know tuition is expensive. "What about normal schools?"

"The *public* school in my—*our* neighborhood is pretty good. Some of the derby kids go there. And I think you've only missed a couple weeks, so you won't be the weird new kid or anything."

"I think I'll still be the weird new kid," I grumble, pushing green beans around on my plate.

"Prince has an old phone for you," Eden goes on, like she's checking things off a list. "I know you . . . don't have yours anymore." She's stiff now. Talking about the fire is the only thing that still seems to make Eden clam up. I feel like I should mention it to break the ice, but I can never bring myself to say the words either.

"Anything else?" I ask reluctantly, guessing what she's about to say.

"Yeah . . . Dr. Greene really recommended you continue counseling here."

There it is. I stiffen, look away.

"She gave me a list of recommended therapists, and you're still covered by Dad's insurance for a while." Eden sighs. "Moose? I know it sucks, but I think it's a good idea."

I don't want to talk about this in the Ikea cafeteria, surrounded by people eating cheap Swedish food next to towering carts of home goods. I can't listen to anyone else tell me about how I need to *process*.

"Fine," I say, mostly so Eden will stop talking about it.

I can tell she's tense. Just like that, the walls are back up between us.

chapter four

THE UPS TRUCK SHOWS UP while Eden and I are dragging Ikea boxes up the stairs to her apartment. I look around for Eden when the driver hops down into the street, but she's just disappeared up the stairs with the new rug, leaving me alone by the sidewalk.

"Got a bunch of boxes here for Morgan Shaker," the driver says, and there's no way for me to pretend he's talking to someone else. *Answer him,* I urge myself, but when I open my mouth, nothing comes out. He's looking at me expectantly, holding an electronic signature pad.

"That's— I'm—" I stop again.

"I just need a signature," the delivery guy says, holding out the signature pad. I don't think he cares if I'm Morgan Shaker, as long as he can exit this increasingly awkward interaction as fast as possible. I'm frustrated with myself, determined to say something, but my chest feels tight again, and I'm getting that feeling like I can't get enough air. Resigned, I sign the pad, and the driver gives me a look before returning to the back of his truck.

"What's this?" Eden's just come down the stairs as the UPS guy starts unloading boxes directly onto the wet grass by the curb.

"Dunno." There it is—the relief as the pressure in my chest dissipates.

Eden frowns and crosses the lawn to peer at the label on one of the boxes. She grimaces and looks back at me. "It's, uh . . . the rest of your stuff from Moab."

"Oh." There's a weird feeling in the pit of my stomach, something like panic mixed with irritation mixed with excitement at seeing my stuff again. "Did you pack it?" I've only been back to our house once since the fire. I have a vague recollection of Eden talking about it in the hospital sometime after I woke up, trying awkwardly to explain that I had to move to Oregon with her but she would take care of all the packing. I didn't really think about it at the time. Did I even *want* to see the house, the reminders of Dads in the dirty dishes in the sink, the remote on the coffee table that needed new batteries, the Christmas cards that they still hadn't packed away? I was supposed to vacuum before we left for the rink on the day of the fire—would the vacuum still be standing in the living room, its cord coiled on the carpet? Papa's hiking boots in a jumble by the door, crusted with orange dust?

But now, watching the UPS driver unceremoniously dump boxes by the curb, it feels wrong to know someone else was responsible for packing up my life.

"Yeah," Eden replies as the driver unloads the last box. "Aren't you gonna take these up to the porch for us?" she asks the driver, who's already behind the wheel of the truck.

"Sorry, busy day," he says, then the truck is peeling away, toward the next, less awkward, less traumatized delivery recipient.

"Asshole," Eden sighs, surveying the six duct-taped cardboard boxes on the lawn. It's not enough to be everything from the house in Finney's Mesa. There were shelves full of books, Papa's scratchy wool sweaters, at least four pairs of skates between the two of them. I want to ask Eden what happened to Dads' stuff. She wouldn't have sold it, would she? But the tension in the car as we drove back from Ikea was thick, made worse by the rolled-up rug shoved between our seats. I already feel like I'm in Eden's way.

"Well," she says, "I guess we're already in the middle of moving stuff." We haul the boxes up to the apartment—Eden much faster and less out of breath than me—and dump them in the second bedroom, already crowded with Ikea boxes. This morning, Eden dragged her bookshelf and drafting table out of the room, and now they're crammed in the narrow hallway until she can figure out where to put them. I feel another twinge of guilt at displacing her stuff, taking over her second bedroom that clearly used to be an office in her already tiny apartment. I probably imagined the irritation on her face as she was moving things. Probably.

Eden goes to the kitchen to order us dinner, and I cut open one of the nearest boxes. It's filled with old spiral-bound notebooks from school, scraps of college-ruled paper and crumpled English assignments falling out. I frown, pulling out notebooks and pencil stubs and my stained JanSport backpack. Is this really the stuff Eden thought I would need? The bottom of the box is filled with tightly rolled clothes that look unfamiliar after months of practically living in the same two pairs of jeans and four old T-shirts.

I sit back on my heels, deflating as I stare at the five other boxes stacked inside the doorway on towels Eden rolled out to keep the new rug dry. I don't even want to open them, don't want to see the pieces of my life that this distant sister thought defined me. Papa, thoughtful and type A, would have known what to pack—my vintage horror movie T-shirts that made him grimace, the suncatchers that hung in my bedroom window, my skates—

No. Not my skates.

I take my box cutter to the nearest Ikea box instead and start pulling out pieces of the cheap particle board dresser, blank and impersonal.

We spend the rest of the evening after dinner browsing therapists online, even though I desperately wish I could fast-forward to my first derby practice tomorrow morning. I'm not exactly excited for it, but it's better than this. I feel like a work in progress, like Eden is just methodically going down my list of problems and googling the solutions. *Spent the entire summer in the hospital unable to socialize with other teenagers* . . . public school. Check. *Mentally and emotionally unstable after a horrific tragedy* . . . therapy. Check.

Eden pulls up Google Maps to show me how easily I'll be able to walk to school, seeming genuinely excited about how great it is that I won't have to wait for the bus every day. I think she's more excited to get me out of her house for six hours a day. Her laptop screen shows a slideshow of smiling, diverse students—studying under a tree together, holding up a trophy on a basketball court, wearing lab goggles and leaning over a beaker. The last slide shows a group of kids holding up a rainbow flag, glitter painted on their cheeks and confetti scattered on the pavement around them. I hadn't even thought about whether there would be other queer people at my school in Portland. There's a weird jolt in my stomach when I see it. Is it jealousy? Excitement?

I'm not paying much attention as Eden scrolls through available therapists, trying to decipher the weird knot of nerves in my stomach at the thought of existing around other gay people who aren't my dads. I was too self-conscious to even *look* at Jenna from freshman English in Utah.

"Moose," Eden prods, and I look back to her laptop. "Come on. I really think you should be the one to make this decision."

"Any of them are fine."

"Oka-ay," Eden says sarcastically, scrolling and clicking randomly. She turns her laptop to show me a wizened old man with crooked glasses, smiling like he's in pain. "Then we'll send you to Dr. Rodney Tuttle starting tomorrow. Oh look, he's accepting new patients!"

"Fine," I snap, snatching the laptop away and ignoring Eden's grin. I give her a look, backing out of Dr. Rodney Tuttle's entry and scrolling down the list again. Eden gets up to make coffee as I pick through the various therapists, not sure what I'm searching for. I click a few, read a sentence or two of their biography, then back out. One bio catches my eye.

Therapy is a collaborative effort. My goal is to foster a strong sense of teamwork so we can work together to empower you in all aspects of your life. The picture shows a smiling woman with her hair in a sleek black ponytail over her shoulder. She looks coolly confident, like nothing could rattle her.

"I want to go to her," I tell Eden, carrying her laptop to the kitchen and showing her.

"Dr. Nisha Parikh. Great," Eden says, scrolling down to scan Dr. Parikh's list of qualifications. Her appointment cost is listed at the bottom—almost three hundred dollars an hour. Over a thousand dollars a month, when Eden is already feeding me and housing me.

"Maybe I could just try a month without therapy and see how it goes," I say quickly, but Eden is already clicking the contact form.

"I'll make it work," she says quickly, shutting the lid of the laptop, but I can tell she's making mental calculations. "You want coffee? Oh, are you—I mean, did Dad let you drink coffee?"

"I got it," I say, finding a carton of coconut creamer in the fridge. *Dad* didn't mind, but Papa's caffeine-free Mormon upbringing made him judgy when I reached for the coffeepot. *We're raising our child to be an addict,* he used to chide Dad, only half joking. Eden doesn't need to know that. "How often do I have to go?"

Eden gives me a long look. "I go to therapy, you know."

"Really?"

"Yeah. I have for years. It's nothing to be ashamed of."

"But . . ." I bite my lip, look away. "You seem so happy here."

"I am, kid," she says. "Partly because I go to therapy every week. It's not just for people with trauma. I think you'll find that a lot of your derby teammates go, too."

"Can I go to your therapist?" Maybe they'll give us a family discount.

"I think it's a good idea for us to find someone new for you to talk to. You know, so you can talk about me without it being weird. If you need to."

I avoid her gaze. She's trying. She's *really* fucking trying. And I'm not making it any easier on her. *She didn't ask to finish raising a teenager,* I remind myself. Eden had her own happy, separate life before I got dumped in her lap. The last time I saw her was at my dads' wedding in Salt Lake City, at a courthouse as soon as they legalized gay marriage in Utah. Years ago.

A nurse told me that, when Eden came to Utah after the fire, she sat in an armchair in the corner of my room for weeks. I was on a ventilator for a month, the inside of my throat so scarred from the smoke that I couldn't breathe without a machine. I couldn't do much more than sit and watch whatever the nurse turned on the TV. My gaze would usually stray to Eden, sitting quietly in her corner, sketching or reading or squinting at her laptop. She talked to me occasionally, trying to fill the silence, but she so clearly didn't know what to say. Especially when I couldn't respond. Mostly, she was just there.

One night, right after they finally took the trach out, I woke to find Eden's rolling cot empty, blankets tossed aside. The blinds over the window were slatted, the kind that let bars of moonlight ripple on the bed when they aren't closed all the way. The door to my room was cracked, and I saw Eden's silhouette in the hallway.

"I just don't know what to do," she whispered, turning slightly so I could see the cell phone pressed against her ear. "I feel like I have to do *something*. But I feel stuck."

I wonder now if she was whispering with her therapist, a late-night panic call about driving a sister she barely knew a thousand miles to live with her. And I wonder if she still feels stuck.

When I get up late that night and pad to the kitchen for water, there's a stack of mail on the counter, a long, pointy metal thing beside it. I pick it up, trying to figure out what it is, and realize Eden must use it to open mail. I don't know why I'm surprised that she owns a special tool just to open envelopes. I guess everything someone does is surprising when you don't really know them.

I slice open one envelope for fun, and the letter inside slides out. There's a red PAST DUE stamp on the front, and I flick it open against my better judgment. *Eden Shaker,* the first line says, *this is your third notice that your monthly Federal Student Aid payment of $253.40 is more than 30 days past due.*

chapter five

"GIVE IT ONE PRACTICE," Eden's saying. "That's all I'm asking. If you hate it and it feels awful, we can leave." We're in the Hangar's parking lot on Saturday, and I'm a melty, nervous blend of anxiety and giddiness. I can't tell if she thinks I'll be freaked out by skating for the first time since the fire or intimidated by the other skaters. She told me yesterday that it would be mostly beginners at today's practice, since we wouldn't be drafted onto teams until we were assessed. I've been skating practically since before I could walk, but I haven't had wheels on my feet since the fire. My body feels so different now—my muscles are gone, my throat is always raw, and I can't hide my trach scar during derby practice.

I follow Eden into the Hangar, where the bleachers are already filled with teenagers around my age. They look like younger versions of Eden's teammates—no tattoos, but a handful of them have brightly dyed hair and multiple piercings. They're textbook Instagram queer kids, even though they all look nervous. I'm starting to realize that I don't look queer at all by Portland standards. I get that same feeling as when I saw the rainbow flag on my future high school's website, a weird mix of envy and vague excitement and something else, like I don't quite belong here yet, even though I'm definitely not straight. I'm suddenly overly aware of myself, wearing scuffed sneakers with leggings and a hoodie borrowed from Eden.

"Go grab a spot with the new skaters," Eden says, signing me in on a table by the door. "I have to gear up with the other coaches, and they'll do a quick orientation before you start skating."

I climb to the top of the bleachers, perching on one end away from everyone else. They're jittery, but most of them seem to know each other, clustered in groups, showing each other videos on their phones, gossiping. They probably all go to school together. Maybe the same school I'll be at starting on Monday. Another wave of anxiety hits me, and I stare around the space to avoid making eye contact with anyone. The track, made up of blue plastic tiles, takes up most of the Hangar. Banners hang along the high metal walls, ads for yarn supply stores and taquerias and an egg donation clinic, whatever that is. There are two old church pews against the far wall where the skaters sat when I watched Eden's scrimmage, and huge industrial fans are propped up in the corners, pointed toward the track. Big trans and rainbow flags are in a place of honor above the track where an American flag would hang in any other sports venue. The Hangar looks cobbled together, like a few people on roller skates stumbled across it one day and decided it would make a decent roller derby venue.

"Listen up!" someone shouts, and the bleachers quiet. Eden's teammate Prince stands at the bottom, not in skates but with a whistle around her neck. I see Eden buckling her helmet as she chats with a couple other geared-up skaters. They look too young to be her teammates.

"Welcome to the Hangar," Prince says, tucking a clipboard under her arm and smiling at all the new skaters. "I know some of you have been here before, and some of you are new." Her gaze finds me, and she winks. "I'm Prince Harming, and I'll be one of your intake coaches. My pronouns are she/they. Before we get you on skates, a couple ground rules.

"One: when a coach is talking, you're not talking. We need y'all to pay attention and listen to keep everybody safe. Two: you're going to fall. It's part of derby. Try not to freak out when it happens, but it's okay if you do. Three: even though you're not on a formal team yet, we're still a team. You can't play derby by yourself. Show respect to your coaches and your peers." She checks her clipboard. "Oh, and we gently discourage dating your teammates. I know, like, love is love and all, but romance can make things messy in derby." A few people in the bleachers giggle and whisper, and Prince gives them a sharp gaze that shuts them up. "Questions?"

I zone out as people ask questions about schedules and renting gear and where to get a mouthguard, looking past Prince at the track. Eden's skating backward, talking to one of the young-looking skaters who's warming up beside her. She's tall and curvy, her black hair tied in two low buns that stick out under her helmet. She skates with the same confidence as Eden, like she's been doing it all her life. Even though she's about to practice and get sweaty, she has dark red lipstick on.

A clamor erupts around me as people stand on the bleachers, clomping down to the concrete floor. I get up quickly, hanging back just slightly and joining the group at the rear. Everyone's headed toward the other side of the track, where a couple parents are setting out rental gear.

Prince claps a hand on my shoulder as I pass her. "What up, Moose on the Loose? You good?"

"Yeah," I say shyly. The derby skaters are easier to talk to than total strangers like the UPS guy, but my voice still barely goes above a whisper. "Uh, does everybody skate in rental gear?"

"Most beginners do. Ripley says you've skated a lot, though, so she can probably get you set up with your own pair before too long." It takes me a minute to realize she's talking about Eden. *Ripley Riot.* She's Ripley here. "You better get over there before the good rentals are gone."

The loaner skates are clearly well-loved, scuffed with worn leather and frayed laces. I scrutinize one that a parent handed me, flipping it over to check the plates. I haven't seen skates like this before—low profile and tattered from many falls—but it's definitely a beginner skate.

Prince is going around helping people put on their gear, and I wave her past me, pulling on the pads with frayed Velcro and a battered helmet. It's weird to feel air on my trach scar after so many months of carefully covering it. I wonder how many people have noticed it. It's hard to miss. Eden already gave me an unused mouthguard from her bag and helped me mold it last night, and I pop it over my teeth.

I lace up the skates, my hands automatically tying them in my favorite pattern that helps lift my arches. I stare down at them, waiting for the panic to hit me. I'm wearing skates. I'm supposed to be feeling the fire, my stomach turning over as I scramble for the window latch, trying to claw my way out of the burning rink.

But they're just skates. And all I feel is that familiar, building anticipation that always comes with wheels on my feet.

I stand, and I don't wobble. Dads always said I seemed more coordinated on skates than my feet. The other new skaters are uncertain, wobbling as they stand on wheels for the first time—but I step easily over the foam barrier on the track, and then I'm *skating*. The surface of the track is weird, the hard plastic tiles clicking under my wheels, but the feeling comes back instantly. I'm lighter, even in these tattered skates and weighed down with gear. I'm pushing out easily, gaining speed, crossing over smoothly in the turns. For the first time in months, I feel like I can breathe without smoke filling my lungs.

The song over the speakers ends, and the next one starts abruptly, all cymbals and heavy electric guitar. I recognize it instantly—"Sabotage" by Beastie Boys. The same song that was playing when the fire started.

At first, I think I'm fine. My stomach roils a little, but I'm still skating, still sailing on the track with the familiar sensation of wheels on my feet. *It's not the rink,* I remind myself. The floor is totally different. There are rainbow flags everywhere. Everyone around me is wearing borrowed gear that stinks a little. I focus on the smell, the vague gear stink, and how alien it is compared to a roller rink. But then the stink turns into fire burning my hair, and I'm choking on smoke. My wheels are sticking in melted tar, cementing me to the rink floor. My hands are shaking as I untie my skates and yank my feet out of them, and the floor is so hot on my foot that I scream. There were so many people screaming when the fire first spread, but now the rink is devoid of voices, smoke filling the air, flames roaring around me, the Beastie Boys yelling over the warped speakers. I'm panicking, stuck, surrounded, alone, and I'm screaming, and—

My face hits the track.

I blink, staring at the blue tiles. My heart's pounding against the floor, and I'm cold, but drenched with sweat. I hear whispering, and the Hangar comes back to me. I fell. In front of everybody. And now I'm on the floor having a panic attack. I want to sink through the track and disappear.

"Everybody to the middle!" I hear Prince shout, clapping. "Hurry up!" Chatter fills the Hangar again as everyone rolls toward the center of the track, and I see a pair of skates in front of me. There's a vague smell of lavender.

"You okay?"

The voice is too soft to be Eden's. I lift my head just slightly and see the skater with the little buns and the dark lipstick, squatting in front of me.

My cheeks grow hot. "Yeah," I say quickly, scrambling to my knees. She offers me a hand, and I ignore it—but I'm shaking as I try to stand, and I slip again.

"Whoa," the girl says, catching my arms. "Damn. You came out guns blazing, huh?"

"I'm really okay."

She studies me for a moment—she's taller than me. Her expression is soft, but I'm pretty sure she could crush my head like a watermelon if she wanted to. "Mercury," she says.

"What?"

She smiles. "It's my derby name."

"Oh." I offer my hand awkwardly. "Moose. That's my . . . regular name. I don't have a derby name yet."

"Cool," Mercury says, taking my hand. Instead of shaking it, she rests her other hand on top of mine. It feels weirdly intimate. "Welcome to derby, Moose. You should avoid ignoring Coach Prince in the future. She doesn't take any shit."

My cheeks flush. "Noted. Are you—" Before I can finish my question, Prince blows her whistle, giving both of us a pointed look. Mercury winks at me before she glides away, smoothly skating to the middle with Eden and Prince. Eden catches my eye. *You okay?* she mouths, and I nod, embarrassed. The Beastie Boys song is mercifully over. Or someone changed it. It's NSYNC now, which is significantly worse musically, but better for my nerves.

Now that my heartbeat has slowed down, I glance around at the other skaters on the track. I can tell most of them haven't skated much—a few of them are wobbling just standing still. They probably think I'm a mess, jumping onto the track and falling on my face before practice even starts. I stare at the ground.

"Everybody, take a knee," Prince says, and the skaters awkwardly drop to one knee on the track. Some of them glance sidelong at me, staring a split second too long. I flush and tuck my chin. "Cool," Prince goes on. "Like I said earlier, I'm Prince." She nods to Eden.

"Ripley, she/her. I'll be your assistant coach."

"I'm Mercury. She/her."

"Mercury's captain of one of the junior teams this year," Prince says. "She'll be here to help out every now and then."

Mercury's eyes flick to me, and I quickly look away. *Great.*

"First thing we're gonna learn is how to fall," Prince says. "Since you'll be doing a lot of it."

Three minutes into practice, it's clear I have no idea how to skate for roller derby. Prince spreads us out on the track and instructs us to start with a slow roll, tap one knee on the ground, then get back up in the same motion. I start out confidently enough, but I can't keep enough momentum to push myself back up without stopping. Around me, most of the new skaters are having the same issue—sliding onto their kneepad, then scrambling back up.

"Try not to use your hands to get up," Mercury says to a skater in front of me, demonstrating the smooth knee tap. "Let your momentum carry you through."

She hangs back to watch me, and I try to pretend she's not there as I perform an awkward knee tap. Mercury just nods and falls back to the next skater, and I feel weirdly disappointed that she didn't have any feedback for me.

My legs are shaking after knee taps, but Prince moves right on to falling. "*When*—not if—you go down, you do an egg," she says, and Eden demonstrates by sliding onto her knees and curling her limbs beneath her, tucking her head in. "If you don't egg, you're asking for someone to run over your fingers or kick you in the face with a toe stop. And you *can* play derby with a broken finger or a broken nose, but it ain't as fun."

We spread out again, practice falling into eggs and getting back up. Prince makes us do it over and over, until I feel like my legs are about to detach from my body. Every time we go down, we scramble back up.

Practice gets a little easier after that. We do watermelons, crossovers, and work on basic skating stride—things I can handle. I'm watching Mercury drift around the inside of the track, correcting people's posture and offering tips. "Sink a little deeper into that crossover, Moose," she tells me at one point, then skates away before she can see my grimace. I'm annoyed at her correction, but she's right. After months without practice, my crossovers are shallower than they should be.

After two excruciating hours, Prince finally blasts her whistle and everyone rolls to the middle of the track, exhausted. I grab my water bottle and accidentally splash half of it down my face. My helmet itches, the foam sweaty against my head, and my legs are shaking. Six months ago, this might have been easy.

"Everybody feel good?" Prince asks, and a few skaters give her exhausted looks. "First practice is always the hardest. You're gonna hurt tomorrow. And some of you won't want to come back. I want all of you to give it a month. Just one month of practice, twice a week, and if you still want to quit, fine. But I guarantee you're gonna keep coming back. Everybody in for a cheer!" She waves us in, and we cluster in a sweaty circle, holding our wrist-guard-clad hands in fists in the middle.

"Mercury, what's our cheer?" Prince says.

Mercury grins. Somehow, even after two hours of skating, her lipstick is perfect. "Skate hard, with a stomp after." I have a brief moment of panic trying to decide whether I'm going to cheer with the group. Before I can decide, Prince is already pumping her fist and counting us off. "One, two, three—"

"SKATE HARD!"

The cheer echoes off the high metal ceiling and seems to hang in the air, ringing in my ears. For a split second, time feels frozen, and loud, and sweaty, and unified. Then the circle breaks apart, and skaters chat with each other as they collect their water bottles and roll back to the bleachers. And I realize that I cheered with everyone else and nobody's staring.

"Nice job, Moose."

I turn—Mercury's right behind me, already with her skates and her helmet off. Even in just her socks, she seems to tower over me.

"Thanks," I say awkwardly. "I promise I don't usually faceplant the second I put skates on."

"Oh, I always fall when I'm doing the most average thing," she says, tucking her helmet under her arm. "I never seem to biff it in gameplay, but skating to the cooler to fill up my water bottle? On. The. Ground." She's trying to be chill and fun, and I'm just staring at her like a weirdo, unsure of what to say to impress her.

"So, Coach Prince," I try, "does she—I mean, uh, they coach all the junior teams?"

"Prince uses *she* or *they* pronouns," Mercury explains smoothly.

"So you can use either one. They just coach the beginning class and the Hot Shots. That's my team."

I want to ask her more—how many teams are there, how hard is it to get on a team, who decides, when do you get to play, how long she's been skating—but then another new skater talks to Mercury, and she gives me a brief smile before she turns away.

I roll back to my spot on the bleachers, pull off my loaner skates and helmet, and watch skaters for the next practice filing in and gearing up. And even though my legs are shaking and my lungs feel like they're going to explode, all I want to do is put my skates on and get back on the track.

chapter six

MY GOOD MOOD DEFLATES on Monday morning when my alarm goes off at seven. Prince came by last night with an old laptop and phone for me, presenting them like priceless artifacts. "This phone is good luck," they told me seriously. "The day I got it, we won a tournament in Salem and I got a hot girl's number. Treat it with respect." I turned the phone over, rubbing my thumb across a worn sticker that looked like it used to be a snake curling around a roller skate. *Salem Serpents,* read a tattoo-style banner below it. The old laptop was similarly aged but worked well enough.

I roll to one side and hit the snooze button, but I'm immediately wide awake, my stomach twisting with nerves. I feel like I haven't gotten a full night's sleep since before the fire. In the darkness of the room, with the sun not quite up and the shades pulled over the window, the stacked boxes from our house in Moab cast menacing shadows. I haven't opened any of the others.

I slide reluctantly out of bed and determinedly ignore the boxes as I trudge to the bathroom to pull my curls into a bun, my go-to for school in Utah when I couldn't be bothered to wrestle with them. But when I look in the mirror, the hair lifted off my face just accentuates the dark red scar on my throat. I pull the hair tie out, fluff it into something manageable, then add a hoodie and Eden's old gray scarf. It'll have to do.

Eden drives me to school on her way to work, talking nonstop about derby and what she has to do at work today and what she's going to pick up for dinner later. I'm learning she does this when she's anxious, probably to avoid sitting in awkward silence. Our dad did the same thing when he was nervous. Whenever we went to the Home Depot in Moab—the watering hole of straight conservative Utahns—he talked the entire time, pretending he knew how to use every tool, like it would help us blend in. I feel like Eden would appreciate the comparison, but she's talking so much I can't get a word in to point it out. "You feel okay?" she asks, finally pausing for air as she pulls into a drop-off spot. She's jittery, and I can't really figure out why. *I'm* the one being thrown to the wolves in a new public school with no friends. I peer through the passenger window at the low brick building, my unscarred new peers talking and scrolling their phones as they head inside.

"Not really."

Eden sighs, which I've learned is the cue she's about to go into parenting mode. "I know this isn't ideal, Moose. But I promise it'll be okay. Kids in Portland aren't like the ones in Utah. It'll take some adjusting, but it'll be okay."

I can't figure out what she means—kids here aren't homophobic? Won't stare?

"If you say so," I grumble, but I regret it as I unbuckle my seat belt, remembering the overdue student loan bill in the kitchen. "Sorry."

"Don't worry about it," Eden says, but she still looks overwhelmed. "Just call me if you need anything, okay?"

"Okay," I agree, but we both know I won't.

Eden waits in her car until I'm all the way inside, like she's worried I'll run off if she doesn't watch me the whole time. I glance over my shoulder once I'm through the glass doors to see her pulling away, and my stomach twists with nerves. There's a receptionist at the front desk of the office, looking expectantly at me. *Just talk,* I tell myself sternly. *Just open your mouth and talk like you talk to Eden. It's fine.* My chest is getting tight, but it only takes a couple breaths this time to dissipate it.

"Hi," I say, and the receptionist leans closer to hear me better. I clear my throat before giving him my name. He scans my file, and his eyes widen slightly when he (presumably) reaches the part about the fire.

"Do you go by Morgan?" he asks.

"I go by Moose." It's a nickname that usually gets me a weird look, but the receptionist looks totally unfazed as he types something in.

"All right, Moose," he says, and the printer beside him whirrs. "Let me get you your schedule and a copy of the handbook. Have your sister sign it tonight and bring it back tomorrow." He pulls a packet out of the printer and staples it, slides it across the desk to me. "I can show you to your first class in a minute if you just—"

"I'll find it," I say, grabbing the schedule and pushing out through the office door. My first class is world history, and I manage to find the room and slip in quietly. The teacher—Ms. Trayhart, according to my schedule—has her back to the class, writing on the whiteboard. I hover by the door, trying to decide if I should go talk to Ms. Trayhart or pick a random desk and hope seats aren't assigned or—the most appealing option—turn around and run back to Eden's apartment before anyone perceives me. I look down at the schedule in my hands and crinkle the edge of the paper, feeling hot. Maybe if I just don't make a decision, time will stand still long enough for me to sink into the floor.

Someone taps me on the shoulder. "Moose?"

I jump and turn to see Mercury standing behind me, remarkably less terrifying in a chunky knit sweater and jeans.

"Hi," I say with a wave of relief. I've only met her once before, but Mercury being here means I have an ally. I wave the crumpled schedule in my hand toward the desks where my new peers are already filtering in. "Are there, uh, assigned seats?"

"Yeah. Have you met Ms. Trayhart yet?" I shake my head, and Mercury gestures me to follow her up to the board. She introduces me to Ms. Trayhart, who parks her glasses on her head and goes to her desk to make a note on her laptop.

"You go by Moose, right?" she asks, and I nod. Mercury, bless her, stays beside me, standing between me and the rest of the room. "It's really nice to meet you, Moose." She hands me a half sheet of paper and a textbook. "Fill this out and get it back to me at the end of class. You only missed a couple weeks. I can get you caught up if you come to my planning period this afternoon."

"There's an empty desk by me," Mercury says, and she leads me toward a pair of open desks by the window. I'm grateful that I made it through that whole exchange without having to talk, but I still feel hyperconscious of myself as I weave through the desks, trying not to hit people with my backpack as I go. Is everyone staring at me? Can everyone see the scar on my throat, hear the rattle in my voice? When I finally reach the open desk behind Mercury's and throw my bag down, my shoulders are heaving, panic and fear coursing through me. The room is tunneling, closing in, getting smaller, suffocating me.

Mercury turns in her seat. "Are you okay?" she asks quietly. I meet her eyes, and force my breathing to slow down.

"Yeah." I clench my fists under the desk, forcing myself to calm down. "I didn't know you went to this school."

"There's a few of us from the league here," she replies, and she studies my face for a moment. Even without the helmet and the skates, she's gorgeous, with perfect red lipstick and winged eyeliner, her inky black hair in low twin buns. I can't fully process how pretty she is because my heart is still racing and I'm trying to push the panic down.

"I'm glad you're here," she starts, but then Ms. Trayhart is clapping to get our attention to start the lesson, and Mercury gives me one more warm smile before turning around to face the front of the room.

I look down at the half sheet of paper Ms. Trayhart handed me, mostly to avoid the lingering stares around the classroom.

Your legal name:

Name you want me to call you in class:

Name you want me to call you when talking to your guardian(s):

Pronouns:

Pronouns you want me to use in class:

Pronouns you want me to use when talking to your guardian(s):

Anything else you want me to know about your identity or gender presentation:

I glance around the room again. With everyone paying attention to Ms. Trayhart, my panic ebbs and it's easier to look at my new classmates. Some of them have dyed hair like Eden and her derby teammates. I see nose piercings, rainbow pins and trans flags on their backpacks. In Moab, just *looking* at Jenna from freshman English too long would get people to call me a dyke. Here, it seems like half the class is queer.

I look back down at the half sheet on my desk, focusing on *Anything else you want me to know about your identity or gender presentation.* I'm not used to being asked my pronouns, not used to seeing other queer people confidently wearing their flags and rainbows and *they/them* pins at school. I could probably be out here, could just tell people that I'm queer right away.

Biting my lip, I pull a pen out of my bag to fill out the half sheet.

Your legal name: Morgan Shaker

Name you want me to call you in class: Moose

Name you want me to call you when talking to your guardian(s): Moose

Pronouns: she/her

Pronouns you want me to use in class: she/her

Pronouns you want me to use when talking to your guardian(s): she/her

Anything else you want me to know about your identity or gender presentation: no

---

I manage to make it through the next week of school, but I'm on edge almost the entire time. I can't figure out where the anxiety is coming from, but I move through the halls with my head down and eat lunch in the library, like making eye contact with any of my new peers will send me reeling into a panic attack. The first fifty minutes of every day, when I sit behind Mercury in Ms. Trayhart's class, are the only easy part. Mercury—or *Sonia,* which I learn is her real name—and I don't talk much that first week, but she smiles at me every morning, and on Friday, she asks cheerily if I'll be at practice tomorrow. My stomach jumps at her words, but not in the familiar anxious way.

"Yeah," I tell her, hoping I didn't answer too fast. "Yeah, I'll be there."

"Good," Mercury says with a grin. "I can tell you're a good skater. We just need to teach you some contact skills."

"Contact skills?"

"You know. Hitting." She mimes punching the air in front of her, then giggles at my startled look. "I'm joking. You can't punch people in derby."

"Oh. Right." The thought of going back to derby practice is the only thing that keeps me slogging through each day.

On Friday, I'm camped out in the conference room at Eden's office, a long line of tabs open beside the take-home English quiz I'm supposed to be doing. Videos of old championship games, message boards about learning tricky footwork skills, a whole database about choosing the right skates, and a long list of derby name suggestions. That's the one I spend the most time on, scrolling endlessly through the names and waiting for one to jump out at me. *Angela Death, Jurasskick Park, Knockems Razor* . . . none of them feel quite right.

When I get overwhelmed by trying to pick a derby name, I open

Instagram, where I've found Mercury's account. All the junior skaters seem to have separate Instagram accounts for derby, with their derby name and number in their bio and emojis to signify which team they're on. Mercury's has her pronouns and a bunch of orange hearts and flame emojis, followed by *Hot Shots Captain:-)*. It's filled with pictures of her skating in a bright orange jersey, looking strong and confident on the track. There's a red ring around her profile picture (Mercury in her helmet and red lipstick, looking coolly to one side in the middle of a scrimmage), indicating she's added a story, but I know she'll see my name if I tap it. Still, my thumb hovers over the picture. It wouldn't be weird to follow her at this point, would it? We've talked to each other every morning this week. But I don't know the social protocol with derby yet.

I close the app without looking at Mercury's story and roll my chair back from the conference table, glancing through the glass door where Eden's taking a phone call at the front desk. She's been leaving work at three each day to pick me up, then parking me in the conference room of her office while she works for two more hours. She told me her boss was okay with it, but I can tell it's a hassle for her to use one of her breaks to come pick me up. "So, what do you do at this job?" I asked her on Monday. Her nonprofit's called Rise Up for Justice Coalition or something, and their website just seems like a confusing jumble of social justice words.

"*I* answer the phones," Eden had answered as she swiped her keycard to let me into the conference room. "The nonprofit builds community and provides grantee partnership support for local organizations."

"Okay, but what does that mean?"

"Honestly, I don't really know," she admitted as she turned on the lights. "I schedule meetings and answer phones. It pays the bills."

Now, when Eden hangs up, I close the laptop lid and cross the office lobby to her.

"How much money did we get from the insurance payout?" I ask, resting my elbows on her desk.

Eden doesn't look at me as she shuffles papers around. "I don't know yet. The lawyer in Utah is still working on the estate." She shuts her computer down and reaches for her coat. "Ready to go?" Eden shuts off the lights before we head out into the hallway.

"I was kind of hoping I could buy new skates. Do you know when they'll be done with the estate?"

Eden locks the office door and gives me a look as we head down to the parking garage. "It's a lot of work, Moose. It might take a while for them to sort out." *I need new skates,* I want to say. *I need the other people in derby to take me seriously.*

"How much do you think we'll get?"

Eden ignores me as she unlocks the car, opens the back door, and tosses her purse in.

"Eden?"

"We need to talk about the house in Moab," she says, avoiding my eyes.

I deflate. "Why?"

Eden sighs and turns back to me, one hand on the driver's side door. The parking garage is empty—Eden always seems to be the last one here, even though she definitely gets paid the least. "The lawyers are asking if we're going to sell it."

"Did you tell them no?"

"I told them I need to talk to you about it."

"Just tell them no."

"Let's talk about it at home."

"I *have* a home." My tone is harsher than it needs to be. "In Finney's Mesa. Why would we sell it?"

Eden slams the car door, frustrated, and it echoes in the empty parking garage. "Because it costs a shit ton of money to own a house we're not even living in." Her words are like a gut punch.

"Sorry my dads fucking died," I snap. "I'll try to be less of an inconvenience next time."

Eden sighs and pinches the bridge of her nose. "No, it's— I'm sorry, Moose. That was shitty." She gestures to my side of the car. "You want a coffee on the way home?"

"I guess," I mumble, chucking my backpack into the backseat and climbing into the Subaru. Eden starts the car and pulls into rush-hour traffic, quiet. I pull my hood up, feeling its comforting closeness around my scar. "Sorry," I say after a while. *She is trying,* I remind myself for what feels like the thousandth time.

"Don't worry about it." We go to the Dutch Bros drive-thru, and Eden orders me a cake pop, even though it's four dollars and I'm sixteen, not eight. But it's a nice gesture, so I take it anyway, spinning it in one hand. "We do need to talk about the house, though," she says quietly as we merge onto the highway. It's dark already, raining, and the red taillights of the cars around us light up the wet road. "It doesn't have to be right now. But it has to be soon."

"I know."

"And—I think Dad would want you to spend some of his life insurance on skates, don't you? As long as you buy them from an actual skate shop where they'll custom fit you, not some cheap website."

"Yeah," I admit. "He would be horrified if he saw me browsing discount roller skates online." Thinking of him hits me hard and sudden, and out of nowhere, my stomach aches, picturing his bright smile, the red suspenders he always wore when we skated at the rink, the melty, sickeningly-in-love way he looked at Papa. When I look back at Eden, I'm suddenly desperate to take down some of the bricks in the wall between us, somehow. She looks so much like the dad we shared, so much like *me*, and I keep pushing her further away.

"Do you remember the wavy floor at the Rollerdome?" I ask. It was a strip of polished wood that rippled up and down like moguls with a carpeted wall at the end that you could slam into to stop yourself.

Eden stiffens and gives me a curious look. I haven't talked about the rink since she brought me here from Utah. "I think so," she says slowly. "In the back by the arcade, right?"

I push down the flash of panic at the mention of the arcade. *You're safe you're safe you're safe.*

"Yeah. They got rid of it when they remodeled the snack bar a few years ago."

"For real? Everybody loved the wavy floor!"

"I think somebody chipped a tooth on it, like, every hour."

Eden waves a hand. "Whatever. Everything *I* did as a kid is too dangerous now."

"Dad used to push me onto the wavy floor when I was still learning how to skate. As hard as he could."

"That sounds like him. I can totally hear your papa yelling at him about safety while he's literally throwing his kid around the rink."

"Yeah. But Dad said it was important to learn how to save myself when I lost control."

Eden smiles, but it looks tired, sad. "He was a good teacher."

"Yeah." We're quiet for a minute, both of us staring at our hands. "I miss him," I say to my feet.

"Me too."

chapter seven

I'M DISTRACTED as soon as I strap on my loaner skates at practice on Saturday. My first therapy appointment is scheduled for immediately after, and my stomach is already twisting.

Over an hour into practice, Mercury skates up to me, somehow looking gorgeous despite wearing sweaty gear head to toe. "How's it going?" I haven't talked to her much at school, preferring to speed walk in and out of the history room as fast as possible so nobody looks at me.

"How do you look amazing?" I ask, gesturing to her perfectly intact makeup before I can stop myself, and I instantly regret it. I can't figure out what it is about Mercury that makes me twitch and fall every time she looks at me—I've been skating practically as long as I've been walking. A cute girl shouldn't instantly send me crashing to the floor.

"Lots of setting spray," she says simply, then nods toward the back of the track. "Come over here with me." I follow her nervously to an empty strip of track near the penalty box. Did I screw something up already?

Mercury turns when we reach the penalty box. "I want to do some contact drills with you."

I blink. "Really?"

"Yeah. Your basic skills are good. I know you haven't skated in a while, but it's obvious they're coming back. It feels silly to make you do knee taps and plow stops when you're clearly ready for the next step."

I hope she doesn't see the flush creeping up my face. *I know you haven't skated in a while*—that's code for *your sister told me about the rink fire where you lost both your dads and had a hole in your neck for two months, and I know you haven't put on skates since your last pair melted on your feet.*

Mercury aligns herself beside me, facing the same direction, and drops into derby stance—knees bent with her butt tucked in, but her torso straight. I mimic her.

"You know about legal hitting zones?" she asks me.

"Sort of. No elbows, right?"

"Right." She runs a hand down her side, starting at her armpit and over her hip, all the way down to her knee. I feel like I'm looking too hard, and my flush deepens. "You can't hit the spine, above the neck, or below the knee. Anything else is fair game. So I want you to hit me with your hip, as hard as you can."

I stare at her. "Just . . . hit you?"

"Yeah," she says with a grin. "Just hit me."

I drop into derby stance beside her. The moment feels weirdly important. I take a breath, lean away, then throw myself into her as hard as possible.

It's like slamming into a tree. Mercury barely moves, and I bounce off her and onto the floor, skates clattering. Track dust floats up around me, and I wince, waiting for Mercury to laugh. But she just spins around and drops to her knees. "Can I touch you?"

"What?" I ask, my mouth dry.

"I want to show you where to load your weight. It's a consent thing, some people don't like being touched outside of gameplay. Is it okay?"

I look down at her soft hands hovering near my left leg. Taking a hip check doesn't seem nearly as scary as someone's hands gentle on my leg. Too much like the hospital, where random nurses would touch me all the time when I already couldn't move. "No," I blurt out. "Sorry. No."

"No problem," she says easily, breezing past it. She stands and mirrors me, shifting to one side. "If you load your weight into this outside leg, you can spring off it to get enough momentum to move me. Make sense?"

I nod, my cheeks still hot at the thought of Merucry touching my leg, but she doesn't seem fazed.

Mercury settles back into position beside me, and I try again, loading my weight and pushing off my left leg. She moves this time, just a little.

"Did you just do that to make me feel better?" I ask.

"Nah. We don't do that in roller derby. Hit me again."

She has me go on hitting her for nearly ten minutes, stopping each time to switch sides or adjust my stance. By the time we finish, I'm drenched in sweat and my legs are wobbling, but I got Mercury to move a fraction more. I count that as a win.

Out of nowhere, Prince blows the whistle to signal the end of practice, and the other skaters start drifting toward the middle of the track.

"You have good instincts, Moose," Mercury tells me. One side of her mouth quirks up in a half smile. "Listen, I think you could make one of the teams before December if you brush up your contact skills a bit. I can coach you one-on-one, if you want."

"Really?" I try not to sound too eager.

"Yeah, team captains are allowed to reserve the track for private practices. I'll check the calendar to find a time. Do I have your number?"

"Nobody has my number."

"Cool. I'll be the first, then. I'll catch you after practice." She starts to skate away.

"Wait!"

Mercury pauses, looks back at me. My mouth is dry, but if I don't ask her now, I'll lose my nerve.

"Can you hit me?"

Her lips twist in that half smile again. "You sure?"

"If I'm going to be on a team, I should know what it feels like to get hit. Right?"

Mercury laughs, shaking her head and pulling me into position beside her. I try not to hyperfixate on how easily she moves me, the way it seems like second nature to put me in the right position to get hit. "Ready?"

"Ready."

This time, it's like the tree is slamming into *me*. Mercury's hip collides with mine, and in a second I'm on the ground, sliding across the tiles on my kneepads. I'm vaguely aware of the other skaters turning toward us, gasping, but Mercury's knocked the wind out of me, and I'm on the floor trying to catch my breath.

Her skates appear in front of me, just like they did at that first practice, and again she kneels, offering me a hand. "Are you good?"

I look up at her, still breathless, her perfectly round face framed by the big lights along the ceiling of the Hangar. Her hit knocked something loose in me, and now I feel nervous in a totally different way. I grab her hand and let her pull me to my feet. "Yeah. I think you realigned my spine. But I'm good."

My blood is still pumping from practice and Mercury's hip check when I push open the door to Dr. Parikh's office. The waiting room is empty, just soft gray walls and hanging plants by the window and a trickling fountain on the coffee table. I feel my energy drop as soon as the door swings shut behind me—it feels so vastly contrary to be in such a serene room when I'm sweaty and red-faced from practice in Eden's borrowed sweatshirt. Maybe my actual clothes, the ones *I* would wear, are buried in the boxes Eden packed, but I haven't been able to search through them more since they got delivered.

There's no receptionist, so I sit in a brown leather armchair, pressing my knees together and tucking my hands in the big pocket of my hoodie. Eden pulled it from the backseat of the car when we parked outside Dr. Parikh's office, insisting it was clean as I did my best to scrub the dry sweat off with a baby wipe.

"Do you want me to go in with you?" she had asked when I finished and pulled the sweatshirt over my head. "I can sit in the waiting room."

"No, it's okay," I told her, glancing out the window. Dr. Parikh's office looked like every other house in Portland, a comforting Craftsman with big square windows. "Are you sure this is an office?"

"A lot of therapists practice out of their houses these days. Moose," she said, tapping my knee to get me to look at her. I resisted the urge to flinch. "Are you good? I know your first therapy session can be scary."

"I'm totally good," I lied. "And you don't have to come in. Just pick me up after."

Eden clearly didn't believe me, but she didn't argue when I got out of the car and headed up to the porch. We still can't quite figure out the correct dynamic for moments like this.

Now I wish I'd asked her to come in with me. I can tell the room is supposed to make me feel calm, but I'm just jumpy—I think I'd feel calmer if I could run around the block a few times. I think about getting a cup of tea from the little cart across the room, but I don't want Dr. Parikh to walk in on me trying to figure out how to work her electric kettle. I'm too sweaty for hot tea anyway. So I sit there, bouncing my knees up and down, trying instead to think about Mercury hitting me so hard that I slid across the track.

"Morgan?"

I start slightly at my name, twisting in the armchair. Dr. Parikh stands in a doorway, exactly like her picture—sleek and calm, the opposite of how I feel.

"Yeah." My voice is too rough. I clear my throat, try to swallow the glass that always seems to linger there now. "Yes. I'm Morgan."

"You can come on back if you're ready."

I follow her down a hallway and into a room with a pink velvet couch, bookshelves along the walls, and houseplants on the windowsills. This room feels calmer to me than the waiting room—it looks more personal, like Dr. Parikh decorated it herself.

"Go ahead and make yourself comfortable," she says, shutting the door behind her. She has a very slight Indian accent. I perch on the edge of the velvet couch, and Dr. Parikh takes the armchair across from me. She doesn't have a notebook or anything—she just settles with her hands in her lap and her ankles crossed, her expression warm, but not quite a smile. "Do you use the name Morgan?"

"Uh . . . not really. Most people call me Moose. But you can call me Morgan if you want."

"I'll call you Moose, if that's how you think of yourself. Where'd you get that nickname?"

"My papa. My hair wouldn't sit flat when I was little, and he used to put it up in two buns. It was so frizzy, he said I looked like a moose. He was, like, blond and ex-Mormon, and it took him a while to figure out how to do my hair." I feel like I'm explaining too much.

"And what are your pronouns, Moose?"

"Um. She and her."

"My pronouns are also she/her."

I'm not used to the question yet. Most people at derby practice introduce themselves with their pronouns, something I never heard people do in Finney's Mesa. I still haven't gotten used to how many other queer kids there are in Portland. It should have been a relief—I should have immediately and joyously come out, posted an Instagram with a rainbow flag tied around my shoulders. In Moab, my slouchy T-shirts and gay dads and consistent lack of homecoming dates made people call me a dyke, even when they didn't know how many hours I spent staring at Jenna from freshman English's Instagram posts. I *still* somehow felt too queer, too out, too visible. But in Portland, where the other kids in my school talk openly about their girlfriends and pronouns and transitioning, I don't feel queer *enough*. These would all be great things to tell the therapist sitting in front of me.

"That's good," I say awkwardly.

"So, Moose, it's very normal to feel nervous the first time you go to therapy. You might feel like you don't know what to talk about or like you don't want to open up to a stranger. And that's okay. We need to build trust with each other to make meaningful work, right?"

"Right," I agree, because it seems like the correct thing to say.

"Your sister told me on the phone that you're new to Portland. How has it been going?"

"It's okay. I've only been here a couple weeks."

"And you're from Utah, yes?"

"Yeah. It's . . . drier there."

"Most places are drier than Oregon. Do you find it a welcome change?"

I look down at my sneakers, surprised when tears prick my eyes. I've tried not to think about Utah, but Dr. Parikh's question sends a deep hurt radiating through me, an ache for the orange mesas and dusty cliffs and huge, wide-open skies filled with stars. For my dads lying on either side of me on a Navajo blanket in the backyard, making up constellations and ridiculous stories about them that made me laugh so hard I wheezed. The big copper wind chimes Papa hung in the back garden that sounded like gongs when a breeze came through the mesa.

"I miss it," I hear myself say. When Dr. Parikh doesn't reply, I keep talking, words spilling out faster than I can think through them. "I didn't have time. I didn't have a chance to see anyone or say goodbye to anything. The people at school would have—treated me differently." I'm saying things that I didn't even realize, things I didn't know were sitting deep within me, waiting.

My cheeks are wet, and Dr. Parikh offers me the box of tissues on the coffee table. God, I've been here for two minutes, and I'm already sobbing.

"Why would they treat you differently?"

"I mean . . ." I sniff and gesture broadly to myself. "Is it not obvious? My voice is all messed up, and I have this huge scar on my neck, and everyone would know my dads died."

Dr. Parikh is quiet, waiting for me to continue. I don't speak right away, my gaze shifting to my hands twisting in my lap. I swallow and feel that tightness in my throat that might never go away, the pull of my skin on the trach scar.

"People don't ask me about the fire," I say finally.

"Do you appreciate that?"

"I guess. I think they're trying to be polite. But they're so obvious. I was in a fucking fire. It's not a secret."

Dr. Parikh leans forward. "What would you say to those people, if you could tell them anything?"

Don't look at me—no, just talk to me. Don't talk to me. Yeah, I was in a fire. Yes, I had a tube in my throat. No, I couldn't talk while it was in. Yeah, it still hurts. No, it's not your business. Yeah, I dream about it. Constantly. "I don't know."

Dr. Parikh can tell I want to say more, but she doesn't press me.

It's pouring rain when I leave her office an hour later, and I can't tell how I feel. I hover on the porch to wait for Eden, watching puddles fill the concrete path.

Dr. Parikh told me to set a goal for myself. "The first year after trauma can feel directionless," she said, "like there's too much hurt for you to even think about processing anything. So by next April, when it's been a year since the fire, what do you want to have accomplished?"

I don't want to think about the fire, or talk about it, or remember it. It seems unreasonably cruel—almost two hundred people got out of the rink safely that night. Only *six* died, and two of them had to be my dads.

I didn't have an answer for Dr. Parikh. It didn't feel like I had anything to accomplish. After losing Dads, the rink, and Utah, I feel hollowed out. "You don't have to come up with a goal today," she said as she opened the door for me. "But let's think about it."

On the porch, I feel the panic deep within me, starting to slowly claw its way up to my throat. My pulse hammers against my scar. It always starts like this—a deep, unsettled feeling, like a creature stirring way down in the hollows of my body. It drags itself up my spine, setting me on fire as it goes. Vertebra by vertebra, flames in its wake.

My hands shake, and the creature pulls me back to the rink that night. The DJ was spinning a Beastie Boys song. The flames didn't reach the booth right away—I remember the song blaring at me from a speaker while I struggled with the window, fire singeing my hair. The song always comes back next.

A car horn blares, and the creature disappears as I start. Eden's just pulled up outside Dr. Parikh's office, waving me toward the car. I feel the panic dissipate, the song fade. I manage a deep, slow breath that satisfies the tightness in my chest. Then I shove my hands into my pockets so Eden won't see them shaking, and head into the rain.

chapter eight

We'll see you at the Hangar at 7 :-)

I check Mercury's text for the millionth time that day, and it still says *we*. Maybe if I were less awkward, I could have responded with a simple *Who's we?* But some irrational part of me feels like Mercury will rescind the whole offer to train me if I question any part of it. Stupid, but I can't shake it.

And who writes smiley faces with a nose? Is she a thousand years old?

"Just text me when you're done, and I'll come pick you up," Eden says, halting the car by the Hangar doors. "Mercury can unlock the loaner gear for you."

"You don't need to watch me?" I say it with a little more vitriol than necessary, and the corner of Eden's mouth twitches. *She's trying,* I remind myself. But the helicoptering is getting to me. Every time I enter the living room, I feel like Eden's either worrying about me or annoyed by my presence, and I can never predict which one it's going to be. I've started spending most of my time in Eden's office-turned-guest-room, trying to be as quiet and small as possible.

"You're just not supposed to be alone. I trust Mercury." Eden probably knows Mercury better than she knows me. If I showed her Mercury's text, she would probably instantly know who else planned to come to our coaching session.

I grab my bag out of the backseat and give Eden a wave, but she doesn't pull away until I open the Hangar door and step inside. It's colder inside than usual, and Chappell Roan is already blasting on the speakers. Mercury's on the track, skating backward and dancing with someone in a fuzzy pink jacket.

"Moose!" she calls as she comes around the turn. Mercury skates to the foam barrier to meet me, trailed by her dance partner—a petite blonde with her hair in two braids, already giving me a huge smile.

"Hi!" the blonde says, doing an abrupt hockey stop right at the barrier and throwing an arm around Mercury. "I'm Carmen."

"Moose," I say, and Carmen gives me a mock salute.

"I hear you're gonna be the next star of the Hot Shots," she says, poking Mercury in the ribs. "Right, Captain?"

"We are coaching Moose out of the goodness of our hearts," Mercury tells her stoically.

Carmen cups a hand around her mouth and stage-whispers, "Merc is desperate for more jammers on our team."

There's a confusing rush of feelings—being wanted, meeting someone new, being vulnerable, all seasoned with the ever-present anxiety that looms like smoke. I push it all down. "So you offering to coach me had an ulterior motive?" I risk a joke.

"Extremely ulterior," Carmen says, stepping over the barrier. "Come on, I'll unlock the loaner gear for you." She takes my hand as I start walking toward the gear cage, letting me pull her along the bleachers. "HEY, MERC!" she shouts as she rolls next to me, her voice echoing off the high metal ceiling. "IS POWERHOUSE COMING?"

"They're on the way," Mercury replies from the track at a normal volume. She's skating backward again, practicing her footwork. I watch her smoothly grapevine across the track, her skates like an extension of her legs. The bruise that appeared on my hip after she hit me at practice the other day twinges.

"So Mercury told me you've been skating for, like, practically forever," Carmen is saying, "and that you basically just need to learn some contact skills and then we can steal you for the Hot Shots."

"How many junior teams are there?"

Carmen gives a short laugh. "Three. So there's not a ton of competition with each other. We have a home season in the fall, then a regional season in the spring." We reach the gear cage, and Carmen enters a code on the keypad and pulls open the door. "Is Moose your real name?" she calls from inside, where I hear something crash.

"Uh . . . yeah. Well, it's not my derby name, I mean."

Carmen reappears at the door, handing me a pair of skates. "My real name's Frances, but I think my teachers are literally the only ones who ever call me that. Even my parents call me Carmen sometimes."

"I don't think these are my size," I say, checking the faded tag on the inside of the loaner skates. "Are there any fours back there?"

"Oh, I just handed you the least scuffed pair," she says, leaning back out of the gear cage to grab the skates. She swaps them for the correct size and hands them to me by the laces. "Anyway, I always try to get Mr. Samuels to call me Carmen, but he only does it if I really make him laugh."

"Who?"

"Oh duh, you're not going to Patterson, are you? For school?"

"I'm going to Green Valley," I say, taking the helmet she passes me.

"Mercury goes there!" She digs around behind a filing cabinet for a pair of kneepads and checks the fraying Velcro on them.

"Yeah, I have history class with her." Carmen piles kneepads and elbow pads in my arms.

"I tried to get my mom to let me transfer, but she says I need to have friends outside of derby. Can you believe?"

"Uh . . . so who's Mr. Samuels?" I prod.

"Oh my god. Duh. Sorry. He's the chem teacher at Patterson. I like chemistry. That's my derby name—Carmen Monoxide."

"I love that," I tell her honestly, and Carmen's face lights up.

"We'll find you a good derby name too." She locks the gear cage and gestures for me to follow her back to the bleachers. "I'm sure Coach Prince has already given you, like, a billion ideas. She's good at those."

Carmen plants herself next to me on the bleachers and keeps talking while I pull on my gear, and I'm relieved by her chatter. She talks fast enough that I don't have to respond and worry about saying something weird or depressing. I realize I've been talking to Carmen, a new person, for five minutes without thinking about my voice.

The Hangar door clangs, and a tall Black girl with waist-length green braids enters, skates dangling over her shoulders on a strap.

"Finally!" Carmen exclaims next to me. "Powerhouse, you're late."

The girl checks the huge digital clock over the penalty box. "I'm literally exactly on time."

"I always tell Carmen to show up fifteen minutes before we need her," Mercury remarks from the middle of the track.

Carmen gives her a look. "Rude."

"Hey," the girl says, stopping in front of me and peering at me through big round glasses. "I'm Powerhouse. They/them."

"Moose," I say, making a mental note to not call Powerhouse a girl, even in my head. I'm struck, again, by how little I seem to know about being queer in Portland. Or anywhere, for that matter.

"We're gonna train Moose to jam so it's not just you and Acid playing back-to-back every game," Carmen tells them.

"You're not a jammer?" I ask her, surprised. Carmen's tiny, almost a full head shorter than Powerhouse.

"Do I look like a jammer?" She pauses when she sees my look of confusion. "Wait, really?"

I glance between her and Powerhouse, afraid to say something stupid. "I just thought— I mean, aren't jammers supposed to be small? To get around people faster?"

"Derby isn't really like that," Powerhouse says, dropping their bag on the floor and taking a spot on the bleachers beside me. Their energy is the exact opposite of Carmen's—low and calm, like they're carefully considering each word. They slide their braids over one shoulder and start weaving them into a plait. "Any body type can play any position. There are advantages and disadvantages."

"Yeah," Carmen adds. "Like, someone small might be able to get around the blockers really fast. But wait till you see Powerhouse jam. There's a reason their derby name is *Powerhouse*."

"It's like getting hit by a freight train," Mercury remarks, skating over to us. "Y'all should start warming up. We only have the Hangar for an hour."

Carmen hops back onto the track to skate laps while Powerhouse grabs their water bottle, heading to the other side of the bleachers to fill it up.

"Sorry." Mercury steps over the foam barrier to sit beside me. "I think I forgot to tell you that I invited Carmen and Powerhouse."

"It's okay," I say truthfully. "I mean, I was kind of nervous, but . . . they're nice. Do you coach them too?"

"Not really—we're all on the Hot Shots together. But it's hard to teach contact with just two people. If we want to get you up to speed, we need more skaters for you to practice with."

I remember Mercury hitting me at our last practice, so hard that I slid halfway across the track. The thought of it makes the bruise on my hip throb again, but I'm excited. Maybe today will start to feel less like skating in circles and more like roller derby.

Mercury has us practice moving as a triangular formation called a tripod, switching positions every few minutes. When I brace, I notice how smoothly Carmen and Powerhouse move together, like they're reading each other's minds.

When my hip flexors are burning and my helmet is squishy with sweat, Mercury pulls Powerhouse and me out of the tripod. "Okay, Moose. You want to try jamming?"

"Better her than me," Carmen chirps.

"Can I ask you guys a question? Why doesn't anybody like jamming?"

Carmen laughs. "Because it's the fucking *worst*!"

"Jamming is just really hard," Powerhouse explains calmly. "The jammer is the only person on the track who can score points, so everybody's watching you, and you have four people whose goal is to *not* let you pass them. So you have to be strong, and have great endurance, and be willing to fail. Because you will, a lot, and a lot of people will be watching."

"Way to hype her up," Carmen says.

"It's definitely not for everybody," Mercury adds. "But I think you should at least try it."

"I want to try it," I say immediately. My mind jerks me back to the rink, flames licking up the walls. When I crawled to the window in the arcade, with the blaze roaring around me and tears streaming down my face, it felt like years. I can struggle on skates for two minutes.

Mercury, Carmen, and Powerhouse set up a tripod, and Powerhouse shows me where to place my weight and how to push.

They don't move.

When Mercury finally calls two minutes, I've moved the tripod about a foot. Even pushing against Carmen did barely anything—for someone so slight, she's able to dig deep into the ground, solid as rock when I try to push her.

"Rotate through and give Moose a break," Mercury says. "Everyone should practice their jamming."

By the time the clock over the penalty box reads five till eight, I'm ready to sprawl out on the track and never get up. It feels like I've been completely wrung out, all the breath and energy leaked out of me with every push against the tripod. "Let's call it a night," Mercury says, checking the clock, and I slide gratefully onto my belly in the middle of the track.

"I think I'm gonna sleep here," I mumble into the floor.

"Welcome to derby," Powerhouse says, sliding elegantly to their knee beside me and ripping open a protein bar. "Wait till your first scrimmage. I got a bruise the size of Oregon on my thigh after three jams."

"I got a pretty good one on my shin at my first scrimmage," Mercury offers, unscrewing her water bottle. It's red, covered in stickers of stars and planets. "But I still think Acid tripped me on purpose."

"That's nothing," Carmen says dramatically. "My first scrimmage, I fell backward and somebody's *wheel* hit me right in the tailbone. I had a big round bruise on my ass for weeks."

Powerhouse and Carmen go on trying to one-up each other with bruise stories, and Mercury sits next to me. "You're gonna have some," she says, touching my arm.

I flinch instinctively, and I'm instantly annoyed with myself. Mercury and her friends have been running into me and hitting me for the past hour, but it's Mercury gently pointing out my bruises that freaks me out? I look down and realize Mercury's right—there are faint yellowish spots on my biceps, promises of bruises to come.

"Sorry," Mercury says, her hand curling into a fist. "Forgot."

"It's cool," I mumble, trying to shake off the startled feeling of Mercury's touch.

"They're like battle scars," Mercury says, and I can see she instantly regrets it.

"It's fine," I assure her before she can start apologizing. I glance over at Carmen and Powerhouse, still swapping escalating stories of their most dramatic derby injuries. "This is, like . . . the most people I've hung out with that haven't acted weird around me in months."

"Weird how?"

I pause, staring at the elbow pad in my hand and trying to decide if I want to keep talking. "For the past six months, the fire is all anyone can see when they look at me. But they don't wanna say anything, so they just stare, but try to act like they're not staring. We were at this rest stop in Idaho on the way here, and this little kid came up to me and asked me why I had a big scar on my neck."

Mercury raises her eyebrows. "Seriously?"

"Yeah, but, like—it was a little kid, you know? I told him I'd needed a hole in my throat to breathe, and he just kinda shrugged and went on with his day. I guess I wish more people would do that, instead of being so weird about it. It makes *me* feel worse about it. Like I have to hide it."

Why am I talking so much?

The door to the Hangar opens, and skaters start pouring in, their voices filling the air.

"The adult teams have practice," Mercury says. "We better get off the track."

"Can we go to Major's?" Carmen hops up on her skates. "*Pleeeeease?* I need a burger."

"It's eight o' clock," Mercury says, like she can't fathom being out any later than this.

"I'll buy you a burger if you come, Grandma." Carmen elbows her. "*And* I'll look at your chem paper."

"Sold. Powerhouse?"

"What's the pie of the month?"

"What is it, September?" Carmen says, thinking. "*Sweeptember* Potato Pie, maybe?" She turns to me. "They do this stupid themed pie every month. Febucherry is the best."

"You wanna come, Moose?" Mercury asks me.

Before the fire, after a grueling hour and a half of throwing myself fruitlessly at three people who are much, much stronger than me, I might have said no. My muscles burned with every movement, my legs trembled when I stood. But Mercury and Carmen and Powerhouse are all looking hopefully at me now, and I can tell it's not a pity invite. Carmen spins on her skates when I say yes.

We retreat to the bleachers as the adult skaters get on the track to start warming up for their practice, and I pull out my phone to ask Eden if I can go. It feels weird to be asking my older sister for permission to do things, but I guess that's where we stand now.

"My phone's dead." I turn to Mercury. "Do you have Eden's number?"

"Yeah, here," she says, entering the passcode and handing me her phone. "I need to sweep the track for the next practice real quick. Be right back."

I navigate to Mercury's message app, and a group message is already pulled up. Bitch Pod, the group is titled, with two lightning bolt emojis on either side. I start to tap away, but then I see my name.

MERCURY

her name is moose

CARMEN

love

MERCURY

I think it's a nickname. she was in an accident before she came here. just be cool

POWERHOUSE

she's coach ripley's sister?

MERCURY

half sister, I think

CARMEN

is this her?

There's a link to an article from the *Moab Chronicle*, dated April 8. One day after the fire. I don't even have to click it, because I know what it says. *Six dead in three bell roller rink fire in Finney's Mesa. More injured. Mechanical failure suspected cause.* I've read it a million times. Dads' names are in the third column of the article, twenty-six words down: *Erlan Shaker, 51,* and *Marcus Shaker, 53.* They're between *Tom Ryder, 40,* and *Sierra Summers, 13.*

"Moose, does that work for you?" Carmen's question pulls me back to the present. I look up at her, her cheeks flushed from exertion and her wispy blond bangs sticking to her forehead. How long did it take her to figure out what a *victim* I am?

"What?"

"Mercury gave me a ride here, so I was saying we can all go to Major's in her car. She can probably drop you off at your house."

"I don't think I can go," I say, sending Eden a quick text from Mercury's phone. *It's Moose. Come pick me up please.* "I have some work to do for school."

"It's *Friday*!" Carmen presses, but I'm already hurrying to the rental cage in my socks to drop off my skates. Mercury's gearing down with them when I return, and I brush off her questions and pull on my sweatshirt and a pair of sneakers.

"I'll see you later," I mumble, because I can't think of anything else to say. My cheeks are burning, and I turn and practically run out of the Hangar and into the rain.

chapter nine

ALL MY MUSCLES ARE ON FIRE the next day. I duck walk to the bathroom while Typo winds around my ankles, wondering how I'm going to possibly skate at the beginner class this afternoon. And how I'm going to face Mercury.

It was just a heads-up, I tell myself as I splash my face with water, studying my ashen expression in the mirror. *She was trying to help.* But it feels like pity, like she had to tell Carmen and Powerhouse what a charity case I am and how they need to be nice to me. And Carmen, posting a link that condensed my tragedy into 432 words. Putting it in that group chat like it was nothing.

I've barely been skating for two weeks, and I'm already a point of gossip in the league.

Eden's making protein shakes for us when I stagger into the kitchen, throwing myself onto the couch to try to silence my screaming muscles. "Morning," she says distractedly as Typo hops up into my lap. I carefully move her to the side, afraid she'll give me a muscle spasm if she tries to knead on my legs.

"I'm not going today," I grumble.

Eden turns, surprised. "What? To practice?"

"I can barely move."

"Skating will actually help your muscles stretch out. If you just sit on the couch all day, they're going to lock up again." She turns back to the blender, and I focus on Typo's head, scratching her ears.

"You okay?" Eden asks, handing me a shake. "I thought you were enjoying derby."

I hesitate. Everything I say to Eden seems to worry her these days. But my frustration is about to boil over, and I have to tell someone besides Typo. "Mercury told Carmen and Powerhouse about the fire before they met me," I burst out. "And Carmen found that article and sent it to everybody."

Eden raises an eyebrow and sits across from me on the floor, knees tucked under her. "How do you know she sent it to everybody?"

"I mean—she definitely sent it to Mercury and Powerhouse. Probably everyone else too."

"There are almost two hundred skaters in the junior league. Those three are hardly *everybody*."

"Forget it," I snap, trying to stand and wincing when my muscles resist. I flop backward onto the couch, glowering at the floor.

Eden studies me for a moment. "Do you know why we made Mercury captain of the Hot Shots this year?"

I shake my head, annoyed.

"It's because Mercury is always looking out for her teammates. Not just on the track. All the time. They call her *Grandma* as a joke, but she really takes care of everybody else like it's her job. Even me."

I look up at Eden. "You?"

"Yeah," Eden says, twisting her hands in her lap. "Mercury was with me when I got the news about—about you and Dad and Erlan. I was giving her a ride home from a practice, and I had to pull over because the Finney's Mesa sheriff wouldn't stop calling my cell. I felt like I was dying, Moose." Her voice wavers. Is she going to cry? I have no idea how to feel about my sister crying. Are we sisters enough for me to comfort her? "Mercury just told me to switch spots with her, and she drove me home. And when we got here, she'd called Prince and some of my other teammates, and they stayed with me all night."

I bite my lip, feeling a wedge of guilt at her words. A totally unrelated teenager knows my sister better than me. "That doesn't make it okay," I mutter. "It wasn't her thing to talk about."

"No, it wasn't. But people fuck up, Moose. Even people just trying to help. I don't think Mercury or Carmen meant to hurt you."

Typo mews at me, pushing her head under my hand so I'll keep petting her. "I just—I don't want anybody feeling sorry for me. It felt like they were gathering around to throw me a pity party."

"Then you should talk to them about it," Eden says, standing. "Nothing will get resolved by just sitting here and being mad about it, right? And you're not getting out of practice today."

She heads to her bedroom to change, and I force myself to stand up. I guess if anything will make me feel less like a victim today, it's putting on skates and crashing into someone.

I'm in my usual spot at the top of the bleachers during Eden's scrimmage, statistics textbook open on my lap. I always bring homework to the Hangar to work on until my practice, but it's impossible to focus with the constant whistles and shouting. I'm not that interested in stats anyway—I always watch the scrimmage instead, trying to keep track of the different start formations and figure out why certain penalties get called.

The first few times I watched roller derby, it just seemed like a chaotic wrestling match on wheels. But now I'm learning to watch the skaters as they set up on the jam line, focus on their strategy.

Eden sets up her tripod at the front. Even from a distance, I can see the firm set of her jaw, the careful strategizing happening in her head as a referee calls five seconds till the jam starts. Eden's jammer gives her the tiniest of nods, and suddenly the blockers all scatter, creating a tangle of limbs and skates, and Eden's jammer darts past the chaos, easily claiming lead jammer.

I make a mental note to ask Eden about that play as the pack rolls forward, shrill whistles filling the air as penalties are called and points are scored. I lean down to dig in my backpack for a pen so I can write down the play, and I see Mercury entering the Hangar, her wavy hair loose around her shoulders and her perfect red lipstick in place as always.

I stiffen when Mercury spots me on the bleachers. She gives me a half smile, as if testing the waters. She's not stupid—she knows I'm mad.

I look back down into my bag, feeling heat creep up the back of my neck as I push aside energy bar wrappers and stats notes. My hand slips, and then the contents of my bag are spilling over my feet and clattering to the concrete floor below. The bleachers vibrate under me as someone walks up them, and Mercury's Doc Martens stop beside me.

"Hi."

I let out a frustrated little sigh, snatching up a fallen pamphlet by my foot. It's the leaflet about body image for burn victims. Why haven't I thrown it out yet? "Hi," I say stiffly, sitting back on the bleachers and resigning myself to crawling under them later to retrieve my stuff. I'm hot, and I want to take this ugly gray scarf off, but I still can't bring myself to leave the house without it carefully arranged over my scar.

Mercury leans down, picking up a flat orange rock the size of my fist that fell from my bag. There's a tiny, perfect circle at one end. "This is cool," she says, hefting it in one hand. "Paperweight?"

"Memento," I mutter, accepting the rock as she hands it back to me.

A whistle pierces the air. *"Black one-nine-seven-nine! Forearm!"* a ref shouts from the track, and I watch Eden curse under her breath as she skates to the penalty box.

"Can I sit down?"

I nod, and Mercury settles beside me, propping her boots up on the seat in front of us. She's quiet, trying to gauge the vibe. Or maybe waiting for me to talk first. It's hard to tell.

"I saw your texts with Carmen and Powerhouse," I say, staring at the track. I don't want to see pity in her eyes. "When you let me borrow your phone."

Mercury nods solemnly. "I figured. I'm sorry, Moose. It wasn't my story to tell."

"No. It wasn't." I pass the orange rock between my hands. I picked it up the last time I went rock climbing in Moab with Papa, not knowing it would be the last time.

"You know, my mom—"

"It's called a hagstone," I say at the same time. I look over at her. "What?"

"Nothing," she says breezily, scooting closer to examine the rock in my hands. "What's it called? A *what*stone?" She looks almost relieved that I interrupted her.

"Rocks with these little holes," I say, flipping it over in my palm. "They're called hagstones. When water hits a rock in just the right way for years, it makes a little hole like this." I hold it up to my eye, peering at her through the hole. "No idea how one ended up in Utah.

My papa told me you can see fairies if you look through it at the right time."

Mercury takes the hagstone and holds it up to her eye, scanning the Hangar with it. When she gets to me, she fake gasps, pressing her hand to her heart.

I crack a smile in spite of myself as she hands it back to me and rub my thumb across the surface. "I know you were just trying to help."

"For the record, I don't think Carmen or Powerhouse would have brought it up if I didn't tell them. They're not assholes."

"It's not that I don't want people to bring it up. It's just . . . I don't want to feel like everyone feels sorry for me all the time, you know? You can say the word *fire* around me. It's not a secret." I finger the scarf around my neck, safely hiding the scar there.

"Do you wanna talk about it?" she asks simply. "The fire?"

I turn the hagstone over in my hands, considering. "Not right now. But eventually. Maybe."

"Just let me know when." She says it so easily, like I couldn't inconvenience her if I tried. I feel like if I look directly at her, I'll start crying, so I just nod and grip the hagstone harder. "So," Mercury ventures, "you still want to try out for our team?"

There's a loud smack—a chorus of gasps and *oooh*s radiate from the track, and we turn to see the skaters gathered around a fallen jammer. "Is she okay?" I ask as the jammer rolls to one side with her face twisted in pain, clutching her ankle.

The Hangar is deathly silent for a moment as the skaters return to their benches and a medic kneels beside the fallen jammer, talking with her in a low voice. Then the jammer sighs, nods, and gets gingerly to her feet to roll back to her bench. The other skaters cheer as she accepts an ice pack, laughing, and sits down to ice her ankle.

"Rolled ankle," Mercury says, letting out a breath. "It happens. She'll be fine." A few skaters give the jammer a lighthearted punch on the shoulder as they head back to the track. I realize my eyes are prickling for real now.

I quickly wipe my eyes on the sleeve of my sweatshirt. If Mercury notices, she doesn't say anything. "Yeah," I tell her, and her face lights up. "I still want to try out for the team."

Carmen texts me that evening with a novel-length apology for sending the article to Mercury and Powerhouse. The constant apologizing would normally embarrass me, but Carmen's text is entertaining enough that I don't care, somehow comparing her misstep to covalent bonds, then going off on a tangent about modern chemistry ethics. She ends with an offer to help me with my bio homework anytime. An hour later, I get a notification that I've been added to a group chat with Carmen, Mercury, and Powerhouse—Carmen's named it Bitch Pod 2: 2 Fast, 2 Bitchy.

When Prince calls us all to the middle at the end of practice on Tuesday, she's brandishing a clipboard and a pen. "We're doing assessments this Saturday, after our regular practice," she announces. "You need to sign up if you want to join a team."

Mercury's gaze finds mine, and she winks. She's been pulling me aside during practice to work on contact and advanced footwork, and today I hit her hard enough to make her stumble. I cross my eyes back at her, and she stifles a giggle.

Prince gives us a sharp look before continuing. "There are three junior teams: Knockout Kids, Hot Shots, and Slamazons. Captains and coaches from each team will be at the assessment, and it'll mostly feel like a normal practice. I'd encourage all of you to try to assess, even if you don't think you're ready. Never turn down an opportunity for feedback on your skating."

"What if they tell us we suck?" someone asks, and a few other skaters titter.

Prince gives her an exasperated look. "Has anyone in the Hangar ever told you that you suck, Lauren?"

"Remember that derby is a team sport," Eden says, a little more tactfully. "Nobody's rooting for you to fail."

"And if you don't assess onto a team this time, you'll have plenty of other chances," Prince adds. When she passes the clipboard around, I eagerly sign my name. Since watching Eden scrimmage every weekend and learning contact with Mercury, Carmen, and Powerhouse, I'm itching to do something more than isolated hits.

"Assessments are pretty chill," Mercury tells me on the bleachers as we gear down. "Most people are just trying to see how close they are to making a team. And all the captains are nice."

Across the Hangar, Prince and Eden are putting cones away by the penalty box—Prince says something, and Eden practically doubles over in laughter.

"Merc," I mutter. "Is something going on with Prince and my sister?"

Mercury follows my gaze. "Oh . . . I mean . . ." Her cheeks grow pink.

"What?" I press.

"You'll have to ask Carmen."

"You're not getting away with that."

Mercury raises her hands. "I have no comment."

"Do you accept bribes?"

Now it's Mercury's turn to look exasperated. "Okay," she says, dropping her voice. "I'm only telling you because she's your sister, but . . . everyone has suspected they're dating for, like, the last year. Carmen knows all the rumors in the league—she has some kind of evidence book with all the observed instances of them flirting with each other."

"That's really weird."

"Yeah. She says it's, like, scientific observation or something."

Mercury leans down to unlace her skates, and I look back over at Prince and Eden. Prince is skating alongside Eden while she sweeps the track, talking to her. At one point, Prince briefly touches the small of her back, pointing out a warped tile in the track so she doesn't trip over it.

It never occurred to me to wonder if Eden was also gay. Most of my life, Eden was just someone my dads mentioned every now and then, more of an abstract thought than a tangible person. *Eden got into the National Honor Society,* or *Eden joined the softball team.* Our dad would go up to Portland to visit her a few times a year, and they talked on the phone most weeks. But I hadn't seen her in years, not since the last summer she visited us in Utah.

There was a folder on Dad's computer full of pictures from that summer—Eden and me kneeling by a bighorn skeleton we found in the desert, sharing a teacup on the ride at Six Flags, squinting in the sun in front of the Grand Canyon. There was one that Dad printed out and put on the windowsill above the kitchen sink, the one he'd stare at while he did the dishes. *So I can look at something I love while I do something I hate,* he used to joke. It's the four of us—Dad, Papa, Eden, and me, at the Finney's Mesa Rollerdome, in the middle of the skate floor. I'm little, probably only five, and the three of them are clustered around me, Eden kneeling at my side with her arm around my waist. I look grouchy, like I always did as a kid—but everyone else is grinning, and Eden's mouth is open in a laugh. The picture's a little blurred from being taken on an old phone. But we're all there. Papa showed us how to make suncatchers that summer to hang in all the windows, and they sent spikes of rainbow light spinning across our grainy faces.

It never occurred to me then to ask Dads why Eden and I didn't know each other better. Moab and Portland are far apart, but not so far that we had to be this distant. But all that time I'd spent with Eden—months in the hospital, driving through the mountains to Portland, living in her spare bedroom—and it took me this long to realize we might share more than looks.

As she drives me to therapy after practice, I almost ask her about it four separate times. If Eden's queer, that could be one more thing we have in common, besides roller skating and a dead dad. One more thing that might make us feel a little less awkward and polite as we tiptoe around each other in her apartment. Someone who's been out and queer in Portland, who might celebrate with me when I come out to her. But every time I'm about to ask, the words don't come.

I tell Dr. Parikh about it as soon as I sit down, because it's the only thing I can think of and I don't want to talk about the fire for the next fifty minutes.

"Would it change your perception of your sister if she told you she was queer?" Dr. Parikh asks me, folding her hands in her lap. It's weird to have someone so focused on you, so I look out the window while I talk.

"I guess. There's this wall between us, because we just don't know each other that well, and she suddenly has to take care of me. And if she's . . . Well, if she's like me, maybe that's one more brick in the wall we can take down."

"Is that the only reason you want to know?" Dr. Parikh asks, raising her eyebrows. "To find commonality with her?"

I look down at my sweatpants, hand-me-downs from Eden. Along with my hoodie, and my sneakers, and the gray scarf that's become a staple. "It's something her friends probably know about her," I say without looking up. "And I'm her sister. I should know."

When I finally look up at Dr. Parikh, she's looking at me evenly, without pity. That's what I like about her—even with all the shit I've been through in the past year, she doesn't seem to feel sorry for me. "Blood doesn't make a family," she says. "It never has. Just because she is your genetic sister doesn't mean you will have some instant bond. Like all relationships, it takes time to build back up. Just because you don't know everything about her after living here for a few weeks doesn't mean you never will. But it takes effort from both sides."

I keep thinking about her words after I step out of the shower at Eden's apartment and wrap my hair, standing in front of the mirror to glare at myself. I still feel like I barely recognize my body—it looks a little stronger now from all the skating I've been doing, but it's still different. There are stretch marks where my skin was smooth before, angles and lines and muscles that all feel new. My arms used to be thicker from rock climbing with Papa, but the combination of weeks in the hospital and playing a sport that's mostly leg-dependent has made them noodly. And, of course, the ever-present dark red scar in the hollow of my throat, the one I haven't been able to bring myself to touch without gauze over my finger. There's a small window in the bathroom that we crack when we use the shower, and I hear rain outside. The bathroom's steamy, but the faint slip of cool, wet air pushes through like a reminder. *You're okay.*

I want to hide in my room after therapy. Besides keeping me out of Eden's way, the room has finally started to feel like mine—my homework on the desk, the rumpled green duvet, a Polaroid of me with Carmen, Mercury, and Powerhouse in our derby gear tacked on the wall. My boxes from Moab, still mostly untouched, are shoved in a corner by the closet with a blanket thrown over them, out of sight. It feels a little safer here, almost a home base in the still vaguely unfamiliar territory of Eden's apartment. I stare at the room for a moment, then pull on a pair of clean sweats and scoop Typo into my arms before heading back out to the living room.

"Hey."

Eden twists around on the couch—she has a glass of wine in one hand and a remote in the other, scrolling through the true crime section of Netflix.

"Hey. What's up?"

I could tell her now, about my crush on Mercury and how it felt when I came out to Dads and how weird it is trying to be queer in a place that's *already* queerer than anywhere I've ever been. We could bond about it, maybe. But it still feels too raw and unfamiliar.

I shrug, and Typo mews, pressing her face into my neck. "What are you watching?"

Eden opens her mouth, then closes it, looking surprised. "I don't know yet," she finally says. "You wanna join me?"

"Can I have some wine?"

"No. But I'll let you pick the documentary."

I smirk, walking around the coffee table to settle on the other side of the couch. Typo sprawls in the space between us, pushing her feet into both our legs as Eden passes me the remote. I scroll through thumbnails of beautiful young murdered women in dramatic grayscale, then lower the remote to my lap.

"Why didn't we know each other?"

Eden glances sidelong at me. "Hmm?"

"I hadn't seen you since that summer you spent with us. Didn't Dad want us to know each other?"

"Oh." Eden leans forward to set her wineglass on the coffee table. "Well. It's complicated."

"So it was on purpose?" I can't picture Dad intentionally keeping Eden and me apart.

Eden steels herself, avoiding my gaze. "My mom got involved in some weird evangelical church group when I was in high school," she says after a moment. "Like the super-homophobic, conversion-therapy, protesting-rainbow-weddings shit. I think she was upset that Dad broke up with her after he realized he was gay and was kind of looking for a reason to blame him for it."

"Oh, shit." I'd only met Eden's mom a few times, when we were younger and meeting her at a rest stop in Idaho to pick Eden up for the summer. "Is she still . . . ?"

"Yeah," Eden says softly. "Yeah, we don't talk. For a lot of reasons. But that's a big one. She made it really hard for Dad to see me for a long time. Which made it really hard for me to see you, too. Do you remember your dads' wedding?"

"A bit." I was little when they got married, and I mostly remember Dads picking me up from school early that day and buying me Wendy's in the car. We drove nearly four hours to Salt Lake City to make it to the courthouse, where we got in line behind two old women holding hands. I remember Dad on the phone for half the drive and being bored while we waited another two hours for their turn to get married. Eden appeared at some point, as if by magic, and she sat next to me in the courtroom, crying while Dads said their vows. I tugged on her sleeve at one point and asked her why she was sad, and she explained in a whisper that sometimes people cry when they're happy, too.

"Dad called my mom while y'all were driving to Salt Lake," Eden says now, "and told her they were going to get married and they wanted me there, and that they would buy me a plane ticket right then." Dads told me later, when I learned about gay marriage being legalized in my government class, that people were saying it would be overturned in Utah within a few days, so they should get married as soon as possible. Eden picks at a hangnail, looking frustrated. This is hard for her to talk about, I realize. Does she feel . . . guilty? "My mom didn't want me to go."

"Are you serious? To your dad's wedding?"

"Yeah. So I called Dad and told him to buy the ticket, and I skipped class and went to the airport, and one of Dad's friends picked me up and drove me to the courthouse."

"I'm guessing your mom was pissed."

"To put it lightly. She wouldn't let me go back after that."

"Weren't you, like, nineteen when that happened?" I try to keep the hostility from edging into my voice, but I'm frustrated that I've lived ten years of my life without her.

"Yeah, but she was paying my tuition, and my housing, and all sorts of stuff. I couldn't really cut her off until I had a job, you know?" She finally makes eye contact with me, and I see the deep regret etched on her face. "But I should have done it anyway. I could have moved to Utah, lived with you guys, transferred schools, something. I don't know. I should have stood up to her. Didn't your dads ever tell you they almost moved to Portland?"

"No," I say blankly.

"Like I said, my mom made it hard. And they didn't want to uproot you when you were so little."

I frown at the carpet. "They should have asked me." So many things could have been different. I could have been out at school. Could have grown up with my sister. If we'd moved to Portland, we wouldn't have been at the Rollerdome on April 7.

"Hey," Eden says gently, resting a hand on my knee. "They weren't perfect, you know. They were so, so wonderful. But they were human. They did their best."

But I could have known *you,* I want to say. But saying that would steer us too far into this emotional sister relationship that we still don't have. So I pick up the remote instead and choose a documentary at random, sinking farther into the couch so Eden can't see my face. I hear her sigh and tuck her hands into her lap, and we sit in silence as the movie plays.

chapter ten

EDEN AND I TIPTOE AROUND EACH OTHER for the next couple days. I'm still trying to wrap my head around everything she told me about Dads and her mom. I find Papa's old Facebook account, abandoned long before he died, and scroll back to December 2013, when he posted a picture of the four of us outside the courthouse, Dads pressed together and grinning so hard their eyes are barely visible. I'm in front, squinting in the sun with Papa's hand on my shoulder, and Eden's kneeling beside me, her arm around my waist. I study her face, trying to tell if she looks tired or sad or like she had just had a blowout fight with her mom before sneaking to the airport. But she just looks teary, overwhelmed, happy. I'm mad at her, I realize. For not trying harder. But how can I be mad when she's uprooted her entire life to take me in?

I decide to channel my frustration into derby and the team assessment instead. It feels like any other practice but with the intensity upped to ten, so we're extra sweaty from our regular drills. Mercury and Eden sit in the bleachers while Prince coaches us through the assessment, and there are a handful of other observers that I don't recognize—captains and coaches for the other teams, I'm guessing.

We go through a long list of basic skills—weaving around cones in under six seconds, skating on one foot, skating backward around the track at speed. I catch Mercury's eye at one point as I'm doing my crossovers and nearly stumble in the turn. *Focus,* I tell myself sternly. My lungs are burning, and I hope the captains don't notice how much harder I'm breathing than everybody else.

"All right, skaters!" Prince calls at the end of the assessment, waving us to the middle. "Y'all did great today. Captains and coaches are meeting right after this to do draft picks, so we'll let you know by the end of the day. If you don't get picked up this time, you can try again in a month, capiche?"

I steal a glance over my shoulder at the bleachers—the captains and coaches have gathered in one spot, leaning in to mutter to one another. Mercury is off-skates today, wearing a baggy knit sweater and Docs, somehow looking even more put-together than she does on skates.

"Question, Moose?" I pull my gaze away to look at Prince, who is raising an eyebrow at me.

"Oh," I say, flushing. "No, sorry. I'm paying attention."

"Great," Prince says with feigned gusto, glancing back down at their clipboard. "If anybody wants feedback, come see me. Otherwise, you're free to gear down." Prince taps me on the helmet with her clipboard as everyone else heads to the bleachers. "I need you to listen when I'm talking, kid."

"Sorry," I say sheepishly.

"The teams don't care about how good a skater you are. It's about whether you can work as part of a team, yeah?"

I nod, popping out my mouthguard so I can talk clearly. "Do you know how long it takes them to decide?"

"Well, longer if I don't get over there soon," she jokes. "Shouldn't be more than a half hour, though. Not many people went out for teams today. Hey, you want to sweep the track and put cones away for me?"

"Sure."

Prince turns to give another skater feedback, and I skate to the other side of the Hangar, where a huge shop broom leans against the wall. I grab the broom, then pause when I notice the row of dusty framed photos behind it. *Knockout Kids, 2011,* reads one, emblazoned beneath a group picture of theatrically scowling teenagers in derby gear. The matte frame around it is filled with signatures in silver Sharpie: *Quantum Fury, #365; Squirrely Temple, #42; Stomps, #527.* One name, written in a familiar, careful hand, leaps out at me: *Ripley Riot, #1979.* I scan the grinning faces and find Eden in the middle row, braces glinting on her teeth. She's in almost every picture of the Knockout Kids until 2012. I had no idea she played derby all through middle and high school. The team picture from Eden's sophomore year is like looking in a mirror—she's all frizzy curls under her helmet, gangly and short, but I can see in the defiant set of her shoulders and head-on gaze that teenage Eden had miles more confidence than me.

I try not to stare at the huddle on the bleachers while I skate around the track with the broom, collecting piles of dust to sweep up later. For the first time, I feel a twinge of nerves.

I'm shaking dust off the broom when the bleachers clatter, and the huddle of captains and coaches breaks apart. I can't stop myself—I'm racing toward the bleachers dragging the broom behind me, abruptly plowing to a stop at the foam barrier where Mercury stands with Eden and Prince.

"Oh, hi, Moose," Prince chides. "Nice of you to stop by."

"Well?" I press, my gaze flitting to each of their faces. Eden and

Prince look carefully neutral, but Mercury is fighting back a smile at the corners of her mouth.

"You'll have to wait for the email with everyone el—" Eden starts.

"You're on the Hot Shots!" Mercury bursts out.

A dizzy rush tears through me and I drop the broom with a whoop, throwing my arms around Mercury before I can stop myself. She gives me a backbreaking hug, lifting me off the ground slightly while Eden shouts about skate safety.

"Really?" I burst out when Mercury sets me down. Her cheeks are pink with sparkly blush, but I think it's more than just makeup.

"No, I lied and we're making you quit roller derby forever," Mercury says sarcastically.

"We *will* make you quit derby forever if y'all don't finish sweeping the track," Prince adds, and Mercury stifles a giggle as I snatch up the broom.

"I'll help you with the dustpan," she says, and she walks next to me as I skate back onto the track. "You'll have to pick a number. And we need to order you a jersey. You probably won't play in a bout till after the holidays, 'cause we'll need to get you scrimmaging for a while first. But god, we really need jammers. Oh, and you need a derby name!" She goes on ticking things off her fingers as I shove the broom in the corner and reach around for a dustpan.

A flicker of doubt hits me, draining the excitement as fast as it came.

"Merc," I say, turning back to her. She sees my serious expression, and her smile falters. "I wasn't, like, a pity draft, right?"

"Moose." She gives me a look. "Come on. Prince and I were *fighting* over you with the other captains. You were the best skater out there today."

I bite my lip. "Promise?"

"What did I tell you that first time you hit me? We don't do shit like that in derby. You've been working hard, and you earned your spot on the team."

Mercury's right. The whole month I've been skating at the Hangar, nobody has once gently lied to spare my feelings. Not in a mean way—but the coaches know that beating around the bush doesn't get you anywhere.

"Okay?" Mercury presses.

I huff, trying to imagine my self-doubt dissipating in the air. Dr. Parikh would be proud. "Okay."

"Good. We don't have time for self-deprecation if we're gonna get to the regional tournament this year."

Mercury joins me on the track, holding the dustpan in place so I can sweep up the little piles of track dust. She smells like lavender, somehow, even in the Hangar that always smells like sweat and old nachos. I'm looking down at the part of her hair, the dark eyelashes against her cheek, the collection of silver rings on her fingers, and I'm talking before I can stop myself.

"Shouldn't we, like, celebrate?"

Mercury looks up at me. "What?"

Fuck, fuck, fuck, fuck, fuck. "Oh, I just mean—like, get fries, or something, but we don't have to— Sorry, I—"

Her smile broadens. "I think your sister has something in mind for the two of you to do. But Carmen and Powerhouse and I will take you to Major's after your first Hot Shots practice tomorrow. Our treat."

"Great," I say quickly, hoping she didn't notice my blunder. But the back of my neck's on fire, so I'm not sure how she could have missed it. "Let's do it."

"I'll text them," she says, taking the dustpan to a trash bin near the bleachers. "They're gonna be psyched. Carmen won't have to jam at practice anymore."

When Mercury shrugs on her jacket and winks at me before heading out to her car, I want to sink into the floor. *Did I just try to ask her out? And did she not notice that I was trying to ask her out? Or was she deflecting?*

Prince, Eden, and I leave the Hangar together, Eden double-checking the door to make sure it's locked. It's raining again, and the parking lot is dark with just Prince's and Eden's cars left.

"See ya at practice, Hot Shot," Prince says, punching me lightly on the shoulder. "Bring your A game. We won't go easy on you 'cause you're new."

"Yeah, yeah," I grumble, but I give Prince a cheeky grin before sliding into Eden's car.

"Hey," she says when she closes her door, turning to face me with a breathless smile. "I'm so fucking proud of you, Moose."

Before I can react, she's pulling me into a hug, and it doesn't matter that I stink from practice. When we break apart, she's beaming so big that she looks like the picture from 2011, all braces with her face scrunched up in excitement. And I think, for today at least, I can forget that Eden wasn't in my life for so long.

"I have one stop to make before we go home," she says, turning the key in the ignition. The car rumbles to life, and Eden peels out of the parking lot, waving at Prince. "Should only take, like, half an hour."

"What—?"

"You'll see."

"Eden?" I ask as we drive along the river, blanketed in fog.

"Yeah?"

"Why didn't I know you played derby for so long?"

She shrugs. "Honestly? It wasn't really a huge part of my life for a long time. I got a bad concussion my senior year of high school and didn't skate again until after college. And Dad was never really into it. That made it hard sometimes."

"Wait, really?" I just assumed Dad would've been super into Eden doing any kind of skating.

"He was kind of an elitist about rhythm skating sometimes." Eden laughs a little, but she seems bummed about it. Did Dad ever go to one of her games? I try to reconcile my version of our dad—always cool, smiling, cracking jokes—with a dad that looked down on roller derby. It feels wrong.

"Why'd you go back?" I ask Eden.

"Bad breakup." She scoffs. "I was living with a shitty boyfriend who I was convinced I was going to marry." My stomach clenches at her words. *Tell her you're gay! Tell her now!* "I went to a practice and took one hit and started just sobbing on the track. Like, really embarrassing, full-on meltdown. The coach, who I'd never even met before that night, stopped practice to make sure I was okay. Drove me home and bought me groceries and everything. That's what derby is. We just help each other. And it was what I needed at the time."

I feel a longing ache for something I can't quite place. "Do you still talk to the coach from that practice?"

"Oh, yeah. They're your coach too."

"It was *Prince*?"

"Does that surprise you?"

"A little. They're such a hard-ass in practice."

Eden laughs. "Yeah. They have a sensitive side, though. Cancer moon."

"I have no idea what that means."

"Ask Powerhouse." She pauses. "Hey, so . . . you're really into derby now, huh? You actually want to be skating?"

"Yes, Eden," I admit grudgingly. "I want to be skating."

"Good," Eden says as the car rolls to a halt, and I lean down to look through her window. We're parked outside a storefront painted bright teal, and I see black boxes and skate wheels stacked up in the lit window. A neon pink sign glows against the rain: FIVE STRIDE SKATE SHOP.

My heart skips a beat, and I scramble to follow Eden out of the car. "Are we—?"

Eden beams at me. "Well, if you're on a team, you need your own skates, right?"

"Okay," Mercury says, twisting around in her seat and slapping a piece of paper triumphantly on my desk. "This is the Hot Shots season roster." She's written the names, numbers, and positions of every person on the Hot Shots, presumably from memory. At the very bottom, after the slew of clever derby names, is my name—*Moose,* simple and one word and boring.

"I really need a derby name," I say, leaning over the roster. Ms. Trayhart left the room twenty minutes ago and told us to work on our study guides while she ran to the office, and then everyone quickly dissolved into doing everything *but* working on our study guides. I really should be looking at mine—history has never been my strong suit—but when Mercury immediately spun around and offered to give me gossip on every member of my new team, I said yes before I even really processed what she was saying.

"Hasn't Prince already given you a million ideas for derby names?"

"Yeah, but none of them are really *me*, you know?" I scan the list. Mercury, Carmen, and Powerhouse are there, along with Ripley—Eden—and Prince, listed at the top as coaches. "How did you choose yours?"

"My mom taught astronomy at Portland State. We had this huge photo book of all the planets, like super high-def, massive pictures. Mercury just always seemed the coolest to me. I *did* pick it when I was ten," she adds. "So there isn't some deep, personal meaning. I just thought it was neat."

I shift forward in my seat, resting my chin on my hands and raising my eyebrows expectantly. "Are you gonna tell me a cool Mercury fact?"

"I can sing the alphabet backward in Korean."

"A cool fact about Mercury the *planet*, not Mercury the Hot Shots captain."

"Ummm . . ." She looks at the ceiling. "It has volcanoes?"

"Smart of you to leave the astronomy to your mom."

Mercury's smile fades a little. "She died."

"Oh." Her words hit me like a confusing gut punch. "So did my dads."

"I know."

I'm quiet for a second, trying to think of something to say that doesn't make me sound like an asshole. It feels especially weird to be talking about this in the corner of the history room, where everyone around us is talking about the homecoming game or volleyball practice or (in the case of a dedicated few) attempting to work on the study guide. I study Mercury's face, the way she's staring at her fingernail, suddenly weird and kind of quiet. I think about what I wish people would say when they hear my dads are dead, what I would want them to do instead of awkwardly backtracking and trying to change the subject.

"What was she like?"

Mercury looks back up at me, surprised. "My mom?"

"Yeah. She taught astronomy. What else?"

"Well . . ." Mercury bites back a smile. "She was mean, sometimes. Just to people who deserved it, you know? She didn't take any shit, and she was confident, and funny, and she made really good pajeon."

"Pajeon?" I repeat, fumbling the pronunciation. "What's that?"

"You are saying it like a white person from Utah."

"I *am* a white person from Utah."

"It's not *pah-john*, it's *pa-jeon*," she says, slower, making a pinching motion with her hand. "Less space between your tongue and the roof of your mouth."

I try not to dwell on Mercury thinking about my mouth and repeat her pronunciation.

"Passable," she says. "Pajeon are scallion pancakes. My mom would drag us to the Korean market on Eighty-Second and buy these gigantic heads of cabbage to make kimchi for them. She fermented it in jars buried in our yard. I'm pretty sure there are still some there, but we've dug up half the grass since she died and haven't been able to find them."

"Can they over-ferment? Maybe you're accidentally making radioactive kimchi."

"You know, I have no idea. I guess it'll be my dad's problem after I graduate."

"So was the scallion pancake gene passed down to you?"

"Yeah, but mine aren't as good."

I lean forward over my desk, tapping my pencil on her hand. "Maybe I should be the judge of that."

"If you think you can handle it. Korean food is spicy."

"I can handle spicy." It feels like we're veering dangerously close to flirting territory, so I'm grateful when Ms. Trayhart sweeps back into the room, scolding everyone for clearly not working quietly on their study guides. Mercury turns back around, but not before she gives me a quick grin that makes my stomach flip over.

HOT SHOTS SEASON ROSTER

RIPLEY RIOT & PRINCE HARMING, *coaches*
MERCURY #80, *captain, pivot*
CARMEN MONOXIDE #51, *blocker*
POWERHOUSE #5, *jammer*
ACID REIGN #653, *jammer*
GAMMA RAZE #666, *blocker*
KICKY LONGSTOCKING #43, *pivot*
TRAIL MX. #8279, *blocker*
D-MONIC #195, *blocker*
FIREBOLT #1775, *pivot*
SYBIL DISOBEDIENCE #7, *blocker*
POUNDSTOOTH #39, *blocker*
HIMASLAYA #90, *blocker*
RAT QUEEN #24, *blocker*
PANIC! AT THE JAM LINE #735, *pivot*
APEX PREDATOR #472, *blocker*
MOOSE

chapter eleven

THE WEEK AFTER MY ASSESSMENT, Eden and I are back at the Hangar for my first Hot Shots practice. It's a rare sunny morning in October, the light illuminating the constant puddles in the parking lot.

"Take it slow with the new skates," Eden tells me as we pull our gear out of the trunk. "You'll need time to break them in. I can adjust the trucks for you if they feel weird."

"I know how to adjust trucks." I know I'm being an ass to my sister, who just bought me brand-new, not-cheap skates, but my stomach keeps turning over, roiling with nerves. "Eden?"

She pauses as we reach the Hangar door. "Yeah?"

"Were you nervous?"

She nods. "Oh, yeah. Super nervous. You're gonna do great." The way she strides confidently into the Hangar now, it's hard to imagine.

"MOOSE!"

I turn with one hand on the door handle to see Carmen sprinting toward me across the parking lot, Powerhouse walking calmly behind. "Hi—" I start, but then Carmen's bowling into me, practically knocking me off my feet. I shouldn't be surprised—despite her size, Carmen is dense as hell, all muscle.

"This is the best day of my life," she says, cupping my face in mock romance. "Someone else to jam so I don't have to."

I know Carmen's not surprised—the minute I got home last night, the Bitch Pod 2: 2 Fast, 2 Bitchy group chat was filled with a string of exclamation points from Carmen that I had to scroll through for a solid six seconds to reach the end. Powerhouse followed it with "congrats." It felt like an equal reaction to Carmen's enthusiasm, proportionally.

"You good?" Powerhouse asks me, holding the Hangar door for me as Carmen darts in.

"Yeah," I say, but Powerhouse looks skeptical.

"Just keep up," they tell me. "You don't have to be perfect. But do your best."

I nod. Their pep talk doesn't do anything for my nerves.

The group of skaters gearing up in the bleachers is much smaller than the beginner class—I count around fifteen people talking loudly, showing off videos on their phones. Fifteen new people I'm going to have to talk to. My throat already feels raw. I spot Mercury on the far side of the bleachers, half geared up and talking to Prince.

"You want me to announce you as our new jammer?" Carmen asks.

"No," I say quickly. "No, absolutely do not do that."

She laughs, but I'm not convinced she'll listen to me.

"Hey," Mercury greets us as the three of us join her on the bleachers. "Thanks, Coach," she tells Prince. "Moose, you ready?"

I wish they would all stop asking me.

"Here's your new draft packet, Moose on the Loose," Prince

says, handing me a ream of stapled pages. "You don't have to read it all now, but get it signed and turned in to me by next practice."

I flip open the packet, skimming the introductory paragraph. *Dating among teammates is strongly discouraged* jumps out at me. My gaze flicks to Mercury. She's sitting now, talking to Carmen as she pulls her skates on. *Of course.* Mercury, the team captain, a model for the Hot Shots—of course she let me down easy when I asked her to hang out after assessments. People here must take it seriously—I feel like Prince and Eden would already be married if teammates dating wasn't frowned upon.

"Get on the track!" Eden shouts, and there's a flurry of movement as dawdling skaters rush to gear up. "We have a bout in two weeks!"

I pull on my new skates, instinctively lacing them in the high arch pattern I always used at the rink. Carmen and Powerhouse are up on either side of me, hopping easily over the foam barrier and onto the track. I pull in a deep breath, then exhale as slowly as I can, focusing on the pressure of my wheels on the concrete. Dr. Parikh calls it grounding.

Mercury slides over, nudging me with her shoulder. "Hey."

"Hi," I say, bracing for her to ask me if I'm ready, to give me some kind of inspiring captain speech.

"Let's kick ass."

As soon as I hit the track, I feel better, the nerves dissolving into focus on my warmups. A couple skaters wave to me, sensing that I'm new. One girl, skating with her long brunette hair loose under her helmet, cuts in too close, glancing back at me as she passes. I sense a weird sort of judgment in her gaze, but then she's turned away again, stretching her hamstrings as she rolls down the track.

Prince whistles us to the middle, the same way she's done a million times at the beginner practices. But this group is clearly different—rather than slowly rolling into the middle and taking a careful knee, skaters zoom into the center of the track, hockey-stopping dramatically so their wheels chatter on the sport court. Mercury's with Prince and Eden, looking important, so I wedge myself between Carmen and Powerhouse, hoping I don't seem too clingy.

"We have a new Hot Shot to welcome today," Prince says, and everyone turns their eyes on me. I redden, realizing that I'm the only new draft. "Moose, you got a derby name yet?"

"Uh—no," I croak, "not yet."

"We're working on it," Carmen says, throwing an arm around my waist and shaking me affectionately. I stare hard at the ground, hoping my new teammates can't see my flush.

"Cool. Get one by your first bout, or I'm making an executive decision about Moose on the Loose. Let's go around and do names and pronouns."

The skaters in the circle introduce themselves, and I try to hammer their names into my brain. *Gamma Raze, they/them. Kicky Longstocking, she/they. Himaslaya, she/her.* There are sixteen of them—some seem to share Carmen's enthusiasm for having someone else to jam so they don't have to, while others just look bored.

The brunette with the sneer goes last: "Acid Reign. She/her. I'm a jammer." She looks right at me while she announces her position.

"Don't get territorial, Acid," Powerhouse drawls, and Acid shoots them a dark look.

"You should be paranoid too," she snaps.

"Easy!" Eden barks, and they fall silent, still glowering at each other. "Geez. What did we say we were going to focus on this year?"

"Teamwork," the skaters reply in unison, and I get the feeling they've said it many times before.

"Good. We're gonna start with footwork—find a spot on the track!"

"Just ignore Acid," Carmen mutters to me as we skate onto the track. "She's always bitter about something."

Powerhouse mumbles something under their breath that I don't catch, and I can't help but think it would take a lot to annoy them to the point of calling someone out.

The first hour should be easy—it's just solitary footwork, stuff I've done a million times. But I keep letting my gaze wander to Mercury as I loop my way through a pair of cones. I'm impatient to get to contact drills, I realize. I want Mercury to hit me again. And I want to show her how much stronger I've gotten.

At the end of the first hour, Prince announces that we're moving on to scrimmage scenarios. My heart leaps—*this* is what I've been waiting for, a chance to actually play instead of breaking down every little individual skill. Mercury picks up a drawstring bag from the middle of the track and pulls out a handful of red and orange helmet covers, which she starts tossing to random people. For some reason, I feel a pang of disappointment when she doesn't specifically throw me a helmet cover with a star. Everyone says jamming is hard, but as the only person on the track who can score, it also seems like the flashiest position. The thought of everyone in an audience watching me should scare me—that many people perceiving me. But if I can learn to jam like the travel team skaters, maybe that's all they'll see.

Eden sets up ten skaters on the jam line and starts talking through a start strategy. "Getting lead is important," she says after talking us through the drill, "because the lead jammer can call it off before the opposing jammer scores any points. Set it up." Eight blockers cluster at the jam line. Acid Reign and Powerhouse are jamming, wearing opposing starred helmet covers. Eden sticks a hand in the air, fingers splayed out. "Five seconds!" she barks.

Even though they're just running a starting play, I see every player on the track hold their breath, notice the electrified gazes passing between them, the way they communicate with the tiniest of nods. Eden's whistle splits the air and her hand cuts down, and two blockers—Rat Queen and Firebolt, I think—shove the opposing blockers so Acid can leap fluidly through, claiming lead jammer.

"Good," Eden says, gesturing Acid back to the jam line. "But going easy on your teammates doesn't do us any favors. Challenge each other more."

The blockers set up again as Mercury appears beside me. "How's it going?" she asks, nudging me with one elbow. Eden's whistle blows, and this time there's more of a struggle; Acid is clearly stuck in a wall while her blockers attempt to play offense for her. I was itching to get to contact drills a minute ago, but now, watching the way the blockers hit, there's a wave of apprehension.

"I'm kinda nervous," I admit in a low voice. "I know I've done some contact with you, but—"

Rat Queen lays a huge hit on Kicky, and she rolls off the track, opening a hole for Powerhouse to zoom through to claim lead jammer. "Keep running it!" Eden shouts.

"You'll catch up quick," Mercury assures me. "Really. Playing with people who are better than you is the fastest way to improve."

Powerhouse has lapped the pack and starts punching through blockers again, this time to score. Acid looks visibly frustrated. *"I need offense!"* she snarls, trying to get her blockers' attention. They're supposed to be helping her get out of the pack.

I start to ask Mercury what Acid's deal is, but then Eden's whistling to call off the jam, waving at us all to pay attention.

"You should try it," Mercury whispers in my ear. Before I can reply, she's skating past me to take a spot on the track. I make eye contact with Powerhouse.

"Just follow your offense," Powerhouse tells me, pulling the star over my helmet for me.

I touch my helmet as I roll onto the track, feeling the stretchy fabric and the lopsided stars stitched on either side. I've imagined jamming a million times, sliding over the wood floors of Eden's apartment in my socks, picturing myself expertly ducking and dodging and leaping over a spray of blockers in my way. But now that I'm on the jam line with the star on my helmet, looking at a tangled knot of my extremely strong new teammates, my stomach flutters.

"Five seconds!" Eden shouts, throwing her hand up. *Oh fuck, already?*

Beside me, Acid gets low on her skates, one toe stop down to propel her into the pack as soon as the whistle blows. *Should I copy her?* In all our private practices, Powerhouse never showed me what I'm supposed to do on the line, waiting for the whistle. I squat awkwardly, wondering how it's possible that five seconds haven't passed yet.

Just follow your offense. I glance up toward the outside edge of the track, where Carmen and Gamma Raze are waiting to clear a path for me. Carmen makes eye contact, giving me a slow, careful nod. *Wait, does that mean to follow her? Or* not *follow her? What the fuck is the drill?*

The whistle blows.

The opposing blockers roll backward, sending me ass-first onto the track. I scramble to my feet and throw myself into them, but they're completely solid. There are two whistles up ahead, indicating that Acid got out of the pack and claimed lead jammer.

"Keep it going!" Eden calls again over the clatter of wheels. "Run it until both jammers get out!"

I throw everything I have into the wall, getting up on my toe stops to grind against them. The blockers are calm, which feels even more demoralizing.

Beside me, Carmen dips into a low squat, digging her shoulder into the opposing blocker's ribs to make space for me. Panting, I attempt to roll around her. For the briefest moment, I can see an expanse of empty track ahead, a clear shot out—then someone collides with my hip, and I'm sprawled on the track again.

Three rounds of whistles end the jam, and Carmen leans over me. "You okay?"

"Yeah," I grunt, and she doesn't extend a hand to help me up. *Part of derby,* Mercury told me at our last private practice. *Gotta be able to get up on your own.*

As soon as Carmen confirms that I'm not injured, she rounds on Acid. "What the *hell*?" she snarls. "You don't hit a new skater that hard, Acid!"

Was Acid the one who hit me? It happened so fast that I didn't even have time to register whose hip knocked me down. Are jammers even allowed to hit each other?

Acid's on the side of the track with her arms crossed, glowering at Carmen. "*You* wanted her on the Hot Shots," she sneers.

"Hey!" Mercury barks, and everyone quiets, turning to her. I've never heard her speak so sharply. "Enough. Acid—play down when you're skating with a newbie. You know better. And, Carmen," she adds, "keep it civil."

Carmen looks ready to throw hands, but Mercury's already turning to Eden, gesturing for her to take over.

"What happened that time?" Eden asks the team as I roll to my knees, slowly dragging myself upright. I stare at the ground as Eden explains the drill again, pointing out what everyone did wrong. "New jammers!" she calls, and I pull the star off my helmet in defeat, handing it to the first person I see. I can tell my face is red, and that makes me more embarrassed. My eyes sting, and I feel that panicked monster start to claw its way up from deep within me, squeezing my lungs like a rope. "Moose," Eden says in a low voice as I pass her. "Deep breath. You're doing fine. Just work on communicating with your offense next time."

"Water," I mumble, grabbing my full Nalgene and sprinting toward the edge of the track. I'm so shaken that I fumble my stop at the foam barrier and nearly flip myself over it—thankfully, nobody sees.

The water cooler is at the back of the Hangar, tucked between the bleachers and the locker room with an emergency door behind it. I leave my Nalgene by the cooler, pushing open the door to breathe. For the first time, I'm annoyed that it's not raining—the cool mist would be a relief on my burning cheeks right now.

I rest my helmet on the doorframe and place a hand on my belly, trying to breathe deep and slow like Dr. Parikh showed me. The back door opens to a narrow strip of asphalt behind the Hangar, with the drooping trees of the nature reserve rising up beyond. There must be a bike path cutting through—I watch a handful of cyclists whiz by, a pair of older women walking with their sweatshirts tied around their waists.

You're going to fall. It's part of derby. Try not to freak out when it happens, but it's okay if you do.

I wipe my sweaty wrist guard across my stinging eyes, squaring my shoulders. My hip is smarting where Acid hit me, and my forearms are already riddled with the yellow promises of bruises. *Maybe this isn't for me,* I think glumly, staring out at the puddles in the asphalt. *Maybe I should take up walking outside with a sweater around my waist.* After barely surviving the fire, strolling the bike path might be a safer option.

Another, angrier part of me rolls its eyes. *You* did *survive,* it chides me. *You can handle getting knocked around on roller skates.*

A whistle cuts through the air, drawing me back toward the action in the Hangar. Outside feels fresh and new and cleansed by the rain, and the rare Portland sun is calm. Safe. Behind me, I hear skates slamming on the sport court, hips colliding, my new teammates shouting at each other over the whistle blasts. The Hangar's muggy and kind of smelly and sounds like bruised hips and frustration. But it's a challenge.

I take a final, steadying breath and close the emergency door, retrieving my water bottle and heading back to the track.

chapter twelve

SITTING IN A CROWDED DINER during Sunday brunch is the last thing I want to do after two full hours of fruitlessly throwing myself at blockers. But then Carmen is offering to drive me, and Apex, Trail Mx., and Rat Queen are saying they'll meet us at Major's, and Eden is telling me it's fine and she'll see me at home.

I thought the six of us would be a nuisance, tramping into the middle of the brunch rush with our sweaty helmet hair and bruised arms and big appetites—but the server at the bar just beckons us in, nodding to an open swath of counter. "Your spot's open, girls!" he barks, turning to grab a tray of fries. Powerhouse and Trail Mx. stiffen at his words, and Carmen shoots back, "We're not all girls!" but it's too noisy for anyone to really hear. I feel like I should be worried about how loud I'm going to have to be in here, how hoarse my voice will sound after two hours of practice and another hour of yelling at brunch. But I realize I'm too hungry to care.

"Robbie can't wrap his head around the nonbinary thing," Trail Mx. says, grabbing a menu from the hostess stand for me.

"He's good at the pronouns," Mercury adds, leading us to the counter. "Just not the more nuanced stuff. You know, 'girls,' 'ladies.' "

"*I* don't even like being called a lady," Queenie grumbles.

"Why not?" I ask, squeezing on a barstool between Queenie and Powerhouse. Queenie introduced herself with she/her pronouns at practice. She and Powerhouse exchange a look.

"Utah," Powerhouse reminds Queenie.

"Ah."

I'm tempted to just shut down, apologize and sit in silence at yet another thing I don't understand about being queer in Portland. But Powerhouse and Queenie don't look annoyed, and I'm desperate to show them I belong. "So . . ." I ask slowly, "no 'ladies' because . . . ?"

"It's just kind of weird and demeaning," Queenie says frankly, sliding a coffee mug down to Powerhouse. She offers one to me, and I shake my head. "At least for me. I mean, I'm trans, so I guess it's *kind* of affirming, but it's presumptuous and weird to call a group of people 'ladies' when you don't know their gender."

"*And* it's outdated," Powerhouse says from my other side, sliding the coffee mug toward the harried server who fills it for them. "No need to use gendered terms to address a group unless you know for sure that all the folks *in* that group are okay with that specific word."

I nod, but I feel like I haven't had enough calories to fully understand what they're saying. Being queer in Utah was black-and-white—you were either gay and therefore an outsider, or you were straight and generally left alone. I'm still not used to how open everyone in Portland is, introducing themselves instinctively with their pronouns, wearing Pride pins on their jackets, filling their Instagram stories with queer memes, and gossiping about ex-partners dating current friends.

"Can I ask . . ." I say slowly to Queenie, "with derby, are you . . . ?"

"The only trans girl?" Queenie finishes my sentence, raising an eyebrow. I nod sheepishly. "Definitely not. It's one of the only junior sports where trans people are welcome, so there's a lot of us."

"Not even just junior sports," Powerhouse adds from my other side, stirring oat milk into their coffee. "Sports in general. Most of them are not kind to trans folks."

"I played basketball all through middle school and my freshman year," Queenie tells me. "I wasn't even *that* good, but I loved it. Then I transitioned before sophomore year, and suddenly there's a rule about only 'biological women' being allowed on the girls' team."

"In Portland?" I say, surprised.

"Nah, a really small town a couple hours from here, near the coast. I'm lucky—my parents moved us up here so I could play girls' basketball, but I sorta fell in love with derby instead."

"People think trans women have some sort of 'natural advantage,'" Powerhouse adds disdainfully. "But I could lay out Queenie here in my sleep." Queenie leans over me to punch Powerhouse's shoulder, but she's grinning.

"And any trans people can play derby?" I ask, still trying to wrap my head around it.

"Sure," Queenie replies. "As long as derby feels like where they're meant to be, they're welcome."

"Well, *I'm* happy you're here," I say. "And you're welcome to lay me out on the track anytime."

"I will gladly take you up on that," Queenie replies as the server reappears and sets a purple milkshake down in front of me.

"Oh, I didn't order—"

"Just drink it, Moose!" Carmen calls from down the counter. "You'll like it!"

My new teammates have filled out their usual spots at the counter with practiced ease, seamlessly making room for me. I still don't know where the milkshake came from, but I'm slurping it down gratefully—my body's desperate for calories after the last two hours.

At the end of practice, Prince had made everyone line up on the track. "You ready for your initiation, Moose on the Loose?" they had asked, directing me to the end of the line.

"What?"

"Team tradition," Poundstooth told me sagely as I skated into place behind her. "At the end of your first practice, you get to push the entire team twice around the track."

I had stared down the line of my sixteen new teammates, most of them significantly bigger and more muscular than me, and all of them grinning back at me, waiting.

"I can't do that," I'd said, and my voice sounded small and hoarse. My lungs and throat were still burning from practice.

"It's not as hard as it looks," Pounds whispered. "You just have to get us rolling."

Everything in me wanted to say no—my legs were already trembling. But Eden, standing in the middle of the track, had her phone out, beaming in excitement as she turned the camera on me. I set my jaw and planted my hands on Pounds's hips. The Hot Shots cheered, everyone dropping into derby stance and holding on to the hips of the skater in front of them.

I popped up on my toe stops and threw all my weight into Pounds. For a second, nothing seemed to happen—my legs screamed in protest, and my arms felt ready to collapse. But then the line began to inch forward. I kept pushing, digging into my toe stops, and everyone began to roll, whooping and whistling as we picked up speed. Soon we were sailing—I stayed at the back, thrusting all my power into the line ahead of me, panting as sweat soaked the pad of my helmet.

When we made it twice around the track, the line dissolved, and the cheering mass of my new teammates swarmed me.

The loud bang of Carmen dropping a textbook on the counter jerks me back to the present. "I don't normally work on Sundays," she's saying loftily to Queenie, "but I'll make an exception for teammates who are about to flunk out of chem."

Major's Diner is far from the bougie, trendy restaurants I've seen so far in Portland—it's all peach and white tile and striped vinyl booths. There are a couple vague suggestions of modernity—a Square reader instead of a cash register, a Bluetooth speaker in the kitchen blasting Aerosmith—but I could have found the same restaurant in a roadside Utah town.

On the other side of Carmen tutoring Queenie over the brunch din, Mercury and Trail Mx. are embroiled in a heated discussion about the elimination of the jammer lap point, whatever that means. I'm half listening, mostly trying to figure out the flavor of this milkshake and feeling grateful that nobody's talking to me. It feels easy to sit in silence in this group—I'm included, but not the center of attention, not awkwardly brushing off stares. When Robbie comes by to drop a couple baskets of fries, I feel his eyes linger on the scar on my throat until Powerhouse gives him a death glare that scares him off.

"It's marionberry."

I half turn with the straw still in my mouth. Powerhouse is leaning forward on the counter, stirring their coffee. Queenie goes to the bathroom, leaving Powerhouse and me alone on this side of the bar. "What?" I croak.

"The shake. It's a crossbred blackberry, or something. People in Oregon lose their shit over them." They pick up a spoon to stir their coffee, and I'm amazed how everything Powerhouse does looks so smooth and calculated, even in the chaotic noise of the diner. "You look beyond confused over there," they add.

I slide the shake back and clear my throat, a little embarrassed. "It's good."

Powerhouse gives me a searching look, like they have no time for shallow conversations about local genetically engineered fruit. "You did good today."

I scoff. "You don't need to lie to me."

They raise an eyebrow. "You really think I would lie to you? I know we've only known each other a few weeks, Moose, but damn."

"I never even got out of the pack."

"So?"

"So, how was I any good if I can't get past a single blocker?"

"That's not the only measure of being good. I saw you skate off the track after the second jam. I could tell you wanted to stop."

I look away, but Powerhouse doesn't quite sound like they're sorry for me.

"You came back," they continue. "That's what makes you good. When you keep trying, even if you're not getting anywhere. Plus, you pushed the line. Not easy."

To my left, our four teammates have dissolved into a near shouting match in their debate, to the point that Robbie has to slam his hand on the counter to shut them up. They wait a split second until he returns to the kitchen, then burst into conversation again.

"Anyway," Powerhouse tells me, looking completely unfazed, "your first practice on a real team always sucks. You'll get better."

Robbie appears again with a tray full of plates. "Burgers," he says gruffly, sliding plates to Powerhouse and me without meeting my gaze.

Powerhouse lifts the bun off their burger, inspecting the patty.

"Sometimes he accidentally gives me the regular instead of the veggie burger," they explain, peeling up the lettuce to check.

"How long have you been skating?"

They drop the bun, satisfied. "Seven years, give or take. Carmen and I went to the same elementary school. She talked me into going to a derby summer camp with her."

"You're really good," I say, hoping I don't sound pandering.

Powerhouse just shrugs, politely overlooking my embarrassment. "You will be too. You have the skating. Just gotta work on the derby skills."

"Did you ever . . ." When I pause, Powerhouse glances up at me, raising their eyebrows.

"Yeah?"

"Did you ever want to quit?"

They give me another long, searching look. I'm starting to realize it's their thing. "No. Never."

"Even when you weren't good yet?"

"I was always good," Powerhouse says, and it takes me a second to realize they're joking. They crack a rare smile at my expression, sipping coffee. "Nah. I liked the challenge. There's always more to learn in derby, you know? Do *you* wanna quit?"

"No," I say quickly, biting my lip. "But . . . I'm worried I *will* want to. Later." Derby, even with all its ups and downs and bruises and hard falls and screaming on the track, feels stable. The first thing in my life that's felt stable since the fire. The other Hot Shots know my name, care about me, folded me effortlessly into their team after a single practice. I feel like I'm digging my fingers into derby to keep it close to me, like if I get too in my head or panic too much or take one hard fall, I'll let it slip away.

"There is no point in worrying about how you might feel later,"

Powerhouse tells me. They dig into their bag, pulling out a little green velvet pouch embroidered with gold vines. "Here," they say, wiping ketchup off their fingers and reaching into the pouch. They pull out a deck of cards, shuffling them deftly and holding them out to me. "Pick a card."

"Powerhouse is fortune-telling!" Carmen announces from my other side, and suddenly all attention is on us.

"It's *not* fortune-telling," Powerhouse scolds Carmen, but she ignores them, shaking my shoulders excitedly.

"Powerhouse is so good at these. It's like mini therapy every time you touch their magic deck."

"Uh—"

"Go on," Powerhouse says, nudging the deck toward me. Painfully aware of Carmen, Mercury, and three of our other teammates watching excitedly, I pick a card at random and pull it out of the deck. I flip it over—it's a skeleton in a flowing robe, holding open the jaw of a much bigger, four-legged skeleton. It doesn't look violent—the skeleton in the robe seems at ease, confident in its ability to peel back the beast's teeth.

"Strength," Powerhouse says. They meet my gaze, unflinching, and tap the card in my hand. "This means you need to trust yourself."

Carmen drops me off at Eden's apartment after brunch, and I finally drop my gear by the door, strip off my stinking workout clothes, and slip into the shower, exhausted.

The shower's been a weird place for me lately. In the hospital, I couldn't shower by myself until I'd spent five weeks in the intensive burn unit getting sponged off every other day. After that, a nurse showed me how to clip a plastic shield around my neck to keep the tube in my throat from getting wet. I showered as fast as I could because I hated the sound of the water hitting it, reminding me it was there. Since Utah, I like the shower—it's a place where I'm completely alone, unseen by anyone else, where I can let myself dissolve in the steam. I usually turn the hot water dial as far as it will go, feeling the water sear my skin and thinking about how I'd known hotter. Then I kill the hot water and douse myself in icy cold, shivering but reveling in the control. The whole time, I think about how I'll have to get out and see the dark red scar in the mirror, see the way my body has changed since April. I stay in the shower as long as I can.

Today, I'm aching and tender and sore as I step into the tub, letting the water mat my hair and spill down the angles of my body. I'm shaped different now. Not like I was before the fire, not like I was in the hospital. Something new. When I look down, I find myself staring at my arms. Not the faint stretch marks on my legs or the dark red scar I can just barely see when I tuck my chin enough—just my arms. The faint yellow patches are deepening into purple and green, spotted along my forearms like paint. There are more on my thighs, peppered around my knees, and one particularly painful lump on my hip where Acid hit me. I turn and wince when the water hits a patch of raw red skin—a Velcro burn from the strap of someone's kneepad.

I run my hands over the bruises, feeling the deep lumps and tender spots like I'm taking stock of myself, inventorying the damage. My muscles are sore, but a satisfying sore. I worked for this. These are wounds and scrapes I can learn to control. *Battle scars,* Mercury called them. I move my hands up my own shoulders and let my fingers rest on my collarbone, thumbs on either side of the trach scar I've never touched. I close my eyes, take a breath, and move one thumb along the curve of the scar, feeling each ridge and bump. Maybe I can learn to control this one too.

When I step out of the shower, bruised and exhausted and still somehow hungry, I feel strong.

chapter thirteen

PRACTICES WITH THE HOT SHOTS don't get easier, but I feel myself getting tougher. I throw myself into every drill, pulling Prince aside to break down skills for me, meeting up with Mercury, Carmen, and Powerhouse every Friday night to work on my contact skills. After every practice, I strip off my sweaty gear, down a protein shake in minutes, and sit crouched at Eden's coffee table or the counter at Major's, tapping notes into my phone about what I need to work on.

After our Wednesday scrimmage, most of the Hot Shots end up at Major's with one or both of the coaches, crammed into the corner booth and passing a small whiteboard around to dissect the strategy we worked on that week.

I'm not surprised that I'm not rostered for the game against the Slamazons. I knew I wouldn't be—I can still barely stay upright during scrimmage—but I'm surprised to feel a twinge of disappointment anyway when Eden gives me a heads-up at the end of practice one afternoon. I never played a sport before derby, unless you count rock climbing with Papa a few times a year. But it's taken over my entire life—I'm thinking about it in school, in the conference room of Eden's office, staring at the ceiling at night while I try to sleep.

"I think you'll be ready after the holidays," she says encouragingly, ever-present coaching clipboard tucked under her arm. We're off to one side by the bleachers as the rest of the Hot Shots make their way off the track, sweaty and tired but energized for the bout in a couple weeks. "This one is still just a little too soon."

"Yeah, I get it," I say, even though I already feel awkward and different and othered from the rest of the Hot Shots.

"Moose," Mercury says, stepping over the track barrier next to us. "Come here, I have something for you."

Eden gives my shoulder a comforting squeeze before I follow Mercury to her bag. She squats and digs around until she pulls out an orange jersey and hands it to me. "Here."

I take the jersey, holding it up to examine the scowling meteor on the front. Prince told me they would order my jersey before my first bout, but that they take a while to come in. "I think it's too big. And I don't even have a derby name yet."

"That's because it's mine," Mercury chides, taking the jersey out of my hands and flipping it around. Her name and number are emblazoned across the back. "That's a spare from when I first got drafted to the Hot Shots. It's for you to wear at the bout this weekend. I know you're not rostered, but we still want you on the bench with us."

I feel a pang of something at her words—*we* want *you on the bench*—and lower the jersey, running my thumb over the *M* of her name.

"Won't I just get in the way?"

"No," Mercury replies simply, unclipping her helmet and shaking her hair loose. "It doesn't matter if you're not skating—you're part of the team."

My eyes prick, and I use Mercury's jersey to rub them furiously while she's not looking.

When I zip up my gear bag and cross the Hangar to find Eden, she's near the door with Prince, staring at a clipboard with her brows furrowed. Prince touches her elbow, but Eden stiffens. Prince's hand drops when she sees me.

"Hey, Moose on the Loose!" she says, and Eden looks up. "We need to get you measured for a jersey."

"I'll measure her at home," Eden says briskly, shoving the clipboard into her bag. "See you."

Prince frowns after her as Eden shoulders her bag and ducks out the door, clearly expecting me to follow.

"Uh . . . see you Friday," I tell Prince, unsure of what else to say before hurrying after Eden. She's already running the car and practically peels out of the parking lot as soon as I get in. "Are you okay?" Eden was okay five minutes ago when she was telling me I wouldn't be on the roster—whatever Prince said in that time must have been enough to piss her off.

"I'm fine," she says stiffly.

I watch the rain snake down my window as we turn out onto the bridge, crossing the gray river. "You don't seem fine."

"Moose," Eden sighs, pinching the bridge of her nose. "It's been a long week, okay? I don't want to talk about it right now." We drive in silence for a few more minutes, and my phone lights up in my lap with a text in Bitch Pod 2:

CARMEN

sorry u aren't on the roster moose. if it makes u feel better, the slamazons are gigantic and mean and will probably knock the shit out of us.

MERCURY

that is a very negative viewpoint to adopt two weeks before our bout.

CARMEN

WELL CAPTAIN I'm feeling negative.

I hesitate a moment and glance sidelong at Eden, glaring at the road and gripping the steering wheel much harder than necessary.

MOOSE

you're not the only one

CARMEN

say more

MOOSE

idk. something happened with prince and my sister and now she's being really weird

CARMEN

lover's quarrel

POWERHOUSE

shut up carmen

CARMEN

maybe prince finally asked her out and they didn't want to make it weird. we know how that is.

I freeze with my thumbs hovering over my phone screen. Mercury's typing bubble appears, then disappears.

CARMEN

I mean like people in derby are always trying to date each other and it's always messy. not about any couple in particular

CARMEN

or any skater in particular

CARMEN

although some are messier than others

POWERHOUSE

THANK YOU carmen that's enough

"Who are you texting?" Eden asks, and I turn the screen off and shove Prince's hand-me-down phone back in my pocket, flushed.

"Just some other Hot Shots."

"Mercury?"

Jesus, does everyone know I have a crush on her?

"And Carmen and Powerhouse," I say, defensive.

Eden just nods. "Sorry for being short with you earlier. I'm having a weird day."

I should ask her again if she wants to talk about it. Or maybe talk about something else to distract her. I'm not sure what the sister protocol is—it still feels like I've only had a sister for a few months. I suddenly feel an overwhelming need to share something with her, to spill some secret that might make us feel a little less like strangers.

"So . . . um . . . have you ever dated someone in derby?" I venture.

Eden pulls up to a stoplight and turns just enough to make eye contact with me, her brow furrowed. "No." She pauses. "Not really."

"Have you ever . . . *wanted* to date someone in derby?"

"No." Another pause. "Maybe."

"And are you . . ." *Just say it just say it just say it.* "Gay?"

Eden bites her lip. Maybe this was not the conversation to have if I wanted to distract her. "Well, first of all, you shouldn't just *ask* people if they're queer. Coming out is a big deal, and you should let the person tell you when and if they're ready for you to know." She's talking fast again.

"Sorry," I say, my voice small. She's right, but I'm desperate to throw a rope across the chasm between us.

"It's okay," she replies, gentler. "It happens. But yeah, I am. And yes, I've thought about dating people in derby."

"Is it easier? Dating someone in derby where everyone is queer?"

"Nah. Dating is always weird and confusing, no matter what community you're part of. And dating in derby can be tricky. That's why we advise people not to date their teammates."

"Do people follow that suggestion?"

"Rarely."

I should tell her I'm queer too. It should be so easy here—in Utah, Dads got dirty looks when they kissed in public, never held hands downtown after dark, picked neighbors to befriend based on the yard signs they put up in the fall. I was only out to my dads, afraid the whole school would come after me if I dared utter the word *lesbian* to describe myself. Nobody knew about my crush on Jenna from freshman English, not even Dads. But almost everyone in derby is queer, almost everyone in *Portland* even.

Eden's waiting for me to say something, expectant. I try to form the words but can't force them out.

chapter fourteen

I WATCH MOST OF THE HOT SHOTS versus Slamazons game from the end of our team's bench, a bag of energy bars and ice packs between my feet. Mercury's jersey is too big on me, but it gives me a sense of authority as I move through the Hangar to fill water bottles and fetch tools to tighten wheels. I'm part of the team, even wearing hand-me-down combat boots and a too-big jersey with someone else's name on it.

I try to study Powerhouse and Acid each time they jam. Their styles are completely different—where Powerhouse punches through walls and forces their way straight up the middle of the track, Acid moves like water, fluidly wrapping herself around the blockers and deftly sneaking through the pack. She's annoyingly good.

In the final jam, when everything hinges on Acid to score a few more points and pull ahead of the Slamazons, Eden beckons our bench to their feet. We watch the last jam standing, linked together, stomping and then dissolving into cheers when Acid scores a tidy three points and calls off the jam, earning us a narrow victory.

"*That's* why she doesn't get kicked off the team," Carmen tells

Mercury, Powerhouse, and me as she drives us to the after-party at Major's. "She's too good."

"That's not true," Mercury says from the front seat, jabbing Carmen in the thigh. "It's because this is a juniors' program, and we can't just kick people off the team because we don't like them."

"What's her problem?" I ask, glancing between the three of them. I can only see a fraction of Mercury's face, lit up in flashes by the passing streetlights. Her mouth looks tight.

"What *isn't* her problem?" Carmen says, and she glances at Mercury, like she's waiting for permission to say something.

"She's just had a hard time," Mercury says calmly.

I can tell Carmen wants her to say more, but she doesn't push it.

"Mercury, the great mediator," Powerhouse mutters.

chapter fifteen

I'VE BEEN LOSING FOCUS DURING SCHOOL, spending most of the time I should be doing homework clicking over to new tabs about derby technique and recordings of old championship games. It doesn't help that Mercury sits in front of me in history, and I spend most of that hour staring at her hair instead of listening to Ms. Trayhart.

"How'd you do on the test?" Mercury asks as the bell rings the Friday after the Slamazons bout. We normally have history first period, but an assembly this morning jumbled the schedule so it's our last class of the day.

"Okay," I say, and Mercury sighs as she slings her bag over her shoulder.

"I just hate that the class is called *world* history but we're still just learning about Europe. Like, there are several other continents we could be talking about, where events significant to humanity occurred."

We stop at my locker so I can grab my derby bag before heading down the hall to Mercury's. "It's better than what we learned in Moab."

Mercury frowns down at her history test as she shuts her locker. "Actually, you know what? I'm gonna ask Ms. Trayhart about this. I feel like this question about Roman aqueducts should have been right. Meet you out front?" Powerhouse and Carmen's school gets out twenty minutes earlier than ours, and they've been picking us up on practice days to drive us to the Hangar.

"Sure." Mercury heads back to the history room as I heave my skate bag over one shoulder and my backpack over the other before teetering out to the front entrance.

Powerhouse and Carmen aren't here yet, so I park myself on a covered bench by the bike racks, dropping my bags at my feet to give my shoulders some relief while I wait for Mercury. The grassy area outside the front entrance is crowded even though it's cold and drizzly—mostly other students in raincoats waiting for rides, huddled in their own little groups, texting. A loose thread from my scarf tickles my chin, and I pull the whole thing off to yank the thread off. I feel the sudden cool air on my neck, and I realize how nice it feels to be unencumbered by this chunky gray scarf that is definitely more Eden's style than mine. I feel weirdly calm about the fact that my trach scar is peeking up from the neckline of my hoodie, probably visible to anyone who would happen to look at me. I bunch up the scarf in my lap, waiting for the panic to hit, but it doesn't come.

I pull my phone out and idly open Instagram. Most of the junior skaters have separate accounts for derby where they post game pictures and selfies from after scrimmage and inside jokes from their teams. I've thought about making one, but I have no idea what I'd put on it—I don't have any photos of myself in derby skates. And even if I did, the neckline of the orange Hot Shots jersey would show the scar on my neck.

As I'm tapping through Carmen's story full of memes about

atomic mass, a text notification pops up—it's an unsaved number with a 435 area code.

Hey, moose?

My brows furrow as I tap into the text. I have no other messages with this person, but it must be someone from Utah.

Yeah? I type back.

Hey!!!!! It's Skatemare!!!!!

I suck in a breath. Skatemare, Dads' best friend from the rink, who was at our house every Sunday to play cards. Who had tried to get me to leave with him when the fire started. I realize, staring at the text, that I haven't even thought about anyone else who survived the fire, the many rink skaters who must have made it out, unlike my dads. There must have been more of them in the burn unit with me in Moab. I realize my heart's beating faster.

Another text appears. **I found your sister on Facebook and she gave me your new number, wanted to see how you were doing.**

My thumb hovers over the keyboard. I have no idea what to say to him. How I'm doing seems to change minute to minute. How am I *supposed* to be doing?

I try to take a breath, but my lungs are constricted again, like I can't pull in enough air to satisfy them. I try again, but it just makes my breath faster. My trach scar feels thick and heavy on my neck, like a leech I can't pull off, exposed to everyone. My vision tunnels as I stare at the text, thumb shaking.

"Hey." Mercury's appeared beside me, hefting her skate bag onto the bench, but I can't look away from my phone. "You okay?"

The panic boils over then, searing, spilling down my back. I feel cool air on my neck, the scar on full display. I chuck my phone away, distantly hear it hit the concrete, see people turning to stare. There's no exit, no path to sneak through. Not when everyone's staring at me, wide-eyed, trying to figure out why I'm having a meltdown on the school's front lawn.

Everything spins, and my vision tunnels, heart pounding. I can't see—no, I can't hear. Why is it so *fucking* loud?

I whirl around again, desperate for an exit, but people are still in my way, jostling each other, too loud, talking to me, looking at me, why is everyone always *looking* at me? My new derby instincts kick in, and I shove past them, hands shaking as I bolt around the side of the parking lot, my sneakers slipping on the wet grass.

The noise mercifully drops away as I round the corner of the building, into the soggy vegetable garden outside the ecology classroom. The raised beds are empty, soil turned to mud as we get closer to winter.

I sniff, drawing in a huge, shuddering breath and gripping the closest handhold I can find, a wheelbarrow filled with rainwater. I'm squeezing the side of the wheelbarrow, trying to slow my breath, but I'm sinking to the ground, breathing harder, and my chest is tight. *I'm going to die,* I realize, clutching my chest and squeezing my eyes shut. *I survived a fire, and I'm going to die of a heart attack in a vegetable garden.*

I can still hear the distant chaos from the front of the school, but now there are also sodden footsteps coming toward me in the grass and a hand on my back. I grip the edge of the wheelbarrow harder, my breath so sharp that it stings my throat.

"Moose," someone says gently. "Open your eyes."

I crack one open, my breath still uncontrollable, heart pounding.

I vaguely make out the shape of Mercury, sitting cross-legged in the wet grass with me.

"What are five things you can see?"

Can't she see I'm having a fucking heart attack? "I—I can't," I gasp, twisting my shirt in one hand. "I'm—"

"You're having a panic attack," Mercury says, firmer. She pries my hand off my shirt, closing it in her own warm hands. "Tell me five things you can see."

I squeeze my eyes shut again, then prick them open, staring around the garden while my heart threatens to burst through my ribs. "The—the flowerpot," I gasp, searching for something else. "M-my shoe. The shovel. That t-tree. You. I see you."

"Four things you can touch," she says softly.

"Your hand. The wheelbarrow." My breath is slowing down. I drop my other hand to the ground, still shaking. "The grass. My shirt."

"Three things you can hear."

My heart is slower now, and I no longer feel like my ribs are going to crack open from the stress. "Traffic, from the highway. M-my heart beating. The wind."

"Two things you can smell."

"The rain." Pause. "Lavender."

"One thing you can taste."

I close my eyes, drawing in a deep, shuddering breath. "Water, I guess." When I open my eyes, Mercury's still there, calmly rubbing circles on my palm with her thumb.

"You're fine," she tells me, gentle but firm. "Do you believe me?"

I release the tension in my limbs, let myself puddle on the ground. My jeans are soaked from the damp grass. "I think so." We sit quietly for a moment. The sound from the front of the school has quieted, cars and buses pulling out of the parking lot as normal. Whatever mess I started seems to have settled.

Mercury reaches into her back pocket and pulls out my phone. It lights up when she hands it to me, and there's a spiderweb of cracks across the screen. I feel a pang of guilt. This was Prince's old phone, and Eden probably can't afford to buy me a whole new one. There's a new message from Skatemare, warped a little under the cracks: **would love to catch up sometime, let me know!!! Miss you kid.**

"Do you wanna talk about it?" Mercury asks gently.

I turn the phone over in my hands. "This guy I know from Utah texted me. One of my dads' friends. It just . . . surprised me, I guess." It sounds ridiculous when I say it out loud, but Mercury nods easily. She's still holding my hand, tracing tiny circles in my palm, and I don't want her to stop.

"Is he a weirdo?"

"No. He's a really good guy. I just . . . I haven't talked to him since the fire." I can't explain why the sudden merging of my two very different worlds—the Rollerdome in Utah and the damp cold of Oregon—overwhelmed me. But Mercury, thankfully, doesn't push it.

"Did everybody see me have a meltdown?" I ask her.

Mercury shrugs. "Who cares?"

I give her a look.

"Okay, a few people saw. Maybe ten. But seriously, who cares?"

I stretch my legs out, leaning against the wet cedar of the raised bed behind me and letting the rain whisper down my face, focusing on the feeling of Mercury's hand in mine. "How did you know to do that?"

"What?" she asks, voice muffled by the spinach and cabbage and waterlogged garden tools around us. Her hair is a little frizzy in the rain, cheeks pink.

"The five senses thing you did. To calm me down."

"I learned it in grief counseling after my mom died. It's supposed to ground you—remind you that you're not dying, that the anxiety will pass."

"I like it."

She glances over at me, mouth quirked in that half smile. For a moment, it feels so easy, sitting in the wet grass like this with her, holding her hand, being *close* to her. *Teammate,* that stern voice in my head reminds me, and I stiffen.

"Mercury," I begin, "what were you trying to say about Acid the other day? When we were going to the after-party?"

Her smile falters. "We dated last spring," she admits, and all the air goes out of my lungs. "*Briefly*. There was this whole thing with our qualifying bout for champs going wrong, then I got captain over her. That's why we're not supposed to date teammates. It always gets messy."

It's my turn to stare at the neglected, overwintered garden through the mist around us. I don't know what I expected—Mercury's captain of the Hot Shots. She has to set an example. She puts her team before herself. I close my eyes, feel the slow, calming circles she's drawing on my palm.

"I think I'm done with the scarf," I say after a moment.

Mercury stops drawing circles on my hand, looking up. She seems surprised, probably taken aback that I brought up the scarf in the first place.

"What changed your mind?" she asks gently.

"I just . . . I don't think I need it anymore. I'm tired of always worrying about it covering up my scar. And it's kinda ugly. The scarf, I mean."

Mercury laughs, her face bloomed into a smile. I hope she doesn't see my flush. "How about this," she says, continuing to draw little circles on my palm with her finger. "I'll knit you a cuter scarf just in case. And we can burn the gray one."

"Deal." My skin prickles, and I realize Mercury's staring at me. No, not staring—she's gazing, her eyes softer than the people who gawk at my scar. Raindrops glitter in her hair like jewels. She reaches up a hand, slowly, so *achingly* slow, toward my face.

"Is this okay?" she asks, her voice barely above a whisper. I can hardly hear her over the rain.

I nod, my heart threatening to beat out of my chest.

She gently spreads her hand over the side of my face, and I don't flinch away. Her touch prickles, but not unpleasantly. Mercury's hand moves slowly down my neck, her thumb just above the scar, and her face is quietly curious, like she's solving a puzzle. Before I can stop myself, I'm reaching up, resting my hand over hers on my cheek. Her lips part slightly, and it takes everything in me not to kiss her.

"Hey!" The chain-link gate around the garden swings open and Mercury jerks her hand back, burying it in her pocket like a secret. Carmen and Powerhouse have appeared around the corner, Carmen carrying a grease-stained takeout bag from Major's. "Let's bounce," she calls, swinging Powerhouse's keys on one finger. "We brought pre-practice carbs."

Mercury's up first, and she offers me a hand. When I take it, there's an unmistakable heat between us. She catches my eye and fails to hold back a grin. When I'm up and we're walking toward the parking lot, she holds my hand a second longer than she needs to.

chapter sixteen

CARMEN, clearly sensing that I need a distraction, spends the entire drive to practice telling us about the girl she's been tutoring in chemistry class. I'm half listening most of the time, sitting in the backseat beside Mercury and thinking about holding her hand. Obviously I shouldn't. But I can still think about it. It's better than thinking about the text from Skatemare and giving myself another panic attack over trying to respond.

"Can y'all come over after practice?" Carmen asks as we pull into the Hangar's parking lot. "My mom's been trying to get me to drive all the way out to Beaverton to go to the specialty paint supply store, and she won't make me do it if I have people over."

"Glad our friendship is transactional," Powerhouse remarks from the driver's seat.

"I have to ask my sister," I say. As much as I want to curl up in Eden's second bedroom and not talk to anyone all weekend, I should probably attempt to socialize.

"Oh, don't worry about that," Carmen says, twisting around in the passenger seat to look at me. "I'm extremely trustworthy. Parents-slash-guardians love me."

"Parents-slash-guardians love you because you make sure all their kids pass chemistry," Mercury says wryly. "Not because of your chaperoning skills."

"I'm hurt that you don't see the difference."

Eden seems exhausted at practice, avoiding looking at Prince the whole time and mostly just staring at her ever-present clipboard. When practice wraps up and we start gearing down, I skate over to where she's deposited her bag on the other side of the bleachers.

"Hey, kid," she says, running a hand through her sweaty helmet hair. "How was school?"

I almost tell her about the panic attack, but the circles under Eden's eyes are heavy, and it's not like she could do anything about it anyway.

"Fine. Can I sleep over at Carmen's tonight? With Merc and Powerhouse?"

"Tonight?" Eden's expression is sad suddenly.

"Um . . . yeah."

"There's nothing else you wanted to do tonight?"

"Is there . . . something I was supposed to do?" Was she expecting me to hang out with her all weekend? "We can do something on Saturday," I offer, but it sounds flat.

"No, no," Eden says impatiently, waving a hand. "You can go tonight. It's fine."

Carmen's house is an eclectic orange Craftsman, the windows strung with bundles of herbs and colorful prayer flags. The trees are hung with ropes of dried cranberries that crisscross over us as we head up the walk.

"There are the champions!" someone crows from the porch, despite the fact that it's forty-five degrees and already pitch-black out at seven o' clock. "Hail to the champions!"

"The game was last week, Ma," Carmen says as we follow her onto the porch. Carmen's mom looks exactly like her, just aged about twenty-five years. Her white-blond hair is loose around her shoulders, and she has a chunky knit green sweater pulled over her pajamas. She has a lit joint in one hand and a mug in the other.

"Frances always downplays victory," she says mournfully to us, looping an arm around Carmen's waist and shaking her playfully.

"Only to you," Powerhouse mutters, and I stifle a laugh.

Carmen's mom's big eyes fall on me, and her face lights up. "You're Moose," she declares. It's not a question. She steps toward me, takes my hands. "Frances has told me *everything* about you. We are so glad you're in our family."

"Uh . . . thanks."

"I'm glad your sister has someone keeping her company around that apartment," she adds seriously. "Ripley spends too much time alone, if you ask me. Now, is Moose your derby name?"

"I don't have a derby name yet."

"Well, these three are great at derby names," Carmen's mom replies. "They'll get you christened and baptized by your first bout."

"Okay, thanks, Ma," Carmen says pointedly. "We've all had extremely exhausting days of being very serious athletes, so."

"All right, all right," she says, waving us off and settling on the porch swing. "I'll finish my tea out here. You all have fun. And, Moose," she adds, pointing to me. "Call me Mama Monoxide. Or Mama Mono. All the kids at the Hangar do."

"Bye, Ma," Carmen presses, ushering us through the door. The house is just as eclectic on the inside—Carmen leads us through a maze of cramped hallways, squeezing between overflowing bookshelves, hutches filled with dried flowers and herbs, easels stacked with half-finished canvases depicting a curvy person in shadow. I notice a hospital bed in one room—it's been stripped of sheets, and there are little painted glass ornaments hanging over the place where you'd lay your head, the railings woven with fabric flowers. It looks like it's been turned into a shrine.

"That's where my grandpa died," Carmen says frankly when she sees me looking. "*Three years* ago. We don't throw things out."

"Mama Mono is one of those weird artist types," Mercury tells me as we turn a corner and file up a narrow wooden staircase. "One time she told me I would always be protected by the 'vortex of the mountains.' "

"The what?"

"I literally have no idea. You just kind of nod and accept it from her." The walls in the stairwell are crowded with paintings of Carmen, from a round blond baby with wispy curls to her leaping heroically over a fallen blocker on skates.

"I'm her greatest muse," Carmen says dramatically, turning the corner and taking us up another flight of stairs. "She and my dad met at Burning Man, which should tell you all you need to know about them. They were devastated to learn that I can't draw to save my life." She opens the door at the top of the stairs, and I step up into a huge semifinished attic room. There's a big round window on one wall, and even though it's dark outside, I can tell the panes are made of rippled stained glass. Carmen flips a switch, and strings of fairy lights crisscrossing the ceiling fill the room with soft light. They illuminate more stacks of books, a round woven rug surrounded by a threadbare couch and mismatched poufs, and abstract art prints hung haphazardly on the unfinished walls.

"Is this your room?" I ask in awe, shutting the door behind me and staring around.

"Nah, spare attic," Carmen says, crossing to an ancient-looking space heater and cranking it to life. "My parents used to use it as a studio, but my mom hates working up here in the cold. No heat."

Powerhouse and Mercury have already deposited their bags and dropped onto the sagging couch. "That practice was exhausting," Powerhouse says, tearing into the takeout bag from Major's. "When did Apex get so strong? She laid me out like six times."

"She started doing CrossFit," Carmen says, and they all roll their eyes.

We talk about practice and the next bout in a couple weeks until Mercury slumps over, snoring, and Carmen drags out an armful of faded pillows and comforters. We make a sort of nest on the rug, just a heap of mismatched pillows and blankets that we pile into, and Carmen flicks off the lights. The only light is the moon from the round window, dappling the dusty floorboards in washed-out color.

I doze off, half sleeping, half thinking about Mercury's touch on my face, the way her lips parted and her eyes softened as her thumb almost touched my scar. No revulsion, no morbid curiosity, just . . . softness. I don't let myself look at her sleeping on the other side of the rug.

The wind rattling the window wakes me up at some point, and I stare at the vaulted ceiling of the attic, picking out silvery cobwebs in the rafters. My phone buzzes on the rug beside me, and I roll onto my side so the light doesn't wake the others up. It's just an email notification from school, informing me that I barely passed my history test. Restless, I open Instagram to see if anyone posted pictures from last week's game yet.

The first thing that pops up is a memory. A post from three years ago, when I had my first phone and Dads reluctantly let me download Instagram. It's Papa and me on either side of Dad, wearing goofy paper hats and pointing at the huge flan stuck with sparklers in front of Dad. Big sugared letters top the round custard, declaring his fiftieth birthday.

Oh my god.

I drop my phone, pressing my knuckles to my eyes. Dad wouldn't have minded. Papa would—he was big on family traditions—but Dad wasn't as sentimental. I remember that birthday—Papa got all their friends to film videos of themselves gushing over Dad, listing endless reasons why they loved him. Dad was red in the face the whole time he watched it, but that night, I heard him playing it again in the living room, over and over.

I grab my phone again, burning with guilt. **Are you awake?** I text Eden. She probably isn't—my phone reads 12:23 a.m. I'll have to lie here, knowing I'm a shitty person, for hours still.

My phone vibrates.

EDEN

yeah.

MOOSE

I'm sorry. I totally forgot.

EDEN

it's ok

MOOSE

I can come home now

EDEN

stay with your friends. I'll pick you up in the morning and we can celebrate then

There's a pause, then a picture: a slightly misshapen flan, a little uneven on the top but an improvement over her last attempt. I suck in a breath, surprised by the sharpness in my lungs.

EDEN

we can eat it tomorrow:)

She's not mad at me, I realize. Probably disappointed. Probably lonely. But not mad.

Somehow, it feels worse.

chapter seventeen

DR. PARIKH SEEMS PLEASANTLY SURPRISED when I tell her about the five senses thing Mercury showed me at school. I don't tell her about the way my entire body buzzed when Mercury touched my face, the feeling of her soft thumb on my neck. Just thinking about it makes me want to bury my face in a pillow and scream, and even my therapist might not be equipped to deal with that.

"That is a great tool to have in your toolbox," she says, nodding as I finish telling her about the incident outside school. "You felt like it helped you stabilize yourself through the panic attack?"

"Yeah," I say, twisting the toe of my boot into the carpet. "I mean, I thought I was having a heart attack."

"That's common with severe panic attacks. It's a sign that your body is overwhelmed, and your stress hormones trigger a fight-or-flight response." I wait for her to go on, but Dr. Parikh is quiet, waiting for me to speak. I hate when she does this—I know she's giving me space to think, waiting for my thoughts to tumble out so we don't have to sit in silence.

"Am I getting better?" I burst out.

"What do you think?"

"I think I'm still having panic attacks and dreaming about the fire and acting like a brat when I don't mean to," I say, a little harsher than I need to. But I'm frustrated with myself. "Skatemare has known me since I was born, but a text from him sent me into a panic attack, and I haven't been able to respond to him. I just . . . It's been six months since the fire. I thought I'd be better by now."

"There's no timeline on recovery from trauma, Moose."

"I know. But . . . I feel like I haven't made *any* kind of recovery."

"You got yourself through a panic attack."

"*Mercury* got me through a panic attack."

"You made the decision to join roller derby on your own."

"Eden made me join roller derby."

"Eden made you *try* roller derby. The decision to *stay* and try out for a team was yours."

"That had nothing to do with the fire."

"It didn't?" I looked Dr. Parikh up on LinkedIn once—she went to law school before she switched to social work. Annoyingly, it shows.

"Look, is there a metric or something?" I press, frustrated. "Some test I can take to tell if I'm making progress?"

"I think you are looking at your treatment too analytically," Dr. Parikh says calmly. "This isn't a math test that you can get a letter grade on. You will have good days and bad days, and you may feel the effects of your trauma when you don't expect it. Do you know about the ball in the box?"

I shake my head.

Dr. Parikh sets her notepad on the coffee table between us. She draws a square, then a large circle that nearly fills the box. "Imagine we have a ball in a box. Every time the ball touches the sides of the box, you feel that pain, or that panic. When you first feel grief, the ball is huge. It's touching all the sides, all the time, and it can feel like too much to bear."

She draws a second box, the same size but with a much smaller circle inside. "The ball never disappears. But over time, it shrinks. Most of the time, you're fine. But occasionally the ball will still hit the side of the box. And that's when it feels hard. Sometimes, you'll feel the same way you felt on the day you lost your fathers. We can never really get rid of the grief that comes with losing people we love. But we can learn how to carry it."

I stare at the notepad on the coffee table, my eyes prickling. "I . . ." I close my eyes, take a breath. "I think I'm ready to set a goal."

Dr. Parikh sits up, listening. She's asked me in every session if I've thought of a goal for the year after the fire yet, and I've deflected every time. But maybe she's right—I won't get better if I don't figure out how to carry it.

"I want to skate in a rink again. There's . . . a roller rink across from the Hangar where we practice. I see people going in all the time. But whenever I look at it, I feel panicky. I like derby, but—if I can skate in a rink, just once, just for fun, then maybe I'll feel like I've gotten better."

"What's different about skating at the rink versus playing roller derby?"

"Everything."

"Such as?"

"Well . . . you don't wear gear at the rink, for starters. It's just for fun—or it's supposed to be—and you just kind of skate in circles and talk to your friends and maybe dance a little. The Hangar is for *derby*. Like, you're there to work and get stronger and play this really intense sport, you know? It's easy to forget about everything else that's fucked up about my life when I'm at the Hangar, because I go into derby mode as soon as I'm there. At the roller rink, it's just . . . skating." It's so much more than that, really. But Dr. Parikh seems to get what I mean.

"Then I think that is a fine goal, Moose. Do you think it's attainable?"

Skate at the rink by April. *It doesn't have to be long,* I tell myself. I just want to get on the skate floor, feel the ripple of the polished wood under my skates without breaking down. I can do that.

"It's attainable."

"Good. We have our goal."

chapter eighteen

YOU CAN ONLY HEAR RAIN from inside the Hangar when it's a downpour. It beats the metal ceiling like hail, the sound ringing through the space over the track. Today, it's the only thing I hear as I lower one toe stop, exhale, and look up. The time between the call for five seconds and the beginning of a jam always seems to stretch into eternity, totally silent. But today, I hear the rain.

Eden's whistle blasts. I shove off, slamming into the tripod in front of me. From the corner of my eye, I see Acid dart past—but my blockers will catch her.

I dig my shoulder into Kicky Longstocking and Trail Mx., testing their link, feeling for a weakness. They're pressed together, strong, barely moving as I throw my weight into them. I flick my gaze toward the inside of the track—their fourth blocker is distracted, leaving the entire inside of the track unguarded.

I twist, exploding to the left and turning on my skates to shoot past the blockers. I streak past Acid, who's still stuck, and Prince blows two short whistles, making an *L* with their hand to declare me lead jammer.

"Good, Moose!" Prince calls. I'm crossing over, building speed, already looking ahead to the pack I'm about to reenter. Acid gets out and sprints to catch me.

Himaslaya is waiting for me, ready to play offense, but there's an open lane on the other side of the track—I dive toward it, slipping past two more blockers and tapping my hips to end the jam. Prince blows three sets of whistle blasts, holding up three fingers to indicate my three points to the imaginary scorekeeper. Acid hockey stops, her wheels chattering on the track, and gives her blockers a dirty look.

"Great job, Moose," Eden says, turning to me, "but that wasn't the drill. We're working on communicating with offense."

I frown at her. "I did communicate with my offense." Didn't I? I swear I said something to Himaslaya, standing there waiting to clear a lane for me.

"I heard nothing," Himaslaya says, and I shoot her a look.

"Every skater on the track needs to be able to communicate with one another," Eden's lecturing. "Overcommunicate, and be ten times louder than you think you need to be."

"But—" I close my mouth instead.

As Eden and Prince start explaining the nuances of setting up an offensive sweep, I pull off the jammer cap and roll backward till I'm between Powerhouse and Mercury. "I didn't *need* offense," I whisper to Powerhouse. "Right?"

"I mean, no, but it's the drill we're practicing."

"Pay attention, y'all!" Prince barks. "We're making the roster for the next game this weekend." I know I'll be assisting on the bench again—Prince made it clear that I probably won't be on a roster until after the holiday break. And I'm okay with it, weirdly. It takes the pressure off in practices.

Carmen leans over Powerhouse to whisper loudly. "If they roster me as a jammer again, I swear to god—"

"Carmen!" Prince barks, and she presses a hand over her mouth, straightening up.

"Anyway," Eden says, going back to her clipboard. "Any questions about pack definition? No? We'll go over it on Sunday too. Before we cool down—" She turns and gestures to Prince, who's disappeared into the bleachers and is now striding back to the track carrying a huge cardboard box. "Prince and I got you all something."

Prince drops the box in the middle of the circle, and we roll forward to peer inside.

"Oh, *sick*!" Carmen exclaims, pulling out a deep-orange-and-red letterman-style jacket. Our mascot, the scowling meteor, is embroidered on the breast, with Apex's name and number stitched in red thread beneath it. They must have been insanely expensive—I think of Eden's past due loan statement in the kitchen from months ago. Did she and Prince pay for these out of their own pockets? We definitely don't pay enough in monthly dues to the league to afford something like this.

"This is not just a gift," Prince says as Carmen dives into the box, pulling out more jackets and tossing them to us. "This is a team-building activity."

"Everything is a team-building activity," Trail Mx. mutters.

"You'll notice that the backs of your jackets are blank," Eden says. "We'd like each of you to find a patch or pin that you feel represents you, get enough for the team, and tell everyone why you chose it. By champs, we should have full jackets."

"Can we cover this up?" Apex interjects, gesturing to the huge logo of a local donut shop on the side of each jacket.

"No," Prince replies briskly. "Work around the donut, folks. They sponsored us and bought the jackets." I'm relieved. "These are so cool," Carmen says, passing me a jacket. There's no derby name stitched on the breast. I still haven't picked one.

"And no skate patches," Prince adds. "We all know you like to skate. Choose something you don't have in common with the whole team."

"Cooldown laps!" Eden calls, and she turns to mutter something to Prince as everyone drifts onto the track to skate in slow circles. Whatever was going on between Eden and Prince a few weeks ago seems to have passed—Prince laughs at something Eden says, and she can't stop grinning at them as she attempts to open her Nalgene.

"They're not even trying to hide it anymore," Carmen whispers as we skate onto the track. She's pulled her letterman jacket over her gear. "Moose, does Ripley just, like, gush over Prince all the time?"

"Not really," I say, shrugging. "Prince is just over a lot."

When I meet Eden by the door, she's with Prince, scribbling something on the clipboard that seems to be glued to her hand. Prince knocks on her head to get her attention, and she tears her gaze away. "Hey," she says, tucking the clipboard under her arm. "I'm gonna drop you off at home, then head over to Prince's so we can make the roster for the next bout. I'll bring home a pizza or something for dinner."

"I thought—" I glance around, making sure nobody's within earshot. "I thought I wasn't allowed to be alone."

"Dr. Parikh says you've been doing really well, you're socializing, you're staying active . . . I think I can leave you alone in the apartment for two hours."

She still seems hesitant, but I don't care. I haven't been alone since April, since before the fire, and the prospect of two uninterrupted solitary hours is tantalizing.

"How are we on a derby name, Moose on the Loose?" Prince asks as the three of us head out into the parking lot. It's raining, as usual, but has slowed to a fine drizzle. "We can get it stitched onto your jacket once you pick one."

I shrug. "I dunno. I haven't thought about it much."

"Can you believe this kid?" Prince asks Eden, throwing an arm around my shoulders. "Most people have a derby name picked out before they even get on skates."

"I have plenty of time!" I protest.

"Get on it," Prince says, winking as she unlocks her car. "See you at my place, Edy."

Eden waves, cheeks pink as we throw our gear bags in the trunk of her car.

"Did Prince call you *Edy*?" I ask as soon as we close the doors.

"What?" Eden asks distractedly, pushing her hair out of her face and turning the key in the ignition.

"I've just never heard her call you that. You hate *Edy*. She usually uses your derby name."

"Mm-hmm."

"What were you two fighting about last week?"

"Coach stuff."

I stare as Eden peels out of the parking lot, heading down the winding road beside the dreary theme park. "Eden."

"Yeah?"

"Are you dating Prince?" I expect her to sputter, maybe deny it, offer a bunch of half-assed other possibilities that make it clear she's lying.

But she gives me a wide, toothy grimace, shrugging. "I think I am."

I gape at her a moment, then punch her in the shoulder. "Really?"

"Ow, Moose—yeah, really."

"How long?"

"Thirty-six days officially," she answers automatically, "but with, like, two years of buildup."

"You know that all the Hot Shots can tell, right?"

Eden groans. "Is it obvious?"

I snort, and she jabs me playfully in the ribs. I look over at her after a moment—she's watching the road but not really, her head clearly somewhere else. I wonder what I would look like with neon blue hair like hers.

"How long did it take you to figure out you were queer?"

Eden glances over at me, curious. "A long time," she says simply. "Coming out was a little harder when I was your age, you know. Even in Portland."

We let silence fill the space between us. I read somewhere that a lot of people come out while driving, or in a car—you don't have to look directly at the person you're coming out to, and there's a clear end to the conversation when you reach your destination, a point where you don't have to talk about it anymore. I came out to Papa in the car when I was eleven—I'd had a grand plan to come out to Dads together on the first day of Pride, with music and a rainbow feather boa from the dollar store. But it was just Papa and me driving to Arches to go rock climbing, and I had his climbing helmet on my lap and was spinning it over and over, staring at the faded rainbow flag sticker on one side. Someone cut him off in an intersection, and he braked suddenly, throwing an arm across me in a move we called *pizza arm*, because Papa once did the same motion to save a stack of pizzas buckled into the passenger seat.

Sorry, kiddo, he said, cautiously peering both ways before inching the rest of the way into the intersection. *Freaking tourists.* I realized that I was still gripping his helmet, palm slapped flat over the rainbow sticker, and I wondered if it was a kind of talisman, some genderless gay deity that had kept us from getting T-boned by a Jeep.

I'm gay, Papa, I said, and he braked so hard he had to pizza arm me again, but this time he threw the car into park and twisted around to wrap me in a hug.

"Eden?" I say now. My heart's pounding.

"Yeah?"

"I'm queer." Palpable relief floods me. No matter how Eden reacts, no matter who finds out, no matter who I want to date—I *said* it.

"Yeah?" Eden says excitedly. She almost rear-ends the car in front of us and slams on the brakes, then turns to face me. "You realize that means that one hundred percent of your immediate family is fruity, right?"

"Oh my god, Eden, people don't say *fruity* unironically anymore."

"Your generation is so boring. What am I supposed to say? 'Slay'?"

"Oh my *god*," I groan, pulling my beanie over my eyes. "The light is green. Please just drive."

Eden insists on stopping for celebratory donuts on our way home, and she fishes a miniature rainbow flag out of her glove box—"From Pride 2018," she informs me stoically—to stick in mine. I try to bat it away and roll my eyes, but there's an entirely new feeling in my chest now, an antsy, swelling feeling at someone knowing me—no, at my *sister* knowing me.

I'm still giddy from successfully coming out to Eden when she drops me off at her apartment, but I have no idea what to do with myself for my first two hours of solitary freedom. I eat frozen Girl Scout cookies out of the sleeve while Typo winds around my legs, stare at Eden's framed art prints in her bedroom, and watch a rerun of *Survivor*. But it's all stuff I would be allowed to do if Eden were here, too. I realize how weird it feels, being alone suddenly. After weeks in the hospital, then months of derby where I'm constantly surrounded by shouting and whistles, the stillness of the apartment is kind of unnerving.

My phone lights up on the counter as I'm feeding Typo.

CARMEN to Bitch Pod 2

taking bets on when we think the roster will go out

MERCURY

it usually takes them the weekend, so probably sunday.

CARMEN

the girl im tutoring in chem wants to buy tickets and she's really fucking cute. i can't buy tickets for her if im not rostered!!

POWERHOUSE

You've been on the roster for every game this year. buy the tickets.

Typo mews at me, and I realize I've paused with one hand in the cat food bag and one on my phone. I dump a couple scoops into her bowl on the counter while I text them back.

MOOSE

I'm pretty sure Eden and prince are doing the roster right now.

A flurry of texts from Carmen follows, speculating about the roster. I'm about to reply when I hear a key in the lock. Typo meows through her chewing as Eden opens the door, her coat dripping and a pizza box in one hand.

"Hey," she says breathlessly, kicking off her boots in the foyer before she steps inside. "I brought dinner."

"Everybody's very impatient for the roster," I say, waving my phone at her.

Eden tosses the pizza on the counter and unzips her jacket. "It was a hard one. We have a lot of great skaters this season."

I grab a couple plates while Eden strips off her rain gear. She darts into her bedroom to change, and I lift the lid of the pizza box.

The black olives are arranged into letters, spelling out *ROSTERED!* across the middle of the pizza.

I blink, then look up at Typo as though she will have the answers for me. She just buries her head in her food bowl again, crunching. "Eden!" I call, looking back down at the pizza.

"Oh shit, did you open it already?" Eden yells from her bedroom. "I did, like, a *Princess Diaries* thing, 'cause you were obsessed with that movie the last summer I stayed with you guys." She comes back out into the kitchen, pulling on a sweatshirt. "I decided not to use M&M's to spell out the letters, though, so our dinner would still be edible." She stops, looks between me and the pizza. "Moose?"

"Is this real?" I can feel my heartbeat in my ears.

Eden breaks into a huge grin. "I know we told you it wouldn't happen till spring, but, Moose, you've gotten so much better these past few weeks—you're working with the team and paying attention on the track, and Prince and I really think it's time."

I drop the lid of the pizza box and sprint to my room.

"Moose?" Eden calls after me. I slam the door, sliding down onto the carpet. *You're playing in the next game,* I tell myself, and it sounds hollow. *You're going to play roller derby in front of people.*

A confusing mess of emotions wells up. There's panic, elation, fear, more panic, and whatever feeling comes up when I picture Mercury watching me fall on my ass. More panic. The room starts to tunnel, and I grip the fabric of my sweatpants, feeling that anxiety claw its way up from my gut. My breathing's fast, too fast, and my heart's beating faster—

Five things you can see.

I force my gaze up, out of my lap. There's a stray kneepad by the closet. My stats textbook. A cat toy under the armchair. Mercury's wrinkled jersey, which I still haven't washed and given back to her. The bed from Ikea that Eden and I put together one night, passing a takeout box of spring rolls back and forth as we tried to decipher the directions.

Four things you can touch.

The carpet under my hands. The fabric of my sweatpants. A frizzy curl tickling my cheek. The strap of my gear bag, dumped by the door hours earlier.

Three things you can hear.

"Moose!" Eden's voice jerks me back into the present, and I twist around, unblocking the door. She's wide-eyed. "Are you okay?"

"Yeah," I say, and even though I'm breathless and my heartbeat is still slowing down, it's honest. "Sorry. Yeah. I'm okay."

Eden hovers, uncertain. "Do . . . do you not want to be on the roster?"

I know she'd take me off the roster if I asked, but there's a faint note of disappointment in her voice.

"I want to play," I say firmly, stuffing my shaking hands in my pockets. "I'm ready."

Eden throws her arms around me. "You're gonna do so *fucking* good!"

Eden gives me permission to tell Mercury, Carmen, and Powerhouse and *absolutely nobody else* that we're all on the roster until she and

Prince can finalize the pods and email parents. Their reactions are pretty much what I expect: a long scroll of a message from Carmen with a billion emojis and exclamation points, a simple *nice* from Powerhouse, and a fire emoji from Mercury.

I stare at that last one way longer than I need to. I'm pretty sure she just means that I'm on fire, metaphorically, but I wonder if she catches the irony of it too. A month ago, it might have bothered me, might have sent me into a panic spiral. But now, for some reason, I kind of like it.

I'm lying awake in bed that same night, staring at the dark ceiling and trying to manifest positive images of myself—getting out of the pack, getting lead jammer, following my offense. It feels stupid, but Carmen claims it works.

My phone vibrates on the nightstand, and I roll over.

MERCURY

we should celebrate getting rostered this weekend:-)

She sent it just to me, not our group chat with Carmen and Powerhouse. My breath hitches in my throat.

MOOSE

what do you have in mind?

MERCURY

idk. I feel like you haven't seen much of portland yet. I can take you around, show you some cool stuff.

MOOSE

what's your definition of cool?

MERCURY

there's this sick yarn supply shop in alberta

I snort.

MERCURY

jk. It's a surprise:-)

If it were anyone else, the stupid smiley faces with noses would be annoying. I tap out an agreement and roll over, but it takes me hours to fall asleep.

chapter nineteen

"DO YOU HAVE ENOUGH MONEY on your card?" Eden asks on Sunday morning as I'm scrambling around the apartment. Mercury's red Volvo is idling outside.

"Um, I dunno. I think so." I check under a throw pillow on the couch while Eden hovers by the counter. "Have you seen my phone?"

"Because you can't expect Mercury to pay for everything for you."

"I'm not," I say defensively, opening the closet to root through coat pockets.

"Okay. I'm just saying."

"*What* are you saying, Eden?" I snap, slamming the closet door a little harder than necessary. "Because you're really not spelling it out for me right now."

"You know what? Nothing. Have a good time." She's clearly irritated as she turns to stomp back to her room but pauses in the hallway. "Your phone's on the bathroom counter."

"Thanks," I grumble, shoving it in my pocket and ducking out the door.

"Hey," Mercury says when I get into her car with a frustrated huff. "Are you okay?"

"Yeah. Eden's driving me nuts."

She offers me a paper coffee cup. "I totally didn't ask if you drink coffee or not," she says, "and I hate coffee. So this is a chai latte."

"You think more people like chai lattes than coffee?"

"I mean, not in Portland. But you're from Utah."

I bump our cups in a mock toast. "Chai latte it is. You know this is, like, more ammunition for people to call you a grandma, right?"

"A title I bear with pride," she replies, regally tossing her hair over her shoulder. Her perfect red lipstick is intact as always, and she's wearing a chunky moss-colored sweater that she probably knit herself. I suddenly feel very scraggly, wearing faded Vans and a huge flannel button-down I found in Eden's closet.

"What did Eden do?"

I'm so distracted by Mercury being extremely pretty and put-together and perfect that I forgot about Eden. "Oh. You know. She's just . . . she's afraid to actually try to parent me, because I think she wants to be my cool sister, so then she just acts all cryptically annoyed when I do something she doesn't like." I take a sip of my chai latte. "I dunno. It feels like every time I make some headway with her, we fight about something stupid the next day." I shake my head. "You know what? I don't want to talk about Eden. What's the plan for today?"

Mercury looks like she wants to talk more about my feelings, but she mercifully moves on as she pulls away from the apartment. "Well, I have a grand tour of Portland planned. We're gonna start at the Rose Garden, then a picnic on Mount Tabor, and we'll stop at Voodoo Doughnut on the way."

"I've lived here for three months and I already know those are all tourist traps."

"Yeah, I would never make you eat the trash donuts at Voodoo.

Plus their name is racist. Navigate for me?" She hands me her phone with Google Maps already pulled up. When I take it, it feels like our fingers brush a moment longer than they need to. Mercury looks straight at me, coy, and I hope she doesn't notice how my cheeks flush. "We have a much more interesting agenda."

Our first stop is a propped-open door guarded by bushy planters. Inside, we're met with the glassy stares of dozens of taxidermied animal heads, filling the far wall.

"What the fuck?" I hiss, grabbing Mercury's arm and staring around. While there's only one wall of heads, the shelves and spindly displays are crowded with animal skulls, hunched silhouettes floating in murky jars, butterflies pinned to frames with their wings spread open, wooden bowls of bones and feathers and crystals. There's a huge spinal column from . . . some gigantic animal curving past the entrance and stretching toward the ceiling.

"Mercury," I whisper. "Where the fuck are we?"

"I need to buy a Christmas present for Powerhouse," she says, like we're sniffing candles at Anthropologie and not looking at a table of dissected piglets. "They're the only one I'm still missing."

"Let me ask again. *Where the fuck are we?*"

"It's an oddities shop. Powerhouse loves this place. It's all ethically sourced, don't worry."

"As if that's what I was worrying about."

Mercury wanders over to look at a little glass figurine of a two-headed calf, and I stare down at the table to my right, where there's a display of taxidermied mice wearing gnome clothes and posed like they're ice skating on a mirror.

"So is this what people in Portland do instead of going to the mall?" I ask Mercury, shoving my hands in my pockets so I don't accidentally touch anything. She's leaning down to look at a shelf bathed in a bluish glow from a grow light, illuminating tiny pots of Venus flytraps.

"We have a mall, too. This stuff is just more Powerhouse's speed." She rubs her chin, thinking. "I feel weird buying them a plant. They already have a million, and I don't know if I could keep one alive until Christmas."

A handwritten sign in Gothic calligraphy forbids sticking your finger in the flytraps' jaws. I had gotten hints that Powerhouse was into this weird, witchy stuff—they were annoyed that I didn't know my birth time so they could review my astrological chart.

"What about this?" I ask, holding up a bright red tin with a portly demon striding across the lid. "'Krampus Greeting Cards'?"

"Oh, that's hilarious," Mercury says, peeking over my shoulder. "Krampus is that anti-Santa monster that eats naughty kids on Christmas Eve or something. That's a maybe."

"Did you know Powerhouse before you started derby?"

"No—they and Carmen literally ran into me at the roller rink and bullied me into joining. You should've seen how tiny Carmen was then. She could barely move the football dummy. Everybody thought she would be a jammer."

"But Carmen hates jamming."

"Exactly. There's no wrong body type for derby. It's cool. Like, my mom used to do these women's fitness programs on the TV, and they were all about having the tiniest waist or arms or thighs. But derby is about taking up space, not apologizing for existing. Any person with any body type can play, and they'll have advantages that someone without their body doesn't." I think about the things that make my body different—the trach scar and the perpetual soreness in my throat and the way my voice gets hoarse when I talk too loud now. None of them seem like things that would give me an advantage in roller derby.

I end up buying the Krampus cards for Powerhouse, and Mercury settles on a necklace with a glass sheep's eye pendant. It grosses both of us out, which Mercury says is a sign that Powerhouse will probably like it.

"Does this mean that you already have a Christmas present for me?" I ask Mercury as we get back in her car, carrying our little black paper bags with stamps in the shape of skulls. I'm joking, but Mercury nods sagely.

"I got yours a month ago."

"A mo— Mercury, you didn't have to get me anything!"

She shrugs, smiling. "I think it's fun."

"Can I have a hint?"

"What? No. You have a whole month left."

"It's more fun if I get to guess."

"No."

Mercury takes me to three more bizarre Portland boutiques—a bubble tea café in an old caboose, a vast vintage store with an entire room of overalls with daisy patches on the knees, and a huge warehouse downtown filled with scraps from other people's craft projects, where I spend thirty cents on a painted clay mask that we decide is definitely cursed. She insists on paying for my ramen when we stop for lunch, primly reminding me that we are celebrating my being rostered for my first bout. I've never had ramen before—Dad always insisted it wasn't good enough in Moab to spend twenty dollars on.

"Okay," Mercury says, pulling into a tiny gravel parking lot. "Last stop."

I stare around—there are no other cars, and we're surrounded on all sides by forest. There's still some weak sunlight, but the early winter darkness looms. "Are you going to murder me?"

"Yes. Come on."

I follow Mercury out of the car and onto a narrow path in the trees, made of stamped-down mud and the occasional weathered plank. The rain stopped hours ago, but the trees still feel saturated. I realize that I've lived in Oregon for three months now, and I haven't been in the woods yet. It's as far from Utah's scrubby orange deserts as I can imagine. We wind between slender firs blanketed in bright moss, step over ferns spilling onto the trail, cross narrow wooden bridges over rocky streams. It feels like we're not supposed to talk. The trail isn't wide enough for us to walk side by side, so I follow behind Mercury, taking in the drippy quiet and stillness that presses in on us. It's humid in the forest, a cold humidity that soothes the perpetual soreness of my throat.

When Mercury finally speaks after nearly thirty minutes of silence, it's jarring. "Almost there."

The trail spills out onto a ridge, a tiny, cleared area tucked between the trees with a wooden railing along the edge. And beyond, the ground drops out and a huge green suspension bridge stretches across the river, its posts shaped like silhouettes of enormous Gothic cathedrals. The rain has cleared away and the sky is lit up with streaks of pink-and-orange cloud. The cars crossing back and forth over the suspension bridge seem impossibly far away.

"So . . ." Mercury says slowly as we lean on the wooden railing. "What do you think?"

"It's so . . . green."

She laughs, and the sound disappears in the vastness of the space before us.

"No, really!" I insist, shaking my head. "Have you ever been to Arches? In Utah?"

"I've been to Korea and Oregon. That's it."

"Okay, it's like—it looks like a different planet. It's bright orange, all the time, even in winter—all the rocks, the sand, the plants, everything. This is just so . . . green."

"Is that a good thing?" Mercury's looking sidelong at me, inquisitive, a breeze lifting fine strands of hair off her shoulders. She looks like she belongs, like she knows the forests and these mossy trees and magic green cathedral bridges as well as she knows herself.

"It's different."

She looks back out over the bridge, like she's not quite sure how to respond. Then she points along the horizon at distant snowy peaks. "That's why I like this spot. One of the only spots in Portland where you can see all three mountains."

"Why is that one flat on top?"

"That's Mount Saint Helens. It erupted."

"Erupted?"

"All three of those mountains are volcanoes. And we're about a thousand years overdue for a giant earthquake that will sink the entire coast into the Pacific Ocean." Maybe I imagine it, but I swear in that moment she steps a fraction closer to me, just enough so our elbows are touching as we lean on the wooden railing.

"It won't happen as long as I live here."

Mercury gives me a sideways glance, one eyebrow raised. "Yeah?"

"Yeah. I've already lived through a once-in-a-lifetime disaster. No higher being would make me do it again. So you're all safe until I go back to Utah."

Her smile falters, just slightly. "So . . . you're going back? To Utah?"

I look away, realizing that the words just fell out of my mouth. "I— Maybe? I don't know. I guess I could go stand in the burned-out ruin of the rink." I hesitate, watching the cars on the bridge flick their lights on against the twilight. I was trying to be self-deprecating, but the thought of actually seeing the rink again, standing in the burned-up, blackened hull, fills my stomach with dread. "I don't really have anything left there, do I?"

"I don't think that's true."

"Eden is my only family besides my dads." My voice is harder than I mean it to be. "There's nobody else. The rink is gone. And Eden wants to sell our old house."

"She hasn't yet?"

"I haven't let her."

Mercury pauses, thinking. "Okay, the buildings and the people are gone. But the memories aren't, right? The orange rock formations that look like a different planet? I mean, you should see the way your face lights up when you talk about it, Moose. It's—" She looks away suddenly, cheeks pink. "Beautiful," she murmurs, then buries her face in her hands. "Oh my god. That was the dumbest thing I've ever said."

I'm glad she's not looking at me, glad she can't see the way my throat hitched at her words and my eyes prickled. I rub them vigorously with the sleeve of my hoodie before she looks up again. She politely pretends not to see. "You can come with me sometime," I say, hoping she doesn't hear the thickness in my voice. "There's this one rock formation in Arches called the North Window—if you stand at the right angle during a full moon, it looks like a giant eye. Cool as hell."

"I would love to," Mercury says gently. Her cheeks and nose are still pink, but probably from the cold—it's getting dark, and the wind is wet and chilly, the boughs around us swaying. The mountains are barely visible now. But it doesn't matter. I'm just looking at Mercury, right next to me, studying my face with soft eyes.

"Moose," she says quietly, and my heart hitches, breath stuck in my throat. She's so close, closer than I've ever been to a girl, even in roller derby. And she's so *here*. In the Hangar, she's strong and solid, like an impenetrable wall. Here though, on this dark, empty ridge, she seems so soft.

My hand twitches, and I start to reach out, wanting to take her hand. She's watching me, evenly, lips slightly parted, waiting.

"Can I—?" I ask, my voice a whisper.

Mercury blesses me with a breathless smile, and her cheeks flush when she nods. Before I can talk myself out of it, I close the space between us.

I kiss Mercury, my hands sliding up to hold her cheeks as hers find my waist. Her lips are soft and open, and she smells like lavender—heady and floral and safe. We're suspended on this ridge, so far above the bridge, with the mountains looking on, alone in the darkening forest with Oregon's perpetual mist all around us. Mercury pulls me closer, gently, and my whole body relaxes into the curves of hers, like we were meant to fit together.

When we finally break apart, our eyes flutter open at the same time. We both giggle, breathless, nervous but not wanting to look away from each other.

"Was that—"

"Are you—" I start at the same time.

She laughs, burying her face in her hands, and she's so beautiful and perfect here in the woods that I never want to leave.

"Sorry," she giggles, "you're just so—I've just wanted to kiss you for so long."

My whole heart turns over at her words.

"I've been kissing you—I mean wanting to—I mean— Oh, fuck." It's my turn to hide my eyes, so flustered I can't even talk straight. But Mercury holds my cheeks, and there's such delight in her dark eyes that I smile anyway.

"I think I know what you mean," she teases. Then she kisses me again. Her hand slides around the back of my neck and into my hair, and goose bumps race down my spine as her finger twirls around a curl at the nape of my neck. Something in Mercury's pocket buzzes, pressed against my stomach in the space between us. I ignore it in favor of kissing her, but it buzzes again, insistently.

"Sorry," Mercury says grudgingly as we pull apart. She keeps one hand on my shoulder as she pulls her phone out with the other. "Let me just mute it." Her face lights up blue as she pulls her phone up, and the starry expression on her face instantly vanishes. "Oh, shit. We have to go."

"What's wrong?" I ask, but Mercury's already rushing toward the trail, turning on her phone's flashlight to illuminate the way.

"I was supposed to pick up my brothers!" she calls over her shoulder. "Crap!" In an instant, we've left the ridge behind.

chapter twenty

"I'M REALLY SORRY," Mercury says, trying to text with one hand as we speed toward the bridge. "I never forget to pick them up. I don't know what's wrong with me."

I reach over and pull her phone out of her hand to keep us from crashing into the river. She's halfway through typing a text to her brothers: **sorry on my—**

"Is your dad not home?" I ask, adding **way** to Mercury's text and hitting send.

She shakes her head, sitting too close to the wheel, like that will make her drive faster. "He works."

"You can just drop me at the MAX stop," I tell her. "The train will take me right to Eden's."

"No way. It's gonna rain soon. I'll only be, like, twenty minutes later if I run you home first."

"Mercury," I say, shifting in my seat to stare at her. "Let's just go get them. I don't mind."

"They're annoying."

"I don't care."

"Don't you have better things to do?"

"On a Saturday night? Have you met me?"

She hesitates as we pull up to a stoplight. The green cathedral bridge looms over us, and it's so much higher over the river than I realized.

"Are you sure?"

"Yes. It's totally fine." I look across the car at her, the deep line that's appeared across her forehead. She's clearly stressed, and trying to figure out if she's regretting kissing me in this moment probably isn't helpful. I hesitate, then reach across the center console to rest a hand on her knee. Mercury stiffens for a second. Then she peels a hand off the steering wheel and places it over mine, gently. My whole body flutters again at her touch.

"What are we picking them up from?" I ask her.

Mercury stifles a snort. "Junior high volleyball, of all things."

"We play roller derby, of all things," I point out, and she bites her lip, smiling.

We drive across the bridge, and I watch the red lights at the tops of the spires, blinking slowly to ward off planes.

I slide my hand off Mercury's knee as we pull up to the school, where Mercury's brothers are on a bench outside the gym, an annoyed-looking teacher beside them. Mercury jumps out of the car to apologize to the adult left to supervise them. Her brothers both look taller than her, somehow, even though they're thirteen, and they trudge to the car in unison. One of them instinctively heads for the passenger seat, and he startles when he sees me, giving me a weird look as he reroutes to the back.

"Hi," I say awkwardly as they pile into the backseat, staring at me like I'm from a different planet. "I'm Mercury's friend."

"Derby," one of them says to the other, and they both roll their eyes. One slouches in the seat and pulls out his phone, and the other conjures a handheld game out of nowhere. I turn back to face the dashboard, wondering if I'm supposed to use Mercury's real name. *Sonia.*

"I'm so sorry," Mercury says breathlessly as she gets back in the car, buckling her seat belt and throwing it into reverse. "I just lost track of time. Did you guys say hi to Moose?"

"Hey," one answers without looking up. The other one has headphones on.

Mercury rolls her eyes, looking remarkably like her brother. "That's Hyeon and Colin. They're delightful." I don't ask about the different names, but Mercury explains anyway: "My dad's white. They flipped a coin for each kid. Mom only won for Hyeon."

"And *Sonia*?" Her real name feels foreign on my tongue.

"Oh, I'm the firstborn. Dad was always going to win that one."

We pull up to a small clapboard house tucked away in far North Portland, pale green siding and a tiny porch. There's already a car in the gravel driveway, and Mercury looks exhausted. Hyeon and Colin wordlessly file out of the car, jostling each other to get in the door first.

"I'm so sorry," she says hastily, putting the car into reverse. "I can take you home, and—"

The front door opens, and a portly man with thinning red hair stands aside to let the twins in, then jogs down the stairs toward Mercury's car. Mercury throws the car back into park, pinching the bridge of her nose.

The guy—Mercury's dad, probably—knocks on the window, and she plasters on a slightly more presentable expression before she rolls it down.

"Hey, Sonia," he says, smiling awkwardly. He ducks slightly, looking past her at me. "Hello there."

"Hi."

"I'm really sorry I'm so late," Mercury cuts in. "We just lost track of time, and—"

He nods, looking a little disappointed. "No worries. Are you okay?"

"Fine. I'll keep better track of time."

He rocks back and forth on his feet for a second. "Uh . . . does your friend want to stay for dinner?"

"She has to go," Mercury—Sonia—says before I can reply. "I'm already late taking her home. There's still seolleongtang in the fridge from last night."

"You want us to wait for you?"

"No, go ahead," she says, like she's already deeply inconvenienced him.

"Okay." He hovers, like he wants to say something else. "Nice to meet you," he says to me instead, and I wave awkwardly in reply. Mercury's dad stands in the driveway as we pull away, watching until we round the corner.

Mercury looks disappointed in herself, wilted, with her eyes glued to the road. I let the silence simmer until her hands relax on the wheel, though there's still a vein pulsing in her forehead.

"Are you okay?"

Mercury lets out a breath, and it's like she deflates—all the tension and tightness dissipating out of her. "Sorry. He didn't tell me he would be home. He could've picked them up."

We're quiet for another moment.

"Do you make them dinner every night?" I ask her quietly.

Mercury doesn't look at me, even though we're at a stoplight. "Not *every* night."

"But most nights?"

She looks down at the dashboard, her face lit up blue from the light panel. "Most nights." She runs a hand through her hair, sighing. "He just . . . He works so much, you know? When my mom died, he just . . . Colin and Hyeon didn't handle it well. Somebody had to step up."

"You don't have to take care of everybody, Merc."

"I know. I'll be in college in a couple years anyway." I can see in that moment that Mercury would delay her life for years to pick her brothers up from volleyball practice and make them dinner.

"And besides . . . I don't know who else would."

"They'd figure it out. Have they ever even been to one of your derby games?"

Mercury finally looks at me. An hour ago, on the ridge, her face was round and pink and soft—now there are shadows under her eyes and her face is drawn, exhausted. *She looks like Eden,* I realize with a jolt. Eden in the hospital, spending her entire summer at my bedside, overwhelmed and worn from taking care of me. Guilt floods me.

"I'm good at taking care of people," Mercury says gently. "And I like being needed."

"Sure, but—do you take enough care of yourself?"

She looks back toward the road and doesn't answer, and I can tell this part of the conversation is over. When we reach Eden's apartment, Mercury puts her Volvo in park and turns off the ignition. We sit in silence for a second.

"So," I venture.

"So."

I'm scared to bring it up, scared to bare myself and give Mercury the opportunity to shoot me down. Teammates aren't supposed to date. Captains aren't supposed to kiss their skaters on a magical ridge in the woods. But I remember Eden telling me about Prince, the way her face lit up when I said their name, the easy giddiness they both exude when they talk about each other.

"Is this okay?" I ask finally.

Mercury reaches across the center console to take my hand, interlacing our fingers with practiced ease. "Moose," she says seriously, "it's more than okay."

I let out a breath, relieved. "Are you sure?"

"I mean . . ." She bites her lip. "We should— Can we just keep it to ourselves for now? I really like you, Moose. I want to keep spending time with you. But we need to be careful."

"'*Dating among teammates is strongly discouraged.*'" I quote the line that's been seared into my brain since I got drafted.

"Yeah. I just— Let's not make it anyone else's business yet. Is that okay?"

There's a confusing rush of emotions. I know Mercury's not ashamed or embarrassed of me. I know it's safe for us to be queer in Portland, safe for us to hold hands and kiss and not worry about being hate-crimed. I know it's about the team. But it still feels weird.

"Of course," I say, and I can't tell if I mean it or not.

Mercury turns in her seat so she's fully facing me, still squeezing my hand. "Thank you, Moose," she says, and the softness of her face makes all my joints feel weak, like I've just survived a two-hour scrimmage. She leans over the console to kiss me, and I want to just live in this moment forever, not worrying about the Hot Shots or Mercury's dad or Eden's judgment or any of it. But we eventually break apart, and Mercury traces a finger down my cheek before I unbuckle my seat belt and climb out of her car.

She waits to drive away until she sees me unlock the front door, and when I turn to wave goodbye, she flashes her headlights once and blows me a kiss. It makes it all feel worth it.

chapter twenty-one

DR. PARIKH'S OFFICE feels like a haven today—the rain's blowing hard enough to pelt the windows, and the branches outside keep smacking the glass. I have a paper cup of chai on the coffee table between us, the first time I've used the little drink cart in her lobby. It feels significant, but I can't figure out why.

"Rostered," Dr. Parikh says, raising her eyebrows. "That sounds like a big deal." I've probably spent too much of my therapy sessions explaining roller derby to her. It's easier to explain the team dynamic of jammers and blockers and getting out of the pack instead of unpacking how I feel about Eden and my dead dads and—the biggest one still lingering in my brain this week—kissing Mercury on the ridge.

"It is. I think. And I haven't been playing very long."

"How are you feeling about it?" She always manages to bring it back to me somehow.

"I don't know—weird. Like, I'm excited, and proud of myself that I made it onto the roster, but then I want to throw up once I think about skating in front of an audience."

I grudgingly tell Dr. Parikh about the weirdness of being a jammer, feeling like everyone's eyes are on you and like the entire game hinges on your ability to score enough points. How I'm worried about not being able to do anything, about spending all my jams stuck in the pack, unable to score a single point while the audience laughs.

Dr. Parikh is talking about grounding or feeling like part of a team or something, but my brain is stuck on the audience watching me. It's not the audience that feels so sinister, I realize. It's the people—hundreds of people, crammed into the bleachers, the track, the parking lot, the Hangar, pressing in, talking, yelling, just existing so close to each other. In my mind, they're not even in the Hangar anymore—it's the Finney's Mesa Rollerdome. Flashing lights streak across the skate floor, and it's crowded with a throng of skaters, pressed together with their voices creating a blur of sound. Then there's smoke, and the voices dissolve into screams, and I'm choking as flames lick my face, searing my skin—the screams stop abruptly, but the fire roars louder. That was the worst part—the moment people just stopped screaming and I realized I was alone in the rink.

"Moose?" Dr. Parikh asks, but her voice sounds so far away. I'm hot, sweating, vision blurring. I squeeze my eyes shut, dizzy, and shove my head between my knees, heaving. I can smell the smoke, black and acrid and filling my lungs. It was dark, so *dark*—the lights went out, and all I could see was fire.

"Moose."

The voice is closer, louder, and there's a hand on my shoulder. I look up with a shuddering gasp and see Dr. Parikh, sitting on the floor in front of me, extraordinarily calm. *Calm*. Because there's no fire—not here. I'm in her quiet office, smelling chai instead of smoke, hearing rain beat against the window instead of screams.

"You're okay," Dr. Parikh says evenly. "Do you want to get on the floor?"

I nod, my chest still heaving, unable to speak. I slide off the couch and flatten myself face down on the rug, feeling the rough fibers on my cheek. My vision slowly tilts back to normal, my breath slowing down. I don't know how long I lie there.

"You're just fine, Moose," Dr. Parikh assures me. "You can stay lying down if you need to."

"No," I mumble, my voice shaky. I push myself off the rug, embarrassed. "Sorry."

"You don't need to apologize for that. Not anywhere, and especially not here. Okay?"

"Okay."

Dr. Parikh arranges herself cross-legged on the floor, leaning against the couch. It feels so weirdly casual, like we're at a sleepover pretending I didn't just have a meltdown.

"I think that was a panic attack," I say after a minute.

Dr. Parikh doesn't say anything, waiting for me to continue.

"I started thinking about the fire. And . . . how many people were there, crowded in the rink." I groan, leaning my head back. "I hate how scared it makes me."

"Moose, have you heard of *reclaiming* as it relates to trauma?"

I shake my head.

"When we ignore our trauma, or try to lock it away before we can process it, it hinders the healing. You can't move on from something if you can't acknowledge that it happened."

I laugh humorlessly. "I don't think I'll forget what happened."

"Knowing logically that it happened and acknowledging it are two different things. Acknowledging it is sitting with it, confronting it, like looking at it head-on and telling it that it won't control your life anymore. Some people have success with reclaiming aspects of their trauma as a means to process. I think that could be helpful to you.

"Take the word *queer*. The LGBTQ+ community reclaimed that word that was used as a slur against them, and now it's a proud part of many people's lives, right? Some people still don't like being described that way, but for many, it's a label that gives them strength. Reclaiming aspects of your trauma can be like that. You could try journaling about it. Some people make art or write music about their trauma."

"I'm not really artistic, though. That's Eden's thing."

"It doesn't have to be art. Some people just talk about it—and it doesn't even have to be to a person. You can talk about it to your cat, if you want. Just having a way to get your emotions about it out of your head and into something else can really help."

She glances at the clock on the coffee table, purposely turned away from the client couch. "You know, we're just about at time, but I would love for you to think about *reclaiming* this week. See if you can come up with something that feels cathartic, something that lets you get that heaviness out of your chest."

Eden can tell I'm panicky when I climb into her car, but she mercifully doesn't say anything about it, just pats me weirdly on the shoulder and hands me a Twix bar. It's become her picking-me-up-from-therapy ritual, pulling up to Dr. Parikh's office with candy for me and a coffee from Plaid Pantry for her. It makes me feel like a little kid, but I don't mind. The routine of it is easy.

We don't usually talk on the way home from therapy—Eden can sense when I'm feeling raw, and she knows not to press me. But today, suddenly, I feel kinetic, weirdly energized. It's like my panic attack was one of those deep, knock-you-out naps, where you wake up feeling kind of groggy but like you need to *do* something.

Something cathartic.

Suddenly, I know what I need to do.

chapter twenty-two

THE HANGAR'S PARKING LOT is nearly empty when we pull in. It's a rare sunny afternoon in late November, but I feel numb as I grab my skate bag and follow Eden inside. She's wearing an orange dress under a red leather jacket, colors that would clash horrifically anywhere else. But here they mark her as part of our team.

The Hangar feels calm inside, but anticipatory—ready for something bigger than a practice or a scrimmage. Someone's sweeping the track on foot, and a pair of volunteers are setting up a snack bar, pouring nacho cheese into a warmer.

"I need to meet with Prince and the Knockout coaches," Eden says, turning to me. "You can throw your stuff in our locker room. We'll do our off-skates warmup at five thirty."

Prince strides up then, wearing a glittery orange blazer. "What's up, Hot Shots?" she greets us, throwing her arms out, even though there are only three of us here so far. "Ready to win?" She sneaks a quick kiss on the cheek from Eden before tossing me a flat plastic package, bright red and orange peeking through. "How you feeling, kid?"

I feel like I'll throw up if I open my mouth, so I give her an awkward so-so gesture instead.

"You'll do great," Eden assures me, shaking my shoulder a little. "We'll be back." She and Prince head into the Hangar office, leaving me standing by the bleachers with my skate bag dangling off one shoulder.

I take a breath and head past the bleachers, ignoring the nervous flutter in my stomach. It's the first time I won't be taking over a swath of the bleachers with my teammates before skating. We get to use one of the coveted locker rooms instead, hidden near the back between a stack of football dummies and a rack of ancient dumbbells. The doors are cracked open today, and there's a piece of paper with *HOT SHOTS* written in Sharpie taped to one door.

I'm the first one here, as expected. The locker room's walls are covered in stickers and signatures, names and numbers of hundreds of skaters that have used the room. There are stickers from leagues all over—Boston, DC, San Diego, London, Sweden. A few people have written messages with their names—*Got high blocked and played the rest of the half with a bloody lip. Best bout ever. Technicolor Dreamboat, #425, 3/14/12*. A plastic bag taped to the wall holds a collection of markers for players to add to the collage. I find a blue marker and a corner by the mirror, where I just write *nervous*.

I drop my bag on one of the benches and sit, the package from Prince in my lap. The plastic crinkles as I pull it off, the orange-and-red jersey sliding out like water. The front is emblazoned with a scowling meteor, its tail spelling out *HOT SHOTS* in a whirl of fire. Holding my breath, I flip the jersey over. A name stretches across the back in bold, angry red letters.

BURNOUT.

There's a surge of *something* as I stare at the letters, something that makes my stomach turn over and my heart beat faster. It starts the same way as the panic, but then it changes, hardens, and the name feels *strong*. *My* name. I unzip my jacket and pull off the T-shirt underneath, sliding the jersey over my head. Tugging it straight, I stand and turn to the mirror.

The orange is bright, loud against my skin. With my arms bare, I can see the slight definition, the muscles that I've built over the past few months, the faded purple bruises. For the first time, I'm not staring at the dark red scar on my throat—I'm staring at myself. And I look *strong*.

The door behind me swings open, and I see Carmen in the mirror, walking backward to talk to Mercury, who's trailing her. Mercury freezes in the doorway when she sees me, and her eyes meet mine in the mirror. I watch as her gaze flicks down to the jersey, reads the name on my back. A huge grin breaks across her face.

"That's fucking awesome."

Carmen twists around, and her eyes widen. "*Burnout?*" she shrieks, and she crosses the locker room in a leap, throwing her arms around me and wrangling me into a hug. "Why didn't you tell us you were picking a derby name?" she yells, and suddenly she's crying, laughing, pulling Mercury into our hug. Mercury's hand is on the back of my arm, and when we break apart, it lingers a second longer than it needs to. If the others notice, they don't say anything.

Carmen starts digging in her bag, tossing aside elbow pads and Band-Aids and energy bar wrappers until she finds a makeup brush and jar of something glittery and orange.

"Team tradition," she says, pointing me toward the bench. "I get to put glitter on everybody."

"It's not a team tradition if you just say you can do it," Mercury says as Carmen twists off the cap and dips the brush.

"Anything is a tradition if I say it is," she murmurs, dotting the brush across my cheeks. The glitter is cold. "Burnout, huh? What do we call you on the track?"

"I dunno," I say. "Does every derby name need a nickname?"

"Only the fun ones."

The rest of the team trickles in, and Carmen goes around the room to douse them all in glitter. Apex and Panic fawn over my new name and jersey while Acid pretends I don't exist. It doesn't bother me—since we're both jammers, we'll never be on the track at the same time.

At an hour and a half until the first whistle, we convene in the parking lot for our off-skates warmup, where I see more cars pulling into the parking lot and a line forming at the doorway. "Ignore it," Powerhouse murmurs, following my gaze. I swallow the lump in my throat.

When we return to the Hangar, they've opened the door to spectators, and there's music pumping over the empty track while people trickle in, picking their spots on the bleachers. Eden and Prince usher us into the locker room to gear up. I feel weirdly calm as I strap on my pads, lace my skates, tighten my helmet strap, and pop in my mouthguard. We have the track first for our on-skates warmup, where Prince whistles us through our drills. The movements are easy, my body automatically remembering where to go.

Fifteen minutes before the first whistle, all seventeen of us crowd into the locker room, wedging ourselves on the benches and the floor so Prince can stand in the middle. Eden leans in the doorway—they both have streaks of orange glitter across their cheeks, courtesy of Carmen.

"Listen up!" Prince barks, and the chatter in the locker room halts abruptly. As Prince reviews our start strategies, I feel my calmness melt away, and I'm suddenly aware of the babble of the crowd outside and the music pulsing in the Hangar. The Knockout Kids are doing their warmup on the track, and I can see them flitting by over Eden's shoulder. They look *huge*—how am I supposed to get past them?

"Hey," Carmen whispers, nudging me with an elbow. "You okay? You look kinda green."

"Just nervous," I mutter, bouncing my leg.

Carmen fishes a Gatorade out of her bag, pressing it into my hands. "Drink," she tells me in an undertone. "The electrolytes will help."

Prince's eyes snap to us, and we both fall silent. When she looks away, I twist off the Gatorade lid, taking a frantic swig.

"We want you to focus on *communicating* today," Prince is saying. "You're all on that track together, with the same goal. Talk to each other. Tell your teammates where the jammers are, where they need to punch a hole, when to follow their offense. Capiche?"

Everyone nods, and I notice Acid looks bored on the other side of the locker room, picking at a loose thread on her wrist guard. Despite her skill, she never seems that interested in being here.

"Ripley," Prince says, turning to Eden. "Anything to add?"

Eden surveys us, and her eyes hold mine. "Remember that this is just another scrimmage. The audience isn't there. It'll sound loud at first, but you'll tune them out." She seems to be speaking directly to me. "Ten minutes to first whistle," she adds, checking the time on her phone. "Go get used to the track. We'll meet on the bench for a cheer at three minutes."

Everybody around me stands and starts to file through the door, swinging water bottles and tightening straps as they go. Carmen pauses when she sees me sitting. "Are you okay?"

"I just need a sec," I tell her. She raises an eyebrow. "Really. I'll be right out."

"I'm coming back if you're not out in five minutes," she warns before she rolls out of the room.

As the team clears, that familiar feeling comes back, like I can't get enough air into my lungs. I squeeze my eyes shut and take a few deep breaths, trying to satisfy the feeling, but it's not working. It feels like smoke in my lungs again, the danger of too many people in the rink and no way out.

"Moose?"

I open my eyes and make eye contact with Mercury in the mirror, hanging back by the door after everyone else went out to the track.

"Isn't it supposed to be *Burnout* now?" I ask, but my voice is thin. I still can't quite get enough air. How am I going to skate if I can't breathe?

Mercury rolls over to me and drops onto the bench. "You're not gonna freak out on me *now*, are you?" she asks, nudging me with her shoulder.

"I don't know if this is a good idea," I burst out. "I've only been playing for a few months. Some of the Knockout Kids have been skating for *years*, Merc. I'm gonna look like an idiot."

Mercury leans back on the bench, crossing her legs. "Well, probably, if you talk about yourself like that."

I give her a sidelong glare. "Aren't you supposed to, like, encourage me? *Captain?*"

"I can pep talk you for hours. But you're the one who has to decide that you're going to get out there and skate. Nobody's gonna force you onto the track."

"Except maybe Carmen, so she doesn't have to jam."

Mercury snorts. "Yeah. Maybe her. But it's up to you to skate. Right?"

I take a deep breath, squaring my shoulders. "Right." I can't quite tell what the protocol is here—should I kiss her? Hold her hand? It feels weird to do in the locker room, when my stomach is in knots from nerves. I crack my knuckles instead, just to give my hands something to do.

"So," Mercury says, "now I'll put my captain hat on and tell you that you're not gonna score any points hiding in here." She stands smoothly, rolling in a half circle so she's directly in front of me, offering a hand. She looks so polished, so ready, her round face glittery and the wings of her eyeliner sharp and perfect. It's the way I felt, when I saw myself in the Hot Shots jersey.

I take her hand and pull myself up, then follow Mercury out onto the track.

There's no pep talk when Prince and Ripley call us into a huddle by our bench. Prince just gives us all a stern look and says, "Kick ass."

"But have fun," Eden adds quickly. "Because this is a juniors game."

"Let's cheer," Mercury interjects, holding her fist into the middle of the circle. We all follow suit, watching Mercury for our cue.

We shout our cheer in unison, stomping our skates in time: "TRACK ON FI-RE, TRACK ON FI-RE, HOT SHOTS!" We throw our hands into the air on the last word, and Apex and Carmen roll around jostling and high-fiving everybody. A month ago, the cheer made me feel raw. Now it fills me with power.

Eden hurries everyone to the bench and consults her clipboard to get the first lineup ready. She hands the starred jammer cap to Powerhouse, and they huddle to decide their play. There are three pods on our bench for this game: three groups of us that will go out and skate together each time. "Second pod will be Burnout, Mercury,

Trail Mx., Carmen, and Panic," she reads, handing me the other star cover. "And Mercury will pivot."

I rub the helmet cover with one hand. The caps we use for games are higher quality than the practice caps—this one's made of stretchy orange fabric to match our jerseys, a flaming yellow star stitched on either side.

"Okay, jammer," Mercury says as she leans toward me. Trail Mx., Carmen, and Panic huddle with us, everybody looking at me expectantly. "What do you want to do?"

I hear myself asking them for a front start, so they can suck back on the Knockout blockers and play offense for me. My anxiety is still there, in my bouncing knee and sweaty palms, but a different, all-business version of my brain has taken the driver's seat. I take a slow, deep breath, relishing the feeling of air filling my lungs.

Across the track, Powerhouse has lined up against Cheery Bomb from the Knockouts. The second the whistle blows, Powerhouse slams into the wall, shoving one blocker to the side, then another. They dodge a third blocker, then sail past the Hot Shots wall. A ref blows two short whistles, awarding Powerhouse lead jammer as they circle the track.

"You ready?" Mercury yells to me over the noise.

"Ready!" I say back, louder than I need to, because it steels me.

Way too soon, Powerhouse calls off the jam, putting six points on the board for the Hot Shots. My legs feel jittery when I stand.

I skate around to the jam line, stopping next to Scary Poppins. "What's up, Moose?" she says amicably as I join her on the jam line. She fist-bumps me. "Good luck."

"You too," I say, but I feel like I'm going to pass out. The crowd is so close, and so *loud*—how am I supposed to hear my blockers over the screaming and the music?

"Five seconds!"

Time slows as we all freeze, counting down in our heads.

Four.

Three.

Two.

One.

The whistle blasts.

I throw myself into the Knockout wall, and they cinch around me, tight. Pop darts past me, and Mercury's wall catches her. I shove against the Knockouts, and their wall flips, catching me again.

"Burnout!" Carmen calls from the other side of the tripod. I try to answer her, but I'm out of breath, panicking. She shoves an opposing blocker out of my way, but I don't have enough energy—someone hits me, hard, and I stumble out of bounds.

I scramble back onto the track, and hear a whistle blast. *"Orange four-three-five!"* a referee yells, crossing her forearms in an X. "Track cut!"

Shit.

I skate to the penalty box as Pop gets lead, circling the track and coming back around to score.

"Deep breath, Burnout!" Prince shouts from our bench as I sit down in the penalty box. "Stay calm!"

I bounce my legs as the official behind me times my thirty-second penalty. The Hot Shots blockers are struggling to catch Scary Poppins—she's already scored eight points. *Stay calm stay calm stay calm.*

When I'm released from the box, I skate the wrong way around the track to reenter, getting confused and going all the way back around while my blockers scream directions at me. When I finally get back onto the track, Pop sails past me, clipping me with her hip and sending me sprawling.

Panting, I drag myself to my feet, skate breathlessly back into the pack, and throw myself weakly into the Knockouts. They hold me easily, and I struggle against them until the jam, mercifully, ends.

I skate angrily back to our bench, pulling off the helmet cover and thrusting it into Eden's hands before slumping onto the end of the bench. Trail Mx. and Carmen drop down on either side of me. "That was a tough wall," Carmen says encouragingly, her blond bangs already plastered to her forehead. "The first jam is always kinda rocky."

"First pancake," Trail Mx. agrees.

I don't answer, taking a swig of Gatorade instead.

Acid makes up the points I failed to score in the next jam, sliding effortlessly through the Knockout Kids to get lead. Powerhouse jams next, doesn't get lead, but steals two points anyway. The Knockouts are leading, and if I don't score any points the whole game, I'll single-handedly bring us to a loss.

Eden crouches in front of me, holding out the jammer cover. "Are you good?" she asks seriously. I set my jaw, nod, take the cover. But the next jam is even worse—I don't get a penalty, but I never get out of the pack, spending the whole two minutes struggling against the Knockout blockers. When it finally ends, I throw myself onto the end of the bench, scowling.

I'm not even embarrassed—I'm mad. Acid and Powerhouse are keeping the score close, but barely. And I'm going out and fucking it up, every single jam. Mercury appears in front of me, stern.

"Hey," she says, taking my hand. It's a gentle motion, but her voice is sharp. "You need to pull yourself together."

"I suck."

"It's been two jams. Take a breath. Pay attention to us. We're telling you where to go. And if you don't get lead, *pass the star.*"

"I should be able to get out."

"Okay. But if you can't, pass the star." She shakes me, gives me a hard look. "Buck up."

When I reach the start line for my third jam, I take a breath, squaring myself, centering. Mercury turns to make eye contact with me, and sudden calm radiates through me at her look.

"Five seconds!"

I lower one toe stop, take a breath.

The whistle blasts.

I spring off my toe stop at the same time Carmen shoves a Knockout blocker to one side, clearing a path for me. My heart leaps as I scramble through—I can see the empty track ahead.

A Knockout blocker swings out of nowhere, flipping around and catching me with her chest. I gasp, stumble, catching myself before I step off the track.

No.

Pop darts past me, and I hear the whistles declaring her lead. But I'm almost there—just one blocker between me and the empty track.

I wind up on one leg, then explode outward, and suddenly I'm out. I don't look back—I race around the corner, hot on Pop's tail. My bench is screaming when I pass them, but I can't hear anything they're saying. I'm focused on the back of Pop's jersey, creeping closer as we careen back into the pack.

She begins to raise her arms to call off the jam before I can score, but Carmen knocks her in the hip, giving me a split second to pass three blockers. Pop regains her balance and calls the jam off, scowling. I look hopefully to the scoreboard—three points appear for the Hot Shots.

"*Yeah!*" Carmen shouts, punching me in the shoulder as we skate back to the bench. "That was awesome!"

Mercury grins at me, pulling off the pivot cover. "Better."

When the game clock is down to a minute and forty-five seconds, it's my pod's turn to go out. We're almost tied—the Knockouts lead by just two points. I stand to follow my pod out to the track, but Eden catches me.

"Hey," she says. "I'm going to put Powerhouse out for this last jam."

My heart sinks. "What?"

"You're doing great, Moose. Really. But it's super close. I know Powerhouse can close the gap."

"Oh."

"This happens sometimes," she says, nodding to Powerhouse as they skate past us to take the jam line. "We need to mix up the rotation to be strategic. But you've done great today."

I sit back down on the bench as the ref blows the five-second whistle. It's weird to see Mercury and Carmen on the track without me—they've been my pod this whole time, and I was just starting to get the hang of following their cues.

"Y'all can stand," Eden tells us, and I stand with the rest of the bench, pushing away the disappointment that I'm not skating in the last jam. I focus on Powerhouse as they lurch sideways, sending Pop sprawling off the track. They whirl around, punching through the Knockout blockers and tapping their hips to call off the jam.

We erupt into cheers as the referee holds up four fingers, putting us two points ahead of the Knockouts. OFFICIAL SCORE flashes on the board, and Powerhouse pumps a fist in victory. We flood the track, surrounding Powerhouse and the blockers in a messy, sweaty group hug.

"Fuck yeah!" Carmen is yelling, throwing her hands up toward the Knockouts. "What now? *What now, huh?*"

"Chill out, Carmen," Mercury says, but she's laughing too—somehow, her makeup is still perfect, not a smear on her face despite her shiny cheeks.

And even though I didn't skate in the last jam, my heart's bursting.

chapter twenty-three

RIGHT AFTER WE DEFEAT THE KNOCKOUT KIDS, right as I'm really getting the hang of derby and itching for another bout, the league goes on break for the holidays. Carmen and Mercury are both out of town, and I'm texting Mercury nonstop while she's visiting her dad's family in Seattle.

MERCURY

ok, I'm officially even more of a grandma than my literal grandma.

MOOSE

what did you do?

MERCURY

I went to bed three hours before everybody else last night, and I got up at 9:30 to tell them they were being too loud and I couldn't sleep.

MOOSE

merc

MERCURY

I know

MOOSE

what were they doing?

MERCURY

playing SCRABBLE

MOOSE

oh my god

MERCURY

I KNOW

MOOSE

remind me not to get on your bad side. I don't think I could handle the lecturing.

MERCURY

I was even wearing a bathrobe

MOOSE

you are nothing if not committed

I catch myself glued to my phone more than I should be, always glancing at it to see if she texted back yet and mentally going through her schedule. *She's at a movie with Hyeon and Colin, so she probably won't text back for a couple more hours. And she has family dinner after that, and she has to help her grandma with cooking.* I never got this far with Jenna—after we finished the singular English project we were assigned together, the closest I got to asking her out was staring at her name in my phone, too scared to actually do it. Now that the euphoria from surviving my first game has subsided, all I can think about is seeing Mercury again, kissing her, skating with her at practice and having my spine rearranged from getting hit by her. In a romantic way.

"Hello? Moose?" I glance up from my phone, distracted, to see Prince in the doorway, hands full of reusable bags with wrapping paper peeking out the front.

"Sorry. Hey."

"I've been talking to you for, like, twenty seconds, kid. Gimme a hand?" I reluctantly abandon my phone on the coffee table and get up to help Prince, depositing the bags by our crooked fake Christmas tree in front of the fireplace.

"What do you keep staring at your phone for?" Eden calls, eyeing me from the kitchen as she puts the finishing touches on a charcuterie board.

"Nothing," I say, too quickly. Prince gives me an annoyingly knowing look as she kicks off her boots.

"Uh-huh," Eden says wryly, clearly not buying it. I'm grateful when she doesn't push it.

Prince wanders into the kitchen to greet Eden with a kiss and get a glass of wine, and I turn my phone over in my hands. I feel jittery, like I've had too much caffeine. Sitting down and holding still feels physically impossible when Mercury might text me any second.

"Be right back," I call into the kitchen, and I duck into my room, pulling up Carmen's contact on my phone. *Is this a bad idea?*

Probably.

MOOSE

hi. Sorry to bother you on christmas eve. do you have a sec?

Within seconds, a typing bubble appears.

CARMEN

I'm jewish and spending christmas eve helping my mom pick out a new kiln. PLEASE give me something else to do.

I hesitate, then start typing and hit send before I can talk myself out of it.

MOOSE

how strict is the no-dating-between-teammates rule?

A typing bubble appears, then disappears. I panic and chuck my phone across the room, and it lands on the bed, startling Typo. "God," I moan, pulling up my hood and yanking the drawstrings tight. Maybe if I can bury myself in this hoodie forever, I will never have to read Carmen's reply.

My phone buzzes, and I reluctantly crawl across the room to grab it.

CARMEN

u hitting on me burnout??

CARMEN

just kidding. I know ur not. It's somebody else.

I groan out loud.

MOOSE

is it obvious?

CARMEN

oh, moosey. It's very obvious.

My phone buzzes again—it's Carmen, *calling* me.

"I'm mortified," I tell her when I finally muster the courage to answer.

"So, the not-dating-teammates thing isn't really a rule. It's more of a suggestion."

"A suggestion with a good reason?"

"Uh. Yeah. There have been . . . incidents in the past."

"Carmen," I say, rubbing my eyes. "Please talk me out of this. I know this is stupid, but I don't know what to do."

She's quiet for a second, a rarity from Carmen. "You know why she and Acid broke up, right?" She doesn't even have to say Mercury's name—we both know who she means.

"Yeah. Acid wanted to get captain over Mercury." A few months ago, this would have seemed ridiculous to me. But now, still amped from my first bout and thinking about roller derby practically every waking minute, it sounds like a perfectly understandable reason to end a relationship.

"Sort of." Carmen hesitates. "There's . . . more to it than that."

I falter, trying to decide whether or not to ask. "What happened?"

"They were in a pod together for the longest time, and they communicated really well. Mercury was, like, the only person who could get her to calm down and work as part of a team. But after they started dating, the pod got sloppy."

"What d'you mean?"

"I mean . . . they started missing things. Getting distracted in gameplay, picking up stupid penalties, fumbling what should have been simple plays. In the game to qualify for the regional tournament last year, we were almost tied with the Slamazons, and Mercury let the other jammer go. Because she was watching Acid."

There's a sinking feeling in my chest. "And you lost."

"We lost," she confirms, and she sounds bitter. "I love Mercury to death, but she puts all of her energy into taking care of other people. And it's not always a good thing. We would have qualified for the tournament if Mercury hadn't been distracted. Merc broke up with her the next day."

I let out a breath, deflated. I should tell Carmen that Mercury and I kissed. She's my friend, and she's on the team, and she cares about Mercury too. But I still feel like I did something wrong by kissing her. And Mercury's right—keeping it to ourselves, at least for now, sounds nice.

"You there, Moosey?" Carmen asks, and I realize I've been silent too long.

"I'm here." My voice sounds small.

"Mercury just cares too much, you know?" Carmen goes on, her voice gentle. "The Hot Shots are family to her, to all of us. And she felt like she betrayed her family."

Before I can fully process Carmen's words, there's a knock at the door.

"I gotta go," I hiss into the phone. "Sorry. Thank you. Sorry."

"What—" Carmen starts, but I hang up and shove my phone under my duvet.

"Moose?" Eden calls through the door. "You okay?"

"Yeah," I say quickly, standing. I leave my phone in my room.

Prince stays over for Christmas the next day, and it's surprisingly festive. Eden makes cinnamon rolls from a can and makes us all wear flimsy paper crowns from our party crackers while we open presents. It's fifty degrees and raining, but it still feels cozy.

I'm not expecting a ton in the way of presents, but there's a fanny pack shaped like a donut from Carmen and a potted cutting of a green-and-white plant from Powerhouse. Mercury's gift, the one she claimed she had ready weeks in advance, is a chunky burnt-orange knit scarf; the inside is lined with matching flannel.

"You're not really a Hot Shot until you own something knitted by Mercury," Prince says as I loop the soft yarn around my neck. "But, damn, she's never made *me* something this luxurious." I flush a little as I imagine Mercury's fingers deftly looping each stitch. I make Eden take a picture of me wearing it, and I send it to her with a string of heart emojis.

Teammate, a stern voice says in my head, and I push the thought away.

Eden chokes up when she opens my gift—earrings I had made from the strings of sea glass that used to hang in our kitchen window in Utah. I pulled them down and tucked them in my pocket after the fire, the first time I stepped into the Finney's Mesa house in months. Dad used to collect them when he lived in California, and he kept the frosted green-and-blue garlands *so I remember what the ocean looks like*, he used to say. It was the only thing I grabbed that day—the rest of the house made me feel too hollow and empty, too many reminders of Dads in every dish in the sink and sticky note on the fridge. Eden had asked me what else I wanted to keep, and I'd just walked out to the back porch, staring at the mesas in angry silence. I feel a pang of guilt at the memory. Eden was probably going through the same shit, and I just left her in the house, alone.

"I love these, Moose," she sniffles now, immediately putting the earrings in. The glass glimmers in her ears. "Thank you."

The last present is big, a flat package for me from Eden. It's a framed drawing, bright orange lines against a deep blue sky. I recognize it immediately—the North Window from Arches, a full moon perfectly positioned in the middle to look like a giant, staring eye. The Delicate Arch is the one you always see on posters, but the North Window is my favorite. It's the one that I made Dads drive me to every full moon, so we could watch the pupil of the eye slowly roll into place. We went twice during one summer Eden stayed with us, standing in a crowd, in awe.

In the corner of the sky, there's a tiny signature in white pen—I see an *E* and an *S*.

"Did you draw this?" I ask, amazed.

Eden nods, a bit sheepishly. "I haven't done colored pencils like that since college, so it's a little sloppy, but I know how much you love Arches, and I know we're gonna go this summer, but I thought until then—"

I'm up before she can finish her sentence, my arms around her neck. Her arms circle me, and she holds me tight, her smooth sea glass earring tickling my cheek.

Mercury texts me as soon as she's back from Seattle: **You busy?** We have two more days until school starts again, and I was planning on spending them on the couch in Eden's apartment, watching footage of old derby games and typing notes into my phone about what I wanted to work on as soon as we got back to practice. I'm still not sure what Mercury and I are to each other. We haven't been alone together since we kissed on the ridge, and our texts during the break have been flirty, but never directly addressing the gigantic, hulking elephant in the room.

Not really, I text back. **Eden's out with her team so I'm just watching old bout footage.**

Her typing bubble appears immediately.

MERCURY

Which bout?

MOOSE

champs 2015, rose v gotham

MERCURY

omg

MERCURY

have you watched it before

MOOSE

NO

MOOSE

IT'S SO GOOD

MERCURY

you kind of jam like shortstop on gotham you know

MOOSE

no I do not

MOOSE

she is so good

MERCURY

SO ARE YOU

MERCURY

I'm saying you should study the way she jams and try to learn some of her techniques

MERCURY

want some company?

MOOSE

yes

I reply before I can talk myself out of it.

MERCURY

be there in 20

When Mercury texts me that she's downstairs, I feel that familiar flutter of nerves I've come to associate with being in the same airspace as her. I race down the stairs two at a time, wondering vaguely if I was supposed to ask Eden for permission for things like this. But I'm already throwing open the door, and Mercury is there, mist in her hair from the rain and holding a bag of takeout and looking gorgeous and perfect as usual.

"Hi," I say, hoping I don't sound breathless.

Mercury grins, stepping off the porch and pulling her hood down. "Hi. You hungry?"

"Always."

I lead Mercury up the stairs to the door of the apartment, and she hands me the takeout bag to pull off her Docs and greet Typo. She moves with practiced familiarity.

"Have you been here before?" I ask.

"Yeah. A couple times. To help Coach Ripley with rosters and stuff." She's squatting on the ground scratching Typo's head, and she notices me watching. "Is that weird?"

"Maybe a little. I just keep realizing how many people know my sister better than I do."

Mercury stands, takes my hand, and squeezes it. "You'll keep getting to know her," she says confidently, and I believe her.

Mercury makes me get real plates and cloth napkins for the burgers she brought from Major's, and she even fills two glasses with ice for the cans of grapefruit LaCroix she brought.

"This is the fanciest way I've ever eaten fries," I say as she arranges the spread on the coffee table, shooing Typo away.

"And isn't it more fun this way?" She's on the other side of the couch, pulling a blanket out of the basket Eden keeps there. "Moose?"

I realize I'm standing awkwardly by the kitchen counter, staring, not sure what to do with myself. Mercury looks so comfortable here.

"Yeah," I say quickly, grabbing my laptop from the counter and setting it on the coffee table. "I was only on the fifth jam. Should I start it over?"

"Obviously," Mercury says, ripping open a ketchup packet and squirting it onto her plate. "You need the entire Rose versus Gotham lore to fully appreciate this game."

I sit next to her on the couch and lean forward to press play.

"Okay," Mercury says immediately, "watch the way Shortstop uses the momentum of the Rose blockers against them. You could easily learn how to do that."

Even though we're watching one of the most dramatic champs games in history, I keep looking sidelong at Mercury, analyzing the space between us on the couch, wondering if I should try to close it. She seems totally enraptured by the game, talking through the strategy and the different starts and how I should work on using my hips more to cut through a tripod.

Halfway through the second period, my laptop blinks with a low battery warning. I lean forward to pause the game. "Let me get my charger," I say quickly, and I practically run down the hall.

I look around, wondering if I should have tidied up a little. Mercury and I still haven't really talked about that night on the ridge. Are we dating now? Should I be expecting her to come in here and want to make out? The thought makes my stomach twist with nerves again. But Mercury's on the couch in the living room, thinking about derby and derby only.

I grab an armful of clean laundry from the bed anyway and dump it in the closet, then hastily start shoving my stinking derby pads back into my skate bag.

"Hey."

I start, turn around, and realize Mercury's standing in the doorway, leaning against the doorframe. "Hi." I hold up a wrist guard. "Sorry. Just—my gear stinks."

"So does everybody's." She glances around the room. "Can I come in?"

"Yeah," I say, shoving the wrist guard into my bag and zipping it shut. "Of course."

Mercury steps into the room, and I stand awkwardly while she looks at the drawing of Arches Eden made for me, the printed photo of the Hot Shots from our last practice thumbtacked to the wall, the short bookshelf filled with Eden's Stephen King novels. Then her gaze lands on the boxes in the corner, still taped shut and untouched.

"What's that?" she asks.

"Just . . . some more of my stuff from Moab."

"You haven't opened them."

I shift uncomfortably. "Yeah. I . . . haven't felt like it."

She finally makes eye contact with me, and I realize she looks nervous. "Is this weird?"

"You already asked me that."

"I asked you if it was weird that I'd been to your apartment before. Now I'm asking if it's weird that I'm in your room."

My apartment. Not Eden's apartment, not *your sister's* apartment. Mercury, I realize, is the first person to name this place as my home. And seeing her standing in my room—*my* room—looking at my stuff, noticing the boxes from Moab, agreeing that my gear stinks, somehow makes it feel true.

"I think it's weird because I can't tell if this is a date or not," I venture.

She looks surprised by my forwardness, but then she's crossing my room in three quick strides, reaching out to take both my hands in hers. "I'm sorry," she says gently. "My dad was being weird, and we had our game right after that night on the ridge, and then I was in Seattle, and I didn't know if you still wanted—"

"I do." I lace my fingers through hers. "Do *you*?" Carmen's words from Christmas Eve blare in my head. *Mercury won't date a teammate, Mercury feels like she betrayed the team, Mercury broke up with Acid.*

"I do," she says quietly, and all the doubts leave my mind as she kisses me again. It's just as soft and heady as our first kiss, but this time it's more confident—our mouths know each other better now, and our hands easily find each other's faces, arms, waists. We step back slowly toward my twin bed, and I sit down first, pulling Mercury with me.

When we finally pause, we're twined together, and my heart's beating hard against my chest.

"Are you okay?" Mercury asks, brushing a curl off my forehead.

"Yeah," I try, but it comes out hoarse. I clear my throat. "Yes. I'm good. I'm so good."

She grins and tugs the collar of my shirt straight. "I have been wanting to kiss you like that since I met you."

I feel myself flush at her words, and I bury my face in her neck to hide it. Mercury laughs and kisses my forehead. "I have never, ever done this," I mumble into her shoulder, and she loops her arms around me, pulling me closer.

"Just tell me if it feels like too much, okay?"

"Okay." I slide up a little so I can look at her, the roundness of her face, her dark eyes, her red lipstick that is usually perfect but is now smudged across one cheek. And for now, I forget about the Hot Shots and the fact that Mercury's my captain and the fire and everything else. And I just let myself exist with her.

chapter twenty-four

WHEN WE'RE BACK AT PRACTICE, we keep winning.

We're bouting other teams now, working our way through the regional tournament bracket. The championship bout, if we qualify, will be May 7—exactly a year and month after the fire. I write the date on a Post-it and stick it to my bedroom wall beside Eden's drawing of the North Window. It's supposed to be a reminder for the tournament, but it mostly reminds me of my goal to skate in a roller rink by a year after the fire. April. The month looms, and I feel no closer to setting foot inside the rink than I did the day I woke up in the burn unit.

I am, however, getting stronger with each bout. I'm learning my teammates' movements, committing our start formations and offense plays to muscle memory, figuring out how to move my body aggressively through the pack. Acid and Powerhouse are still way better than me, but I'm getting out of the pack, scoring more points, even claiming lead jammer a few times each game. Mercury comes over and shows me footage of Shortstop and other famous jammers between making out in my room and holding hands under the blanket on the couch when Eden's not looking. When we're not skating, I'm studying recordings of our bouts, scribbling notes, sprawled on my stomach in Carmen's attic with a whiteboard and a set of magnets and breaking down strategies.

"Passing the star does *not* mean the jammer failed," Mercury's explaining at one such gathering. Carmen and Powerhouse are here, of course, but Panic and Trail Mx. have joined us too, having been standing nearby at the end of practice when Carmen started roping in everybody she could find. Colored light filters through the big stained-glass window—the days are getting longer as we creep closer to spring, and it's still light out close to six. Mercury and I have gotten pretty good at acting normal around the rest of the Hot Shots. It feels weird to keep this secret from them, but I know it's for the best. We need to focus on getting to champs, and stirring up a bunch of drama on the team right before our qualifying game won't help anyone.

Despite the familiarity of Carmen's attic, I'm on edge. Eden left her laptop open on the kitchen counter yesterday, and a picture of our house in Utah practically screamed across the apartment at me. I'd quickly skimmed the email while she was in the bathroom—it was addressed to a real estate agent, asking about commission prices for listing the house. Eden's avoided the topic of selling the Moab house with me since our argument about it, but I know she wants to. It makes sense: I don't live there anymore, and it's costing her money just sitting empty. But the thought of someone else's dishes in the sink, someone else's clothes in my dads' closet, makes my stomach turn over. I'd reached for the keyboard before I could stop myself, hitting the delete button with more force than necessary and watching the email swoosh into oblivion. Eden will be mad when she figures it out. But that's a problem for future Moose.

"If the pivot is in a better position, like this, it makes sense to pass it," Mercury goes on, scooting four of the magnets around on the board. The elliptical track is drawn on with Sharpie, creating a permanent strategy board that seems to travel around the team. Someone—probably a Hot Shot from long ago—drew the scowling meteor on the back of the board, claiming it for our team.

"Plus then, the jammer can revenge hit the enemy blockers," Carmen chimes in, twitching her shoulders like she's checking someone.

Mercury gives her a look. "Do *not* revenge hit," she says sternly. "We can't afford penalty spirals. Not during regionals."

"I never get penalties," Carmen tells Apex and me in a stage whisper.

"That's a bald-faced lie, and you know it," Apex replies.

"O-kay." Powerhouse yawns, leaning back to stretch. "I need a break. Anybody else?"

"God, yes." Carmen sits up on her knees as Powerhouse digs around in their bag. "I thought you'd never offer."

Before I can ask, Powerhouse pulls out a Ziploc bag of orange gummy squares. They hand the bag to Apex, who fishes one out and immediately pops it in her mouth.

"You don't have to take one, Moose," Mercury says, accepting the bag from Apex. She deftly cuts one in half with Powerhouse's pocketknife and pops it in her mouth, and I hope she doesn't notice me staring. The rest of the team has mostly converted to calling me Burnout, but Mercury still calls me Moose off the track. I let her—it makes the name feel special.

"What is it?" I ask, feeling like I should know the answer.

"One-to-one THC and CBD," Powerhouse says as Panic declines the bag, passing it straight to Carmen.

I look at them blankly.

"It's weed," Carmen finally says, digging one out of the bag. "Mercury won't let us smoke in case it messes up our lungs."

"We're athletes," Mercury adds sagely, and Carmen rolls her eyes.

The bag finally gets to me, and I peer into it like the gummies might bite me. "Hey, you really don't have to take any," Powerhouse says. "It's just good for relaxing."

That convinces me. Before I can talk myself out of it, I pull a square gummy out and toss it in my mouth. It's sugary, but with a weird herbal aftertaste.

Within an hour, I feel myself mellowing out. Someone clicks on the Christmas lights strung across the ceiling, bathing Carmen's attic in a soft glow. Everyone but Mercury has abandoned the strategy board—Carmen is trying to gather them around her phone to watch a video of Mongolian throat singing.

I lean back against the couch, running a thumb along the scar on my throat. With the filter from the edible, it doesn't seem quite so awful. I have a sudden urge to look at myself, to stare at my own face. It's gotten better—I'm not using Eden's scarf anymore, but I still avoid most mirrors I see, still catch myself tugging the collar of my hoodie up if it slides down too far. I stand abruptly, and everyone looks at me.

"Bathroom," I say roughly, then I'm hurrying down the narrow attic stairs. I close the door of Carmen's bathroom, lean against it. The mirror is there, an old medicine cabinet above the sink painted with little yellow flowers. Waiting.

I take a few hesitant steps toward the sink. Place one hand on each side of it, look down at my fingers against the porcelain. Then I steady myself with a breath and raise my chin.

My face looks fuller than I thought, my eyes weirdly shiny. I push my mane of frizzy hair back, lifting my chin and grazing my fingers over the ridge of the scar. When they pulled the tracheostomy tube out of my throat in the burn unit, the doctor said, *It's incredible, what the human body can survive.* It made me want to shrivel up inside myself even more, to knock the mirror out of the hands of the nurse who offered it to me. But now I just want to see myself more. Clearer. I want to see more of the face that looks so much like my sister's, like our dad's. I want my hair to look like a queer calling card, like everyone else on the Hot Shots with shaved heads and vivid dye. I want to see myself again above the scar, keep something under control while someone else buys the house I grew up in.

When I burst back into the attic, I'm breathing hard, like I just skated a two-minute jam. "I want to cut my hair," I gasp.

Carmen, half-asleep on the floor, gasps and scrambles to her knees. "I have clippers!" she announces.

"Shit," Trail Mx. says, "we give Burnout some weed one time, and she tries to reinvent herself."

We all crowd back into the bathroom, only this time someone's phone is blasting Doja Cat over tinny speakers and Carmen is yelling over everyone's hair suggestions as she tries to find an outlet for the clippers. Trail Mx. manages to wrestle the clippers away from Carmen and pass them to a stoned Powerhouse, who somehow seems even calmer than usual.

"You could do, like, an undercut sorta thing," Carmen is saying, pulling the lower layer of my hair back to see how it would look. "Or just a side. Or, like, a fade, and leave it long on top. Or—"

"All of it," I say. They all stare at me.

"*All* of it?" Carmen asks after a moment.

Powerhouse clicks the clippers on, and the buzz fills my ears. "You sure?" they ask, placing a hand on my shoulder.

I meet my own gaze in the mirror. "I'm sure."

I close my eyes while Powerhouse slides the clippers along my scalp, feeling tufts of frizz brush my hands. Carmen and Panic are keeping up a running commentary. “It looks amazing,” Carmen keeps saying. “Powerhouse is so good at this. They’re good at everything. Powerhouse, do you wanna shave my head next?”

I don’t notice how tight my grip on the sink is until I feel a familiar hand on top of mine. I force myself to unclench and turn my hand so Mercury can hold it.

chapter twenty-five

I FEEL FASTER, skating with all my hair buzzed off. Like how swimmers wait until their big tournament to shave their legs—I'm lighter and freer. I'm also significantly less drenched in sweat at the end of practice.

"I love it!" Eden had exclaimed when Carmen dropped me off the next morning. "Do you want to dye it? If we both have blue hair, we could *really* confuse some people at practice."

"There's not much to dye," I'd said, running a hand over the short crop of curls left on my scalp.

Her excitement is short-lived when she's scrolling through her email later that day, brow furrowed as she searches for the email from the Realtor that I impulse-deleted. I'm beside her on the couch, my laptop playing an old champs game, but I keep glancing at her phone screen in my periphery. When I watch her tap the deleted emails folder, I know I'm done for.

"Did you delete an email off my laptop?"

"Yes," I admit, not looking at her. No point in hiding it, I guess.

To my surprise, Eden says, "Why don't you come with me to tidy up the gear cage?" League membership for the adult teams requires a certain number of volunteer hours each month, and Eden often makes an extra trip to the Hangar to fix up loaner skates.

"Why?" I ask, and she gives me a look that makes it clear it's not an optional outing.

Eden drives us to the Hangar in silence. The track is empty when we arrive—it's a rare window of time between practices, where the only other people in the Hangar are a couple volunteers hanging new sponsor banners on the walls. It's weird to see it so quiet, and I glumly follow Eden around the empty track to the gear cage tucked in the corner, which houses tidy rows of frayed pads and aged skates.

We work in silence for a few minutes, Eden pulling loaner skates off the shelves and replacing the worn laces before passing them to me to check the plates.

"You can't just delete stuff off my laptop, Moose," Eden says after the fifth skate.

"I know," I grumble, flipping the skate over in my lap and testing the trucks. They're way too loose for a beginner skate, and I grab my skate tool and start tightening. "I'm sorry."

Eden looks tired as she takes the tightened skate and hands me another one. "I know you don't want to sell the house. I know it sucks, and it hurts, you don't want to talk about it. But we need to."

I shake my head. "Why does it have to be right *now*?" I ask, a little sharper than necessary. I've been in Portland for almost five months now, but it feels like an insignificant amount of time compared to the sixteen years I spent growing up in that house.

"It just—it doesn't make sense for us to keep paying for a house we don't live in. I'm trying to be cool about things like this, Moose, but I have to make good decisions for both of us now. And you need to trust me to do that."

"But it's my *house*."

Eden doesn't answer, but she looks so worn, so stressed, that I feel yet another ripple of guilt at being dumped in her lap. I focus on the skate in my hands, the wheels fastened so tight that they can barely spin.

"Sorry," I say quietly. "I know . . . I know we need the money."

"It's not really about money. Your dads made sure we would be okay. It's just a lot of work to keep a house in a totally different state, and—"

"Wait," I interrupt. "It's not about money?"

Eden looks confused. "No. We're fine with money. They both had life insurance, and retirement savings, and—"

"What about your student loans?" There's an angry edge in my voice as I process what Eden's saying. "I found the bill a couple months ago, saying you were past due."

"I missed a payment while we were in Utah. It's fine now. Why are you going through my stuff?"

"Why didn't you tell me?" I shoot back.

"Tell you what?"

"That we had money?" My voice is hard. "Eden, I've spent the past five months feeling like I'm this huge burden on you because you don't make enough money for two people. How much do we have?"

"We have enough," Eden says, trying to keep her voice even. "Moose, it's not your job to worry about money, okay?" Her voice is grating, dredging up an anger I didn't realize lived in me.

"We have all this cash, and you're still rushing me into selling the house?"

"I'm not—"

"No, Eden!" I burst out, dropping my skate tool with a clatter. The volunteers hanging banners glance over at us, and my face heats in shame. "Forget it." I abandon the skate and head for the Hangar door, grimacing. Eden doesn't call after me, and I can't tell whether or not that makes me madder.

When I push open the door, I nearly slam into Mercury.

"Whoa," she says, steadying me when I stumble.

"Sorry," I murmur, ignoring the way my heart flips at her touch. Really? *Now,* of all times? Mercury's not dressed for skating, and we don't have practice tonight. "What are you doing here?"

"Monthly team captains meeting," she says, pulling me away from the door so someone else can head inside.

"Sounds boring." I'm being an asshole, but I can't make myself stop.

Mercury frowns at me. "What's wrong?"

I finally look at her, simultaneously excited and jealous that she always looks so beautiful and perfect. "Eden wants to sell our house in Moab," I admit, and it feels like a weight off my chest. "I fucking grew up there. But she wouldn't know, because she hadn't bothered to see us for ten years before my dads died. *And* she just told me she has tons of money from life insurance, or something, so she doesn't even *need* to sell it! It's my *house*, you know? And she didn't tell me—" I break off, looking over Mercury's shoulder. The roller rink is across from the Hangar, parking lot filled with cars and the neon sign lighting up in the already-darkening sky. I haven't been working very hard at the goal Dr. Parikh and I set—just looking at the roller rink makes me feel sick, and April is coming up faster than it should.

I brush past Mercury and start speed walking through the parking lot toward the rink.

"Moose?" I hear Mercury's boots on the pavement as she follows. "Where are you going?"

"To the roller rink," I call back, not pausing to look at her. If I take too much time to think about it, I'll chicken out. I have to do it *now*. If I'm going to lose the house I grew up in, I might as well do something to impress my therapist.

Mercury catches up with me. She's tall enough to match my stride easily. "Why are you going to the roller rink?"

"I have to go inside and skate," I say briskly. "By the one-year anniversary of the fire, I have to have skated in a roller rink again without having a meltdown."

"Uh . . . why are you doing it now?"

"Because I don't know what else to do!" I burst out, not looking at her as I continue to power walk toward the rink. The huge building is looming now, and I survey it all too quickly—there are barely any windows. I don't see any fire exits. I hear music pulsing through the walls, see the disco ball winking inside, a crush of people lined up to get in. Too many.

"Moose, will you just—" Mercury grabs my arm, but I shake her off. If I stop walking, I won't go in. But the panic is clawing up, squeezing my stomach, sour in my throat. The corners of my vision blur. *Not safe not safe not safe not safe not safe not safe.*

"Moose!"

I stop abruptly and realize how tight my chest feels. I'm a hundred feet from the doors into the rink, and a few people waiting in line are staring at me.

Mercury appears beside me, sets a hand on my shoulder. "Hey. Take a breath." I do, and the air burns in my lungs. I feel jittery all of a sudden and like my legs are about to give out. Mercury takes my hand—which still makes my stomach flutter, even though I'm pissed at Eden—and leads me away from the rink, back through the cars toward the Hangar. My breathing evens out.

We reach Mercury's car, and she opens the door and directs me to sit before digging around in the backseat. I lower myself onto the threadbare fabric seat, sitting sideways so my legs are still outside, and stare up at the rink in the distance.

"Here," Mercury says, handing me a bottle of water. I crack it open and take a sip.

"How is this cold?" The bottle's sweating on the outside, like it just came out of the fridge.

"I keep a cooler in the backseat." Mercury says, going around to sit on the passenger side.

I swing my legs into the car so I can see her. "That's—"

"A grandma thing, I know." She gives me a long look. "Moose, I get setting a goal, but . . . you shouldn't do something you're not ready for."

I look down, rubbing my thumb across the condensation on the water bottle. "I don't feel like I'm ever going to be ready. It's already February."

"Which means you still have time."

We're quiet for a moment, watching cars pull up and skaters from the Slamazons filter out for their practice. They sling heavy gear bags and skate leashes over their shoulders, wave to one another as they head into the Hangar. A couple of them notice Mercury and me and wave, and I smile halfheartedly while Mercury waves back.

"Eden's pissed at me," I say finally. "Because I'm not ready to sell the house."

"Is that what she said?"

"It may as well be."

"I'm sorry, Moose," Mercury says gently. "I can't imagine. Maybe Eden would compromise? Wait to list the house until you've had a chance to see it one more time?"

"Yeah. Maybe."

"And, Moose. You don't have to deal with this all by yourself, okay? Lean on me and Carmen and Powerhouse. It's why we're here. We're not just your teammates."

What are we, then? I almost ask her. "Okay," I say instead, twisting the lid of the water bottle shut. "Thanks."

We get out of the car and Mercury hugs me, a little tighter and longer than she might have if we were *just* teammates. But we're in the parking lot before practice, when it basically turns into social hour among all the skaters heading in. So she leaves it at that as we walk back into the Hangar. She gives my hand a quick squeeze before heading to the office, and I sigh and slink back toward the loaner gear.

Eden's still dutifully adjusting loaner skates like nothing happened. She doesn't look up when I rejoin her at the workbench, just slides a skate tool across the counter to me. I pick it up gingerly and reach for the next pair of skates on the pile, flipping them over to check the trucks.

"Sorry," I say to Eden after a couple quiet moments.

Her shoulders unclench. "Yeah. Me too."

"I know we need to sell the house. But I'm not ready. Not without seeing it again first."

Eden pulls a frayed lace out of the skate she's working on. "Pass me a fresh lace?" I untangle one from the pile and hand it to her. "What about May? We can drive down to see it one more time before we sell."

The thought of selling it at all still twists my gut. "Okay. I can do that." I think.

chapter twenty-six

BY APRIL, Portland blooms out of nowhere. Just when I'd gotten used to the sun setting at four thirty, pink and white flowers burst from the trees, coating the wet sidewalks with petaled carpets. It still rains, but the sunny days start to outnumber the gray, and it's warm enough to shed down to a denim jacket most days. At practice, we wheel open the huge Hangar doors meant to fit an airplane, letting the breeze drift over the track while we skate.

Eden and Prince seem immune to the pleasant weather, working us harder than ever. We have one game left against the Benton Brawlers before the championship teams are determined—if we win, we skate for the regional trophy. I'm exhausted after every practice, two hours of pushing to learn more drills, hone strategy, perfect footwork. But it's a satisfying exhaustion—each time I collapse into bed after the post-practice shower, covered in bruises and scrapes and Velcro burns, with my muscles shaky from exertion, I'm energized, thinking about the game. Every time Eden and I pull into the Hangar's parking lot, I avoid looking at the looming roller rink on the other side of the park.

Eden and I haven't really talked about money *or* the house since our fight in the gear cage. We're both busy and tired most of the time from getting ready for the upcoming champs games. But in the rare moments where it's just the two of us, in the car or making dinner, things feel strained. Eden's back to being overly polite, and I'm spending more time retreating to my room instead of hanging out with her. It feels like all the progress we made in the past few months got erased by this one fight. But every time I think I should go out to the living room, I remember Eden not telling me about the money, not trying harder to be part of my life until our dad's death forced her.

The Saturday before our qualifying game, I'm alone in the apartment, trudging through my bio homework with the big bay windows open. Typo sleeps in the windowsill, the breeze ruffling her fur and sending the hanging stained glass pane spinning. It throws colored light across my homework each time it turns, dancing patches of yellow and blue and orange. Eden lets me stay home on Saturday mornings while she's at scrimmage, and the apartment's quiet.

The sticky note on my wall with my goal for skating in the rink again—*April 7*—seems to mock me now. Neither Eden nor I mentioned the date—not the weeks leading up to it, not the day of, not the two weeks that have passed since. I feel like I should have commemorated it somehow, but I just wanted to get past it, avoid people pitying me and asking if I was okay. I glare at the sticky note for a second before flipping open the cover of my school planner. Weeks ago, I used the printer at Eden's office to print a copy of our team photo from my first bout with the Hot Shots. At the end of every game, all the skaters and coaches from both teams gather on the track under the scoreboard, different-colored jerseys intermingled under the scores that feel meaningless at that point. I look sweaty and small between Mercury and Pop from the Knockout Kids, but I'm smiling so big my eyes are barely visible under my helmet and frizzy hair.

My phone buzzes, giving me an excuse to stall working on Punnett squares. It's from Bitch Pod 2.

MERCURY

can we do something tonight?

I purse my lips. Mercury's not usually the one to initiate plans, especially on weekend nights when she's often in charge of haranguing her brothers into helping her cook dinner.

Carmen is already typing a reply.

CARMEN

yes please. What are we doing

MERCURY

literally anything.

CARMEN

pls narrow down. I have a billion ideas

POWERHOUSE

oaks is open tonight. we should check it out.

Oaks Park, the tiny theme park that houses the Hangar, doesn't fully open until school gets out. But our spring break was last week, and they're leaving the park open an extra day this weekend.

BURNOUT

I'm not getting on the roller coaster.

POWERHOUSE

there are rides besides the roller coaster.

CARMEN

and it's a TINY roller coaster.

MERCURY

im with moose. We have a qualifying bout next week. not risking flying off the track and dying in a Final Destination accident

CARMEN

ok grandma. You and burnout can ride the merry-go-round.

"Is your homework done?" Eden replies when I ask if I can go. She's just barely walked in the door after scrimmage and brought Prince with her, both of them holding iced coffees.

"Almost," I say truthfully. Eden raises an eyebrow. "It's Saturday. I just have bio, and I'll finish it first thing after practice tomorrow. Promise."

She hesitates—Eden's been awkwardly toeing the line between responsible guardian and cool older sister lately.

"Please, Eden. I'll even have Carmen check it before I turn it in."

"Okay," she relents, dropping her derby bag just inside the door. "Are you staying over at her place after?"

"Probably."

"Just let me know by, like, ten at the latest, okay? And take your gear so you can go straight to practice in the morning."

"You ready for the bout next week, Moose on the Loose?" Prince asks me, scooping up a purring Typo to scritch her chin.

"I think so. Powerhouse says the Brawlers are really good."

"Maybe," Prince says with a shrug. She winks at me. "But we're better."

"Everyone is good, and we are all playing just for fun," Eden chides from the kitchen.

Prince holds up Typo's paw like she's whispering to me. "And we're playing for *blood*."

By six, I'm standing awkwardly in front of the mirror in my room, looking at the two sets of non-workout clothes I regularly wear: a pair of jeans and an oversized T-shirt, or denim shorts with an unremarkable black sweater. I pick up the T-shirt, frowning at it. I look at the boxes Eden packed for me from our house in Moab, still shoved in the corner by the closet, mostly untouched. I push aside the one I opened last fall, filled with old scraps of schoolwork from freshman year and clothes I'd never wear again, and hesitantly strip the packing tape off the next one.

My vintage horror movie T-shirts are stacked on top, rolled in neat bundles. My breath catches as I pick one up and shake it loose to reveal the faded *Halloween* logo, and I paw past the shirts to find my scuffed Docs and Dad's old leather jacket from the nineties. Then my hand finds a folded packet of tissue paper, tucked safely between the shirts. I pull it out, feeling beads and chains and thin metal as I unwrap the tissue paper. It's one of the suncatchers Papa used to make, the one that hung in my bedroom window and sent sprays of rainbow light across my bedroom as the sun rose. I picture Eden in the Moab house while I was in the hospital, carefully and lovingly sliding the suncatchers off the curtain rods and packing them away for me, knowing I would need them even in Portland, where the sun lay dormant for months and months.

Eden *did* know what to pack.

I gently rest the suncatcher on my desk and cross to the door, cracking it open. The big square window in Eden's bedroom is open, and she and Prince are sitting on lawn chairs on the roof outside, leaning over Eden's clipboard.

"Eden?"

She twists around, shades her eyes with her hand so she can see me. "What's up?"

"Can you . . . uh . . . help me with something real quick?"

She untangles herself from the lawn chair, and I'm painfully aware of the hand she rests on Prince's shoulder before she climbs through the window.

Eden raises an eyebrow when I close the door behind her, biting my lip. "I don't know what to wear," I admit, feeling silly. "All my clothes are too . . . casual."

Eden doesn't miss a beat. "Skirt or no skirt?"

I blink. "Uh . . . I don't know. I don't usually wear skirts."

"Got it. Be right back." She slips out, then comes back a moment later with an armful of clothes on hangers, which she drapes across my desk chair. "You look really good in these bold eighties colors," she says, sorting through the hangers. "Like Dad did. Here, try this." She hands me a button-down shirt, color blocked in yellow, red, and blue. It's not what I would have picked for myself, but I gave up dressing myself in anything other than sweats after the fire.

I pull my T-shirt off and button the shirt over my sports bra as Eden fishes out a pair of pale denim jeans. "So," she says, holding them up to test them against the shirt, "are you dressing up for anybody in particular?" I freeze, panic jolting through me. Eden's eyes flick up, and her face softens. "You're not in trouble, Moose. You're just not as slick as you think you are." She pauses. "It's Mercury." It's not a question.

I look away. "I haven't done anything," I say, too fast. "I know I'm not supposed to—"

"Moose," Eden says gently, grabbing my shoulder. "Did you hear me? You're not in trouble."

"But we aren't supposed to date teammates."

"We *recommend* that you don't date teammates. But it's not breaking any rules." She studies me for a moment, tugging the shirt straight. "Remember how I told you that Prince and I liked each other for two years before we started dating?"

"Yeah."

"We both thought we'd get over it. Didn't want to mess with the team." She looks up at me, cheeks pink. "And you know what I've realized since we said *fuck it* and just started being together? That we'd make it work. If anything came up with the team that tested our relationship, we would figure it out together. Because that's what she means to me." Eden's eyes are bright, and the way she glows when she talks about Prince makes my heart hurt. It's how Dad looked at Papa, held his hand while they swirled and danced around the roller rink, snuck up behind him at the sink to wrap his arms around him, kiss him on the forehead before he left the room.

"I don't even know if Mercury wants to date me."

"You won't know until you ask her." Eden holds the jeans out to me, and I slip out of my sweatpants and tug them on. She turns me around to face the mirror—I look more put-together now, almost cooler. The buttons on this shirt start below my collarbone, so my trach scar is visible—but it's almost like a shadow now, not really there. "Just be honest," Eden says, squeezing my shoulders. "That's all anybody can ask of you." She spots Dad's old jacket from the boxes lying on the bed and picks it up, gesturing for me to hold my arms out so she can slide it on. She's not even trying to hide her grin as she surveys her handiwork.

"So," I say slowly, tugging the jacket over my shoulders, "does this mean that you condone me dating Mercury? As my coach?"

She holds her hands up, shaking her head as she leaves the room. "I haven't heard anything, and I condone nothing." But she pauses in the doorway, turning to give me a wink before she climbs back out onto the roof.

chapter twenty-seven

THE SKY IS PINK with impending sunset when Carmen pulls into Oaks. It's already crowded. The Ferris wheel moves in lazy circles, and flags ripple along the midway. Oaks is a tiny amusement park, mostly a collection of historical street fair rides on a stretch of asphalt overlooking the Willamette River. I look darkly at the flashing RINK sign on the roof of the roller rink. "Okay, I'm getting on the roller coaster," Carmen declares, pushing the driver's door shut with her hip. "You're missing out, Moose. Do you know how many roller coasters Oregon has to offer? Two. In the whole state. And this is one of them."

"That roller coaster laid in the parking lot in pieces for four months before they finally put it together," Mercury comments.

"I'm good to stay on the ground," I say.

Carmen and Powerhouse lead the way to the ticket booth, leaving Mercury to fall into step beside me. She's wearing a cornflower-blue prairie dress covered in little white flowers, and her hair hangs loose and wavy around her shoulders. I force myself not to stare.

"Can you believe I almost brought Hyeon and Colin?" she asks, bemused. "Like they're six-year-olds for me to keep track of. My mom used to use leashes on them when they were little."

I snort, and Mercury looks offended for a split second before she dissolves into giggles too. "Maybe you should see if the leashes are still in your basement," I suggest, and she punches me lightly in the arm. "My dads were probably *too* hands off. There are pictures of me crawling around on those rock ridges before I could even really walk."

"Without a leash?"

"Yeah, just letting a literal baby roll around on the cliffs."

Mercury giggles, and I wonder if this is what my grief will look like someday. Mercury can so easily bring up her mom, laugh about her, tease her even after she's gone. Her ball is smaller now, only hitting the box every once in a while. Maybe mine will be too. Someday.

The midway is just starting to come to life, the game booths lighting up as people crowd along their counters. Over the tents, a huge spinning ride rocks up into the air, lights flashing as it inches closer to a three-sixty with each swing. We get in line for a tame-looking ride with fake cars that drive on a tilted path, and I feel sick to my stomach by the time we stumble off.

"That was not a good idea," I grumble, finding a bench outside the ride and dropping my head between my knees. "Fuck."

Carmen disappears momentarily, then returns with a tray of corn dogs, popcorn, and four overflowing Icees. "This will help," she says confidently, handing me a corn dog in a paper sleeve.

"How is that supposed to help?" Mercury asks while I stare at the corn dog.

"Gives you something to throw up," she chirps. "Feeling nauseous on an empty stomach is just endless nonrelief. Sisyphean."

Powerhouse rolls their eyes, but I take a bite of the corn dog anyway and I really do feel better. "I just need to sit here for a minute," I say, waving my corn dog at them. "Y'all go on—I'll catch up."

"I can stay," Mercury says, and I hope she doesn't notice that my mouth misses the corn dog at her words. She plucks an Icee from the tray and sits beside me, adjusting her dress. "You two go ride the roller coaster."

"Okay, but you have to come watch Powerhouse screaming on at least one run," Carmen says, and Powerhouse smacks her on the arm, scowling. "Ow. But seriously," Carmen says in a stage whisper as Powerhouse turns to go. "It's insane. They act so big and tough on the track, then the minute the coaster takes off—"

"Carmen!" Powerhouse snaps, and she scurries after them.

"I am really not a ride person," Mercury tells me, accepting the other corn dog I offer her. "Just watching them makes me sick."

"Why'd you want to come here if you don't like rides?"

"I dunno," she says without looking up at me. "Something to do. I had to get out of the house."

"Is everything okay?"

To my surprise, she doesn't stiffen, doesn't brush away the subject. For some reason, this little metal bench tucked between two grinding rides full of screams and laughter is an acceptable place for us to talk. "I told my dad I'm done," she says, taking a bite of her corn dog. "Done playing mom."

"Really?"

"Yeah. There's a line between me helping out with my brothers and running the household, you know? And they don't do shit. It wouldn't kill them to do a load of laundry every once in a while."

People jokingly call her the team's grandma, but Mercury, at seventeen, knows who she wants her family to be, knows who appreciates her and loves her and wants her there. I want to take her hand so badly.

"You want to walk around?" I ask.

Mercury finishes her corn dog and wipes mustard off her fingers with a napkin. "Yeah. I love people-watching here." We move up and down the midway, pressed close together by the crowd, and I feel a jolt each time our hands brush. I know Eden didn't exactly give me her blessing, but she also didn't stop me. Even here, where someone from derby could easily see us, it feels like the barriers have lifted away, and there's just Mercury and me, navigating through the crowd together as the sky gets darker and the carnival music and twinkling lights on the rides drift overhead.

A huge group of middle schoolers pushes past us, almost separating us, and Mercury grabs my hand. "Better than a leash," she says with a smile. I want to call her *Sonia*, want to say the name like it's a secret between us.

"Okay," I say instead, "which of these rides *won't* make me throw up?"

Mercury glances up the midway, and her face lights up. "Come on," she says, and she's taking my hand and leading me through the crowd, purposeful.

The carousel is at the center of the park, under a huge gazebo with lights strung all across it. A few people ride the bobbing wooden animals, but there's no line. "This is about the only thing I would ride," Mercury says as we pause by the fence, watching. A little girl keeps slipping off her mount, checking to make sure the ride operator can't see her, then running to a different one, scrambling up onto its back while the ride is moving.

"Let's go."

Mercury looks sidelong at me, eyebrows raised. "Really?"

"I think I can handle slow circles," I say, and Mercury stifles a giggle.

When the ride stops next, the operator opens the gate to let us on. Mercury steps up onto the platform first, extending a hand for me. I take it, and I realize I love the way her hands are always warm and smooth, so different from when I grab her wrist guard during practice.

The light under the gazebo's roof is warm, bathing the carousel animals in gold. There are more than horses—I see a wooden zebra, a white tiger, a rooster, a roaring lion. "Come on," Mercury says, and she grabs my hand. Time seems to slow as I follow her, winding through the chipped horses and dragons and elephants. She looks back at me, just once, and the lights are like jewels in her hair, her eyes, the glittery blush on her cheeks.

We reach a row with a yawning giraffe and an ostrich side by side, their legs outstretched in a race. "This one's my favorite," Mercury says, swinging herself up onto the giraffe.

I grab the bar protruding from the ostrich, throwing one leg over its back and settling into the plastic saddle. The carousel shudders to life, and Mercury's giraffe rises first, gently lifting her toward the twinkling lights while my ostrich dips down. I can't stop myself from watching her—she throws her head back like she's riding her giraffe into battle, her blue dress rippling in the breeze, a devious grin on her face.

And then—then she looks at me.

Mercury's eyes catch mine, and her gaze softens, her grin faltering like she's seeing me for the first time.

When the carousel grinds to a halt, it feels like it's only been seconds. Wordlessly, we slide off our mounts, and Mercury takes my hand again. This time, she threads her fingers through mine. My heart feels like it's going to beat out of my chest. *Don't overthink it.* I'm suddenly overcome with a need to impress her, to show her how confident and comfortable I am, to do something brave and maybe a little bit stupid.

"I need a break," I blurt out, and Mercury looks back at me, puzzled.

"Huh?"

"I just—I wanna get out of the crowd for a sec." I tug her hand, an idea blossoming in my mind. "Come on."

We wind back across the midway and through the parking lot, and dart through the cars to the Hangar.

"Moose." Mercury laughs as we go around the side of the building, away from the main entrance. "What are we doing?"

"This side door always sticks," I tell her, grabbing the handle and jiggling it. "I've seen Eden open it, like, a million times. She never remembers the code for the front door." The door clicks. I pull it open, ceremonially gesturing Mercury through first. She ducks inside, taking my hand and pulling me in after her.

The door clangs shut behind us. The Hangar is dark except for an emergency light at the back, illuminating a single turn of the track and a square of bleachers.

"I've never been in here alone," Mercury says, her voice echoing in the high, empty room. She strides out to the middle of the track, then spins on one heel to face me and holds out a hand, one eyebrow raised. "Ever taken a whip?"

I blanch. "Excuse me?"

Mercury grins mischievously. "In *derby*. Get your mind out of the gutter, Burnout."

I skip across the track and clap my hand into hers, and Mercury swings me around her, hurling me toward the other side of the track. I stumble over my own feet and almost faceplant, but Mercury catches me by my other arm and hauls me back up, laughing. "I'm not wearing *skates* right now, Captain!" I sputter, shoving her playfully. "You can't just fling me around the track!"

"But it's so much fun," Mercury replies, and we both realize she's still holding my arm. Her grip softens slightly, but she's probably already squeezed it hard enough to leave little fingerprint-shaped bruises. They'll join the ones I already have from derby practice this week. She doesn't let go of my arm, and I realize I don't want her to.

"Should we do something bad?" Mercury asks coyly.

"What did you have in mind?" My heart is in danger of beating out of my chest.

"I know where they keep the key for the bar." She spins again and jogs off the track to the beer fridge in the corner, only opened for adult games. I follow her, unwilling to lose sight of her for even a second.

"Not very captain-like of you."

"I don't care anymore," Mercury calls from where she's disappeared behind the bar. She emerges with a key held triumphantly aloft. Emboldened, I go to the cabinet by the front door while Mercury opens the beer fridge. I've pulled scrimmage caps and Sharpies and spare skate laces out of the cabinet before, and I know there's a basket of emergency candles and a lighter for power outages shoved in the back. I glare at the lighter, daring it to trigger my panic. It doesn't. I feel powerful in here, sneaking around and breaking the rules.

"And those are for . . . ?" Mercury asks as I turn around with the basket under one arm.

"Ambiance."

Mercury gives me a sly look as she turns around with two cans of wine. She jerks her head at me to follow her. I don't quite recognize this impulsive, rule-breaking Mercury, but I follow her anyway, heart thudding.

We go around the bleachers to a flight of narrow metal stairs. They lead up to the mezzanine, a rickety balcony where the announcers and scorekeepers sit during games to see the action easily. I confidently climb the stairs after her, following the hem of her blue dress.

There's a threadbare Persian rug on the mezzanine, and Mercury kicks off her sneakers while I line the scorekeeper's table with candles. "We are definitely not supposed to be up here," she says, but her voice is giddy.

"You're setting a terrible example as my captain," I tell her, but I feel giddy too, like I've been up all night and everything is funny. I push down the safety on the lighter and click it to life. There's a hot flicker of fear when the flame appears, but I point the lighter downward, lighting the wicks of the candles on the table to bathe the mezzanine in a warm glow. Mercury sits cross-legged on the Persian rug and opens her can of wine. She drinks probably too much of it, too fast.

I open the can Mercury offers me and take a sip because it seems like the right thing to do. The wine is bitter on my tongue, but it also feels heady, light, like kissing Mercury. I follow her lead and take a longer drink. When I lower it, Mercury's watching me, her dark eyes reflecting the candlelight. She's looked at me like this before—on the ridge and in practice and in Carmen's attic and in my bedroom and every single time I see her.

I lean over toward her, and I love kissing her here, in the darkness of the Hangar, a little buzzed from stolen wine and in a cavernous space we're definitely not supposed to be in.

"Captaining the Hot Shots isn't everything," she says. "I don't think I realized it until that night we had to pick up my brothers, when you told me that I didn't have to take care of everybody."

"What about the team?" I ask quietly. Her face glows in the candlelight, a halo around her hair with the vast darkness of the Hangar around us.

"I'm tired of worrying about the team."

Mercury kisses me. I reach up to touch her face, and her hand finds my hip, sliding up my waist. When she touches my bare skin, creeping under my shirt, something deep within me flutters. Then there's only Mercury, and I'm breathing her, lost in her, floating from the bubbly wine and the candlelight and the thrill of being somewhere we're not supposed to be, doing something we're not supposed to do.

I'm dizzy as Mercury leans into me, her hand tangled in my hair. Cautiously, her tongue parts my lips, and then everything is sharp breaths and teeth and lips.

When we've kissed for what feels like decades, we lie facing each other on the worn carpet, our legs tangled, the dark, open space of the Hangar yawning above us. For a while, neither of us speak—I just study every line and mole on her face, reach over to brush her dark hair away from her forehead. She takes my hand, threading her fingers through mine. The world pitches a little from the wine, but Mercury's face stays steady.

"I think this is my favorite place in the whole world," she says softly.

"The Hangar?"

"Yeah, but . . . specifically here. Now." Something in me swells at her words, and I shuffle closer to her, like I can't close the space between us enough. She wraps her arms around me and holds me there, and I feel so incredibly safe against her, like I haven't felt in months. Here, tucked into the high corner of the Hangar that nobody sees, in a pocket of candlelight, nothing can touch us.

Far below, miles away, the Hangar door swings open.

Mercury and I both freeze, our grips tightening on each other as a flashlight beam sweeps across the ceiling. We shuffle back, away from the edge of the mezzanine, and my foot kicks one of the open cans of wine. Mercury lunges for it, but it's already out of reach, rolling off the edge. Cold dread spills over me as the can hits the bleachers below with a metallic clang.

"Hello?" someone calls, and the flashlight points up toward the mezzanine. Mercury and I sit squeezed together, pressed against the wall. I'm gripping her arm so tight I can feel her pulse.

"Let's go," I hiss, and start to pull her toward the stairs at the end of the mezzanine.

"Go *where*?" Mercury whispers back, tugging her arm out of my grip. There's only one way off the mezzanine—the steep, corrugated metal stairs—and the back door is right at the bottom. If Mercury and I can just be faster than whoever's entered the Hangar, we can get out the door and into the woods behind the parking lot before we're caught. But we have to go *now*.

"Merc, come on," I whisper, grabbing her hand again and practically dragging her toward the stairs. The flashlight is still pointed at the mezzanine, and we stay ducked behind the wall, just out of its view. My heart is beating in overdrive, and for a second, I swear I see smoke behind her, menacing, gathering near the ceiling. *No. I'm imagining it. Mercury blew the candles out.*

We reach the top of the stairs and Mercury halts abruptly. "Moose, just—"

"Please," I mutter frantically, trying to drag her with me. I'm spiraling back to the rink, choking back sobs as I struggle to unlace my skates on the melting skate floor. I can't lose Mercury too. "Mer—"

My foot misses the first stair, and then I'm falling, pulling Mercury with me. My vision spins—sharp metal and the dark, faraway ceiling tilting over each other in a blur until we hit concrete at the bottom.

chapter twenty-eight

THE SILENCE IN THE CAR IS HEAVY. I watch Eden through the windshield, her back to the car as she talks to the park security guard who found us in the Hangar. The parking lot is emptying now, park-goers drifting back to their cars even though the Ferris wheel is still lit up and spinning cheerily.

"Are you okay?" My voice is hoarse. It's not from the smoke—there wasn't any smoke. Not really. Maybe it's from screaming. When I woke up after the rink fire, at least I knew why my throat was raw.

"Yeah." Mercury's voice beside me is small. I can't look at her—I don't want to see her curled up, her hands and shins bandaged from both of us falling down the metal stairs, her pretty blue dress shredded at the hem. I don't want to see the way my mess has gotten all over her.

Outside, the security guard claps Eden on the shoulder and returns to his golf cart. I see Eden's shoulders sag in a sigh before she turns and heads back to the car. I stare at my hands—scraped up and raw like Mercury's—as Eden settles into the driver's seat.

"Mercury," Eden says, and for some reason, her voice is hoarse too. "Did you get ahold of your dad?"

"He's working," she mutters. "He can't have his phone on him."

"I'll take you home." She turns the key in the ignition, and the radio automatically turns on, an upbeat Taylor Swift song crackling through the speakers. Eden practically punches the radio in her haste to switch it off.

My phone vibrates, and I turn it over. The screen is still cracked from when I threw it across the school lawn months ago. I'd fired a quick text to Carmen and Powerhouse when Eden got to the Hangar—*Merc and I had to run. Talk tomorrow.* Carmen replied with three lines of question marks that went unanswered.

The car stays silent as Eden pulls out of Oaks and onto the main road.

"Coach," Mercury finally says after ten uncomfortable minutes.

Eden holds up a hand, not looking at her. "I can't right now, Mercury. We'll talk tomorrow."

When we reach Mercury's house, she climbs out awkwardly, pulling her sweater around herself as she walks up to the dark porch. She risks a tiny glance back at the car, but I can't tell what that look means—it's too fleeting, too far away.

I stay in the backseat while Eden drives us back to the apartment, pressing my forehead against the window. I feel like I'm coming down off a high, crashing back into reality with a headache and a sick stomach. My skin still feels hot where Mercury touched me. I feel like the whole car smells like smoke, but it must be in my head. I smelled it for weeks after the rink fire, even in the pristine hospital. I worried then that it would never go away.

Finally, we pull up outside the apartment. Eden puts the car in park and makes no attempt to get out, staring at the dashboard. "What were you doing, Moose?" she finally asks, and her voice is hollow.

When Eden's car screeched up outside the park office earlier, she'd stumbled out of it in a panic, choking back sobs, her face streaked with tears. The security guard who called her wasn't clear enough, just said there'd been an accident and we were okay but she needed to come pick me up. She had crossed the office in three quick strides, pulling me into a hug, shaking. I felt like a dead animal in her arms, unable to move, think, feel. Now I hear the cold disappointment in my sister's voice.

"We just wanted some privacy," I say finally. "It was really crowded."

A sliver of Eden's face is lit orange from the streetlamp, and I can just see that her eyes are hard. "The Hangar isn't your clubhouse," she says. "You can't just go whenever you want and steal alcohol and hang out with your friends. Y'all are lucky nobody else was hurt."

"Eden—"

"No, I'm not done, Moose." She cuts me off, shifting in her seat so she's looking back at me. "Do you understand what that building is for so many people? There are people who don't have homes, don't have family outside of derby. It's all they have. And you disrespected that. The park owner has been talking about kicking the entire league out of the Hangar for two years, and this doesn't help our case."

"What? But nobody was hurt," I say, pleading. "And it was minor. It's not like we burned the building down."

"It's *not* about the building!" she snaps, her voice so loud it makes me jump. "It's *more* than that, Moose! You violated my trust, and the trust of the entire league! God, I—I know you've been through hell this year, but you can't just do whatever you want!"

"I did one thing!" I say incredulously. "Don't you know the shit other people my age get up to?"

"I'm not talking about other people." Eden turns around, takes a deep breath, steadies herself. "I can't talk about this right now," she mumbles, unbuckling her seat belt and shuffling out of the car. She slams the door harder than she needs to.

I jump out after her. "So, what, am I grounded?" I call, following her up to the porch. "Putting me on suicide watch again?"

Eden whirls around. "I don't know, Moose!" she yells. Her voice breaks. "I need to talk to Prince and the league coordinator. Just—just give me a minute to think!" She turns back to the door, fumbling with her key. Her hand is shaking, missing the lock. "*Damn* it!" she snarls, kicking the door in frustration.

I'm silent, watching a lone car drive slowly down the street, headlights illuminating crushed petals on the road. "Am I getting kicked off the team?"

"I don't know," Eden says, quieter. She finally jams the key into the lock, turns it, pushes the door open.

"You can't kick me off," I say, a note of panic in my voice now. "Eden. Seriously. It's—" *It's all I have.* I stop before I start crying too.

Eden storms up the stairs to her apartment door, unlocks it, points me inside. "Just go to bed, Moose," she says, angry and exhausted. "We'll talk in the morning."

I want to fight her, demand an answer, walk her through the night so she understands why she can't kick me off the team. This wasn't how the night was supposed to go—I was supposed to get home on cloud nine, heart bursting with thoughts of Mercury, curl up on the couch to talk to Eden about it late into the night. We were supposed to be sisters. At least for tonight.

She's in the kitchen now, clutching the edge of the sink with her back to me, and I can see the tension in her shoulders. She doesn't want to talk.

I go to my room, slam the door, and lie awake for hours.

I'm still awake when Eden knocks on my door in the morning. I stared at my broken phone all night, waiting for Mercury to text me. About fifty times, I went to type out a new message to her, but my thumb just hovered over the cracked screen, uncertain. Once, around four a.m., I saw a typing bubble show up. It vanished after a minute, and a message never appeared.

Eden doesn't look like she's slept much, either. "Get dressed," she tells me stiffly. "We need to be at the Hangar early."

I feel a surge of hope at her words. "I'm still on the team?"

"I don't know," Eden says, and the air leaves my lungs. "We're getting there early to talk to Prince and the league coordinator. She'll have final say."

Both of us are silent the whole way to the Hangar. I brought my skates and my gear, cautiously, like having them in the trunk would help my chances of not getting kicked off the Hot Shots. I fiddle with a loose thread on my sweatshirt, hoping I'll have a chance to actually skate today. Skating would help. I think. There's a smear of glitter on the side of my hand from Mercury's blush last night, one that somehow lasted through the hours of tossing and turning. I wonder if she'll be at practice. My stomach turns over.

The Hangar is nearly empty when we get there, most of the floodlights over the track switched off. I feel a waver of dread as I look up at the mezzanine, half expecting to see a menacing black smoke stain on the ceiling. But it looks the same as it always does. The fallen can that doomed us is still under the bleachers below the mezzanine, probably lying in a sticky puddle of spilled wine. Prince and a tired-looking brunette woman are in the office by the track, the door ajar.

"Wait here," Eden tells me, and she keeps walking, slipping into the office and closing the door behind her. The league coordinator pulls a shade over the window, her disapproving eyes catching me for a split second.

I slump onto the bleachers, dropping my gear bag at my feet. Instinctively, I pull my phone from my pocket. No messages. I even open Bitch Pod 2 to make sure. The Hot Shots group text is suspiciously silent, too. Did they already hear about what happened? Are they icing me out? They probably started another text without me. *Did you hear the new girl freaked out and pushed Mercury down the stairs?*

The Hangar door squeaks open, and I turn, too fast. Mercury freezes by the door, clutching her rolling gear bag. She's not wearing any makeup, not even her red lipstick, and she looks drawn. Her shins and hands are still bandaged up, and her thighs are ribboned with more bruises than usual.

"Hi," she says. She's awkwardly far from my spot on the bleachers, and her voice echoes.

"Hi."

Mercury fidgets for a second, then takes a breath and drags her bag toward me. She sits, just a little too far from me on the bleachers. Stares at her hands, twists a silver ring around her thumb.

"Mercury."

She looks up at me.

"I'm sorry."

Her hands still. "For what?"

"I shouldn't have opened the door. This is my fault."

Mercury shakes her head. "I'm not a little kid, Moose. I should've known better."

Before I can reply, the office door opens. Mercury and I both turn, and my heart feels tight in my chest. Prince's face looks exhausted, and Eden's pinched. Behind them, the league coordinator shuts the door again.

"Okay," Prince says, crossing their arms. "You're both still on the team. Mercury, we're letting you keep your captaincy because this is the first time anything like this has ever happened. But one more situation, and it's gone, okay?"

Mercury nods, her face ashen.

I look from Mercury, to Prince, to Eden. "What's the catch?"

Eden gives me a look. "You're both benched for the next bout."

My heart plummets. "What?"

Eden raises a hand to stop me. "It's not up for debate."

"The next bout is the Benton Brawlers," I say, casting a glance at Mercury. She's just staring at her feet again. "You can't bench both of us. The Hot Shots'll get slaughtered."

"This isn't about the game," Eden says, strained. "Last night could have been much worse. There need to be consequences for your actions, Moose."

"At the expense of the team?" I snarl, my voice getting louder. Eden gives me a warning look, but I press forward. "You're gonna fuck over all the Hot Shots for the whole championship, just to teach us a lesson? Punish us *after* champs!"

"Moose," Prince says, their voice warning.

"We'll get destroyed without three jammers! And Mercury's the best pivot on the team—you know that!"

"Stop it," Mercury hisses.

"You want us to lose now, after all the work we've been putting in?"

"*ENOUGH!*" Eden shouts, and her voice echoes in the empty Hangar. The door creaks, and we turn. Himaslaya and Apex have just entered, looking at us with wide eyes. Whispering, Himaslaya pushes Apex back outside.

I turn to meet Eden's gaze, glaring.

"Enough," she says again, pinching the bridge of her nose. "I'm *this* close to benching you for the champs game too. Don't push it."

"But—"

"You want to be off the team for good?"

I fall silent, fuming.

Eden pushes her hair back, and I notice her hands are shaking. "Get geared up," she says, her voice hard.

I seize my bag, heave it over my shoulder, and storm toward the door.

"Where are you going?" Eden calls.

"I'm not skating."

She catches my arm, and I twist around, glaring at her. "Yes, you are," she snarls. "Grow up, Moose. This is a team." I hold her gaze, furious, until she breaks first, dropping my arm and heading to the other side of the bleachers. Prince trails her, touching her arm comfortingly.

I turn back to Mercury. "Seriously? You're just going to let her bench us?"

"We broke the rules," Mercury says, her voice hollow.

"Mercury, come on. They're gonna get destroyed without us next week."

She raises her hands, defeated. "Please, Moose. I just want to focus on practice today."

"Fine."

I retreat to the other side of the bleachers, glowering at the ground as I yank my gear on. From the corner of my eye, I see Mercury retreat to our usual spot on the bleachers. The rest of the team starts to trickle in, and I glance up when I hear Carmen's familiar voice. She and Powerhouse join Mercury, and she casts a curious glance my way.

I look back down at my skates, lacing them way tighter than I need to. My feet are going to cramp within fifteen minutes, but I don't care.

When we gather in the middle of the track for announcements, Mercury stays on the other side of the circle, not looking at me. Carmen drifts around the back of the circle to my side, poking me in the ribs. "Why did you two leave last night?" she whispers. "Mercury wouldn't tell me."

"Don't worry about it," I say stiffly. Carmen looks frustrated, but she doesn't press it. Acid's openly staring at me, but for once, she doesn't look hostile.

"Okay," Prince says, glancing at her clipboard. She's off-skates today, her curly hair piled on top of her head in a bun. "Coaches have been asked to remind everybody that this building is off-limits when there is not a practice or a game happening. And juniors are not allowed on the mezzanine without supervision. Capiche?"

"I heard they're kicking us out of the Hangar," Acid says, and I shoot her the most withering glare I can muster. To my surprise, though, Acid looks genuinely worried at the prospect of us losing our practice space.

"Why would they kick us out of the Hangar?" Carmen asks. I stare hard at the ground.

"Nobody is getting kicked out," Prince replies calmly.

"But they might not renew our lease for next year, right?" Acid presses. "Because someone stole alcohol?" Around the circle, my teammates whisper. I risk a glance up—Carmen is looking back and forth between Mercury and me, her brow furrowed.

"We don't know anything for certain yet," Prince says. "And there's nothing we can do about it right now. But it's a good reminder that we need to treat this space with respect, just like we treat each other."

"But—" Acid starts.

"We have a couple new skaters today," Prince continues, "joining us from the recent draft. Y'all want to introduce yourselves?" Acid looks annoyed at being cut off, but she doesn't interrupt again. Guilt floods through me. The whole league—not just all three junior teams, but the three hundred adult skaters and officials and volunteers too—are going to lose our venue because of Mercury and me. But mostly me.

There are two nervous-looking skaters to my left, one wearing skates that are at least three sizes too big. "I'm Marie," she says, giving us all a hopeful smile. "She/her pronouns. I don't have a derby name yet."

"Brawlee Pocket," the other says. "They/them. I'm transferring from Salem."

Prince has us go around and do names and pronouns for the new skaters. I watch Marie the entire time. She looks exactly like I did six months ago, jittery and self-conscious, but hopeful. Gamma Raze says something to her, and they both giggle. It makes me feel even sorrier for myself, and *that* makes me angry.

Mercury avoids me during the whole first half of the practice. I partner with Queenie for the pushcart drill, and I ignore Eden completely when she comes around and tries to correct my posture.

"Yo, you okay?" Queenie asks when Eden skates away, shaking her head.

"Mercury and I are off the roster for the next game," I say bitterly.

Queenie's face pales. "What? No way. We'll get destroyed."

"I know. Tell the coaches that."

We move into scrimmage scenarios, and Eden splits us into two groups, one on either side of the track. Mercury and Carmen are in the other group, while Powerhouse hovers near me. Powerhouse, mercifully, doesn't ask me if I'm okay or try to talk to me. They just give me a knowing look, as if to say *relax*. It only works for a second.

Acid takes the star for my group, and I snatch the other jammer cap out of Prince's hand before anyone else can get to it. I skate onto the track, orienting myself to face the wall. I prop myself on one toe stop on the jam line, waiting for the five-second whistle. I'm determined to show Eden and Prince what a mistake they're making, prove that taking me off the roster is a mistake. The anger radiates off me in waves.

Prince blows the whistle, and I spring off my toe stop, slamming into the wall. I shove my shoulder into Apex's ribs, harder than I need to, and she twists to one side. Queenie catches me with her chest, but I juke sharply to one side, then the other, tricking her into diving in the wrong direction. I skirt around her, and Prince whistles twice, declaring me lead jammer.

We're supposed to stop skating when we clear the pack so we don't run into the group on the other side. I make it into the turn before Acid appears out of nowhere. She slams into me from behind, catching me off-balance and whipping past me, not even turning to look.

"Acid!" I snarl, and my voice cuts above the rest of the sound in the Hangar. She's skating toward the other group, just trying to outpace me.

I reorient myself and run on my toe stops, building speed.

"Stop!" Eden shouts, but I'm chasing Acid into the other pack, my face hot, teeth bared. She darts through the blockers, and I'm right on her tail, doubled over, shins burning. A blocker steps into my path, and I light them up without thinking, slamming my shoulder into their chest and sending them sprawling to the ground. I jump over them, flipping around to skate backward and hitting Acid in the turn. She stumbles, losing her balance, and goes down, sliding across the track.

I lower a toe stop, sliding to a halt, my chest heaving. The Hangar is silent. Half the team is staring at me, and the other half is gathered around the blocker I knocked down.

"What the fuck, Burnout?" Apex asks harshly.

Panting, I look over at the downed blocker.

It's Marie, the brand-new draftee with the too-big skates. She's on her back, breathing fast, with Prince and Carmen kneeling at her side.

Fuck.

Out of nowhere, Mercury's rolling toward me, her face screwed up in rage. "You *don't* hit a new skater like that!" she shouts, and everyone's staring now. "You could have injured her!"

"I—"

"Not everything is about you, Moose!"

There are too many people staring, too many whispers. Marie is crying on the floor, and my shoulder feels hot where I hit her in the chest. Mercury's in my face like she was last night, but this time she's furious, boiling over, and she looks ready to punch me in the face.

Panic claws up.

I push past Mercury, skating off the track as my breath tears my throat. It's too sharp, too hot, too many people. The air's too thin. I can't breathe.

I push open the Hangar door and roll into the sunlight, sucking in a breath. The air is fresher here, not stale and sweaty like in the Hangar. The door clangs shut behind me, and I double over, clutching my knees. The ground tilts. Anxiety squeezes my lungs. I drop to my knees, then my stomach, my breath heaving against the ground.

I should do the five senses thing to ground myself. But the only thing registering is the blood on my teeth. I bit my lip at some point. Or maybe I got high blocked. Either way, the coppery taste lingers on my tongue.

I close my eyes, breathing out slowly.

The Hangar door opens, then clangs shut.

I peel myself off the ground, grimacing. I fucked up. I'm off the team.

But it's Powerhouse kneeling down next to me, their long green braids brushing the pavement. "She's okay," Powerhouse says calmly. "Just winded. She'll be fine."

I'm crying then, out of nowhere, and Powerhouse kneels beside me, rubbing my back. They don't say anything, and they don't need to. There's nothing to say.

chapter twenty-nine

EDEN AND I BARELY TALK THAT WEEK. I half-ass my homework in my room, the door closed. Dr. Parikh is on vacation, so I don't have to deal with therapy. I think about texting her. She gave me her cell phone number and told me to contact her if I'm in crisis, no matter what time or day. But stewing in my own anger in my room feels more satisfying, so I leave my phone face down on the nightstand. Typo cries and scratches at the door at first, then gives up, leaving me alone. Eden doesn't even try.

Mercury doesn't text me. She avoids eye contact with me in history, coming in right before the bell and rushing out as soon as we're dismissed so she doesn't have to talk to me. Bitch Pod 2 is silent, and I'm sure they've gone back to their original group text, probably talking about how insane I am. Carmen texts me three times (**What were yall doing?? Was it you and merc in the hangar?? Are you dating??**) and I don't answer. Powerhouse texts me once (**Moose, are you okay?**), and I ignore them.

I barely sleep, lying awake and staring at the popcorn ceiling. Once the light under my door is off and I hear Eden's door close, I touch the thick scar on my neck. I work my way down each unfriendly bump of it until it ends at the hollow of my throat. It feels like the rubbery scar is growing further into me every night, eating away what's left of me.

I don't want to go to the Brawlers game on Friday, don't want to see Mercury's disappointment or Acid's contempt. But Eden knocks on my door for the first time in a week, holding my crumpled orange jersey against her hip.

"You're still part of the Hot Shots," she says. She sounds exhausted, shadows under her eyes. I don't think she's been sleeping either. "It's important for you to be there and support your teammates."

"They don't want me there." I turn over in bed, staring at the wall.

Eden pauses, sighs. "You don't get to decide how they feel, Moose." From the corner of my eye, I see her toss the jersey. It lands on my legs, a splash of violent orange against the green bedspread. I hear her turn and leave the door ajar. I check my phone. No messages.

Maybe there's a chance I haven't completely fucked this up. I sit up, holding up the jersey and flipping it around. My derby name, *BURNOUT*, seems to taunt me. I pull off my T-shirt and slide the jersey over my head anyway.

The Brawlers bout is a daytime game, and the Hangar doors are thrown open to usher in the warm spring air. I linger in the parking lot before following Eden inside, glancing over my shoulder at the roller rink. I haven't made it any closer to going inside the rink, the goal I set for myself with Dr. Parikh. It feels completely insurmountable now that a year has passed.

The bleachers are empty when I trail Eden into the Hangar, soon to be filled with parents and skaters from the other teams and random people that want to watch teenagers reenact *Whip It* on a Saturday afternoon. I perch on one of the benches while the rest of the team trickles in, heading to the locker rooms to gear up, laughing with their hair in braids and their skates bouncing against their hips.

I should join them, apologize, try to ease back in. I should pull Mercury aside, try to talk to her. I've just stood up when I spot Acid crossing the Hangar to the locker room, trailed by D-Monic and Firebolt. Acid somehow zeroes in on me from the other side of the track, giving me a cold look before she disappears into the locker room.

I sit back down.

The referees shoo me off the bench when it's time for their warmup, and I drag myself to the locker room, lingering outside the open door. I can see Carmen inside, sitting cross-legged and laughing as she paints orange glitter on Queenie's face. Everyone's talking, pulling on their jerseys, tightening their wheels, ripping open applesauce packets to down a few last-minute calories. I don't know what feels worse: knowing that I'm not gearing up with them to play or knowing they don't want me in the locker room.

"Oh."

I turn—Marie, the new draftee that I slammed into last weekend, is standing awkwardly outside the door, her arms full of freshly filled water bottles. "Sorry," she says, sidestepping me. "I'm just—"

"Marie," I try, but she's already slipping into the locker room, passing out water bottles. Someone calls her name, and she laughs.

I slouch outside the door, shame prickling my neck.

Prince appears, heading for the locker room with their clipboard in hand. "Get in there, Burnout," they tell me. "Coach Talk starting now."

“I’m not skating.”

“You’re still part of the team, and thus can benefit from Coach Talk.”

Reluctantly, I slide into the crowded locker room, immediately feeling the heat and gear stink of so many skaters pressed together. Mercury glances at me for the barest second before her eyes flit away. She’s wearing a knit red sweater in lieu of her jersey, orange ribbons braided through her hair and glitter sparkling on her cheeks. It feels wrong to see her in the Hangar without skates on. She still looks mad.

“Okay,” Prince says, shushing the Hot Shots. “I know we’re down a couple key skaters today. But we’re not gonna let it faze us. Acid and Powerhouse will be our primary jammers today, and we’ll cycle in Bolt and Carmen when they need a break.”

Carmen looks like she’s going to throw up.

When Prince finishes her pep talk, there’s a halfhearted team cheer before everyone gets to their feet, filing out of the locker room to do warmups. I hover near the door, staring at the ground. Mercury walks right past me. Carmen looks hurt, but reaches out to squeeze my hand anyway when she and Powerhouse go by. I’m angry, and I want Acid to say something bratty so I can scoff and roll my eyes the way she’s always doing to me at practice. But she just rolls silently past me, not even meeting my gaze. It makes me madder.

I find a spot in the bleachers near our bench when the game starts. Marie is already perched on the end of the bench, wearing Mercury’s jersey and armed with ice packs and snacks. I’m pretty sure she doesn’t want to talk to me.

The Benton Brawlers look intimidatingly stronger than us. Their warmup was like a full-on scrimmage, and when they line up for the first jam, they’re firm, immovable. The whistle blows, and the

Brawlers jammer immediately springs forward, easily winding around the Hot Shots blockers before Powerhouse even touches the wall. Two short whistle blasts give the lead to the Brawlers.

This is going to suck.

Eden is supposed to focus only on getting the next lineup of skaters ready, but she keeps glancing over her shoulder, biting her lip in worry as the Brawlers shut our jammers down. My pod seems lost without Mercury's sharp directions—Apex has taken her place in our pod, but nobody seems to know where they should be on the track. The Brawlers move like a well-oiled machine, cleanly breaking up our blockers for their jammer to get through, then re-forming at lightning speed to catch the Hot Shots jammer. Even Acid is struggling, her face twisted up in frustration as she throws herself fruitlessly at the pack.

I look up at the scoreboard: the Brawlers are leading by ninety points, and it's not even halftime yet. My legs bounce up and down, frustrated. I study Acid's movements on the track—she's too caught up in her head to notice the spots where she could sneak through the pack. They're all getting flustered, spiraling into penalties.

When halftime finally comes, we're behind by over a hundred points. Eden and Prince call the Hot Shots in for a huddle, and they all look dejected already. I see the top of Mercury's head as she gives them a pep talk, probably trying to soothe the sloppy chaos on the track.

"Rough game," the guy beside me remarks. "Hot Shots aren't usually this scattered."

I jump off the bleachers when the Hot Shots break apart to refill their water bottles for the next half. Mercury's still at the bench, talking to Eden and Prince. They all turn to look at me when I reach them, and Mercury's gaze is cold.

"Put us in."

Prince sighs, and I see a vein pulse in Eden's neck.

"No, Burnout."

"We can use loaner skates. We have time to gear up right now. If you put us in, we can turn it around." Mercury's staring at me like I've gone insane. "I'm not saying I'm the best jammer," I say quickly, "but Powerhouse and Acid are exhausted. They're not scoring, and the alternates you're putting in don't know how to jam and aren't scoring either. You need one more person who actually practices jamming in the rotation."

"Moose," Eden says sharply. "You're not skating. End of discussion."

"But—"

"Don't ask again." She throws her clipboard onto the bench and walks away, running her fingers through her hair.

The second half starts even worse. Carmen spirals, getting so many penalties that she fouls out and is ordered off the track by the refs. Her face is red when she skates back to the locker room, and I can't tell if she wants to cry or punch someone. Mercury keeps walking up and down the bench, trying to calm the flustered Hot Shots, but it's making them worse—every jam, the Brawlers easily disintegrate the Hot Shots' walls. We go seven jams in a row without scoring.

When there are fifteen minutes left on the clock, I'm clenching my fists in my lap, biting my lip. I twist around to look at the gear cage. I know it's stupid, know how much trouble it could get me into . . . but I can't let the Hot Shots lose this badly.

I shuffle down off the bleachers and punch the code into the gear cage, flicking on the light. I'm barely thinking as I grab kneepads, elbow pads, a pair of scuffed skates and a worn helmet. The Velcro on the wrist guards barely sticks anymore, but it'll have to do. I find my mouthguard in my sweatshirt pocket and pop it in, scrambling to pull the gear on while the crowd screams and groans outside.

I roll out of the cage, not bothering to close the door as I skate around the bleachers and onto the bench. Marie is the first one to see me—her eyes widen, and she nudges Mercury.

I ignore them both and go straight to Eden.

She turns. "No."

"Put me in," I almost shout, lisping around my mouthguard. "I'm geared up, I'm ready—"

"No!" Eden yells, and the Hot Shots on the bench jump. "You're not skating, Moose! How many times do I have to say it?"

"We're not going to champs if you let them keep playing like this!" I fire back, waving an arm at the track. The referees are looking now—someone calls a time-out.

"You should've thought of that before you broke into the Hangar!"

I whip around, addressing the pod waiting to go out onto the track. "You can't let them rip up your defense like that," I tell them hurriedly. "You're fucking up the start formation."

"Stop it!" Mercury's standing now, glaring at me. "Shut up, Moose! We're not playing for the fucking Hydra!"

A referee appears, his mouth a hard line. "You need to take this off the track, or you're forfeiting the rest of the game."

"That would be better than this shitshow!" I yell, and I instantly regret the words. The Hot Shots are all staring at me with mingled expressions of hurt and anger.

"Locker room," Eden snarls, pointing. "Now."

I push her hand away, ripping off the loaner helmet as I skate to the locker room. I kick the door open and throw myself onto one of the benches, yanking off my pads. I'm throwing them down, losing them in the piles of everyone else's stuff. I don't care.

The door opens again, and Eden's filling the doorframe, her face screwed up in rage. "What's wrong with you?"

"Are you kidding me?" I yell, pulling off a loaner skate. "I find the one thing that makes me not want to die every time I look in a mirror, and you take it away? What's wrong with *you*?"

"This is a team, Moose!" Eden's clutching her clipboard so hard that her knuckles are white. "You don't talk to your team like that. And you don't disobey your coaches like that!"

"You're my sister!"

"I'm your *coach* on that track!"

"Okay, *Coach*," I snarl, "sorry for assuming my *sister* would have some fucking sympathy for me."

Eden's hair is frizzy, an angry vein pulsing in her forehead. "I put my whole life on pause for you—and you *still* act like you can do whatever the fuck you want without any consequences. Grow up, Moose!"

"I don't need you!" I shout. "I don't fucking need you, Eden!"

"If you thought about someone other than yourself for half a second, you'd realize you're not the only one whose life that fire *ruined*!"

Silence.

Eden and I hold each other's furious gazes for another second before Eden's face crumples. She covers her mouth with one hand. "Moose," she says, her voice hoarse. "I didn't mean— It's just really hard, you know, suddenly being responsible for somebody else—"

I pull off the other loaner skate, drop it harder than I need to. "Don't bother," I mutter, and I push past her. Eden's calling my name, but I'm already at the gear cage, grabbing my shoes and sweatshirt and darting out the side door.

The door clangs shut behind me, muffling the music and the

whistles and the cheers. It's still light out, but the sun is sinking lower, the sky turning pink. It'll be dark by the time the game is over.

I take a deep, shuddering breath, waiting for the panic to come. But there's nothing. I feel weirdly numb. Eden's words ring in my head. *Ruined.* I don't know why I'm surprised—she made a choice to not be in my life for ten years. Of course she's relieved to get rid of me.

The door doesn't open. I hear the game keep going, the groans and sharp whistles. When there's an underwhelming smatter of applause, I know we've lost.

I slide down the exterior wall of the Hangar, pulling on my shoes.

The noise inside the Hangar starts to die down, and I hear car doors closing, the crunch of gravel as they pull away. I should go back inside and find Eden. But I can't drag myself off the ground.

It's dark by the time the door finally swings out, almost hitting me, and I shuffle to the side, bracing myself for Eden's fury.

But it's Acid looking down at me, her skate bag over one shoulder, her long hair thrown up into a sweaty bun on top of her head. There's no malice in her expression. She looks legitimately surprised to see me.

I don't say anything, and Acid steps outside, letting the door fall closed. We watch each other for a second, both of us trying to figure out the mood.

"We lost," she says finally.

"Yeah. I figured. Is Eden pissed?" I ask. I don't have the energy to be mad at Acid anymore. She was right, after all—she wasn't the one who broke into the Hangar. Acid sighs, fishes a vape out of her skate bag, and takes a hit.

"You could say that." She rolls her eyes when she sees me looking critically at the vape pen. "I have no plans to go on to play professional roller derby, or whatever. I can wreck my lungs if I want."

"Okay."

She raises an eyebrow, like she was expecting a fight, and blows a puff to one side.

"Hey," I say after a moment, twisting a loose thread on my sweatshirt. "Can you give me a ride?"

"You're not going with your sister?"

I scoff. "She doesn't want anything to do with me. Trust me."

Acid shrugs, nods toward her car. "Let's go."

Acid's car is messy, the floor and passenger seat littered with crumpled takeout wrappers. "Just throw those on the backseat," she says, dumping her skate bag in the back and sliding behind the wheel. Acid rolls down the window as she pulls away from the Hangar, taking another hit from her vape before tossing it in the backseat. "Where am I taking you?"

I flip my phone over and over in my hands. An idea's forming in my head. It's stupid, and I'll get in even more trouble. But I'm past caring.

"Is there a train station in Portland?"

Acid looks over at me, skeptical. "Seriously?"

"Yeah. Eden doesn't want me here."

Acid studies me a moment, then accelerates way too fast up a hill, and the seat belt nearly chokes me when she brakes. "You sure?"

"I thought you'd be happy to get me out of here," I say wryly.

"I don't hate you, Burnout," she sighs. "God. But if that's what you want."

I study her a moment. "Do you still love Mercury?"

Acid's jaw tightens. She doesn't look at me.

"Is that why you're always glaring at me and trying to mess with me in drills?" I press.

"It's complicated."

"Is it?"

"You want to get to the train station?" Acid snaps.

I shut up.

A long silence stretches between us. Acid pulls onto the bridge, coasting the car across the river. "We lost our shot at champs last year because of Mercury."

"Yeah. Carmen told me."

Acid scoffs. "Yeah. I'm sure she did. She tell you how?"

"Kind of."

"I used to be the jammer in Mercury's pod. She stopped paying attention to the gameplay. I'd sprained my ankle the month before, and she was worried about me being safe skating in the qualifying bout. She was watching me when she should've been watching the track, and the Brawlers got through and won." Acid taps on the steering wheel, lips pursed. "She broke up with me right after that bout. Didn't even wait until they'd swept the fucking track."

"Acid—"

"I'm not telling you this so you'll be my friend or something. I'm telling you because Mercury decided that she's always gonna care about the Hot Shots more than she cares about any one person. And when she ages out of the junior program and joins an adult team, she's gonna care more about them. She'll fall for you, then something will happen and she'll realize she betrayed the team or whatever, so she'll ruin it. Derby is, like, her whole fuckin' life."

"Why shouldn't it be?"

Acid glances over at me. "My mom played derby too, you know."

"How would I know that?"

"She was on the adult travel team for a couple seasons. Big deal while she was around. She started skating when I was a kid, after getting out of this really crappy relationship, and she got totally addicted to it. Then she got one too many concussions, and the doctor told her she had to choose her brain or derby. So she quit. And nobody even remembers her. She doesn't do shit anymore, doesn't even come to my games, because she says it's too loud and it hurts her head."

There's a weird twist in my stomach, like pity. "Sorry," I say awkwardly, because I'm not sure what else there is to say.

"I guess what I'm saying is, it's not always going to be there. At some point, you'll get a real bad concussion, or break your ankle in just the right spot, or you'll get to practice one day and realize you aren't having fun anymore. And you'll retire, and your team will say they'll miss you, but they'll forget you exist within a season. And the only thing you'll have to show for it will be your old jersey and fucked-up knees."

"Then why are you still here?"

Acid laughs humorlessly. "Just because I'm aware of how cultlike this is doesn't mean I'm immune to it."

"Derby isn't like that for everybody."

"You haven't been here that long. It'll get there. When it's all you care about and it gets taken away, you're left with nothing."

Is derby all I care about? I stare out the window as we head toward downtown, trying to tally in my head. I cared about Eden, but I was just in her way. Mercury, but I fucked that up too. Dads, but they're gone.

I'm silent until Acid pulls up to the station, a squat brick building with a clock tower rising up the front. There's a light-up sign flashing on the tower—GO BY TRAIN.

I reach into the pocket of my sweatshirt—I have my wallet, but that's about it. It's enough. My phone is almost dead. I could ask Acid for a charger, but Eden will be able to track it if it's on. I shut it off and shove it in my pocket instead.

Acid gives me a long look. "Promise me you're not gonna do something stupid. I'd actually feel guilty."

"I'll be fine." I unbuckle my seat belt. "Thanks for the ride, Acid."

She pulls away, and I'm standing alone outside the dark station.

chapter thirty

THE TRAIN WINDS ITS WAY DOWN the West Coast, leaving the imposing pine trees behind in favor of blue skies and grassy fields. I feel like I should *feel* something.

I tuck my feet up and sit cross-legged in the seat, read an abandoned newspaper three times before I get bored and leave it in the empty seat beside me. I wander down to the concessions car at one point, stomach growling, but they only have flat, rubbery-looking hamburgers left. When I transfer trains in Sacramento, I beeline for the gift shop in the station and buy four Kit Kats, a bottled smoothie, and a cheap paperback. There's an ATM in the hallway. I could take all my cash out, let my trail go cold in California. I consider it, turning my debit card around in my hand, then shove it back into my wallet.

I suddenly feel an overwhelming urge to talk to *somebody*. I'm hundreds of miles from Portland, running out of money on my card and probably bound to be stopped by security at some point. A sweaty teenager traveling without any bags or a phone isn't exactly inconspicuous. I spot my reflection in the gift shop window as the cashier hands me my receipt and pull the collar of my hoodie up.

As I turn away from the cashier, I spot a pay phone, grimy and tucked between a trash can and a water fountain.

I turn back to the cashier. "Do you know if that phone still works?"

"No clue."

"Can I get change?" I trade her a dollar for four quarters and cross the shop to the phone, biting my lip. Before I can change my mind, I slide three quarters into the coin slot, wiping the receiver on my sweatshirt before I press it to my ear. The phone crackles to life, a dial tone humming through the speaker.

I raise my hand to the keypad, then realize I don't know anybody's number. I haven't had to memorize a phone number since . . .

Before I realize what I'm doing, I'm dialing. *Four, three, five, six, three, two* . . . The phone starts to ring, and I realize my hand is shaking. No way. There's no way—*"Hi there!"* A tremor shoots through me at Papa's voice, and I grab the pay phone stand to stay upright. But when I open my mouth to respond, he keeps going: *"You've reached Erlan, Marcus, and Moose Shaker. The only people who still call this landline are telemarketers, so please don't leave a message."*

I sink to the tile floor, and I'm clutching the phone so hard I feel like I might break the receiver. It's not the waves of panic moving through me, though—it's something else, something more raw and biting, like a burn. I blink, and a tear rolls down my cheek.

In the background of the voicemail, I hear another voice, distant. *"Why do we still have that th—"*

The voice cuts off, and there's a beep, beckoning me to leave a message.

"H-hi, Papa," I whisper, my lip trembling. "Hi, Dad." I don't know what else to say. *Eden took me in, but I ran away? I joined a roller derby team, but I fucked it up? Why is Eden still paying for landline service to our old house?* I close my eyes, replaying their voices in my head.

A loudspeaker in the terminal crackles. "*California Zephyr with service to Reno, Salt Lake City, Omaha, and Chicago departing in three minutes.*"

There's so much I want to tell them, so much I wish I could pour into a voicemail that might somehow find its way to them, wherever they are. I want to hang up and redial, just to hear their voices again. But I force myself to lower the receiver back into its cradle, clutching the side of the booth, rubbing my eyes furiously with the dirty sleeve of my sweatshirt. I know if I stay a moment longer, I'll be glued to this stupid pay phone forever. And it's not like anyone is waiting for me.

I turn, sprinting to catch the train.

When the sun rises on the second day, it lights up brown rocks and stretches of low, flat-topped mesas. After we transfer from the train to a bus in Green River, I leave the paperback forgotten on the seat beside me, lean my forehead on the window, and watch the sun rise in a vivid blue sky, the pits and dust of the Utah fields spreading out beyond. I can tell I'm disgusting. I haven't showered or brushed my teeth in three days, and all I've eaten are candy bars and a couple limp veggie burgers from the concessions car.

The landscape turns more vivid as we wind south. Soon huge orange rock formations dominate the horizon, contrasting sharply with the cloudless sky. A confusing mix of emotions hits me when I see the first sign for Moab, and I fight the urge to cry and scream simultaneously.

I step off the bus and into the Greyhound station, stuffy and crowded with hikers and climbers with big backpacks swinging around in everybody's way. I push past them toward the exit, but a display outside the gift store makes me pause. There are racks of postcards and lawn ornaments and Utah magnets, but a board of orange enamel pins catches my eye. Before I can talk myself out of it, I'm pulling pins off the board, counting under my breath until I have eighteen cupped in my sweaty palm.

It'll take the last of my money to buy them all, but I carry them to the counter anyway, carefully piling them on the register. I look down at the counter while the cashier rings them up.

"Ninety dollars and fifty-six cents," he says, and I look up at the familiar voice.

"Skatemare?"

The cashier does a double take, and we take each other in at the same time. I see his eyes latch on to the scar on my neck, and I stare at the mottled, waxy burn scars running up both his arms.

"Moose?" He's still wearing his trademark denim jacket with his skate name embroidered across the shoulders. He breaks into a wide smile. "It's so good to see you, kid. Did you get my texts a couple months back?"

"Yeah," I say, feeling faint. I grab the counter to steady myself. "I— Sorry. There was just . . . a lot happening."

"You're in Washington now?"

"Oregon," I correct. "I—I forgot you work here."

"Oh, yeah," he says, sweeping my pins into a paper bag. "I'm good with the tourists." His smile fades a little. "It's different out here, you know? Without you and . . . well, your dads. They left a big hole."

"Yeah." They left a big hole everywhere. "Do you . . . see anybody else? Who made it out?"

"Oh, yeah," Skatemare says easily. He was never one to linger on depressing topics. He prints my receipt and rips it off, tucking it in the bag. "We started a support group, still meet every other Wednesday. We're doing good." He slides the bag across the counter to me, and looks at me again, just now taking in my dirty hoodie and disheveled appearance. "You doing okay? Here with your sister?"

The phone rings before I can answer, and Skatemare gives me a *hold on* gesture and picks it up. I stare at the burn scars along his arm and feel a sudden aching longing for my people in Utah, the rink community that meets every other week to process together, where they undoubtedly cry and laugh and heal and reminisce. Skatemare looks good—happy, even. He's been through the same horrible shit as me, but he looks okay. Like he's getting through it.

Why don't I feel that way?

Skatemare's eyes slide to me as I grab the shopping bag and shove it in my pocket. "Moose," he says, lowering the receiver slightly.

"Thanks, Skatemare. It's good to see you," I say quickly.

"Moose, wait—" he starts, but I duck past a tourist and out the door before he can finish, my cheeks hot with some emotion I can't quite figure out.

I start walking without thinking, my feet carrying me down a familiar street. Moab is small enough that there are no public buses, so I walk the whole way, down tree-lined roads and past strips of cafés and hiking supply shops. I keep my eyes down to avoid making eye contact with any of the climbers and road-trippers crowded around patio tables.

I can feel the first deep twinges of an approaching panic attack, so I push Skatemare out of my mind and focus on my steps, heading down a quieter residential street. The sign welcoming me to the Finney's Mesa neighborhood is sun-faded, the wood painted with imitations of the Ute cliff dwellings. An unfamiliar Jeep is parked on our cul-de-sac—I'm used to recognizing every car that drives down this street. Papa would stand at the window when an unfamiliar vehicle appeared, watching suspiciously until they turned around. It was the most white Mormon thing he did, according to Dad.

There's a FOR SALE sign outside our house. It mars the dusty brown yard, stark against the pale green siding. The door is propped open, a sandwich board on the porch declaring an open house.

Eden listed it.

I stop on the sidewalk, taking in the bare concrete porch, the shades drawn over the windows in the living room. We hung Papa's suncatchers in that window, dozens of them dangling from the curtain rod and sending spinning glints of light across the living room. The ground outside looks prickly, freshly turned, and I wonder if the real estate agent is having grass planted. *Real Utahns have brown front yards,* Papa used to say. Behind the house, Finney's Mesa guards the horizon, casting the neighborhood into shadow.

Without thinking, I'm following the familiar path down the driveway, up the two steps to the front porch, and through the open door.

The living room is staged with furniture that isn't ours, the once vibrant yellow walls painted impersonal gray. There are no suncatchers in the window sending fractals of rainbow light spinning across the carpet. A diffuser spits artificial lavender into the air, masking the smell of cloves and jasmine candles and Dr. Bronner's soap that used to permeate this house.

"Oh, hi there." A man in a blazer has appeared from the kitchen, clearly surprised to see me. "Sorry, didn't hear you come in. You're lucky you came early! This place will be packed before long."

I just stare at him, trying to piece together the picture of this polished, blazer-clad intruder in my home. I realize it's been months since I've been alone with a cis man, and my brain has no idea how to process him.

"So . . . the house is in great shape," he says awkwardly, handing me a pamphlet emblazoned with a glossy, professional photo of the front of the house. "Really well-cared for. Updated HVAC, and the roof is just three years old." I was in middle school when they replaced the roof—we stayed in the Embassy Suites in Moab, and I spent the entire three days at the pool, my hair crunchy from the chlorine.

"Okay," I say, because the Realtor is clearly expecting me to say something.

"Now, I know the listing price is high," he goes on, "but I think the seller can be talked down." *The seller,* meaning Eden—who promised not to list the house until I was ready. "To be honest," the Realtor's saying, "I had to really badger the seller into finally listing it. They asked to price it high. Almost like they didn't want it to sell right away. But if you hang tight for a week or so, I'm sure they'll take a lower offer."

I hand the pamphlet back to him. "I actually just want to look around."

"Oh, sure," he says amicably, tidying the stack of pamphlets on the coffee table. "I'll be in here if you have any questions."

After the cold impersonality of the living room, stepping into the kitchen feels like breathing clean air again. The walls are wood paneled, cabinets out-of-date, countertops still the diamond-pattern pink tiles they've always been. Papa was always begging Dad to let him renovate the kitchen, but Dad loved what he called the *vintage charm*, glossing over the double ovens that broke every year and the tarnished cabinet pulls. This is probably the cleanest our kitchen has been in years.

I run a finger along the valleys of grout in the countertops, the late-afternoon light spilling into the sink. I'm thinking of Dad standing at the island trying to frost my birthday cake, frustrated because he didn't let it cool and it melted all over the plate. The year Papa got him a Polaroid camera for his birthday and the fridge was covered in overexposed snapshots of me squinting into the flash. Dad holding my hands as I scooted nervously across the linoleum in my first pair of pink roller skates. Sitting at the kitchen table with Papa as he showed me how to string beads onto the suncatchers. Dads weeping together at the counter while they watched news coverage of a shooting at a gay nightclub. Papa buying trans and rainbow flags to hang on the front porch that summer, still afraid of the judgment of the rest of Finney's Mesa but no longer willing to hide.

Then, in the confusing swirl of emotions, I see the answering machine. It's ancient, white and bulky from the nineties with an actual cassette tape inside. Dad, ever the fan of *vintage charm*, bought it at a yard sale for twenty cents when I was in elementary school. I cross the kitchen to it and hit the eject button. The lid swings up and a tape pops out—the tape that holds Dads' voices.

I feel like I should stay in the house, see the bathroom where I spent hours wrestling with my hair, and the backyard, where Papa planted tulips. But standing there, staring at the tape, the relief I felt when I stepped into the kitchen starts to dissipate, fast. Even amid the memories, I'm still standing alone in this cold, empty house once bursting with sunlight and noise and card games and rainbow flags in June. I wonder what Dads would think of me, standing here caked with dust and sweat and feeling raw.

“Excuse me,” the Realtor says behind me, and I turn to see his eyes flit from the open answering machine to the tape in my hand. “You can’t touch—”

I push past him, feeling the panic clawing up. The tape is clutched in my sweaty fist as I duck back through the living room and out the front door.

chapter thirty-one

MY PANICKED, HYPERALERT BODY leads me straight to Bishop Street.

It's on the outskirts of Moab, where the roads turn into long stretches of half-empty strip malls and flat brown land in the shadow of Finney's Mesa. Just over the ridge, I know the sunset will soon light up Arches National Park, turning the famous curving rocks an otherworldly orange. The mesa casts shade over the empty lot ahead, where a chain-link fence guards a blackened square of land.

The sign is still there. It's the first thing I notice, two cartoonish bighorn sheep in roller skates, holding a banner between them emblazoned with FINNEY'S MESA ROLLERDOME. It's angled so I can see the back of the sign, covered in black ash. There are fake flowers and framed pictures and stuffed animals crusty with orange dust around the base of the sign, a makeshift memorial for the six people who died. Someone added a photo of Dads at a jam skate night two years ago, holding hands and laughing on the glossy skate floor, their faces lit up by the disco ball.

I'd gotten in trouble for something stupid the night they took that photo—forgetting to take chicken out of the freezer for dinner, or being late to the bus that morning, or something equally mundane that Papa had yelled at me about when I got home from school. We'd been frosty toward each other all afternoon, until Dad got home from work and brandished our skates at us. "We're really gonna miss jam skate night to sit here and be mad at each other?" he'd asked. I'd grabbed my skates and gotten in the car with them, still fuming, but my anger dissipated by the time we were all on the skate floor together, under the disco ball and party lights that always made your problems seem less serious. I was probably just out of frame in the photo, off to the side with Skatemare, maybe rolling my eyes at Dads' affection but secretly glad they were on my team.

I can feel the floodgates about to burst, all the panic and pain threatening to pour out of me if I look at their smiling faces a moment longer. So I pass the little shrine, my sneakers kicking up burnt earth underfoot.

When I touch the chain-link fence, the metal's cold, quickly losing warmth as the sun sets. The lot looks smaller than it should be, smaller than the Rollerdome. I'd have thought they would have had crews come through to clear it out by now, but a skeleton of the rink remains—a broken pillar, half the concrete wall of the snack bar, the melted shell of a vending machine. The rest of it is just blackened, twisted ash.

The gravity of it hits me. I had Dads, then I didn't. I had the rink, then I didn't. I had Eden and Mercury and Carmen and Powerhouse and the Hot Shots and roller derby. And now I don't. Every person that's cared about me, every community that made me feel safe. Gone.

My fingers slide down the chain link as I go down on my knees into the ground, the tears coming. Everything in me is raw, a gaping wound, and I can't tell if I'm screaming or crying or both. The remains of the rink pitch and tilt as I press my forehead into the dirt, tasting burnt earth when my mouth opens in a sob. The vast, imposing silence of the mesas looks down on me, unflinching against the aching emptiness of what the Rollerdome used to be.

Light spills over me, and I sit bolt upright, shoulders still heaving, unable to catch my breath. I know my face is streaked with dirt and tears and ash, and the panic threatens to completely undo me as a pair of headlights moves slowly down the road. I scramble to my feet, briefly considering bolting through the broken chain-link gate and into the ruins of the roller rink—but the thought of stepping into where the ticket booth used to be makes my legs shake. I clutch the fence, breathing hard, mouth sagging open, squinting as the car stops, headlights pointed at me.

My mind rapidly puts the pieces together as the driver's door opens. I feel my body shutting down in panic as the driver leaves the car door ajar and steps into the beam of the headlights.

Mercury.

Mercury, with the light floating around her like a halo.

Mercury, cutting through the wild emptiness of Moab toward me with her arms outstretched.

I'm frozen, staring at her, willing her to be real. Then she staggers into me, arms tight around my shoulders, and I realize she's here—impossibly, perfectly, *here*.

The shock in me breaks, and I'm sobbing into her sweater, clutching her as if she might float away. She pulls me closer, and I feel her draw a shuddering breath as her fingers tangle in my hair.

When my sobs finally abate, there are tears in her eyes, streaked through the grime on her face. I reach up to touch her cheek, hardly able to believe she's real.

"How did you know I'd be here?" I finally whisper.

"Don't worry about that," she breathes, and her voice cracks. She takes my cheeks in both her hands, giving me a stern look through the tears. Her palm feels so normal against my skin. Unafraid. "I came to take you home."

"I don't—" I try to steady myself, but my voice shakes. I twist to look at the rink, the little shrine with the picture of my dads. "I don't have a—"

"Moose," Mercury says, gentle. "You *do* have one."

"They don't want me," I whisper.

"Who?"

"The Hot Shots. The whole league. And Eden—Eden didn't even come. She knows people here; she would have come to get me herself—"

"*I* told Eden I would come," Mercury says at once. "She was freaking out without you, Moose. She needs you too."

"She doesn't—" I start, but Mercury's words register a second later. *She needs you too.* I try to process the confusing muddle of emotions around someone needing me, wanting me. Things I didn't think I'd feel again. Not after the fire.

"But—the Hot Shots—I screwed everything up."

"First of all," she says seriously, "*I* was also responsible for what happened in the Hangar. Second, you think nobody else on the Hot Shots has ever screwed up?"

"Not like that."

She raises her eyebrows. "Carmen once threw a Hydro Flask at Acid's head in the middle of a game and got ejected."

I look down at my shoes, dusted in black ash. "I'm gonna get kicked off the team, though. And we lost because of me, because you and I couldn't play. We can't win champs."

"Moose," Mercury says, and I look up at her. "Nobody has said you're off the team. And we're still playing in champs—just not for first place."

"What's the point?"

She gives me a wry look. "I know you didn't join roller derby to win a championship. And I didn't come here to get our third jammer back. I came here for *you*, Moose. To bring you home."

And I realize that here, the burned-up, blackened remains of the Rollerdome, really isn't home anymore. "So . . . what do we do?"

Mercury half smiles. "We go back to Portland, and we kick ass for third place."

I reach up, brushing a stray hair off her face. She looks exhausted. She must have driven all night to get here, without even knowing exactly where I'd be.

"You ready?" Mercury asks softly.

I sniff, wipe my tears with the filthy sleeve of my hoodie, and stare out at the dark ruins of the roller rink. There's something nagging at me, something pulling me to the rink that isn't quite ready to let go. Then my gaze lands on the flowers and stuffed animals at the base of the sign.

I dig my hand inside my pocket and pull out the cassette tape from our answering machine. "Your car can play this, right?"

Mercury nods, and we climb into her car and sit with the doors swung open as Mercury starts the engine. I push the cassette in, and Mercury holds her phone up to the speakers to record Dads' voices for me, one last time. When it's done, I push eject and pull it out, slide out of the passenger seat, and go to kneel beside the makeshift shrine. Mercury stands beside me as I carefully prop it in the dirt against the framed picture of Dads.

Back in Mercury's car, I twist in my seat to watch the ruins of the rink drop out of sight. They don't loom quite so threateningly anymore.

I direct Mercury back through downtown Moab, where bulb lights are strung over the sidewalks and people stroll along the gift shops. It'll be dark soon, and I roll down my window, drawing in a long breath of the familiar, dusty air.

Mercury drives us past downtown, following my directions a short way down the highway. We pass the strip mall with Papa's favorite outlet stores, the park we used to ride our bikes to. When we near a familiar intersection, something catches in my throat, and I reach over to Mercury, putting a hand on her arm. There's one last thing I have to do in Moab, I decide. One last thing for me.

"Can you turn here?"

She obliges without question, driving us down a long, curving road. I find my National Parks pass still in my wallet, faded and creased, but it's late enough in the day that the ranger just waves us through. Arches Scenic Drive winds through tall walls of orange rock until one side drops away, revealing the vast, stony desert awash with scrubby grasses. In the distance, the La Sal Mountains rise up from the horizon, icy and gray against the fiery rock around us.

"Wow," Mercury breathes, eyes wide as she stares out at the desert.

"It's a different kind of mountain." I feel simultaneously hungover from the panic of the last two hours and giddy at Mercury's amazement, like I'm showing her a secret.

I direct her to the parking lot, a loop with just a few cars. The Parade of Elephants marches along one side, a row of towering sandstone arches shaped like lumbering animals. But when we step out of the car, I take Mercury's hand and lead her in the other direction, through the rough desert grass. The darkness hasn't quite reached the desert here. As we walk, the rock around us lights up in a vivid, otherworldly orange, a sharp contrast from the heavy blue sky.

"Moose," Mercury says as we follow a narrow trail. "Where—" She falls silent as the North Window looms into sight, a massive oval arch. The sun's light strikes it, makes it glow, and it looks like a portal to another world, a stern blue eye staring down at us.

"You told me about this," Mercury says breathlessly, her eyes following the curve of the arch. The setting sun lights her hair up deep red, like it's rimmed with flame. "Right? The eye?"

I nod, but I can't look away from her. Even under the fiery splendor of the arch, all I can see is Mercury—circles under her eyes, sweaty from the road, more ragged than I've ever seen her—but staring in awe, like she's never seen anything this beautiful.

"Can I ask you something?" I say, and my voice feels small in the vastness of the desert.

She turns to me, and she's washed in orange-pink light.

"How did you know I'd be here?" I ask again. She never really answered me at the rink.

"Acid told me she took you to the train station. I figured you only had one place to go."

"I mean . . . the rink," I say, and I'm surprised to find that the words don't stick in my throat like they once did.

She gives me a long look, then her gaze drifts to the massive rock formations before us. "You told me. Months ago, when we hiked up to that lookout over the bridge."

"You . . . remember that?"

Mercury holds my gaze. "Of course I do."

Finally, I turn to look at the arch, and I realize how light I feel. Like I've finally exhaled after holding a deep, painful breath for over a year. For the first time since last April, it feels like the ball has shrunk, no longer pressing so hard against the sides of the box that I can't breathe.

"Look," I say, suddenly realizing what I'm seeing. The moon has begun to rise, its huge round crown just visible at the bottom of the arch. Mercury's breath hitches in wonder, and I reach out, taking her hand. She holds my arm with her other hand, pressing close to me, wide-eyed as we watch the moon slowly roll up into the center of the arch. By the time it forms a pupil, gazing down on us, the sun is nearly gone, and the stars are spread across the sky above us. There's no one else in this desert, no one else in the world. I squeeze her hand.

Her fingers curl around mine, and we watch the moon roll past the arch and up into the sky.

chapter thirty-two

EDEN COMES RUNNING OUT of the apartment when we park, wrapped in a huge Portland State sweatshirt with shadows under her eyes. I feel a hitch of trepidation as I open the door, but then Eden's hugging me. It's a stark difference from the awkward hug I got from her in the hospital, once I could finally move again. This is a hug from someone who knows me.

"Eden," I say, pulling back, and her eyes are filled with tears. "I'm sorry."

She answers by holding me tighter. Over her shoulder, Mercury hovers near her car. She looks uncertain, like she can't tell if she has a role in this reunion.

Eden reaches for her, pulling her into our hug. "Thank you," she whispers to Mercury.

Mercury excuses herself so I can rest, and she squeezes my hand before she leaves, giving me a soft smile. I want to kiss her, but Eden's still there, and I can't quite figure out where I stand with Mercury and Eden and the whole breaking-into-the-Hangar thing. We didn't talk about derby during the fifteen-hour drive through the desert, past the Great Salt Lake, up through the foothills of western Idaho and into the mountains along the Gorge. I told her about my dads' wedding day at the courthouse in Salt Lake City, our vacation to Yellowstone where I sprinted all the way down a trail and was too tired to walk back up, the countless nights we spent at the rink with Skatemare. She told me about visiting her mom's family in Korea and meeting dozens of cousins she didn't know she had, getting lost in a massive shopping mall in Seoul with her brothers, the way her mom would wake up the whole neighborhood banging pots and pans at midnight on New Year's.

Now I follow Eden up the stairs and into the apartment, the same way I followed her months ago. But this time, the bay windows are open to the late-afternoon sun, and the tree outside is flowering, and it almost feels like home.

Eden breathes a heavy sigh, tossing her keys on the coffee table and kicking off her shoes. The gravity of the situation hits me: I got in a screaming match at the last bout, cost us our chance at the championship, and ran a thousand miles away without telling anyone. I pick up Typo and clutch her to my chest, feeling suddenly very small.

"Eden?"

She turns from the kitchen, where she's pulled down two mugs and turned on the electric kettle.

"Yeah, kid?"

I swallow. "Am I off the team?"

"Oh, Moose." Eden comes around the counter. Typo hops out of my arms, and Eden wraps her arms around me again. I feel the emotion welling up. "You're not off the team."

Something in me breaks in relief, and I lean all the way into her, letting my sister hold me up and rub slow circles on my back while I cry into her shoulder. She leads me to the couch, and I crumple into her lap, the exhaustion and emotion and fear from the past week pouring out of me.

When my breathing finally slows, Eden smooths my hair off my face. "I was going to come get you myself," she says. "But when Mercury and I realized where you'd gone . . . I figured you needed a sister more than a parent."

I rub tears out of my eyes with the collar of my jacket. "What do you mean?"

"I mean . . . look, the adult thing for me to do would have been to fly to Moab myself, right? Call the police or something and have someone pick you up and make sure you were safe until I could bring you home myself. Dad would probably be pissed that I didn't. But I think, sometimes, being a sister means giving you space to figure shit out on your own, you know?"

"You weren't freaking out?" I ask reluctantly, not sure what I want her answer to be.

"Oh, no, I was completely freaking out the entire time. But I trust you, Moose. I knew you would be okay. I called Skatemare at the bus station, and when he told me he saw you, I figured you were heading to the house."

I'm silent for a second, processing. "They had the blinds closed."

"Over those big windows?"

"Yeah. The best part."

Eden shakes her head. "Dad always had those blinds open, even in July when it made the living room a thousand degrees."

I stare at my hands in my lap, peppered with bruises from practice. "When did you put it up for sale?"

"I listed it last week," she says gently, "but I asked the Realtor to take it off the market yesterday. I should have asked you, I should have—"

"It's okay," I say, and weirdly, it is. "I'm sorry for being so stubborn about the house. I know we need the money. It was just—hard to let go of. But when I went in . . . they're not there anymore. Dads."

Eden puts one hand on my knee and taps her heart with her other hand. "Yeah. They're with you now."

I hesitate for a second, staring down at my hands twisting in my lap, afraid of saying what I really want to say. "Eden," I venture finally, still unable to look at her, "it really sucks that you weren't in my life for ten years. I feel—I feel like I missed so much without you."

"Moose. Look at me."

I do, reluctant, and she gently takes my nervous hands out of my lap and holds them tight.

"I am *so* sorry, Moose. You're right. I should have been there for you."

"I know your mom made it hard, and you didn't have your own money, and—"

"Sure," she interrupts, "my mom made it hard. But I should have fought for you. I should have fought for Dad. And I'm sorry I wasn't there then. But I want to be here now. It's not about wanting or not wanting you in my life, Moose. I may not have chosen this for myself, but you are *family*, and you always will be. Nothing you could say or do would ever make me not want you."

My eyes prick. "Are you sure?"

"Yes. Surer than I've ever been in my life." Eden, who I idolized when I was little. Eden, who was there from the moment I woke up in the hospital. Eden, who has always been my sister first and everything else—coach, parent, guardian—second.

"I don't think I'm ever gonna move on," I say after a moment. "But I feel like I can set it down. Like, put it on a shelf. Know that it's there, and it might come back up, but I have another home, and another family, and I'll be okay."

Eden gives me a sad, proud look, squeezing my hand. "Yeah, kid," she tells me. "You'll be just fine."

I'm allowed to play in the last game of the season that week. Eden tells me when she gets home from a long meeting with Prince and the league coordinator, a takeout bag in one hand.

"It's conditional," she says, kicking off her boots. "You need to talk to the rest of the Hot Shots first. Some of them are kind of freaked out."

I think of Marie, the way I slammed into her and sent her sprawling to the ground in her very first practice. There's a twinge of shame. "Do *they* want me to play?"

"You have to ask them, Moose."

I want to play in champs, but more than that, I want to erase the revulsion and fear in my teammates' faces when I screamed at Eden during the last game.

Before we leave for the Hangar the next day, I pack my derby bag slowly, strapping down the Velcro on my pads and arranging them neatly. I sit cross-legged on the floor of my bedroom and tighten the wheels on my skates, change the laces, tuck a rolled-up pair of socks inside. Finally, I find a small paper bag in the mess on my bed, thumbing the crinkly paper before I tuck it into the pocket of my gear bag.

I feel a weird hitch of apprehension when we pull into the parking lot, one I haven't felt since my first practice with the Hot Shots. The Hangar has always felt like home since then, but now it looms over me. The massive plane doors are open, and there are only a few people inside, sweeping the track and hanging up sponsor banners and arranging the merch booths as sunlight glints off the sport court.

"You okay?" Eden asks.

I swallow and nod. I'm wearing my Hot Shots letterman jacket, and I suddenly wonder if I should pull it off, ball it up, and throw it in Eden's backseat. Will it look cocky, striding into champs wearing the jacket of a team I humiliated? But Eden's already out of the car, opening the trunk so I can grab my gear. I unlock my phone and tap my message thread with Mercury, studying the most recent message for the twentieth time that day.

MERCURY

it'll be fine. leave it on the track.

Eden's wearing her orange dress with her red leather jacket again, and she's re-dyed the blue of her hair to a brilliant, fiery orange in celebration of the championship game. Tonight will be a doubleheader—the Hot Shots will play first against the Bend Banshees for third place, followed by the Benton Brawlers versus the junior team from Fresno. A huge sign at the entrance declares the doubleheader, and I feel a pang of guilt when I see that we're not listed as competing for first place.

"Can I talk to the team in the locker room?" I ask Eden.

She nods, sweeps out an arm for me to lead the way. I falter when I reach the doorway, those familiar notes of panic creeping in.

"You coming in?" I turn to see Mercury beside me, looking beautiful and perfect and scary all at once with her oiled buns and red lipstick and sharp eyeliner. She's also wearing her Hot Shots jacket, her gear bag dangling over one shoulder.

"I can't," I choke out, biting my lip. "I— They're all going to hate me."

Her face softens, and she holds out a hand. "You won't know until you get in there."

I steel myself, then let out a heavy breath and take her hand. I'm clutching the little paper bag in my other hand.

The smell of ammonia hits me. Carmen is sitting cross-legged on the floor between Powerhouse's knees while Powerhouse applies vivid orange dye to her white-blond hair.

"*Burnout!*" Carmen shrieks, flying to her feet to hug me. "Oh my god. Are you okay? Did you have the most transformative and life-changing running-away?"

"I'm okay," I tell her, leaning back from her hair that's crusty with orange dye and wincing at the smell. "Are you seriously doing this in the locker room?"

Powerhouse's plastic gloves crinkle as they give me a defeated look. "Do you think I had a choice?"

"If I tried to do it at home, my mom would have tried to dye it, like, leopard print or something," Carmen says, giving me a loving pat on the cheek before examining herself with a hand mirror. She has a ragged towel draped around her shoulders, barely covering her jersey. "This is the safest way." Her expression softens a little. "Are you sure you're okay?"

"I'm sure. Look, Carmen, I'm sorry I ignored all your messages. I was just—I was embarrassed, and worried you'd be mad about Mercury and me, and—"

Carmen throws herself into my arms again, and I'm pretty sure her hair leaves a streak of orange on my cheek.

The door opens behind me, and Acid walks in, her nose scrunching up. "Gross. Can you do that outside?"

"There's plenty, Acid," Carmen says, grabbing the brush from Powerhouse and brandishing it at her. "I don't want you to feel left out."

"Hey, Burnout," Himaslaya says as she walks in behind us. "Good to have you back." Marie enters the locker room behind her and I catch her eye, waving her over before she can duck away from me.

"Hey," I say quietly. "I'm really sorry for hitting you like that at practice. That was way out of line."

"It's okay," she says, but her voice is thin.

"It's not. I know better than to treat a new skater like that. I'm really glad you're on the team," I tell her seriously. "And I can't wait to skate with you more."

She smiles, finally—still looks a little nervous, but I think it's the first time she's smiled at me. "Yeah. You too. Hey, what do you think of Tyger Bomb for my derby name?"

"I think it sounds badass."

Marie beams.

"All right," Prince says, raising a hand to quiet us. "This is what we've been working for all season, folks. Any announcements before we get geared up?"

I take a breath, then raise my hand.

"Burnout," Prince says, all business. "You have the floor."

Everyone turns to me, and I swallow the lump of fear in my throat. There are such a range of faces: Marie, who looks scared I might light her up again; Acid, who's trying and failing to look nonchalant and bored; Carmen, giving me an encouraging nod. Mercury squeezes my hand, then lets go. But she's still there. Across the locker room, the mirror stares back at me. I look different now. Stronger. My jersey doesn't hang off me the way it did that first game. It hugs my torso now, cut above my shoulders to show the new muscles. It takes me a moment to remember the scar on my neck, and even then, it barely registers. It's still there, still thick and raised and prominent—but I don't care about it now. I slide my gear bag off my shoulder and take a deep breath, then one more to make sure my lungs are filled with air.

"I'm sorry," I say first. "I was a huge asshole at our last game, and I jeopardized it for all of us." My ears are hot, and I hope nobody notices. "When I started playing derby, it was something I could use to distract myself from . . . everything. It didn't give me time to think about the way I look or how I sound or my anxiety or . . . anything else. When I joined the Hot Shots, you all showed me that derby is more than that."

I take a breath, steadying myself.

"What I mean is— I— Derby gave me a family when I thought I'd lost everything. I had nothing left, and I thought nobody would ever see past what happened to me. But you all gave me a home, and a family, and now you're letting me come back and skate with you even though I was such a bitch at that last game."

"And our last practice," Acid adds, but it's matter-of-fact, not mean. Carmen glares at her, but she's right.

"Yeah. At practice too. So . . . thank you. And sorry."

I open the bag, reaching in and pulling out a tiny enamel pin of an orange arch. I turn to Himaslaya on my right and hold it out to her, pressing it into her hand. "These are from Utah," I say, reaching into the bag for another pin for Apex. "They're for our team jackets." I hand a pin to Acid, and she gives me a dry smile. "I wanted this family to have part of my old one." I walk around the circle, handing out the rest of the pins until my bag is empty.

There's a beat of silence, where the awkwardness of my apology presses down on me and I feel like everyone is about to laugh.

But then, beside me, Himaslaya loops one arm around my shoulders. "We're family," she says, gesturing for Apex to join in. She does, and the rest of the team stands and surrounds me, and we tangle in a big, messy hug, stepping on each others' feet. The Hot Shots surround me in a protective wall, jostling me and touching my arm and all talking over each other at once. My eyes prick, and I squeeze them shut, letting the heat and the voices and the mess and the love pour into me. The house in Moab wasn't quite right, and neither is my room in the apartment. This—my team and the mess that is roller derby—is home.

chapter thirty-three

I'VE NEVER SEEN THE BLEACHERS in the Hangar this packed. The audience is pressed shoulder to shoulder, and the music's already shaking the walls. I spot Carmen's mom in the front row with a sign emblazoned with her name beside Mercury's dad and brothers.

"Your family's here," I say as Mercury and I skate to our bench to drop off our water bottles.

She grins. "Yeah. First time they've seen me skate in years." I feel a pang of jealousy, wishing my dads could be in the bleachers with them.

The refs clear the track, and we filter back to our individual benches. The energy is palpable. Carmen is practically bouncing up and down in her skates, her newly orange hair still damp under her helmet.

"Bring it in," Eden says, and we gather in a close circle. Apex and Mercury, on either side of me, loop their arms around my shoulders, and I do the same. We're a tightly wound thicket of limbs and helmets. Eden takes a long, steadying breath, gesturing for us all to do the same. "Remember," she says, and the calmness in her voice contrasts starkly with the excitement of the crowd behind us. "Communicate. Breathe. Control. We are a strong team. Okay?"

A few skaters nod. I feel like I'm going to be sick.

"Captain?" Eden says, turning to Mercury. "Anything to add?"

Mercury thinks for a moment, then looks around at all of us, her eyes bright. "Bring everything you have into this game. And leave it on the track."

The rest of us dissolve into cheers at her words. Coming from gentle, steadfast Mercury, the words feel like armor.

"Let's cheer," Prince says, sticking her hand into the middle. We join in, and Mercury starts the skate stomp.

"TRACK ON FI-RE," she starts, and we chant along with her. "TRACK ON FI-RE! TRACK ON FI-RE!" Apex has her hands cupped around her mouth and is wailing like a siren. "HOT SHOTS!"

Eden hustles us to sit on our bench while the announcer welcomes the audience and the referees cluster in the middle of the track. The game starts, and I feel a twinge of nerves as I shake out my arms, bounce my knees. I have to sit through two jams before I can actually skate, get the jittery anxiety out of my arms and legs.

Acid only manages to score two points in the first jam because the other jammer starts blocking her out of the pack—it's legal but annoying, and Acid is already seething when she rolls off the track. So much for staying calm.

"Is it weird that I'm mad they messed with Acid?" I ask Carmen.

"Yes," she says instantly, and Panic shoves her playfully.

Powerhouse claims lead in the second jam, managing a full pass and four points before the other jammer gets out. They're already sweating when they get back to the bench, sliding the jammer cap onto my helmet. "Fuck 'em up, Burnout," they say, jostling my shoulder.

I roll to the jam line, hoping the audience can't see the jitters in my knees. Cereal Killer, the Banshees captain, is jamming against me, and she gives me a high five as I skate up next to her.

Focus. Breathe. I face forward, toward the imposing backs of the Banshee blockers. As my blockers set up in front of them, Mercury catches my eye and gives me the tiniest of nods, a silent confirmation. *We're ready.*

"Five seconds!"

I drop one toe stop and level my gaze, ignoring the enemy jammer beside me. *Focus.*

The whistle sounds and a shoulder slams into my ribs, sending me staggering to my knees. Distantly, I hear the audience gasp.

I'm winded, struggling to catch my breath as I scramble to my feet. The pack is already in motion ahead of me—Cereal Killer is chopping her way through my blockers.

"Foul!" Carmen's shouting at the refs, but they don't call anything. Cereal Killer's hit on me was dirty, but legal—and it seems to have jolted the nerves out of me. I catch my breath, spring to my feet, and zip through an open space on the outside. A Banshee blocker shoots out of nowhere, aiming for me—I duck around her, using her momentum to propel myself out of the pack. I speed around the track, my shins burning, and manage to slip again through the pack untouched.

"Call it!" Prince shouts from the bench, and I tap my hips. A whistle blasts through the Hangar, and my points go up on the scoreboard.

"Yeah!" Carmen screams from behind me, and she slams into me, throws her arms around my waist, and picks me up. "That was fucking awesome!"

"Great job," Eden says as we skate back to the bench. I hand her the jammer cap, and she can barely contain her excitement. "Awesome, Moose. That was perfect. Keep it up."

But the Banshees step up their game. They're hitting harder and scrambling our plays. I can feel myself—and all the Hot Shots—running out of steam. We hold on to the lead, but narrowly. By half-time, we're ahead 92–90. *Way* too close.

"It's time to amp it back up," Prince tells us in the locker room. Everyone looks exhausted, slumped on the benches and guzzling Gatorade, passing around the bag of protein bars. "They can see that y'all are getting tired, and they're using that against you."

"I don't know if our jammers can last another half," Apex mutters. I don't think she means it cruelly, but it stings all the same.

Acid throws her a sharp look. "You wanna put the star on and throw yourself into those walls for two minutes straight?"

"Easy," Eden says, her voice a warning. "Now is not the time."

"Coach," Mercury says. She's on the bench opposite me, her cheeks pink beneath all the glitter. "Can I talk?"

"Go ahead," Prince tells her.

"Let them think they've exhausted you." She glances over at me. "Burnout's good at that. She pretends to be stuck in a wall, saving energy, until the right moment. As soon as they let their guard down, you use a blast of force to get past them. The Banshees want us tired."

I want to look down at my skates so nobody can see my cheeks reddening at Mercury's compliment, but Trail Mx. gives me an affirming nudge, nodding in agreement.

We stay neck and neck with the Banshees throughout the second half. It's brutal. I'm drenched in sweat after every jam, chest heaving, and barely have time to compose myself before it's time to go out again. Even Powerhouse, undeniably our strongest jammer, is struggling. But the Banshees are getting tired too. I can see it in their sluggish rolls to the jam line and the pinched looks on their faces as they tussle with the Hot Shots blockers for position.

Acid seems to get a penalty every jam, and she's getting more and more wound up each time she goes out. At her seventh penalty, an official comes to our bench to tell Prince that Acid's fouled out.

"Fuck," Powerhouse breathes beside me. Acid is skating to the locker room to take her gear off, livid at herself. I glance at the scoreboard—the Banshees are leading 124–112.

"How are we going to close that without Acid?" I hiss to Powerhouse. Even though she was getting sloppy, Acid's still a powerful jammer. Without her, it's down to Powerhouse and me. Maybe that's what the Banshees were hoping for.

"Time out!" Eden calls, gesturing to the referees. She gathers us in a huddle at the bench. "Everybody stay calm," she says, consulting her clipboard. "There's no reason we can't still pull ahead."

"We're down to two jammers," Panic titters. "I think that's a pretty good reason."

"Listen," Mercury commands, and Panic falls silent as everyone looks to Prince and Eden.

"Powerhouse, Burnout," Prince says, turning to us. "I know you're tired. But we're almost done. If you can close this gap and keep it closed, we can cinch this bout."

"If you don't get lead," Eden adds, "take the jammer cap off right away." She gives me a pointed look. I almost never pass the star to my pivot—it feels like failure, even though I know it's not.

The pods get all mixed up without Acid jamming, and I end up skating with Powerhouse's usual pod. I glance at the clock. There are only a few minutes left in the game. Powerhouse will skate the last jam, but this will probably be my last time jamming in this bout.

I center myself on the track, take a long, deep breath. No ghosts. No fires. Just my blockers and me, going over our plan in my head. I'm skating against Cereal Killer again. She's bigger, but I'm faster. If I can outskate her, I can get lead.

"Five seconds!"

I lower one toe stop, dip my body so I'm low and bouncy on my knees, stare hard at the seam I'm about to punch.

The whistle blasts.

I launch myself into the Banshees' wall, throwing all my weight against them. They're sucking back on me, surrounding me, holding me in place. They've learned my strategy, but they don't know our plan.

Himaslaya rolls back and slams into the Banshees' brace, causing the tripod to stumble. I take advantage of the mess, springing forward to race out of the pack.

Behind Cereal Killer.

Shit!

She must have gotten out a split second before me. I grit my teeth, legs burning as I cross over, so close I can hear her sharp breath in her throat.

Cereal Killer is about to call the jam off, but if I can jump over the blockers' legs on the apex, I can sneak in a few points before she does. I push past her, heart pounding, all the screaming of the audience and my bench and my coaches tuned out.

And then something makes me look into the stands.

Dads.

Time stops as I stare into the audience, heart hammering. It's them—undeniably. Dad sitting forward in focus, hands folded, and Papa wearing his familiar, overexcited smile. They're here, in the Hangar. Watching me. I realize I've started the jump, and I'm in the air, and my dads are here.

They can't be.

Someone hits me, hard, and my dads flicker out like a candle flame.

chapter thirty-four

THE SOUND FLOODS IN ALL AT ONCE as I crash to the ground, landing in a tangle of skates and legs. Someone is shouting, and the audience is gasping, but I'm just panting on the cold track, twisting around to try to see the bleachers. My vision shifts, but the spot in the crowd is empty. Nobody there.

The pain hits me then. I can already feel a deep bruise forming on my ribs. I hear a ref asking if I'm okay, but her voice is distant, underwater. The other skaters are backing away from me. A whistle blows.

"Medic!" someone shouts, and I hear footsteps pounding toward me, shaking the plastic tiles under my cheek.

I curl in on myself, cradling my rib cage and still trying to catch my breath. There's a jumble of black-and-white stripes around me, and I realize that the refs have formed a wall in front of me, blocking me from the audience's view.

"Moose," says a familiar voice, soft. When I roll toward the voice, blinking, I see Mercury looking down at me, her eyes calm. "Can you squeeze my hand?" I do.

"My dads," I breathe, but then there are more people gathering around me, asking me questions. Mercury rolls back a bit, out of the way.

"Did you hit your head?" the medic asks.

"No," I say quickly, though I can barely get the words out. "Just—my ribs."

There are more people now—I see the corner of Eden's glittery orange dress, Mercury's helmet as she kneels on my other side. Someone squeezes my hand.

The medic touches my ankle gingerly. "That hurt?"

"No." I try to take a deep, steadying breath. "I tried to jump the apex."

"Didn't quite make it," Eden says on my other side, and I'm struck by how calm she sounds. "That's okay."

"I think I'm fine," I tell the medic. My heart is still hammering out of my chest, but the pain in my side is dissipating. It'll be a huge, ugly purple bruise tomorrow, but for now, adrenaline is pumping through me, numbing the ache. "I can still play."

"You sure?"

I nod. They can't remove me unless I'm visibly injured or I hit my head. "Can you help me up?" The medic takes one arm, and Mercury takes my other, and they lift me to my feet. I shake my legs out, roll my shoulders. "I'm good," I assure them.

"Moose," Mercury says, "are you sure?"

"I saw my dads," I whisper.

She blinks. "What?"

"Orange jammer," a ref interjects, and Mercury backs up, eyes wide. "Are you staying in the game?"

I nod firmly.

"We called a low block right before you fell. You need to go serve your penalty. And back to your bench, please," she adds to Mercury.

I take Mercury's hand, squeeze it as I skate toward the penalty box. I hope I seem confident.

I drop into the jammer chair in the penalty box, still breathing hard, and force myself not to look at the bleachers. They're not there.

"Moose."

I look up. Eden's kneeling in front of me.

"Are you sure you're okay?"

"I'm fine."

"Okay. I called a time-out, so you have a minute to catch your breath. The Banshees called off the jam right as you jumped. So you're skating the last jam."

"What?" I breathe. If a jammer is still in the penalty box at the end of a jam, they're still the jammer for the next one—but they have to start later than everyone else, and it's much harder to get lead. With the score this close and me starting in the penalty box, our chances are slim.

"Your usual pod is out there. You have a full thirty-second penalty. Be ready to pass the star if you need to."

"I have to score at least twelve points," I say, and it comes out like a desperate plea. It sounds impossible, especially if I'm starting with a penalty.

Eden rests her hands on my shoulders, leveling her gaze with me.

"Don't pay attention to the scoreboard. I want you to get out there, skate your hardest, follow your blockers, and *breathe*. Do the best you can possibly do. That's all I want."

I meet her gaze, and I wonder how I went so many years without really knowing her, how long she was just an occasional Christmas card or a brief summer visitor. When I woke up in the burn unit, Eden's was the first face I saw. I thought it was me at first—thought I was dead, in some purgatory where I had to judge myself. But when I realized it was Eden, a sister I barely knew anymore, some small part of me unclenched.

I want to tell her about seeing Dads in the stands, the way they were watching so intently, how they looked so real. But I need to focus. So I just nod, and Eden gives me a high five and a smile before she goes back to our bench.

The refs call an end to the time-out, and I pull the jammer cap back onto my helmet. *Don't look at the scoreboard. Don't think about all the ways you could fail. Focus.*

From across the track, Mercury glances over at me, and I swear I see her wink as the officials call five seconds. My stomach flutters.

The whistle blasts, and the Banshees jammer takes off, slamming into Carmen and Panic. They cinch tight, bracing themselves on Mercury. The Banshees are disorganized. I watch them aim for different blockers, miss their hip checks, uncoordinated. They're getting flustered.

Beneath my wheels, the whole floor of the Hangar is shaking. People in the bleachers are screaming themselves hoarse, and I realize that both team benches are all on their feet, arms linked, screaming.

"Orange four-three-five, stand," the official behind me says, and I jump up, nearly taking out the penalty box chair. I take a long, deep breath, drop one toe stop like I'm on the jam line.

The Banshees jammer breaks free.

My heart sinks as she whips around the corner, panting, and two whistle blasts declare her lead. She'll call the jam off before I have a chance to score. *Breathe.*

Focus.

We're not finished. Not until the clock runs out.

"Orange four-three-five," the official says, and my heart turns over. "Done."

At his word, I catapult out of the penalty box, entering the track right behind the Banshees jammer.

She should call it now. They're ahead, and they would win even if she didn't score. But she slams into the Hot Shots tripod, panting, throwing all her weight against them.

I aim for the Banshees, doubled over, heart pounding. The sound presses in on me—clattering wheels, grunting, the crowd screaming so loud the track is shaking.

Their jammer must be exhausted, not paying attention to her bench coach, who's screaming at her to end the jam.

A sharp whistle interrupts my thoughts, and I hear the refs call a penalty on the Banshees jammer.

"*Yes!*" Carmen screams, immediately spinning to play offense for me. I feel an unsteady hammer of fear and excitement—*now* we have a chance.

But as the Banshee blockers converge on me, there's another whistle, a penalty called on Trail Mx.

My legs are shaking, giving out. *No. No fucking way.* I didn't go through all this to collapse in the last jam. But I'm out of energy, and the Banshees have me pinned.

I feel myself start to deflate. The crowd is still screaming, but I can't push anymore.

Then, from the corner of my eye, there's a flash of orange as Mercury coasts backward to play offense for me. But I realize her path is totally clear of blockers.

"Don't!" I shout at her, and she falters as I yank the jammer cap off my helmet and press it into her hand.

Then Mercury disappears, streaking past the Banshees and out of the pack.

The Banshees release me. They're shouting, ready to catch Mercury when she comes back into the pack. I quickly cross the track to join Carmen and Panic as a blocker, glancing over my shoulder.

Mercury's coming around the turn now, pulling the jammer cap onto her helmet.

"Sweep!" Carmen commands us, tugging my arm. In one smooth motion, we throw ourselves into the Banshees, clearing a path for Mercury. She streaks past us, and the referee throws up four points.

"Just a few more points!" Panic yells, pulling Carmen and me away from the Banshees. "No problem!"

Where the rest of us are exhausted, Mercury suddenly skates with new life, jamming for the first time in the game. She's not as fluid as Acid, or as punchy as Powerhouse, or even as explosive as me—but something else entirely, spinning past the blockers that try to stop her, leveraging their own momentum to propel her through the pack. She manages two more scoring passes, and we're tied.

The sound is deafening now, and I struggle to tune it out, focus on Panic's instructions.

"Jammer's coming in," she shouts, and I glance over my shoulder. The Banshees jammer finished her penalty, and she's skating back into the pack, hot on Mercury's heels.

One more point—we have to get *one* more point for Mercury, and we can win.

Blockers come out of nowhere, busting up our tripod. Everything seems to slow down. I see the Banshees jammer recovering from a stumble, laser-focused on her clear path out of the pack. And I see Mercury, just behind me, about to hit the Banshees.

"MERCURY!"

Her eyes meet mine across the track. I seize her elbow, pulling her away from the Banshees. Mustering all my strength, I swing her around and whip her out of the pack.

The whistle shrieks, ending the jam.

I whirl around, trying to remember where the scoreboard is.

"What's the score?" Carmen's yelling at the refs, grabbing my arm. "Did we—?"

The scoreboard flickers.

HOT SHOTS: 128 / BEND BANSHEES: 125 / OFFICIAL SCORE.

I'm suddenly on the floor, my limbs giving out. I think I'm crying, but I can't tell. Everyone around me is screaming, and there are hands on my back, grabbing at my jersey. Carmen and Panic have melted to the ground beside me, tears streaming down their cheeks.

"WE FUCKING WON!" Carmen screams through her tears, pulling me into a fierce, sweaty hug.

I'm exhilarated, overcome—I scream with Carmen and Panic, crying into Carmen's orange hair, my arms and legs shaking. Mercury sails toward us and drops to her knees, sliding across the track and slamming into us, weeping.

"That was amazing!" I yell into her ear.

"*You* were amazing!"

I think there are more sounds—the announcer declaring us third-place winners, the rest of the Hot Shots flooding onto the track, the audience losing their minds in the bleachers. But it doesn't matter—I'm here, with my team, exhausted and sweaty and shaking, and we *won*.

I turn my head, and Mercury is there, laughing through the tears streaking through the glitter on her face. I pull her toward me, and I kiss her, not caring about the sweat or the glitter or the screams around us, not caring that our helmets clunk together and both of us are shaking. All that matters is that I'm here, and I feel alive.

epilogue

CHARACTERISTICALLY, the first day of summer in Portland starts with rain.

"It doesn't get really nice until the Fourth of July," Eden told me last night as we sat on the roof outside her bedroom window, her with a glass of wine and me with a much, much smaller glass of wine. "But summer here is the best. It's worth putting up with the rain for the rest of the year."

"How hot d'you think it'll be in Moab?" I'd asked, nudging her with my foot.

Eden had groaned. "God. Like a billion degrees. But worth it." We're leaving next week, driving Eden's car all the way down the West Coast to see Dad's old roller rink in LA before cutting up to southern Utah. Even though the house in Moab sold three weeks ago, the new owners agreed to let us come see it one more time. Maybe with Eden at my side, I'll feel Dads' energy there again. All the good things that happened within its walls, all the warmth and safety.

But today, we're driving to the theme park under the cool mist of early summer, the road I've now been down a million times. The clouds part as we turn through the gates, and Eden attempts to navigate her Subaru through the crowded lot. The park is full of people, the Ferris wheel spinning in spite of the damp asphalt. Eden turns away from the rides and up toward the Hangar, but then makes a left, finding a spot on the other side of the lot.

She cuts the ignition and we sit in silence for a minute, listening to the engine click as it cools down. It feels like the first day I came to watch her derby practice, when I peered through the window and felt my stomach hitch when she said *roller derby*.

But now I'm staring at a larger building with low, sloped roof, narrow windows along one side, a light-up sign on one wall: RINK.

"You sure about this?" Eden asks, just like that first day at the Hangar.

I take a long, deep breath. My heart's pounding, but I will it to slow down. It feels like Arches again, watching the sun drench the valley orange. Like staring at the blackened, twisted remains of the Finney's Mesa Rollerdome. I didn't make it here by April 7. At one point I didn't think I'd make it here at all.

"I'm sure."

Someone raps on my window, and I jump—but it's just Carmen, grinning excitedly at me with her skates over her shoulders. Her hair is back to blond, woven in twin braids that hang down to her overalls. I roll my eyes at her, opening the door and climbing out.

"I'm psyched," she says the minute I'm out of the car. "I haven't been to the rink in, like, three years. It's always so crowded." Powerhouse stands beside her, acknowledging me with a nod.

"Hey, Moose on the Loose!" calls Prince, untangling herself from the seat belt of her car. "Good to see you!"

"You're at our house, like, every night," I say, and she ruffles my frizzy hair affectionately.

"Yes I am. And it's still good to see you." She turns to greet Eden with a kiss, and I glance around the parking lot.

"Where's—?"

"She got here before us," Powerhouse says. "I think she's waiting inside."

I push down the pang of disappointment. Walking into a roller rink for the first time since the fire would have been easier with Mercury by my side.

Eden and Prince lead us toward the rink, holding hands. Behind them, Carmen and Powerhouse flank me like bodyguards. My hands are shaking a little, and I shove them into my pockets. Carmen notices and loops her arm through mine, prattling about the upcoming roller derby convention in Vegas that we're all attending. I'm grateful for the distraction.

When we reach the rink, I stop abruptly. The doors are glass, and I can see the ticket booth beyond. It looks just like the one from Finney's Mesa, the one where Gemma would sit and slip me candy every night.

"Moose?" Eden says, turning. "You good?"

I bite my lip. I can't back out now, after I asked them all to come. But what if it's crowded inside? What if there are too many people, too few emergency exits, the smell of fresh wood polish on the floor that could send the whole building up in flames?

"Hey," Eden says gently. She stations herself at my other side, taking my hand. "We got you."

I take a long, steadying breath. There won't be a fire. It's just a roller rink. And I'm safe.

The cool air hits me as we step inside the rink, and a tidal wave of memories crashes over me. The carpet is blue space print, and the old walls are '70s-style wood paneling that's woefully out of date. Tiny theme park lockers line the walls and there's a teenager behind a counter, tightening the trucks on a pair of rental skates. It all hurts, how much it feels like home.

"Wait," I say, looking around. "There's nobody here."

The rink is quiet, only a couple lights on over the skate floor. And there's one person skating on it—Mercury turns, and her face lights up at the sight of me. There's a feeling like pressure lifting off my chest.

Mercury skates over to us, rolling off the polished wood skate floor and onto the carpet. "We thought it might be easier if it were empty," she tells me, her voice echoing off the space meant to hold hundreds. "Quieter."

I wish I could articulate how much it means to me, how much my heart aches at her thoughtfulness. But I can't, so I kiss her instead. She smiles into my lips, a comforting hand in my hair.

"Okay, we get it," Prince says, clapping a couple times to break us up. "Get your skates on, Moose on the Loose. Mercury only bribed the rink manager for an hour." Mercury squeezes my hand as we break apart.

I sit on one of the carpeted benches, pulling off my sneakers and sliding my feet into my skates. They're my derby skates, but they feel so different here. With no safety gear on, no loud whistles or shouting refs or slamming bodies, it's just skating.

By the time I finish lacing up my skates, the others are on the floor, streaking easy circles across the wood, voices echoing. I hover at the edge, watching the stationary disco ball over the floor. The light from a window hits it, and it glitters.

Mercury rolls over to me, coming to an easy halt. “Ready?”

I take one more deep breath, put my hand in hers. “Ready.”

Mercury links her fingers through mine, and I step onto the skate floor.

ACKNOWLEDGMENTS

Taking this book from an unruly Word doc on my laptop to the real book you are holding in your hands took hard work and love from many people.

My incredible agent, Faye Bender: Thank you for answering my emails in minutes and for always being a fierce, warm, and passionate advocate for my work.

My editor, Andrew Karre: Shaping this book with you has been the most fulfilling creative endeavor of my life. Thank you for your passion for skating (with wheels instead of blades!), your love for queer stories, and for pushing me to take risks. This book would not be what it is today without you.

The whole team at Dutton and Penguin Young Readers, especially Anna Booth, Danielle Ceccolini, Rob Farren, Ilana Jacobs, Madison Penico, Vanessa Robles, Julie Strauss-Gabel, Natalie Vielkind, and Rye White: Thank you for all your expertise and hard work.

My cover artist, Beatriz Ramo: Thank you for creating the most stunning cover that made me cry when I saw it, and for letting me be nitpicky about making sure the skates had the correct toe stops.

My mentor, Laurie Frankel: Thank you for your immense help with this manuscript, but also for all the Zoom calls, letting me crash on your couch, explaining many publishing mysteries, and your continued love and support for everything I do.

The incredible folks from Reese's Book Club's LitUp Fellowship: My fellow All Stars, Allison King, Ashley Jordan, Bora Lee Reed, and Tolani Akinola; Gretchen Schreiber, Reese Witherspoon, and the Hello Sunshine/Reese's Book Club team; Dhonielle Clayton, Zoraida Córdova, Tessa Gratton, Natalie C. Parker, and the We Need Diverse Books team; Sharon Cameron, Curtis Sittenfeld, Jasmine Guillory, and Adrienne Young. Thank you for the opportunity that helped a lifelong dream come true.

Early readers of this book: Jamie Factor, Asha Whittle (Bolt), Karen Benson (Danger Moose), Morgan Oberweiser, Sprout Frattalone, Tasha Dethlefs (Tazzberry Jam), and Whitney Mccool (Thor's Slammer).

Jen St. Jude: Thank you for the early encouragement and insight into how weird publishing is, and for always making me feel welcome in author spaces.

Tanvi Berwah, my very first critique partner: Thank you for your critique and support back when I was writing very different books, and for being a cheerleader for me ever since.

My friends who stood by me and rooted for me every step of this journey: Dakota and Kalven Link, Emily Hamilton (Shamrocket), Kate Walford (Jurasskick Park), Kelsey Ryan (OSHA Violation), Alexia Zhang (Lexsanguination), Mae Schuttler (Mae Dae), Mal Copeland (Judge Booty), Mia Palau, Peter Kukla (Adam Splitter), Rachel Sullivan, Roxie Stewart, Sam Fulan, Trinity Boothe, and Valeria LaChapelle.

All my teammates and coaches from Ohio Roller Derby, Crow City Derby, and especially Wreckers and High Rollers: This book is for you and all the ways you make roller derby magical.

The many incredible skaters who let me borrow their derby names for this book, because I am not good at puns: Quantum Fury,

Tyger Bomb, Stomps, Firebolt, Sybil Disobedience, Technicolor Dreamboat, Cereal Killer, Knockems Raezor, Gamma Raze, Squirrely Temple, Poundstooth, Scary Poppins, Jurasskick Park, Angela Death, D-Monic, Kicky Longstocking, and Cheery Bomb.

Thank you to Kevin Smith, who let me ask all sorts of probing questions about what it's like to have a tracheostomy and how teenagers behave in the hospital burn unit, and to Victoria Jamieson, who paved the way for books about roller derby.

Kim Stegeman (Rocket Mean), the executive director of Rose City Rollers, who graciously allowed me to set my book in the very real Hangar in Portland, a space that means so much to me. Thank you also to Nicole Williams (Bonnie Thunders) and Drew Flowers (OMG WTF) for allowing me to use Five Stride Skate Shop's name in this book.

Arianna Kupras: I would not be here today without you, for so many reasons. Thank you for always challenging me to grow.

Susan Cramer: There have been so many points in this journey where I've wished I could call you. I miss you terribly, and I hope you're enjoying lots of uninterrupted time to read.

My wonderful family, who have seen me through many stages of both writing and life: Auntie Deb, Uncle John, Mom, Dad, Abby, Tae, Lesley, CJ, Jack, Teddy, Holly, Zach, Freya, Heidi, Oscar, Ethel, and Clove.

And Hannah: my best friend, my biggest fan, my love, my favorite person. You make everything fun, including writing a book. I love every single thing about you.